Julianne was born in Berkshire and grew up in the rural part of Oxfordshire. In 1998, she moved with her husband to Hampshire.

Not really knowing what she wanted to do as a career, she went down many different roads. She tried Dentistry, Financial Services and Pharmaceutical Companies. She then became a GP Medical Sales Representative. She was very successful in all these areas. Julianne never enjoyed sales but was incredibly good at it.

As a child, she suffered from Bipolar depression. This was managed when she was younger with medication.

Later in life, medication was not required and the condition seemed under control. That was until she started having a problem with alcohol.

Bipolar depression and alcohol addiction took her down a very dark path and due to that path, this book was written.

Writing was what Julianne has always wanted to do.

Julianne is working on her second book, which continues to follow her painful journey on the road to 'recovery'.

To the many people who stood by me when they thought all was lost and so did I.

Julianne Harper

IDLING IN A RETROGRESSIVE GROOVE

AUSTIN MACAULEY PUBLISHERS™

LONDON • CAMBRIDGE • NEW YORK • SHARJAH

A CIP catalogue record for this title is available from the British Library.

ISBN 9781528914086 (Paperback)
ISBN 9781528960762 (ePub e-book)

www.austinmacauley.com

First Published (2019)
Austin Macauley Publishers Ltd
25 Canada Square
Canary Wharf
London
E14 5LQ

To the one from the *Dark Side* who came into the light. I could not have written this book without his knowledge of addictions, prison, homelessness and hitting rock bottom so many times.

He was able to tell his story of the start of a new life and help me tell the beginning of mine.

Prologue

Last night the nightmare was like the truth. How funny that my first husband and my last partner were both in the same dream.

Michael and I had met a few times over the last year. He was still in love with me and wanted us to get back together. My relationship with Gee was anything but perfect, it was hard work and I felt time and time again I should leave, as we had little in common. I stayed as I was scared to be alone and that thought took me back to my childhood. Alone and abandoned. Both, Michael and Gee, I felt safe and secure with. However, Michael would be causing more problems. I had complications with Adrian as it was. He was still in my life. In many ways, he was selfish and though only thought of himself. I was his best friend by all accounts, he had never had anyone do as much for him as I had and he relied on me to make sure his finances were okay. I was weak and should have said, "Enough is enough, Adrian, we both have got to live our lives without each other." But I didn't.

Michael, don't pick me up. He tries to do a fireman lift but we don't get that far; we fall over on the pavement close to the road.

Michael said, "Gee is here." He walks into my kitchen with his white Reebok trainers on.

Your children, Michael, they are in the dream too, but how, I don't know. We then skip.

Adrian, his instant savers account had been overdrawn by £22.50. Will he ever listen to me? I said to him there was nothing there if he wanted the money. Why didn't he ask me to move it? He is so frustrating.

I'm in trouble, I need to find my car. Which car park did I put it in? The car park attendant said there is another car park. He tells me where but it's far and I'm lost. I will get lost. I can't find it. I haven't tried yet.

The bus. Can I use the bus?

More folders. Car folder. This folder. I'm in Adrian's flat. I'm packing away the folders that are not relevant. His car folder, his

9

MOT that is due. Lilly is here. She sees me. I see her. No words are spoken. She just looks at me. She is doing things, collecting things. She leaves.

The flat is in a rough area, all concrete grey buildings. It's awful. I don't want to be here.

Adrian, he doesn't look right—he is different, his face is haunting, his eyes too big for his face. "Adrian, why are you smoking a cigarette?" It's a roll up.

He's lost weight, his legs are thin. He's in jeans. He is skinny.

I'm looking at the cigarette. "Old behaviour, Adrian, next you will be back on drugs!"

"You are on drugs, you are on drugs, you are on drugs. Why am I repeating it?"

He admits it. He's not at work. "What about work, do they know?" He looks like I know the answer.

People, loads of people, what are they all doing in his flat? It's like his past; all these people, are they all on drugs? Lilly is not there. I want to get away, get out, I feel trapped by the amount of people; I can't move. They are all junkies.

I look at Adrian's hands. Where has all his jewellery gone? The three rings I brought him. My granddad's ring. Where is my granddad's ring?

"Adrian, who have you sold my granddad's ring to? Tell me, I want to buy it back. Tell me."

He looks at me. He is sick. He doesn't care. "Cathy, do you think they care? Whoever is wearing it doesn't care. I don't know who I sold it to."

"It would have been passed on down the line."

"I don't have a crystal ball."

All his chains have gone, his bracelet, his necklace, his cross, all that I gave him over the years.

He has changed, gone back. He is going to hurt me. He wants my jewellery that I am wearing. What did he say once? Oh yes, to inflict as much pain as possible.

He has me. There are three people. They are close but not too close. I shout for help; I shout for help. They ignore me. They don't even look at me. No. It's "fire" you need to shout. It's fire. People turn and will help if you shout fire. I can't shout fire. I'm still shouting help.

I'm on a counter. People are working. They do not look at me. Why are they not looking at me? I'm here. Adrian is here. He is going to hurt me. They will not help me as they will not look at me.

Inflict as much pain and damage as possible, Cathy. My self-defence classes, what did they say? I know some of it but I can't think quick enough. I go to kick him. I'm on the counter, kick him in the face. Will he get my foot or my leg? I try to kick him. He's going to get my leg; he has my foot. Use your palm. Use your palm, break his nose. Hit him in the face with your palm.

"Why have you relapsed, Adrian?" Was it Lilly?

He replies, "Yes, Lilly but another also, she was not good; she did it."

"How did she do it, Adrian?"

"I was with them." He says more but it's a blur.

"Why did she make you relapse?"

"Because I was surrounded by them," is his reply.

My voice. It's in a dream, it's distant, it's far away. "You should have stayed with me. I would have reminded you of what it was like and not to go back; I would have kept you on the straight and narrow. Lilly has led you in to a false sense of security."

I wake up, I'm in a cold sweat, I'm wide awake. Now was that a mixed-up nightmare? It's been nearly two years since the break with Adrian. It's Boxing Day, 2016. It all ended on 4th January, 2014.

Not nightmares like that of Adrian as well!

It's going to be 2017 in a few days; my life has got to change. I thought it was complicated back then but I'm making it worse. I have got to change. Things in my life have got to change.

I have choices, we all have choices. Good, bad, sad and some completely mad. They are still choices. I now needed to make the choices and act on them!

Chapter One
Christmas 2016

*Sorry works when a mistake is made but not when trust is broken.
So in life, make a mistake but never break trust. Because forgiving
is easy, but forgetting and trusting again is sometimes impossible.*

This had got to stop, not another nightmare about my mixed-up crazy life. I haven't moved on, learnt from my mistakes. Everything is being repeated. Text Adrian, Adrian texts me. Speak with Adrian, meet Adrian. Look after Adrian. Sort Adrian's money out. Christmas presents. Adrian's mum, Frankie, Ida, Anna, now Lilly. It's been two years now that Adrian and our relationship changed quite drastically. Which it needed to. Also, Lilly came. My present. I, however, didn't really want or need a present. *Why did I...Why was I doing it?* Buy my present from Adrian with Adrian. I was doing it for the sake of doing it. Buy Adrian a present. Never easy with him. Always the same; him just being difficult, not listening. Jewellery and watches have always been easy. Clothes and shoes just a nightmare. Still trying to get him to look after decent clothes and shoes so they lasted. How many times had we been down this road? Buying clothes, then he wouldn't wear them. They just stay in the wardrobe. That hadn't changed. Shoes, trainers, try on first pair, that was it. Many very heated discussions in shops to try on more than one pair to make sure they fitted and were what he actually wanted? The tracksuit this year was no different, a couple tried on. Impatience set in. "Oh come on, there's nothing here."

"Adrian, we haven't looked."

"No, I haven't got time for this. I've got to get home. I'm sick of looking. I'll try one more on."

Adrian did try one more on. That was it. That would do; he liked it. The two items were returned straight after Christmas. I then had to go through the same procedure again, only to be told that I was a nightmare. *What?* My head was spinning with the whirlwind steamroller chaotic self-obsessed effect he had on me. I wasn't taking two items back because 'the tracksuit bottoms made a squeaking noise when he walked'. Just a minor detail which with Adrian would be a major problem and issue. He just didn't learn in some areas. Patience is what he needed in practically every area of his life. He had none. It had to be 'now'.

Had the liberation of clothes changed? He was working at the day centre and people donate clothes for the homeless. As with so many charities, the staff more often than not had first choice of clothing that came in. Adrian in all fairness would only take the odd T-shirt and a few other items but I still had an issue with it. More often than not, they went back to the day centre to be given to the homeless.

Was he still doing that? Going in the wardrobe only to look at them a few years down the line. Adrian saying I'm never going to wear that or this. What had I said when he brought them home? "Are you really going to wear that?"

"Of course, I am. Look at it. It's Armani, Lacoste," or another designer name, another item of clothing you would never supposedly get anywhere else. They were then back in a black bin liner and taken straight away to the 'Day Centre' where he worked. The bin liners could not stay in the flat. They had to go straight away. This sorting out was not without problems. It was chaotic. Mess everywhere. He would not listen to me about how to sort his wardrobe out in a methodical, quick manner. Everything was chucked out of the wardrobe.

Then the bin liners and clothes would have to be removed from his flat that moment, no delay, that instant. Adrian could not deal with having clutter or items like that around him or in his flat. Quite bizarre. So the clothes had been returned to where they should have been. With me thinking, *I said to him right from the start that he should not have these items*. There were people in more need than him. The homeless. Adrian, of all people, should know that; I was more than happy to tell him that. There were a few hours of sorting through his wardrobe. "It needs sorting out, Cathy. It won't take long. We'll work as a team." Then the steamroller effect, not listening to how to do it methodically. Taking twice as long as it should do, with my head spinning. I wasn't doing that anymore. Was Lilly?

Wasn't I better off without him? Sure, life was calmer in many ways. I did miss him, the company, some of the fun. Even the 'dark side'. It was easier now. I didn't torture myself anymore. I felt happier about things. I just needed now to make sure that I didn't continue down the road that I had been travelling for so long. Getting, as they say, the same results and doing the same things.

Adrian, in so many ways, was fundamentally still the same. As he put it, a "*A self-obsessed c**t*". I agreed. There had been changes. Were they changes or was he always like that? But now they were coming through so you could see him, his other side, not the just the *'dark side'*. In so many areas, his life had changed.

I need to move on. Change and get a different result; I needed a goal.

The first goal would be book one. The nightmare. It got me thinking in more ways than one. I went straight to my notebook on my iPhone. Typed it. I needed to remember this one. It was Boxing Day.

I spent the day thinking about the nightmare. That was it. That's what I needed. I had tried to write books and started many. I had so much written but nothing really passionate. I felt something was missing. I kept on thinking. If I knew what to write, I'd do it. But what?

Now I knew what I should write. This nightmare is where the passion and the desire lay to write it. All I needed now was to do it and get it down on paper. Boxing Day, I started again on my book. This time, my goal and focus were there. Not only the goal and focus but the information. I had most of it written down in diaries. Some was handwritten. That didn't matter. I could read and put down what was required or what I thought would be required. There were also many Excel spreadsheets in the forms of diaries, along with much more information, like the medication that I was on. Appointments with doctors and consultants. Other mental health appointments. Alcohol Anonymous. *That would be interesting.* See what I wrote based on how I felt about it. In all fairness to AA, it did keep people sober, and maybe I should revisit it in 2017. Loads of people who I got on incredibly well with went. Look at Adrian, what I would call a real rock-bottom desperate case; if he could be clean and sober for twelve years…He must be an inspiration and hope for many out there who really did not think there was a way. I had written down about my drinking so I had all the information. Just now how to do it and what to put in. I hoped I knew how to and could put it in a readable form that would appeal to a broad spectrum of people.

The other area that needed to be carefully thought about and written about was Adrian. His cooperation, acceptance of what I would need to write. It did have to be true; certain things could not be written and people named.

AA was there to help people. The people who went needed to respect the anonymity of other AA members. The yellow card said, '*Who you see here, what you hear here, let it stay here.*' I most certainly could relate to that. I didn't want people to know about my addiction. I was ashamed. Adrian would call it denial. *It was.*

2016, another year that I had not got the drinking under control. I did, however, spend this Christmas sober. I didn't have to drink a bottle of wine on the way this year, so I didn't throw up. After Christmas 2014, I had no intention of spending Christmas at home. It was just too painful. I would, however, have had to go through some of the pain by re-reading my diaries. One of the reasons was the book. The other was just plan morbidity.

When Gee and I arrived in Norton Sub Hamden for Christmas, it was nice to go straight to the apartment. It was lovely. An upside down apartment in a listed building. It had a fireplace, so we could have a log fire going. The owners had provided us with a basket of wood for our first fire. We were shown around; there was an indoor swimming pool. That was always a criterion. However, I had lapsed and had put on nearly two stone due to drinking, no exercise and eating the wrong foods. I'm normally very much into my fitness and eating healthy; low GI food being a priority and what I would mostly eat.

There were beams in the apartment and it reminded me of a cottage. All cosy and homely but spacious, or it seemed that way. A large bedroom with an en suite wet room. The washbasin was in the bedroom with a mirror, which I really liked. Upstairs was an open plan kitchen, dining room and lounge. The fire, to me, made it. That would take a bit of work on my behalf. It didn't come naturally to me, even though in the second property my parents had in Chinnor the only heating was an open fire.

I remember the three-day week from the late 60s to early 70s well. Quite a bit of cooking was done on that open fire. The power normally went off about 5 p.m. It was darkness with candlelight and an oil lantern. Never quite sure when the power came back on.

I fell in love with it. It was the type of place I felt at home in. That was the type of property and area I wanted to live in. The swimming pool was there, so my intention was to get back into swimming. We arrived on the 23rd, I was in the pool 7:30 a.m. on the 24th. I swam every day.

Gee and I had packed the car up. Well, my crossover 4X4. It was chock-a-block. There was all the food to take, Poppy, our Border Collie, her food, treats, etc. Cases, presents, and not forgetting Gee bringing things that really weren't required or used again—a remote control plane and quads.

This year, the plan was for me to drive. In 2015, Gee had slipped on Christmas Day. We landed upside down A&E in Torbay; we had gone to Dartmoor for Christmas. Gee had broken his wrist; this was before 8 a.m. in the morning. Gee did not drink, or very little. We had taken his BMW but it really wasn't the area for a BMW 135IM Sport. It was 4X4 land. There were the normal arguments that married couples have when the other partner is driving their car. However, the argument were probably worse for the two of us as we just did not get on. Plus, I don't even think Gee likes me. So why did I stay? Good point. Gee was a good person in so many ways. He was reliable and hard working. I stayed as I was scared to leave and when I did want to go and was going on a few occasions, he was so upset that he begged me to stay. So out of weakness, I stayed. Even though Gee was a good man, he could have had met someone else who would have made him a great deal happier than me. I did not make him that happy. We could not do anything together without arguing about something. Simple things like walking the dog just didn't work, there would be arguments and bickering the whole walk. Gee was controlling, so if I wanted to stop and talk with people, he didn't like it. Taking photos of wildlife and flowers on the walk annoyed him. I came home feeling frustrated and down. I did point this all out to him and he had said that he would change when I agreed to stay the last time. The changes only lasted a few months and then we were back to normal. I should have just walked out the door and said enough is enough, it would have saved both of us a great deal of pain.

We took my 4X4. I had, however, lost my licence. I will state at this point, in the past, I should have lost it on many grounds. This time, I lost it on personal grounds. I had in July seen a completely new SPR. Female. First time I gave her all the information. My past drinking, which had really been bad. In 2004–2006, at times I was on six bottles of wine at any one time. That was not the case now. I could not drink that quantity—one of the reasons was that I passed out quite quickly. The other, I didn't wake up quickly. Now I passed out between 3–6 hours at a time so the quantity compared to the past just wasn't possible. There was no 5 a.m. getting out of bed; I was lucky to make 7:30 a.m. and get to the co-op at 8 a.m. buying two bottles of wine. I informed her about when my last drink was—13th June. I had a key worker to help support me with my drinking; things were going well. I spoke about my affair with Adrian, and that I was still in contact with him. My libido was mentioned. It had increased, not decreased with age. I was honest.

I lost my licence by unfair means on 25th November, 2016. The next SPR I saw was male Asian. I did not trust him. His opening statement was, had I contacted the DVLA with regards to my bipolar depression? No, I hadn't. I got what I called a full-blown PowerPoint presentation on the DVLA along with him immediately opening a book on the page showing me that I should. How important it was, along with the DVLA coming down quite hard on this. He was not interested in the change of medication that had happened six weeks prior, and I found it difficult to cope with it and wanted it readdressed. That didn't happen. The short story here. I saw him three times; each time, the DVLA was mentioned. Each time he had no problem with my ability to drive. Three care plans went to my GP and me stating this. What was also included was that I had contacted the DVLA, and he would be happy with me to drive.

I felt he had an issue with my sex, my relationship with Adrian, my drinking. His letter to the DVLA was unfair and was based on things going back to 2006 and before. I had drunk fourteen times in total in 2016.

I had no choice, Gee drove my 4X4. Again, the normal argument that a married couple have with regards to them driving the other partner's car. Along with what must have been even more annoying for Gee, "I've passed my advanced driving course. You haven't." I will leave that to your imagination what was said between the two of us.

The area was lovely. The walks were great. The weather was nice. Mostly sunny and cold. Great for going out with Poppy. She was in her element. So was I. I could see myself living in an area like this. It took me back to my childhood. Open space, farms, peace and quiet, villages, friendly people, a proper community.

The few areas which were of concern to Gee were my drinking and bipolar depression, when I would go into a state of not leaving the home and not speaking to people. In the past, I had support from neighbours, friends, the club I attended, (Solent Hotel; I was a member) and sort of my family.

My main concern was the swimming. I really wanted to get back into my fitness routine and my swimming, lose the weight that I put on when I had these drinking periods. Adrian called them MIA (Missing in Action). I called them AWOL (Absence without Leave). Both were the same. That is what happened when I started drinking. I had gone from being a functioning alcoholic to one that was not.

If I drank, nothing happened. That was it—drink only. Admittedly, not high quantities now. Nothing happened, nothing got done.

I swam every day I was down in Somerset, along with doing all the exercises for the multitude of injuries I had accumulated due to sport. When I got home, I would continue. My last swim, however, was 3rd January, 2017. Disappointing. This time, however, it was not drink. I'm not sure what it was. *Was it Gee's retirement, my licences or had I lost interest?* I did, however, have a goal. The book. I spent every day from Boxing Day onwards writing the book. I had a reservation that this would change when I returned home. That was not the case.

Christmas 2016 was different from 2015 and definitely 2014. Christmas Eve, Gee and I took Poppy to Ham Hill. It was an old quarry that had been transformed into walks. It was perfect for Poppy (another reason to move). We parked near a pub called the Prince of Wales. I'm not really a pubby person. After our walk, we decided to have something to eat and a cappuccino. There were dogs and owners all over the place outside. Not thinking they would allow dogs in, I went in to look at the menu. They allowed dogs in. We took Poppy in, ordered our food and cappuccino. The atmosphere was lovely; I got chatting to the landlord. I had forgotten to pack my apron and mentioned this to the landlord asking if he had a spare apron that I could have or buy as I like to cook at home with one on. He went in the kitchen and brought one out for me.

Both Gee and I had noticed the glasses that people were drinking from. We assumed cider. At the bar, there were labels saying mulled wine but also a non-alcoholic spiced apple. We had one. It was lovely. I went and asked if they had a take-away cup and a couple of shots of it. I'd be happy to pay. Their person behind the bar gave me a whole take-away cup full of it. This was going to make Christmas Day dinner better as at least I had something that resembled a seasonal drink. (I'm still drinking it today.)

The pub had a fantastic atmosphere. The landlord played the trumpet. Christmas carols were sung; it was great. Gee and I went to that pub every day. Every day it was packed. Down there, while going out on walks and visiting National Trust Properties that had land and were suitable for dogs, I fell in love with it. Both of us thought it was great. We looked at a few properties again as always there are criteria which you want for a new home. Mine was village, fireplace and beams.

I was feeling happier about things. I wasn't sure about my feelings for Adrian. On the 24th of January, 2017, I had a moment. I knew at that moment that Adrian and I would not be getting back together again. When I saw him that evening, he met me at the co-op and we went up as normal to Whiteley Village. After our meal in Prezzo, we did a few bits and pieces. Then we went to Costas, where I told him about my feelings. I saw his expression, which didn't give much away. I asked him what he thought about us being together. His reply was, "Well, not at the moment." He did, however, wanted to ensure that he had my friendship; that what was the most important thing to him.

End of 2016, Adrian's words to me were that I was the best thing that had happened to him. The impact that I had on his life was so great that for the first time financially he was in a good position. I had made him think ahead, had shown him a different life that he felt was never achievable, introduced him to new things and new people. He had, for the first time, got a true friend, someone who meant the world to him. Whom he loved in many ways. If I had not been there, with all the emotional baggage he had, and the company he was keeping at the beginning, which was causing more emotional baggage. Adrian would almost certainly have relapsed. I gave him the stability he needed and sorted his life out in every way possible.

I also knew him. The true him. He could not hide from me. He could not lie to me. I would know. I knew him better than anyone.

He had said similar words before to another. He did need to go down further before he could get better and listen. I was there at the right time and stopped his decline, emotionally, from what could have had a drastic adverse effect on him. 'Angie.' *Boy did he know how to pick the wrong women.*

Even me!

Angie was in his life before me and was really fucking him around. I felt that was one of the things that drew me to Adrian, I could see the pain he was in over his life and over Angie. He played a record to me by Smokey Robinson and the Miracles, *'The love I saw in you was just a mirage'*.

The words to the song was just how Angie was to Adrian.

Chapter Two
December 2006

2007 would be a very different year for me, in about every way possible. For the first time in my life, I would just give up. I broke down completely. It would also be the year that I met Adrian.

In 2007, I was working for a pharmaceutical company called Pharma. How I landed up working for them on the Specialist Division, I have no idea. I sold in the vaccines and prostate cancer palliative care areas.

Prior to that, I had worked for a contract company for the pharmaceutical industry called Kudos, and that will go down as one of my best-liked jobs. With the best and most likable people, it was a very special contract team that you very rarely see; we were all happy, all worked hard and everyone was nice. I started working for Kudos in January, 1999. I had moved down from the Home Counties, which is where I grew up, to Hampshire in April, 1998. How different Pharma would be compared to Kudos.

In 2002, I joined a pharmaceutical company Pharma. At that point, I would say I was, if I am honest, a functioning alcoholic. For years, I would say I was a problematic/binge drinker. In AA, they would call that denial; true, for years I would be in denial. I would also say that I never had alcoholic tendencies; again, that would be denial. I would blame pressure from work, which probably escalated it; again, that would be denial.

I can't remember much from January–March 2007; it really is a blur. I just know for the first time in my life, I just gave up. The killer instinct in me with my work ethos went. Well, it had seriously been dwindling. One of the things that I didn't like about Pharma was they expected more than 100%. In all my jobs, I had always given more than 100%. Always went the extra mile. Outperformed most people in all areas. With Pharma, it was the fact that they expect so much more and I was resentful; I wanted it to be my choice not them making me, the must-do attitude they had.

At the end of 2006, this is what I wrote about how I felt. However, what is more disturbing was what I wrote on 13th September, 2007. I had re-read those notes.

I called it burn-out because that is how I felt.

Maybe it isn't the depression, maybe I am not an alcoholic, "I just have a drinking problem."

The last appointment I had with my doctor made me think. It was what he said. We discussed my depression; I explained I had taken a turn for the worse. After three excellent months, I'd gone from being this vibrant girl who couldn't wait to get up in the morning, going back to the gym (that had suffered; as in, I hadn't been). I had just got back into it. Just like a flick of a switch, I just couldn't face the day. I couldn't face any of it, getting up, going out, seeing people, speaking with people, taking the dog 'Holly' for a walk, having a shower, brushing my teeth, making myself something to eat, putting clean clothes on, picking the post up, opening the post. The post was something I had begun to dread. The bills, the bank most of all.

I said to my GP that this all happened just before my period (it must be hormonal). That's what I said. I explained that I had been off the drink. Had been very positive about everything, was getting back on track and felt good about the job, well, better. Everything was great, I was cured, the new pills had worked. They had stopped me drinking, along with the anti-depressant that I had been on and off for five years (Prozac). Yes, I was better. It was the drink; I was going to stay clean. That was it. Never, never again. No more.

"Oh my God, who have I spoken to on the phone? What time is it?" Followed by the guilt, the retching that would follow at a certain point during the day. (I would later learn in AA from the big book that these are called the Four Horsemen—Terror, Bewilderment, Frustration, Despair.)

It is also from the bible 'The Four Horsemen of the Apocalypse'. 'The Lamb of God', or 'Lion of Judah'. Jesus Christ opens the first four of the seven seals, which summons forth four beings that ride out on the white, red, black and pale horses. Although some interpretations differ, in most accounts, the four riders are symbolising conquest, war, famine, death, respectively. Not much in the two interpretations. Describes perfectly how I felt at those moments in time when I drank.

Gee, my husband, did not handle my drinking very well. In fact, he handles none of our relationship well. If I kept my mouth shut and did all that he wanted, I stood some chance of having a reasonable day but on the whole, I was treated like a child always in trouble. If I drank it was, *why had I done it, didn't I realise that I couldn't drink?*

He'd had enough; he didn't want to carry on like this. He dreaded coming home. I dreaded him coming home.

Alcoholics tend to be very selfish people when they drink, and I wasn't any different. What was Gee's excuse for his behaviour? Drunk or sober it was the same.

There would be the verbal abuse from him and at times, the physical abuse. Throwing me out of the house, trying to strangle me. All in a fit of rage. Either I was unconscious or drunk. (I would not have liked to come home to that.) What is so ironic is that one of my criteria for a boyfriend was that they were not a drinker.

I was never physically violent when drunk; I just wanted to be left alone. I would either sit in front of the TV or at the table and just get sozzled. Just wanted to be alone and wanted to escape and feel nothing. (Pretty much how I had been on and off since end of 2009).

Again, this is what I wrote:

It was hormonal, my last period. It all happened after my last period, and I really, really wanted a drink. (I'm writing this and it's like today. Well, not 'today' but what has been happening on and off since the end of 2009. This is quite frightening for me to write. I am sat here unable to believe that in 2017, nothing has changed. I have not had a drink so I have got to do things differently; that, I know for sure or this book will not be written.)

All through my period, my whole system just didn't seem to calm down. I felt lower and lower. The period pain, although not agony, just never went and the breast tenderness continued. In fact, I wrote: 'My breasts have remained rather swollen.' (Another thing mentioned in AA is that women must be careful around their menstrual cycle.) This is actually quite frightening to be reading this and then writing it. I am finding it quite unbelievable that nothing has changed.

I was trying hard with my low mood. Trying to stay motivated but I was getting lower. I was sort of doing the gym and walking the dog, cleaning the house. I had gained weight and didn't look my normal slim, well-presented self. I wasn't fat but not happy with my appearance.

Then bang, the flick of the switch happened; I could do nothing. Over the last three months, I had spent some time talking with one of the girls down the gym, Murtel. I had found her much more approachable than others. This was since, earlier in the year, she had been diagnosed with breast cancer. Murtel had been very open about her treatment, medications. I didn't feel that I couldn't ask her a question or talk about it. There had been several women down the club I belonged to (Solent Hotel) who had breast cancer, and all of them had been very open about it. It was not a taboo subject. During these three months of talking, I mentioned my depression. Murtel had noticed over the last few years a change in me. (You never notice it yourself.) I had gone from this absolutely-had-to-go-to-the-gym, where some of my friends were, to missing a week here, three weeks there. A few days. I wasn't aware that people had been so observant and noticed such a big change in me. I was just living it; I didn't see it.

I was regarded down at the club as one of the most liked, popular members. A good laugh, fun to be with and helpful. I also was the one that got everyone talking. By that I mean new people would come and I would get to know them. I was social. The social for me was only for small periods of time. The gym equipment people used would only be on it for so long. That would stop conversations and I liked that. The club gave me a safety net. Members had work to go to. I would have limited time to talk. Although I was regarded as a very social and talkative person, I could only do that and be like that for short periods of time. Long periods would cause me serve anxiety.

When I wasn't there, other members would say it was deathly quiet without me, and they didn't have the laughs that they did with me.

I was incredibly motivated, a good athlete, would enter most of the competitions and normally won. Other members would say that I was what they were aspiring to be like. I guess I was good.

Murtel had said her bit. Ali, my very good friend, had also really noticed all the changes in me that I had had those three good months. Ali said to me, "Cathy, you haven't had much time off lately."

My reply was, "I've changed my gym program and feel much more motivated." That wasn't the case.

During one of my discussions with Murtel, just before the relapse completely kicked in, I had mentioned that I thought the depression was hormonal. The discussion we had was about the similarities between me and her daughter, Nik.

Nik reached fourteen, all the hormones kicked in, and Nik changed completely. Nik became depressed and started drinking, which just made matters worse. Murtel was sure that it had been hormonal with Nik. We both agreed that there was very little help in such a situation. Now this, what was this, drinking, depression, hormonal problems. This, today, is still the case. Mental health issues are not dealt with very well; to get someone into rehab for drinking or other addictions on the NHS can take months; by the time they get in, they probably won't want to go. For someone who wants to clean themselves up from either drink or drugs, you must do it when they are ready, not when there is a space.

Hormones can have a big effect on the body and state of mind for many women. I have no idea if that was the case with me. Probably not.

I do however remember being on an awful tasting pink medicine when I was very young and having to attend hospital appointments. I remember my Nana saying to me when I came off the pink stuff that I should go back on it as I was so over-active and nervous and the medication had calmed me down.

Murtel and I agreed that with these low periods, Nik and myself were very much alike. For me, it was give me a drink, any drink. Nik's drug of choice in the end was not alcohol. It was methadone. I never asked but I should imagine that Nik had been on heroin. The methadone was prescribed to her on a regular visit to her GP for a prescription. One holiday, Murtel had to find out whether they would take this medication on the flight. They flew out with the methadone on board. This made me realise that Nik had been in this state for quite a while and was not getting better, just continuing the same.

With all my low moods, I had seriously thought of suicide. I did not, at that time, trust my state of mind. I felt there was no joy, desire, motivation, my self-esteem was low and I had no confidence. Let's not forget the really big one—paranoia. It felt like a complete black hole and that someone had taken over my body. I had no control over my drinking; I did it to escape. I was a spectator in my life.

My appointment with my GP was about the hormones. In AA, there is a great deal of talk about changes due to your menstrual cycle. (Women are more at risk due to this. They need to be extra vigilant as this can cause them to pick up the drink again.)

We discussed my options. The pill was mentioned. I wasn't convinced. My reply, which was a bit rich, was, *"I don't want it interfering with my body make up."* Classic from someone who went on these drink benders. My GP did mention it very diplomatically. So, the pill it was. That was going to fix a few things in the next couple of days. I'd be back to my old self. My happy, vibrant, athletic, organised, determined self. I would lose the weight I had put on, get back into all my clothes; I was in quite a few of them, but not all.

I was motivated to do all these things and keen to do my job. *'The contraceptive pill'* was going to restore my life!

My GP started to talk about the wobble that I had had with the drinking. Was it every day? How much and what did I drink?

Should I or should I not confess? I told my GP the truth and this would continue for all the years that I saw him; I just didn't want to lie as he had been a very good GP to me. *'I would learn later that most GPs ask patients who have problems about their drinking and then double the amount, which in fairness is probably more accurate'.*

It had not been the two to three bottles of wine a day that I had been drinking before my good three months of absence. It had not been the six bottles of wine that I had drunk per day several years earlier when I was very new to Pharma. That had stopped completely, mainly because I passed out well before drinking the second bottle of wine. I then spent more hours passed out than I did drinking.

Over two weeks, I'd had the odd bottle of wine. It was two days off, one day on, then three days on, which were awful, with two bottles of wine on each of those nights. However, I excelled on the third day and drank three bottles. That session had been particularly bad. I drank two bottles, went to bed, woke up around 2:30 p.m., walked down to Spar and brought another bottle. I must have been in a right state. I vaguely remember it; no shower, a baseball cap on to hide my hair that I hadn't washed. What they must have thought of me, intoxicated, unwashed. I have no idea who served me; that is even more worrying. I can remember my friend Jackie saying this to me and they possibly may have thought this (However, I doubt it today.) that I was some bored middle-class housewife (I was working). That was after a work colleague of mine had called an ambulance when she came around to my house and I was drunk. I refused to go to hospital as I was coherent, just; I did not need to be hospitalised that time. I was, however, in a state. (I was pretty pissed at her and then even more pissed at her as she had left a message on Gee's phone telling him what a state I was in. He was flying back from Hong Kong and would pick it up when he landed the next morning). I'm glad I didn't go to QA Hospital. I would, however, land there before I went into the Priory in 2007. My GP at this point said they probably thought I was some burnt-out employee. His words, not mine. I am not normally lost for words, but nothing came out.

It got me thinking. What I said to myself was not what I was really thinking.

I'm not burnt out, that happens to others; I'm fine, I'm depressed, it's hormonal. That is what I thought after the appointment.

The pill was prescribed and I was told to come back in a few months to see how I was getting on.

Then I wrote burnt out, burnt out, burnt out.

12th, I saw my GP, burnt out, burnt out.

24th, Can't sleep. This burnt-out lark still there. The morning of the 24th, I made some decisions about my life which was burnt out. Today, I am writing this—I did not follow them through. These changes should have been made. Why? I wouldn't be writing this book if they had.

These changes. It was not just my job that was awfully stressful. Plus, I hated it and really did not think much of some of the people whom I worked with. My social life needed addressing since it had disappeared completely. I had none. Home life was awful, along with my married life. I felt controlled, restricted, and money was out of control. Gee and I had very different opinions and outlook on most things. Gee was not interested in socialising with my family; I hardly got to see my nephews and sister. Gee never wanted to go and see them and join me. Very different with his family. They could come. He'd make the effort. He didn't go upstairs to use the computer or watch the TV. He moaned about going out with my friends or having them around for a meal. In all fairness to Gee, I was inclined to get very drunk with them on occasions. So, I could understand that. However, even before the excessive drinking, Gee made the whole thing awful. Gee would spend weeks complaining about it. I can remember our engagement party. For two weeks, Gee did nothing but complain about it. This caused me a great deal of pressure. I wanted a social life and when we got together in the late 80s, I wanted to have fun, go out, see friends and have them around. That happened rarely.

When we moved to Hampshire in 1998, by the time 2007 came, there was none of it. No socialising with any friends or family. He had been terrible about my mum. She suffered from COPD, was on oxygen 24/7. He did not want her or Ralph in the house and was very negative towards them when they came to stay on several occasions before my mother died. Ralph even mentioned to Gee, "You *don't* want us here, do you?"

Gee replied, "No, I don't." He could, however, palm me off to my relatives when he felt he couldn't cope. He did that on a few occasions.

Both times were a complete disaster.

One time I went to Mum and Ralph down in Devon to give Gee a break for a week. I took Holly my dog with me. Gee went home. I found drink and would get up in the night and drink but replace it the next day by going to the shop and buying it. It wasn't noticed to start with but then it was and Ralph confronted me. I confessed and stopped drinking until Gee picked me up.

The next occasion the palmed me off was to my dad at a weekend. He took me down Saturday morning. I was drinking a bottle of wine on the way down. When I got to my dad, Gee dropped me off and left. I wanted to drink so my dad let me drink a little, then got fed up and angry. I walked out of the house and went and booked into a tavern. Then drank myself stupid at the bar and was put to bed by the bar staff. The Brighton football club had been there. I was probably the sight everyone was looking at. Especially with two female members of staff having to put me to bed. I got to know this as on my way back to my dad, which was very difficult as I had no idea where I was. I remember I had ordered a bottle of wine and it was in my room that night but wasn't there when I got up the next morning.

My dad was overjoyed to see me. I told him about the wine, and he said they should have left the wine as I had brought it. I phoned the tavern only to be told I was so drunk that two female members of staff had to put me to bed and that they removed the wine for my safety. I could go and pick it up as they had it behind the bar. I never did.

Sunday was a disaster since I drank a whole bottle of brandy at my dad's before we went out to lunch at no other than *'Brighton Football Club'*. I drank most of the wine at the table. Gee was there and so were two of Dad's friends. I had to be put in the car while everyone finished their meals.

There was no respect for my possessions by Gee; I had no say over things, no help financially; he just dug his head in the sand. We were living an upstairs-downstairs life. Gee downstairs, watching what he wanted. I was upstairs, normally working. We didn't have meals together. We were living separate lives.

It wasn't just Pharma; it was my whole life. A total mess. Looking at it today, reading what I had written.

No social life. I continued with the stress of the job, along with their pointless business plans, regional divisional meetings. *I did bring the business in.*

Pharma kept on changing what they wanted us to do. How many ways did they want us to try? It was pointless! If you brought the business in, why change what was working?

In 2002, I had joined Pharma. I had been bullied, victimised, accused of not doing things. Most was by the general division. This was as I knew them on the territory which I worked and so did they, Hampshire, that was when I worked for Kudos. I called them '*The coffee shop kids, and I'm going home reps.*'

They would be on territory and meet other reps in coffee shops. I was out speaking to or seeing the doctors or making appointments either on the phone or going into their practices. I work hard to get appointments and meetings. They complained about the call rate and not being able to achieve it. It was obvious why. They were worried I would grass them up. I had no intention of doing that. They could get on with it. It was their job and choice, not mine. Three regional team members of the specialist division I now worked for were awful; Bruce being the worst, then Ray and Caroline. All of this contributed to me going on Prozac and probably contributed to the excessive drinking. The regional and divisional meetings didn't help as there was so much drinking involved. It was expected of you to be in the bar, drinking with the management, the so-called team building. It was just a massive piss up. Some would stay up until 5 a.m. in the morning drinking after starting at 5 p.m. I was not in that league. My tolerance for drinking had reached its peak. At one point, I was drinking, over the day and night, six bottles. The only way after that amount to get you through the next day was to drink again. It was now declining rapidly. If I was in the bar at 5 p.m., I was in bed plastered at 8 p.m. No duty of care on Pharma's behalf with that. However, there were more people promoted, given good pay raises by joining in than not. People whom I saw were by far more suitable for positions, and were better qualified, were passed by.

Back to what I wrote.

I felt isolated, lonely, and I had withdrawn from most things. I couldn't cope. I had been good at multi-tasking, due to the work overload and my head feeling cluttered. Where do I start? I was just blanking things out. I had no say. I just couldn't cope with the bullying, and I was just burnt out.

Was it just the job? That was making me feel like this. It wasn't just the job; there was a list of things that added to this feeling of not being able to cope.

For 16 years, I had been in sales. I had always over-achieved and been one of the top performers, if not the 'top performer'. I had never felt this was my calling in life, and I often thought if I really enjoyed or liked what I did, how much better would I have been. I had enjoyed working as a GP rep for Kudos. I loved the team; they were great, along with the management.

I had just got stuck in a rut with sales. Not only a rut but golden handcuffs; there were so many benefits that I felt it impossible to leave due to the financial implication. Plus, I was afraid to pursue what I really wanted to do. I find that quite difficult to believe based on my sales skill; surely, I could sell myself after what I had done in sales.

As a GP rep, it's a good idea to try and have a good relationship with the receptionist and practice manager they will help you get in if you have built up a good rapport with them.

When I joined Pharma, that is when everything started to go wrong for me, and things spiralled out of control. My mood became low, I had lost my motivation, and I wanted to escape from everything.

With Pharma, I felt like a caged animal which paced up and down. It seemed the more I did, the more they wanted. This made me want to do less. I felt that I wanted to blank things out. The sales targets, reports, business plans, exam after exam. They seemed to be endless. How, between January and March 2007, I passed all the exams, I have no idea. I know it felt like there was an exam every day. The text messages, conference calls, the duplication of everything which had no bearing on productive business and getting results. The management who demanded this was reactive not proactive. Pointless.

The job had changed. I was no longer a specialist rep. I had to do training in general practice. This, I did not want to do. I was no trainer and no teacher. I also had no desire to be one. I felt myself switching off completely and losing all that I had ever had. My drive, determination, self-starting drive, motivation, wanting to succeed and bringing the business in, I just didn't care about any of it, and I was just unable to do it. For the first time in my life, I did not care. I was completely empty and had nothing to give. *The job, management, being bullied, the pressure, the depression and drink were killing me.* All of this had to stop or go. I had to take it one step at a time. I did, however, need to do the steps. This was one thing I was not very good at anymore; taking the first step to move forward. I kept on going backwards because I was doing the same things over and over again. I just didn't seem to be able to break that pattern and there was the real fear factor. Job. What would I do? Gee, can I leave him? All of this was just too much for me at that moment.

These changes that needed to be made would not be made immediately or even for a few years. It would take several years, a great deal of pain, and then I would move forward and things would start to change.

There was an article in the Daily Mail that I wrote down. If I had taken note of this, I might have been saved sooner and achieved a great deal more than I have, which is basically nothing in ten years except making my life a bigger mess than it had been.

The article read: '*You can change direction in a career. You need to find out about it, read up on it, consider it.*' If I had done that after leaving the Priory, along with taking on board what was said about recovery, I am sure I would be in a much better place. However, I then would not have this story.

If I could achieve so much when I didn't like it, in some cases hated it, what could I achieve if I did like it?

Chapter Three
January to March, 2007

I cannot tell you many things that happened between January to March, 2007 except I vaguely remember the company 2007 conference. I think, but I can't be sure, it was in the London Metropolitan Hotel as usual. I can also remember that I did not win any of the achievement awards. That could be down to two things. Firstly, the new divisional manager Carol did not like me. I had sung her praises to get the job. Once she was in the job, I wish I never had. She was a great disappointment to me and others in how she treated people. It was also obvious that she had her favourites. She was mean. By that I mean she didn't give us rewards for work well done and going above the call of duty.

For the last three years in a row the flus season had been a nightmare for every single rep and every single company that dealt with the flu vaccine. Carol was also what many would call a 'Little Hitler'. 2006 had been another year of doing more than the call of duty. Also, I do not feel that I performed that well towards the end of 2006; this was due to the pressure that was put on the whole division. From October, the workload was just awful. You would just get on top of things, or think you were on top on things, then more would be added. In the end, you were just behind on everything. I can remember one of my team mates Tanuja saying to me that she just didn't know where to start. *Thank God it was not just me who thought like that.*

I was working, that is, we were all working all the hours God gave us. Weekends were to catch up with all that you were behind on, only to know you were still behind Monday morning.

Working in the specialist division for Pharma, which was flu vaccines and palliative care, one of the most important things for the company and the rep was to have a good flu season, with the flu business signed up at the latest by the end of March. If you hadn't done it by then, it really was unlikely to happen for you. Your whole target depended on those three crucial months. I have no idea if I did it. I think I had done a fair bit before Christmas of signing up flu business with practices for the following year. Most of the practices getting to the end of giving the flu jab. They had targets and they needed their flu clinics to be up and running by October, with the target 'at-risk patients' mostly vaccinated by December.

I remember Pharma had informed us that we would be taking over palliative care in the hospitals. My heart sunk. Didn't we have enough to do? Now we had another person's job on top of everything else.

I did one day of the hospital training and then called in sick, which was genuine. I had sciatica in both my legs and sitting down was just too painful, and I need to see the physio about it. I didn't go back as I really did not want to do the training or work hospitals. I hated them and I really didn't want that along with everything else I had to do or we had to do as a team.

The other things was meeting we had as a division. There are two things that I remember about that. One was a phone call one of the guys was making; Scot was his name. His words were, *"It's the normal negative crap which you really do not need to hear which makes you really demotivated. Most of it could have been done in few hours over one day. Two days weren't really required."*

Then in the ladies' loo, another one of the reps, Bev, was singing '*Take that look off your face*'. She really was concentrating on the '*I bet you couldn't wait to bring all of that bad news to my door*'.

How apt was that. She was sensible; she got another job with the competitor Aventis. Pharma really had changed and was going downhill with regards to how they were treating people. They got worse!

I felt I needed a career move and by chance an opportunity arose, working within hospitals.

The hospital job which I would not have minded doing was with their Biotech division, selling a drug called Enbrel. Although I was not keen on working hospitals, if I got this job, I would only have one area to worry about. Not a multitude of different ones, which were doing my head in seriously now.

I had the interview. I was not in a very good space then. I know I was all over the place. I never should have gone for the interview. I knew that I was a better rep than the other candidate who was going for it; her name was Liz. However, I did not perform well in the interview.

I knew Liz before I came to Pharma. She belonged to the group I called 'the coffee shop kids'. These were the reps who knew all the locations you could go to, to have a coffee with the other reps. I rarely met other reps for coffee and did not know all the locations or wanted to. Liz would come onto the territory; we could all be waiting outside a practice. Whichever rep got to the practice first would go in first and submit their card. You just had to wait for the practice to open. On my territory, which was hard access, you would get to a practice as close to 7 a.m. as possible. It was a very good time to network with other reps and pass on information or share meetings. This would help you progress in the job very quickly if you were new. As a GP rep, the first six months were crucial; you needed to work out which surgeries booked appointments and when. You didn't want to miss that day. Basically, your diary had to be set up from September–December for the following year. If you didn't do that, you were in for the long haul, which would not be nice. I got this sorted.

Liz, however, didn't and would turn up to speck a doctor (specking is turning up at a practice with no appointment, hoping to see a doctor. Some doctors only saw via speck on certain days, other appointments only.), hoping to get in. Not only that, with a 7 a.m. start, you sat in your car outside a practice with other reps waiting for the doors to open and the first rep there submitted their card to see a doctor later or saw a doctor then. You could say one down two to go at this point. After that 7am spec and waiting, she would be going home or for coffee, with the intention of coming out later. Liz did very little except say it couldn't be done. I was getting it done. Liz had been one of the reps who had victimised, bullied and made accusations about me. The list was endless.

Liz got the job. I recall her saying something at one of the conferences which I just remember. Her words were, "It's impossible to sell in an area like this, there are just too many problems with primary care. Trust, consultants, access." The list went on. I had the same problems with the territory. I was doing it. She got the job; I didn't.

That is what I remember today. However, I do have notes dated the 13th September, 2007; these I wrote after reading my notes from December, 2006. I think I blanked a great deal out over the years. This was done, I should imagine, for self-preservation on my behalf. I would have nightmares about Pharma for years. They have become less frequent over the last year, 2016. At least every two weeks, I get nightmares about Pharma. I would always wake the same way.

Disturbed, which I carried around with me for most of that day, trying to analyse it and why. I never resolved it.

Then there was another nightmare. I now regard this one as a warning; I think at the time as well I did but chose to ignore it. It was always the same dream and the same person, but it was related always to Adrian.

My nightmares with Pharma mostly were about Kay. I never really trusted Kay; I have no idea why not. In my dreams, she was there, always looking, always asking for more. Acts, behaviour that I did not trust or understand. Kay would be doing these. Talking to people about me. Her face always the same, a cold stare. There was always pressure.

My other nightmare was always about Martin, one of my boyfriends when I was young. The relationship ended because he was seeing someone else. He never said he was seeing someone else. I felt he was. I had a very strong sixth sense about this. I remember telling my mother about it. At his 21st birthday party, my mother claimed that if he was seeing someone else, he would have her there. I did not believe this. At the party, one of his relatives was talking about his marriage, break up and how it was always the man (referring to himself) that found out last about the affair. I said, or the woman. I was referring to myself. I found out a year later at my brother Joggy's 18th birthday party that Gareth was DJing for him. Gareth Martin and I had been at college together and I pestered Gareth that night about Martin and he came clean and told me Martin had been seeing someone else. I was devastated. I had ended our relationship a year ago after Martin's party and now I was getting married!

The nightmares were always confusing, about Martin leaving, me wanting him back, trying to get him back. Wanting to change. It was always abandonment and not quite getting there. I felt these nightmares were a warning about Adrian. My sixth sense with Adrian could not be wrong in all areas. My sixth sense was warning me when I suspected him of seeing someone else. Plus, he had done so and was mirroring Martin's behaviour. On so many occasions, I wanted to challenge Adrian over this.

I had, all my life, suffered from insecurities, lack of confidence in so many areas. Along with feeling inferior, and paranoia, what happened to me at Pharma did not help either.

Most of these issues were from my early childhood with my family. My own parents, brothers and sisters. I never fitted in at school, had few friends, tended to mix with younger children rather

34

than my own age. I was bullied at every school I attended, which were four in total. Did I have a tattoo 'come bully me'? College was different; I was never bullied there. I have no idea why that was. This is where I met Martin. We got together halfway through the year. Martin made me feel totally insecure.

Adrian and Martin had a few things in common. Martin was born 4th September, 1961, Adrian 6th September, 1953. The same calendar month. They both acted like thugs and morons. Martin pierced his own ear; it looked ridiculous. Adrian had done the same but out-performed Martin by doing both ears with two piercings in each. Martin talked about tattoos. Adrian was a walking tapestry. His arms were covered in multi-coloured tattoos. By all accounts, the red ones were petals; I always thought they were lips. Other things looked like something from a horror movie. He had Bob Marley on his left shoulder at the top. At the top of his chest, on the top of his left pectoral muscle, it said, 'Once forsaken', and on his right, 'In God, we trust'. When having them done, that is how he felt. Neither was capable of being faithful to a partner. (I think I'm in the same category). Adrian was born in Willesden and grew up Bedfont Middlesex. Then he lived with his dad in Alresford. He moved in with an Irish family in Farnborough, Hampshire, after his dad kicked him out. Adrian stayed there till he was 15.

Martin was from Buckinghamshire, Naphill, near High Wycombe, and lived in a five-bedroom house with his parents and sister Donna. He had been privately educated and his parents owned two top-end men's wear shops; many designer brands were sold in the shops.

Martin had a stable upbringing, with parents staying together. However, Adrian's upbringing was very different to that.

I used to think the world of Martin. I can honestly say I really thought the world of Adrian too; I really liked being with him. I can't be sure if I loved him. He just drew women to him, a complete woman magnet. Adrian and I would remain close for years despite all that had happened. God knows how.

Adrian was incredibly hard work to be around and would have my head spinning and render me unable to think while I was in his company. I would be flustered by his self-obsessive compulsiveness and chaotic behaviour. *Chaos was all around Adrian.*

This would cause what we need to sort out, i.e., tidy a wardrobe, not to be done so quickly with mistakes being made. If we went shopping, instead of trying a few things on, Adrian wanted to try one thing on only and that would be it. We ended up disagreeing and had heated discussions in many shops. That would be an understatement. Adrian also used to act like a child and walk out. Adrian would excel at that one. It was probably very amusing to the person serving us. One of them said, "It's different from the normal customers." The shop assistant was often trying to hard not laugh and mentioned about the time going quickly. Others looked shocked and didn't know what to do. It was a complete comedy act. Adrian had no class or taste and had a foul mouth; every other word was either the F or C word. Adrian knew all the London rhyming slang. His speech, you could say, needed serious attention. He was common. I would accuse him of sounding like someone from Billingsgate Market. However, I had never heard or spoken to anyone from Billingsgate. I was forever correcting him on his speech. Martin did use the F word, but I never heard him use the C word. I only ever went up to London shopping with Martin. It was relatively calm and a controlled affair, with nice stuff being brought out and tried on properly.

Some of Martin's relatives lived in London Wimbledon, the nice part of London. Martin wanted to know the London slang and speak it. He also wanted to speak with a London accent and would try. Why he aspired to be like that, I have no idea. I guess he wanted to be common; at times, he was loud and uncouth. Adrian would excel with regards to being common, foul and loud-mouthed. How on earth did I fall for Adrian or have any form of a relationship with him, which turned out very differently to what we both expected, I have no idea.

Both would have me in tears. Martin over his jealousy and ending the relationship for something as simple as speaking with another guy or going out with my friends. This caused me to feel totally insecure, and I ended up dropping most of my friends due to his issues. He was very controlling and, in some ways, hard and unkind. Adrian had me in tears with his attitude and the 'dark side' he had. I would say to him, "Have you gone over to the '*dark side*'?" Along with his demanding attitude and his quick temper, everything had to be done '*NOW*'. He used to send me a text saying I treated him like a c**t, which I never did. He would then not answer his phone, switching it off, not replying to texts. The one thing that Adrian would have over Martin. There would be no contest here. He couldn't speak, he shouted; didn't talk, it was a very raised voice most of the time. He was a loud, foul-mouthed person. His 'dark side'. All this caused much pain and at times many tears. Apologies would follow, and I genuinely believed he was sorry for his behaviour. In many ways, I feel that Martin was by far the colder person. Both had their own insecurities.

Adrian would always be on time for things; he would always check that I was going to be there, and that we were meeting that night. It was like a record player put on repeat. It was never said just once. Possibly an insecurity issue from his past, I would say.

At the early stage of our relationship, I was always there for him. Even later, I tried and was there in so many ways. If Adrian was late, there was always a reason like traffic. Martin was late for most things. Both were full of themselves and incredibly vain. Both had issues with their teeth. Martin was terrified of the dentist and required fillings. Adrian had issues as a result of his lack of teeth due to being beaten up hit by a baton; lack of oral hygiene had to be one of the top reasons.

Adrian was a recovering addict. Martin drank a fair bit when we were together; he also, early on in our relationship, smoked a few joints. I didn't; for me it would always be drink. Whether Martin landed up with a drink problem or drugs, I have no idea. I could see a potential drink problem being there when we were together.

With both Martin and Adrian, especially at the beginning with Adrian, although it didn't improve much later on, it was me who usually paid for things. I would give more to both and they would take it. While at college, Martin earned £10 per week working in his parents' shop. After he had paid for bus fares and our drinks on a Saturday night when we went out, he normally had no money left. During the week, I tended to buy the drinks and pay for things. I worked as a waitress for the local hotel in Thame, The Spread Eagle (Martin would make sexual comments about the name). My earnings were over £20 a week plus I got tips so that helped.

Martin could be smutty and would have naked women on his wall. Adrian, surprisingly, was not smutty and didn't have any porn or pictures like that in his flat. Not even when he was on drugs. Just when he was with prostitutes, they would watch porn films as he was lonely but they were never his films. '*In his world then drug addict dealer's prostitutes porn films were the norm.*'

Pharma meant I could buy nice clothes, pay to go out. However, I would have coffee with friend at times but that was it. I was relatively independent. The first time in my life there was money, something I was not used to. Both my parents had been bad with money and we had precious little as children. Most of the money was spent either on cigarettes or gambling with my dad. I would end up living in a council house in Thame with my mother and her new partner Ralph, who just so happened to have been my father's best friend.

Although Adrian had no shame with regards to me paying for things early in our relationship, later he would be much better.

Martin was a good-looking guy, well presented in his appearance, but did not have the charm and magnetism that Adrian had. Martin could be smutty in his talk. Adrian surprisingly was not. Now that is hard to believe but true. Adrian was not attractive; he had a hard face and steely cold grey slits for eyes. Plus he looked like a convict, the one that should be behind bars.

He was, however, a woman magnet. I have no idea how or why. Adrian had nothing that should attract a woman. He was, as I've said, fun to be around; very funny, people liked him and his company. Women just loved him despite his past background and behaviour.

Martin had taste. Adrian did not. His appearance was poorly thrown together, at times grubby. Ticky-tacky fifty dirty things surrounded Adrian at all times. He had very little idea about general cleanliness in the home. When he moved from sheltered accommodation, one of several comments were, "You're a filthy pig," and, "Even the hoover needs to be cleaned." His face was quite a picture, hard with raised eyebrows. His flat would become the *Hammer House of Horrors* later in our relationship.

When I look at both, in so many ways they were different but the same. Vain, conceited, unable to be faithful. Both had their insecurities.

They were born on opposite sides of the track.

I felt that I was not good at close relationships with the opposite sex.

Now the nightmares were about Adrian. Yet for years, the confusing, insecure, abandonment nightmares had been about Martin. I always felt it was a reference to Adrian.

On 13th September, I re-read my notes and looked in my diary that I used for work, personal appointment and other events.

It would be just under nine months before I would read what I had written at Christmas, 2006. How I truly felt. Much would pass in that period to make me seriously look at my future and for the first time, admit defeat in many areas of my life. (This defeat was not as great as it should have been and today, in 2017, I can honestly say that I have admitted defeat with the drinking). I can't and don't want to do it anymore.

I cannot really remember much about going back to Pharma after Christmas 2006; everything was very vague. Not until the 29th March. Although things that happened on the 28th would hold some memories, in between blackouts.

Christmas had not been great; I had tried my best to make it as enjoyable as possible. Gee's dad had come to stay. Sue, a friend of mine (another of life's takers), came around Christmas Day. Melvin joined us Christmas Day morning and Boxing Day morning. Melvin's mum had died a few days before. It had hit Melvin hard, even though it was expected. His face said it all. It was painful to see as there was nothing that could be done to ease the situation for him.

I had done some drinking over Christmas, which ranged from moderate to heavy whenever I could got hold of the stuff and hide it.

I would return to work the week commencing 8th January, with that sinking and dreaded feeling of complete emptiness. Being hollow.

I would lie about my call report on the 8th and 9th (first time ever) and be drunk most of the day. I couldn't do that on Wednesday as I was seeing the occupational therapy doctor. I went sick but drunk. (I should imagine I cancelled the doctor but I can't remember; that is what is written).

I would cancel my appointments on Thursday as I couldn't cope with them. Now the drinking was really getting a hold. It was really taking over as I couldn't deal with how I felt. Plus, an addiction like that is cunning, powerful and mutilative. (AA big book).

Now the burnt-out feeling and the addiction both had a hold that I would not be able to get rid of for many months. The addiction, never. The burnt-out feeling could be cured with time, but I would not want to deal with that sort of pressure again, so it would have to be readdressed.

This is what I had wrote:

It seems funny that I have chosen this period 13/9/2007 to re-look at and read what I had written. All this week I have felt drained, lacked energy and enthusiasm. But that could be due to events that have transpired over the last four weeks, which were not my best ideas. They never should have started or happened. Now I have woken up from a dream. That I am around Adrian's flat, I am drugged up on prescription medication, I am telling him I won't remember anything tomorrow. I cannot work out why I am here. There is a wedding dress veil with the price tag hanging up on a coat stand, which he says belongs to his niece. Adrian goes out to get a take-away. I am left with his friend under instructions to keep me in bed. But I am all over the place, staggering around the room, outside opening the boot of my car.

It's bizarre. Thinking about it now, I feel it was a warning of things to come between us and the effect his relationship would have on me. Adrian had fucked me once and had no intention of seeing me again. I was confused, hurt and wanted more. Moth to a flame, Icarus to the sun.

I had decided to avoid AA meetings that Adrian went to. He's at AA St Mary's occasionally, so I just had to deal with that one but the rest, just steer clear. It would be at St Mary's meeting that one of the AA guys would have a go at Adrian for getting involved with me as I was a newcomer and he would ruin my recovery. Adrian was not happy with this but looking back, did our involvement ruin my recovery?

My recovery would come when I wanted it and was ready to do what it would take.

I gave Adrian a very wide berth. It upset and hurt me. I am pretty sure it was my pride and I was feeling hurt and rejected. Yes, rejection is one thing I knew only two well. I don't need this to be a relapse trigger for me, which sends me back down this very slippery slope of drink from which there was a chance I would not return from.

January, 2007, Friday: worked and the business was good but morale low and burn-out high with the drink always in the background.

Saw the occupational doctor on 17th January. Made sure I had not drunk for a few days.

Was meant to have a phone appointment with the occupational doctor on the 23rd. It didn't happen as I was in an appointment. The meeting with the occupational doctor was, Kay, my manager's idea; it had not gone well on the 17th. I don't know why. Could possibly have been my attitude or the fact at this point I was very ill and on the verge of a breakdown. I have no idea.

The rest of January, I could maintain some work in the field. Had little time off. 31st, 1st, 2nd being my birthday, I was drunk all day so nothing was achieved. (Being drunk for my birthday was going to happen a great deal in the future. Well, completely out of my head all day and night more like.) This was a bit like New Year's Eve 2006, drunk all day, then Gee would not open the champagne at 12 to celebrate it. That caused the typical argument an addict/alcoholic would have to get their drink/ fix.

6th February, another telephone appointment with the occupational doctor; this was achieved.

13th February, Benchmarking Day at Birmingham. This was awful; I could not understand why it was necessary for reps who were already trained.

14th February, Admin Day, drunk, felt the pressure to be great.

28th–1st March, off, drunk. Don't know what I put down on the call report. (This is dreadful, reading and writing this, what a state I was in.)

2nd March, didn't make evening meal with Geoff, drunk.

16th March, drunk.

20th–23rd, hair appointment cancelled, God knows what happened the other days.

24th, drunk.

26th, drunk.

27th, drunk, hair appointment cancelled.

28th March, drunk. This was the day I phoned Sarah, the occupational nurse. I was plastered. I told her about the pressure of the job, drinking and the depression; how I couldn't go on. (I would call Sarah on the 28th many times in and out of blackouts. At one time, I can recall today that she was not shouting but saying she would help; she was distressed. I would also call my doctor three times. I can't remember that; I was told at one of our appointments that it *was pitiful).*

Gee was at home that day; he was in and out. I'd had enough; I wanted out. I wanted out there and then I did not want to last another day on this planet. Well, not another second. I took an overdose of codeine, hoping that would finish me off but all that it did was land me in A&E at QA hospital, which I never want to return to. (I would spend many times in A&E at QA for overdoses, from 2010–2016; saying and writing that I didn't want to return was another thing that didn't happen).

I couldn't even get that right. As I was lying on the bed in the hospital full of self-pity, feeling that Gee would just leave me there this time.

After several hours, he did come to see me, very distressed and upset. Made me eat some soup, which I threw up. It seemed like a hundred years before I saw the psychiatrist. I was being sick throughout the appointment. I went all through my drinking, what I had been like. The amounts, the absence. Couldn't she just give me some anti-sickness tablets and Libram to bring me down as the withdrawal was beginning to be horrendous?

I'm now sitting here writing this thinking to myself, how the hell can I go back to that job which has contributed to the stress, the burnt-out feeling and the heavy drinking which turned me into an alcoholic?

I am now feeling down about the mess I've got myself into and the rejection there. Thinking am I good enough? That really wasn't one of my better ideas. I am hoping that his (Adrian) heart is broken. Well feeling like, he felt too much for me. Yeah right.

That is what I wrote. How did it all lead up to this? How did I meet Adrian and what happened?

Chapter Four
Marchwood and Adrian

29th March, 2007, I was admitted to the Priory Hospital in Marchwood. Occupational Health at Pharma had sorted it out. I had company personal health insurance so I wouldn't have to pay for it, and I would be there for a month.

This is where I meet Adrian. This is where it begins.

I was in a very bad state when I arrived at the Priory. It was in the morning and I had to wait for a room. I was in the waiting room being ill. I think at this point I had several bottles of red wine a day. I am not quite sure how many at this point. Four, maybe six at times.

The only way I knew how to deal with the withdrawal was to drink. That normally stopped the vomiting after a few glasses. The withdrawal is due to the level of alcohol in your system reducing too quickly, you need to maintain a slow reduction in alcohol levels. Not only that, it is dangerous to stop drinking quickly. You need medical help for that. The worst thing anyone can do at this point is to stop that person drinking, thinking they are helping them. They are not. They are putting the drinker in a life-threatening position. I learnt that in the Priory. You could have an alcoholic fit or seizure. This can happen anytime between 3–5 days of stopping drinking. That is why medical intervention is needed.

It felt like an eternity that I was in the waiting room. There were many people coming and going with appointments. I was there being ill. I'm convinced that they leave you in that waiting room for the sake of it, so you go through the humiliation of being there. My room, when I got there, had been available for ages.

A doctor came to see me and went through a load of medical details but I can't remember much about that part. The only part I remember is he offered me the anti-sickness injection. In hindsight, I should have taken it. Instead, I opted for the tablets, which I threw up. My question to him was, "Do you think I need to be here?" His reply was yes. Of all the stupid questions, probably for the first time in my whole life, medically this was the one time I needed to be under medical care. I was put on medication. Libram—this was used for alcohol withdrawal. It helps with the withdrawal symptoms. There are many—sweating, hot and cold, shaking. It is not really any help with the *delirium tremens (DTs),* which is a rapid onset of confusion usually caused by withdrawal from *alcohol. When it occurs, it is often three days into the withdrawal.* At that point you are quite doped up on the Libram, for which you start on a high dose and it is reduced over 5–7 days. If you find it difficult with the withdrawal, you can request some in between your normal doses. Vitamin B compound and Thiamine, these are used to protect your organs or in some cases help to improve the poor condition they are in. After my blood test, my liver function test was fine. I was one of the lucky ones; many weren't, and they had to have the vitamin B injections.

I was on Prozac when I arrived. I would be taken off the Prozac by the consultant later in my recovery. He studied me for over a week once I started the four-week treatment plan. I went into a manic high mood. I was over the top, probably annoying and manic to be around; I needed to come down from that. Prozac supposedly had that effect on people. It wasn't the anti-depressant that was used for my type of depression, he claimed; I had bipolar so I was put on mood stabilisers, one of them being Seroquel. Today I am still on that drug along three others.

My consultant, who was a psychiatrist, came to see me when I was first admitted. He wanted to know how I felt. We discussed it. I didn't feel great about anything. The medication which I was on, Libram, was helping with the withdrawals. I was however very drowsy and would spend a fair bit of time in bed sleeping.

The worst part with the withdrawals was at night I would sweat badly and on a few occasions, had to change the bed as it was soaking wet. During this short period, I had improved my general hygiene, which had gone almost completely prior to being admitted, and I took more pride in my appearance. My consultant was pleased with this. There was talk about my treatment, a four-week treatment plan. This would take up most of my time. It would start 3rd April, 2007.

I could not start the treatment plan any sooner; I was too ill along with being doped up on the Libram.

When I did start, Carolyn, one of the patients there, came to meet me on the 3rd at reception. She would take me to meet the group. *I thought she worked there to start.* Carolyn was the same as me—an alcoholic. I went into a room and there were several people there. Jane, Jo, Mark, Martyn and John. Carolyn, Jane, Jo, Martyn and I were in-patients at the Priory; Mark and John weren't. They both lived in Southampton and got the bus daily to Marchwood. There would be an issue with John; not many of us liked him. He was distant, wasn't a team player and didn't join in. I have no idea what happened to John once he left Marchwood.

We were all the same in one way: *'Drinking alcoholically being unwell with a progressive illness'.*

Every time you went back to drink, relapsed, had a slip, picked up, fell off the wagon, call it what you may, you went back at the same level you finished when you last drank; it progressively got worse. There are so many saying about this progressive illness. One being, 'It is not the second or third carriage of the train that kills, you it's the first'. *That means it is the first drink you take on a relapse that will or could kill you.* Another, each time you got off the train (stop drinking), when you restart you don't get back on the same carriage, you get on further down the line. When you get to the last carriage, when you get off that one you either get clean and sober or you die. *That means with each relapse, you are getting closer to dying of an alcoholic death if you continue with the drink. The last carriage is the last chance, but we never know which carriage we are getting on and off.* Throw the bipolar depression on top; it doesn't come alone but rather brings other things with it. Not just manic highs and lows. Petrol is already being poured on to a raging fire, *water is not going to put that out.*

Our backgrounds would be different, along with our stories of how drinking started and what happened.

I did not realise how seriously ill I was with the addiction and bipolar depression. I didn't have the right attitude in the way I came in to the Priory, although I was beat in so many ways and didn't think things could get any worse. I was not beaten and they did and would get worse.

I did not take on board what was said about my alcoholism or my bipolar depression. It was treated rehab like summer camp. *I can see that very clearly now.*

I was arrogant without realising it. I was un-teachable without realising it. I gave more through to my clothes, appearance and jewellery than I did taking in the actual information which was going to keep me alive. I at this point did not understand that this illness kills you. To get better, **'You have to change everything.'** *I didn't. I would carry on the same and get the same result but not*

45

only the same results, they got worse and brought more friends to my two illnesses.

There was a weekly timetable of sessions broken down into daily sessions. Every day one of us could be doing *'our story'* or step work; there were videos to watch, meditations, art work, classes, plus much more. All these sessions had to be attended and the work required completed; this was not optional. There was work we had to complete in our own time when we were not in the therapy groups. This was mainly reading and completing paper work and it also required a daily diary and inventory.

I had become obsessed with the gym again. One of the friends of bipolar depression and addiction.

Amongst the AA twelve steps to recovery, steps one, two and three are the most important steps you take with any addiction. *If you want recovery with AA, you have to take these steps seriously, not just put pen to paper. That's what I did and I didn't realise.*

Along with step work, we had to tell our story about our background, how we started drinking, what happened and how we ended up there.

We all read the AA big book (Alcohol Anonymous), Living Sober. Along with the Twelve Step program which aids recovery. You would complete while you were in rehab the first *'Three steps'.*

The books were handed to me when I went into my first session.

These sessions always started at 9 a.m. We would meet as a group by ourselves and one of us would read from the book *The Promises of the Day.* We then discussed what it meant to each of us.

At 9:30 a.m., the counsellor would come in. The group would discuss their daily diary, how we felt the day before and what had happened along with the inventory of the day. *'How you felt about the forth coming day.'* These had to be handed in before 8 a.m. that day so they could be read by the counsellor before the session began.

These are my daily diaries; I had been in the sessions then for a week. The diary was compulsory along with daily inventories, which were completed in the morning before the sessions began. There would also be a week-ending diary to complete.

Monday, 9/4/2007

*I had a VERY/GOOD/INDIFFERNT/BAD day today (*express your feelings.) I had circled 'good'.

This was because:

It was great to get back to the group therapy session as on Sunday, I had felt a little bit isolated and depressed.

Today, I learnt:

That recovery is all about the steps, following the steps and what they mean. You cannot do this alone. Well, I couldn't. (That is part of the Alcohol Anonymous step program.)

Today, I enjoyed: hearing everyone's diaries. Most had a positive weekend. In addition, getting my step one paper work along with Jo. I felt I was moving forward with the twelve steps. (There are twelve different steps to complete; in rehab, you complete the first three. In AA, you get a sponsor to take you through the steps). Having Gee and Holly, my dog, over for a few hours. The AA meeting was one of the best I have been to. Powerful message and guidance but some very humorous comments.

Today, I did not enjoy:

The situation with Callum (a new arrival). I felt nervous and very threatened when I got back from the AA meeting.

Today, I feel I have made progress in the following areas:

That I need to follow the steps. Listen more and understand more of what is expect of me for my recovery.

I am aware of the need to make progress in the following areas:

By concentrating on one step one at a time but to be aware of all the twelve steps to read. To read all the texts from step one intro and guidelines and put step one in my own words.

I intend to make this progress by:

Reading *Living Sober*, which John recommend yesterday.

Other things I felt about today:

Wanting to concentrate on step one. There is still so much for me to learn.

Anything else…

I felt a bit unsure about having Callum sitting in on the group; I really couldn't understand why he was there. I felt it took the emphasis away from our work and the focus became more on him, what he was doing, why he was doing it etc.

My inventory for 12/04/2007:

I will not use any mind-altering drugs/chemicals today. (.)*This sentence was given to you by the counsellors. All patients wrote these words at the top of an A4 piece of paper)*

Feeling great, I had dreams about work. When I went to the gym, my mind was still on work. I was thinking they will be on their way to the regional meeting for two days. How I hated them! I never liked being away from home. Then I guess it was my higher power saying how peaceful, safe and happy I felt here. How I was enjoying my therapy and realising that my last drink was two weeks ago today. The world hadn't ended, I'm still here, it's not been that bad, not having a drink is quite easy. Then I remember someone saying to me when the student is ready, the teacher will appear. I know that I am in the right place at the right time for my sobriety.

Cathy: I will not use any mind-altering chemicals today.

That sentence was put in by you to keep you focused and to set up one of the goals for the day. *'Not to relapse.'*

That was the format. These had to be completed.

12/04/2007, that is the day I met Adrian.

My introduction to Adrian was at the Marchwood AA meeting on Thursday night, 12/04/2007. I can't tell you if I had seen him at any of the other AA meetings I had to attend. At the end of the meeting at 9 p.m., Adrian came up to me and grabbed my arm, causing me to turn and look at him. His words were, "You so much better." I must have looked bad when he first saw me for him to make that type of comment. That was not Adrian's style. He normally was not interested in other people or their recovery.

I was quite taken back by this. Shocked that someone had touched me. However, I was flattered. He was scruffy, arms covered in multi-coloured tattoos, his teeth needed attention and he was common. His shares in AA meetings overall would be funny but there was a serious message there. His shares from the floor when I first meet him were quite painful on occasions. He was liked, very blunt, outspoken, I regarded him as a thug and a moron from the wrong side of the track. At first he made no real impact on me.

I would later find that something attracted me to him. Adrian should have been the least likely person for me to fall for and want anything to do with.

Adrian would make me feel good. I would look out for him at meetings and try to talk to him. One time, I recall him saying to everyone, "She always has a different outfit. Imelda Marcos." I did have an excessive amount of clothes, shoes and handbags.

My first AA meeting was at Romsey; I didn't want to go. I felt I was above that. It was only the dregs of society who wore trench coats, sat on a park bench with a brown paper bag with their drink in it that go to AA. Not people like me. This was quite a contradiction in terms as in the end, all I wanted was a park bench and a bottle of wine and to be left alone to get on with it. That is the insanity of the illness.

AA was compulsory in the group; we had to attend four a week; Totton Monday, Romsey Wednesday, Marchwood Thursday and

Saturday. If you went home for the weekend, it had to be after the morning AA meeting.

I said to the group when I was going to my first AA meeting that I didn't want to go. If I went, I wanted a balaclava. I was scared someone I knew would see me there. I have no idea why I thought like that. I did not know any alcoholics. Apart from the group I was with and they all looked okay; they weren't and hadn't ever been someone sitting on a park bench with a brown paper bag and a bottle in it, wearing a dirty black coat. Before I came to the Priory, I was sat at home with a bottle of wine in filthy clothes that hadn't been washed for day. What I wore to bed, I got up in, stayed in and went to the co-op in. *I was worried about someone seeing me at and AA meeting well-presented in clean clothes and washed!*

My consultant tried to reassure me, saying that doctors and many professional people attend these meetings. I found that hard to believe. However, it was true. The paranoia I felt when I went to my first meeting was awful; all the way in the taxi, I was not happy. When we got out of the taxi and I was walking there, I felt like the lowest of the low. In the meeting, I was pleasantly surprised; they all looked normal, and there weren't any down and outs.

While in Marchwood, I attended the AA meetings that I was required to, and I noted that Adrian went to most of them. I would be looking out for him. Not the best reason to be there. After I left Marchwood, that would be a reason for me to go to an AA meeting in that area to see Adrian.

That would not be good for recovery. I should have been there for me and my recovery, not to see Adrian. *I had no recovery. It was a relapse waiting to happen.*

One of the most bizarre things with Adrian was that I had never wanted or tried to see, be with anyone, or found anyone remotely attractive while I was married to Gee before this.

At Marchwood as individuals, we went through our stories' steps 1–3 and recovery plan with the group. We knew each other well. I got on incredibly well with Mark, Jo and Martyn were close, Jane had been really good friends with Carolyn, and we all would see Carolyn at aftercare Tuesday evenings or one of the Marchwood AA meetings. Carolyn was discharged a week after I arrived; she had completed the four-week treatment plan. There was a slight cross-over with the group; as our group started, another group was finishing, With Carolyn being in that group. The two groups became like one. We all attended aftercare. My network of recovering alcoholics was expanded.

I had participated well, got on with everyone, and did not feel like an outsider as I did in many areas of my life. I was pleased not to be at home and didn't want to go back. *A form of escapism.*

For the first time in my life, I was happy to hand the whole lot over to someone else to sort out my work and the appointments I had. In many ways, I feel that I had a complete breakdown, which would explain why I just didn't care about it anymore.

Instead, I had started going to the gym while I wasn't in rehab to get myself fit; I was also running outside. I could see me being able to take part in the *'Great South Run'* in October.

There were ponies in the field that I used to go down and feed everyday with carrots or apples. My Priory should have been about my recovery, not getting fit and back into shape and spending time with ponies and feeding them. *I didn't see it then.* I do now.

It was on one of these occasions in the evening that Adrian turned up at about 6 p.m. in a Mercedes 190 E Red, an old G, possibly H, about 30 years old. It looked like a wreck to me. I was quite shocked to see Adrian in that car. I was not impressed. He stopped the car, asked me to get in. I didn't want to but he persisted. I would later learn that Adrian persisted until he got his way. I would also learn that it was easier to say yes to him quickly than go through the long *'No'* process as Adrian was relentless.

I got in, we drove to the car park and chatted, then another AA member turned up. Adrian and he were going to a meeting down in Poole. Adrian was doing a share down there. This just increase my interest in him. I then thought, *he likes me!* I was getting better, I thought. I was not thinking as straight and my attention was elsewhere, not on recovery but on Adrian.

My last day in the Priory Marchwood was Saturday, 28th April. The group had brought each other goodbye presents. It was quite a sad time for us. I left Marchwood with my recovery plan that had been approved by the counsellors. It was written well and had all that was required in it for a good recovery. Academically, A +. Reality, 0.

I saw my consultant. I was very excited when he said that it would be three months before I could return to work. I was over the moon, even more so when he said it would be a staggered return; X number of hours to start and then increased over a six-week period. I did not want to return to Pharma. For the first time in my life, I wanted to walk away from the problem. In the past, I had wanted to walk from problems but never did; I stayed and resolved them. This would not be the case in this instance. The nightmares had started and I always woke up feeling anxious, disturbed and restless, along with a feeling of pure fear and a cold sweat. My day would always be tainted if I had a nightmare. I was edgy and nervous; I couldn't think straight. My thoughts all day returned to the nightmare, trying to understand it but I never really did. The only thing I was sure of was it would not be in my best interest in any way to return. Pharma had caused me more problems and the cost had been too high. I would see that much later.

Aftercare was there as a support base for people who had come into Marchwood. It was on a Tuesday evening for the recovering alcoholics but also for their partners. It was two separate groups. I have no idea what was talked about in the group which Gee attended. This support would be there for up to a year. When you reached a year, you would get a one-year chip (like a coin). People were incredibly proud of these chips. The idea was you could hand your chip on to someone later who had reached that milestone.

It would be nice to say at this point that I would get better and go on to live a better life. That didn't happen. Instead, I got myself into a bigger mess and my recovery from alcohol and depression would be short-lived. I would relapse in June, after six weeks of leaving the Priory. I didn't know why! Just went to the Spar and brought not a bottle but a box of red wine. It would be one of the many occasions I would say to myself, '*Just one bottle/box. I will stop tomorrow.*' It never happened.

I went back to Marchwood 40 days later.

A very short-lived treatment. I went in on Thursday and Friday. Then insisted I came home at the weekend, which I did. I should have driven myself back on Monday, 18th June. I didn't. I stayed at home to drink and got drunk.

Gee would come home, storm into the house Monday afternoon demanding why I had not gone back in and accusing me of having no intention of going. Which was true. I returned on 18th, completely drunk and out of it.

I would find out years later how he found out I was at home. I had been down the club over the weekend swimming. On Monday morning, I did the same, went to the club and had a swim. I was talking with Melvin and Dee about returning. Dee had offered to take me back as I was unsure of driving. I said I'd be okay; I'd get there. Melvin then spent the morning phoning Marchwood Priory and eventually got through to the consultant I was seeing for my bipolar depression. Melvin asked if I had returned. I had not and, the consultant, after checking, confirmed that I had not returned but would make a few phone calls to see where I was. He phoned Gee. *Hence, the reason he returned from work.* This interference by Melvin that I was informed of years later, I would not be happy about, even though Melvin had my best interests at heart.

Gee took me back to the Priory on Monday. Tuesday, I insisted on going home. I had gone to the canteen with Neil, who was now just doing aftercare and had done his four-week stint in rehab, and Mark; The three of us always had a laugh. I had told Neil I wanted to go home and he had agreed to take me if Gee wouldn't. It was all planned.

The only funny thing that happened that day was that while in the canteen, Mark showed Neil and me a text, A Harry the Hamster. It was one of those loud, noisy, humorous texts that you watch. We were in stitches, laughing, not just at the picture but the fact that Mark was trying to turn the volume off as it was so loud and the whole canteen had gone quiet, and everyone was looking at the three of us. One of our saving graces was that, at least, we were on a table by ourselves. With the Priory, you must understand that it deals with depression, eating disorders as well as people with addictive problems. Carla, one of the counsellors, was not happy. She came over to the table and pointed out to the three of us that it was inappropriate, people with many and varied problems were in here, and some, who although might hear only the audio, would find that text disturbing. We were well and truly reprimanded.

After leaving the canteen, the three of us went outside. Gee was there. I insisted he take me home. Carla tried very hard to talk some sense into me, saying that my addiction had really got a hold of me and taken over. *It had and I needed medical help for it.* I would not listen and insisted I return home. At this point, it is pointless trying to help someone when they are determined to drink; you might as well let them get on with it. They will find a way to drink. The only person who will land up distressed and upset will be the person who is trying to stop them. They will be the one who suffers the most. The best thing for them to do for themselves is walk away or just let the addict get on with it. *The addiction had got a real hold on me, I just didn't realise it.* Again, denial.

Gee took me home.

My relapse in June–July lasted 40 days on and off.

I went back into the Marchwood Priory for three weeks and came out on 3rd August. While in there for three weeks, it was very different. There was a great deal of conflict. I didn't get along that well with the new group; this was due to my bad attitude and the excuses I would make that it was my depression that needed sorting. That did need addressing but the alcohol was a big problem. I did not get on well with the counsellors Virginia and Peter. I especially didn't like Peter; I felt he was a git. Carolyn had relapsed along with me. Hers had been quite spectacular. Carolyn had gone back to America and had hoped to get back with her husband; that did not happen. Carolyn had checked in at the JFK airport to return to the UK and her son had taken her to the airport. However, she had no intention of getting on that flight but checked in her luggage. Then Carolyn walked out of the airport and booked herself into the hotel next door or close by. I think it was the Crowne Plaza; they had no normal rooms, it was 4th of July, the American Independence Day. The only room available was the penthouse. She took it, went upstairs, opened the mini bar and drank herself stupid. She had fantastic view of the fireworks that night. All her family were frantic about finding her. As she had checked her luggage in and left the airport, the FBI were looking for her. Her family found her the next morning. Her husband came to collect her and pay the bill. Carolyn said in the group session when telling us this story that her husband had gone very pale when he saw the bill. The FBI did not press charges since this was typical alcoholic behaviour.

Peter was all over Carolyn; it was annoying. He said, Carolyn, "I was so worried about you when I heard that the FBI were looking for you." It was sickening, the way he said it. He was very good at making Carolyn cry over her broken down marriage. Her husband was with another woman; Carolyn still loved him and wanted him back. Peter took great delight, I felt, in making Carolyn open up and talk about it more than was necessary. I personally felt that Peter liked Carolyn in tears.

Peter and I got on very badly this time. Well, it hadn't been great the last time, but it was tolerable and with no real issue. This time we clashed. I felt that he and Virginia picked on me. I became very upset and walked out of one of the sessions. I was in a bad way due to drinking and coming back into rehab. The medication I was on for the bipolar depression was not doing its job for three reasons. One being all of it said avoid alcohol, the other I didn't take much of it anyway, and I would find out later that I was actually on the wrong medication but that would take ten years.

I felt things were not handled very well. I did try but again, my attitude was appalling at times. I would still, after this, do things completely wrong. Three times in one year in rehab and still do it wrong. However, it did get worse!

I would see Adrian again. He didn't see me when I first came in. Thank God he was one of the people I definitely didn't want to see me like this.

Again, I was constantly sick; they provided me with a sick bowl this time. Most of the time, I spent outside, being sick. They kept me waiting for my room. Once I had my room, Gee left. Carolyn was very good to me and even took me to the canteen when they were having their evening meal. I couldn't eat anything. The AA meeting was on that evening and Carolyn suggested that I attend. I did. I was a total mess; I hadn't had a bath or put clean clothes on for day. Most of the people knew me. Only one made a comment. That would be a week later. The guy said I saw you last week when you came back in. "You looked dreadful." Even the nursing staff had commented on it. I was again a total mess.

I went through the same program as before. I did okay. I didn't enjoy it as much due to the group and my issues with the counsellors. I met new people. Kim I really did not like, and she felt the same about me. Natasha I liked; she was young, and I felt for her. In her early 20s, incredibly attractive. Simon was okay; he didn't really say much but what he did say was relevant and sometimes challenging.

Before Simon left, he told everyone he did not want recovery and that once he left here, he was going to go up into the hills with his tent and his St Bernard and drink. He had no intention of staying sober; it was not what he wanted.

Although the group spent many hours trying to persuade him differently, it had no effect. As I have said before, there is no point in trying to help someone when they are like that. They will do it anyway. Recovery only happens if you've hit your rock bottom or something has happened in your life that makes you want to recover. You have to want it. Then accepting it will be hard work. You will then stand a chance.

Then there was Richard. He was gay and incredibly upset with his liver function test results; they were very bad by all accounts. Peter would have an issue with Richard and put him down and ask the group if we felt Richard had put any effort into his story. Richard had only spoken a few words and then Peter made that comment. How could Peter make any judgement when he hadn't heard his story from start to finish? This I pointed out and it did not go down well.

Before I left, I had to have a signing-off session with Peter. He had seen Carolyn and sung her praises, seen her on time and spent time with her. With me, he was half an hour late; it was the quickest signing-off session in the history of time. His words were that no one in the group wanted anything to do with me. I said that was not strictly true but some were wary of me. I did not pursue the conversation any further; we were going to get nowhere. I left.

Adrian saw me after I had been in there for a week; it was on the Thursday in the evening. Gee was there. I said, "Hi." He gave me a hug and looked at Gee. That look that you give someone to check out the competition. I said, "I'm still here."

His reply was, "Good, it's the best place for you."

I had been very judgemental of Adrian. I was sure he would find it difficult to get a girlfriend or any girl be interested in him. *That was not the case.* How wrong could I be! He was a girl magnet. They loved him.

My recovery *again* took a nose dive since I was thinking about other things. Not recovery but ways to get to know Adrian and to be with him. I find this quite difficult at times to understand as I had been with Gee for years, and although our marriage was dreadful, I had never been unfaithful to him and never wanted to be unfaithful to him before getting to know Adrian.

Chapter Five
37 Days Sober

August, 2007 is when I would get to know Adrian much better.

I had sat in many AA meetings listening to Adrian sharing his stories. There were two that I remember well. One was his anger management that he had decided to go back for counselling. This was partly due to Angie, a girlfriend who would come and go. Adrian was obsessed with Angie and thought the world of her. He thought he loved her. She had hurt him terribly and Adrian could not cope. He would later call her a c**t.

His words, not mine. In this share, he also stated how they had got back together and she had behaved. He wasn't specific about what happened. He indicated that she had made him feel worthless. For the first time in his life, he knew what jealousy was and how it felt. I would learn later that Angie had sex with other men when she was with Adrian. This was at Marchwood, the Saturday AA meeting. I went over to him after the meeting and spoke with him very briefly, saying that he was not worthless. Adrian was a broken person at that point. He was in recovery but not recovering. His past held him back. He had lost so much to drink and drugs. Although he was clean and sober, he was barely hanging on by a thread. He, however, did have a recovery.

Adrian had turned up with Angie once at Marchwood. It was when I was in there for the *third time.* They both walked in later. Adrian, as usual, strutted ahead of Angie. Angie was attractive and very slim, I remember. I was actually quite upset about this and I had no idea who she was. It would be later that I would find out all about her.

Angie would cause total chaos, emotional pain, insecurities, jealousy and anger. Quite a bit. Adrian admittedly was in a state due to drink, drugs and many other things. Angie was just a neurotic anorexic self-centred, self-obsessed lying bitch. She would wreck every relationship she got into. The fall-out for that person would be awful and at that moment in time it was Adrian.

Adrian, being three years plus sober, did not need this. He might have been three years sober and at this point quite a few addicts are getting their lives together. Adrian was not. He was clean and sober but his life was a total chaotic mess in everything. Adrian was still very ill and very vulnerable.

He had closed himself down in so many ways, so he didn't feel pain. He hadn't closed himself enough down to avoid the pain that Angie would bring.

I heard him share from the floor at Marchwood at the Thursday evening AA meeting. His statement before my recovery was, "I thought a good night in was watching a porn movie with a couple of prostitutes and a bottle of Jack Daniels." I did actually ask him about that a few years later. Why the prostitutes? Adrian said he did it because he was lonely and wanted to be with people and the only people he knew were dealers, addicts and prostitutes.

On another occasion, Adrian chaired one of the Saturday morning's Marchwood AA meetings. I was still in rehab. There was a normal format for the meeting. Then you went around the room and people would share from the floor, one after the other, if they wished. One of the guys was sharing from the floor and was renowned for going on too long. Not only that, he was depressing to listen to. Adrian had little patience and tolerance at the best of times. It was obviously not one of his better days with regards to that as Adrian's words were, "Dave, this is a large meeting. There are many people who would like to share. Can you please hurry up and let someone else have a chance?" It was, however, one of his better, more controlled statements.

Another outburst which came a few years later, was again at Marchwood while I was not there; I was at his flat waiting for him to get back from the meeting. A new guy who had just started therapy was sharing from the floor all his tales of woe, why recovery wasn't working for him and how had he landed up in here. Adrian did not like what he was saying. He interrupted him and stated that was the reason he was there. The guy replied to Adrian, "Big mistake," to justify what he had said and reiterate it. He was promptly told by Adrian, "That's exactly what I mean and why you are here."

Adrian was very short with people and very vocal. You normally do not interrupt people who are sharing from the floor. You should respect what they are saying since it is important to them. When he returned home, he mentioned this and said he'd have to avoid that meeting for a while. No one challenged Adrian about

57

his behaviour. He wasn't the type of person whom you would challenge. The only exception would be me. I would do that big time. I could get away with speaking to Adrian as no one else would. A better person than me would not have got away with it. He most certainly would have done or said something very vindictive and threatening to them at that time in his life.

Adrian had a very colourful past, which he shared openly in the AA meetings. He was very capable of making people laugh when he was speaking. It was at one of the Marchwood Thursday night AA meetings that I would wait for Adrian outside the room after the AA meeting. He was speaking with someone else. (Adrian was very popular.) When he came out, I went to speak to him and told him I liked to be at a meeting when he was doing a share and were there any coming up? His reply was that he had done quite a few recently and had nothing planned. They tended to come in fits and starts; that's how it worked. He asked for my mobile number but I didn't give it to him. I took his and called him the next day and we met at Marchwood.

I was still in treatment for alcoholism and depression, which was ongoing at Marchwood certain weekdays. Aftercare treatment was on Tuesday evenings and depression groups early Thursday evenings. Along with a one day therapy group on alcohol recovery.

AA recommended not to make any drastic decisions or changes. Buy a plant. Make your bed each day. Don't go out with the intention of possibly fucking around and throw yourself into any more emotional turmoil.

I took the fucking around and emotional turmoil route.

I didn't realise just how much of a mess physically, mentally, emotionally and financially Adrian was in that moment in time when he was ill. He was actually more messed up than me. I couldn't see it then but saw it quite quickly after spending time with him. At this point, I did not know what a profound effect I would have on him and him on me.

I phoned Adrian and he suggested we meet at Marchwood. I had to go home, collect Holly, my dog, as I couldn't leave her any longer. I then went to Marchwood to meet Adrian. We did not discuss anything there. I would follow him in my car to St Mary's in Southampton. Adrian at this point drove a green soft-top MG. It was a crap car and cost him a fortune. I would later call it the Money Gobbler (MG).

I worked the area as a pharmaceutical sales rep. I knew it was one of the worst places in Southampton. It never occurred to me that it was full of drug addicts, dealers, prostitutes, pimps and other unsavoury types. I just thought of them as lowlifes and never thought about it anymore than that.

We parked in a car park. He was going to take me for a meal at the Kurdish restaurant. Adrian could speak a few words of Arabic and understood more. They would not let us in the restaurant with Holly. Instead, we drank a coffee outside and brought some Kurdish cakes. When I refused the meal, he asked if I had an eating disorder. That was not the case with me. I did eat. I would find out later that Angie had an eating disorder.

I can remember when I had parked the car up, I was more interested in Holly being okay than I was about the car. I wouldn't leave her in the car and the Kurdish restaurant wouldn't let Holly in. Standing outside the restaurant, I remember three black guys walking past. This was only the second time I had heard Holly growl at people. I have no idea why except they looked unsavoury, along with everyone else who was walking about. Adrian and I went to the park to talk on the swings.

We spent a while talking. Adrian gave me a great deal of information about his background and what he had done. There were a few things that Adrian told me that I felt he should not have disclosed to me. He didn't know me. Yet the information he gave me was information you would only give to someone you truly trusted. This was also his first lie. When I asked his age, it rolled off his tongue so easily and without a second thought. Like it had been so well-rehearsed that you would not doubt him. His answer was 47! I didn't challenge it; he easily looked that age. Not older (drugs must have preserved him). In truth, he was 54.

There was also the statement that he had gone to a priest to confess some of the information to gain absolution from his drinking and drug use. At this point, I couldn't understand why it was a priest he went to and not a vicar. At this point I belonged to the Church of England. I would later revert to Catholicism. Adrian told me some of his past. He mentioned his first wife, how they met; I was shocked that someone wanted to marry him. His wife-to-be proposed to him! That was a shock. They split up as he'd been unfaithful and landed up in the hospital with a broken leg as he had relapsed with another drug user. He was lucky to be alive. He had passed out with an overdose. Jackie was the other drug user's name. She was trying to wake him by putting his head in cold water in the bath. That was dangerous and could have killed him. Jackie had, however, called the ambulance.

When Adrian's wife came to visit him in hospital, her question was, "Who called the ambulance?" Adrian told her it was Jackie. She left, flew back to America and filed for a divorce. There was no discussion.

Adrian relapsed badly. His words were, "I was only going to take a couple of days off to make myself feel better." It didn't happen. His relapse lasted over three years. This would be the worst period of drinking and drug use.

Jackie and Adrian went on two holidays. They went to Egypt and had to leave early as they ran out of money for drugs Then they went to Sri Lanka. Here, they landed, walked out of the airport, only to see great big signs saying, *'Any possession or handling of drugs will result in a death sentence.'* They were *offered 'brown sugar' (Heroin)* as soon as they got out of the airport. They both started using. Jackie was a complete nut case. One night, she was swimming in the sea in the pitch black. No one could see her. A Sri Lankan guy went to help her, only to be told to f*** off. I was shocked by Adrian's honesty.

I knew very little about Adrian's past, only what I had heard in AA meetings. This had been quite enlightening. I wanted to see him again and he wanted to see me. Before I left, he tried to kiss me but I could not do that. That was Friday 17th August, 2007. I was 37 days sober. We would meet again very shortly.

The little I knew now about Adrian when I first met him and the information that he gave me when we meet up just made me more curious about him. I wanted to know more.

I would constantly ask him questions about his past over the next few months. I would repeat questions several times and this enabled me to get the truth. I found that each time I asked a question, the reply would be different. I would challenge this, and I did get the truth eventually. He was a compulsive liar in almost all areas.

The first lie was about his age being 47 (one of many). He was 54. I found this out later in our relationship by accident, after a year of knowing him. He thought he had been speeding and had not passed his test long ago. This would be the second time, and he wanted to check on his licence that he wouldn't have his licence taken away and have to redo his test. I did not want to drive back to his flat yet again. He insisted. With Adrian, you might as well do what he wanted at the start because he would continue to go on until you did it. That I would learn very early on, like right from the start. That would be one of the many big issues between us.

His licence gave away his date of birth. I kept on repeating it and said I thought you were 47. He muttered something which I can't recall. Later, he asked me to phone him. I did. He was quite remorseful that he had lied to me and tried to explain the reason why. He was ashamed that he had started his recovery so late at that age. I was 46; it seemed the best age to give. At this point in our relationship, although it was by far a long way from a good, healthy one, I just didn't seem to be able to let him go. He intrigued me and I wanted to know more about him; the drugs, prison, the whole lot. He was such an enigma. I wanted to know more. I was having a very profound effect on his life.

I was surprised by the phone call; just how upset he was about the lie and there was fear in his voice and pleading for me to understand his reasoning. This was another indication of his insecurities.

Time and time again, I would catch him out on his lies. He had no idea how to lie and be successful at it. He would forget what he had said, or I would put words in his mouth to see how he played along with it. If he agreed with what I was saying, usually I was suspicious at that point. I would be proved right as his reply would be, "Oh, yeah that's right, that's what happened." His whole tone and body language was different, defensive, with the attitude that will do, that will get her off my back. *But it didn't.*

Adrian's words to me in 2016 were that I changed his life completely. I was the best thing that had happened to him. If I had not come along, he doubt very much if he would be clean and sober or even alive and if that was the case, his finances would have been in "dire straits".

Financially, he had no idea how to handle money and his bank account. This would be an area that I would help him with in the future. That would not be an easy thing to do. Adrian's idea of budgeting and spending money was way different to mine in many ways.

The financial side would come about when he became badly overdrawn. This would be in 2008, when Angie came back again. She had returned many times, but this time Adrian thought it was the real deal. When Angie came back, Adrian wanted to take her out and give her things. He didn't think about the consequences of spending too much and not budgeting. Budgeting was not in his vocabulary. He was charged a fortune by his bank in charges for that one week with Angie. Angie left with the normal, devastating, emotional and now financial mess behind her as he had spent a load of money on her.

I looked at his bank letters; they were not great, with really high charges and bills not paid. At that moment, he asked me to take over his money and finances, which I did. This was not without problems. We clashed badly. I was all for paying the bills and buying food. Adrian was all for CDs, DVDs, tropical fish, one-minute wonders and many other things. We ended up shouting and screaming at each other many times over this budgeting stuff. He was unable to listen to me about many things. As I said Adrian's Way or the highway'. His life skills were limited. Emotionally, I put him back on track after a long time; he had someone who, ultimately, he could rely on. Physically, I sorted out every medical condition that came his way. There were many! I introduced him to the Solent Spa Health and Beauty Club, where I was a member. He now started to mix with new people from a middle-class background. Not the streets! He would go swimming, get a personal trainer, took classes, started doing body pump, walked and went sea swimming. Even in Hurricane Bertha he went in the sea. He really could be an idiot. He would, however, change for the better in many areas that required it. Adrian would be incredibly draining on me with 'Adrian's Way'. That all comes much later.

Adrian, the good, the bad and the ugly. 'The Dark Side'!

Chapter Six
The Colourful Past of Adrian 'The Dark Side'

Adrian had, as I've said, a very colourful past. Over the years, I found out a great deal.

The good, the bad and the ugly.

Most of what I found out about Adrian was from him.

Our relationship would be different. When I was around Adrian, any peace, calmness, and security left me. This was replaced instead by complete and utter 'chaos'.

Adrian as I've said was self-obsessed, unorganised and irrational. He was quick-tempered and extremely untidy. *I would call him a clutter bug.* He had little patience or tolerance. He was completely selfish and loud mouthed. The F and C word were part of every sentence plus most people were '*c**ts*'. The world revolved around him. He came first. He had problems listening to reason or anything rational or sensible. Along with that he suffered paranoia over certain things, felt totally insecure, and was incredibly vain.

That is putting it mildly. I learnt other things about Adrian from other people. He never really disclosed our relationship to people or talked much about me. I helped him get on his feet and had a profound effect on his future. I felt hurt and rejected by this act. In many ways, if it had not been for me, he would not have what he's got today. There would have been no change, and he would have relapsed due to the company he kept. The women whom he associated with always came with a load of problems. So did I.

Adrian and I were more alike than I realised. *We both had many similar traits.*

Adrian was a Londoner. When I asked if he was a Cockney as he knew all the slang, he was quite specific about it. His statement was. "No, I'm a Londoner. Cockneys were born in the east end and could hear the sound of Bow Bells."

Born in Willesden, Middlesex, he had lived in Bedfont, Middlesex, Four Marks and Alresford. At 15 he went to live for a while in Farnborough with an Irish family for a short period of time.

His home life had been violent, no feelings shown or allowed, no crying as that was a sign of weakness, no hugs were allowed. His father was a notorious womaniser. *So was he.*

His dad had been in the army and prison. Adrian came home from school one day when he was very young and said that some guy was going to be waiting for him after school to beat him up. He told his dad this and his dad said, "Don't ever come home to me and say that some guys are waiting for you. What you do tomorrow morning is you go up to the biggest one and say, 'Look I don't want any trouble'. You then punch him in the nose and if he falls down you kick him as well." That was his dad's advice. That's what he did and he never got bullied again.

His parents were forever splitting up and then got divorced. His stepfather was racist, homophobic and a bully. He never hit Adrian, but all this added to him feeling insecure about most things. This would be very apparent when I met him and became involved with him. He would be forever saying, "You are meeting me tonight," or, "We will be doing this, we will be doing that." He would always want reassurance of the arrangements. Adrian is still like that today! I think I am the only person he never stood up and to a degree he never let me down. If he couldn't make what we had arranged, he would let me know.

His stepfather mentally bullied one of Adrian's friends, who was going out with his sister. His stepfather wouldn't let him use the toilet, called him a *'Paddy',* along with other unpleasant remarks. His friend turned up one night and rang the doorbell. His stepdad answered the door and the friend slashed his throat. His friend's sentence was light as the judge recognised that he had been treated badly and bullied.

His mother had a child by his stepfather, neither Adrian nor his sister would accept or like him. The reason he was his stepfather's son and was being treated differently.

Adrian attended many schools due to the divorce of his mother and father. His schooling, as far as he was concerned, finished at nine; he did, however, turn up at times. The schools that he should have attended were Hounslow Primary and Secondary School, Alresford Secondary Modern and Farnborough Secondary Modern. Adrian was very popular at school but somehow didn't mix well and didn't like others.

As a boy, he wanted to be a *'junkie'* like his rock-star heroes; Keith Richards, to name one. He was trying to score before anyone would sell him drugs.

He went to Four Marks in Hampshire at 11. His father lived there. His mother had thrown him out as she had had enough of him and his behaviour; Adrian was uncontrollable. Adrian went back to his mother's, who threw him out again at 15. He was now smoking and getting into trouble with the police.

His behaviour in Hampshire became worse at 13; he got a three-year probation order at Alton Juvenile Court for store breaking and stealing. This happened in Four Marks, where he lived. Not the best or most intelligent idea, robbing your local village shop. That was *'conviction number 1'*.

1st June, 1967: He never used an alias name or date of birth. His CRB would be six pages long.

Impressive!

11th January, 1968: Store breaking and stealing. Fine £5.00. Obviously didn't learn*! 'Conviction* number *2'.* They weren't drug related; it was tobacco and sweets related.

This was probably the start of what would make Adrian a very interesting character to know and talk with. Adrian would become a mine of information and knowledge in many wide and varied areas. He was not thick. Just stupid. His teacher at school when he was eight said he was highly intelligent and could go far with that. With his intelligence he did go far but not down the legal route.

At 15, Adrian started using heroin, which he got in the west end of London, Gerard Street, bought it from the Chinese.

He got kicked out by his father and went to live in Farnborough with an Irish family for a while. He worked for them for a while as a hod carrier and did a bit of plastering. He went back to his dad, then ran away from home to Hammersmith and started to use more drugs. Pep pills, weed, drink, Dexedrine, which he would crush and inject.

The first time he got drunk was at 15. He went to party, got drunk on gin, tried to get his wicked way with a girl. Projectile vomited, abused someone, started a fight, blacked out, it was a complete nightmare. Then passed out. This was early in the evening; he didn't make it to 9 p.m. *I don't think he was invited back! He never drank gin again.*

The people who he looked up to, at this time in his life, were skinheads; that's what he wanted to be like.

At 15, he never went back home or to school. *Well, he'd hardly been at school anyway.*

Adrian was homeless; he started to live in squats, hotels, and bedsits. That was the luxury end. Doorways, tunnels and subways were the lower end and would continue on and off in his life for many years.

At 25, he landed up in jail. However, not for '*conviction number 3*'.

All the convictions he would have would now be drug related.

'*Conviction number 3*' 17th November, 1978 was at Brentford Magistrates Court. Impressive, with seven different offences.

1. Handling (drugs). Imprisonment 6 months, wholly suspended 2 years.

2. Submitting Forged Document (stolen prescription pads). Fine £50. Compensation 13.05.

3. Theft. Imprisonment 6 months wholly, suspended 2 years. Fine £175.00.

4. Theft—shoplifting. No separate penalty.

5, 6 and 7 conviction were all the same. Obtaining property by deception. No separate penalty.

Adrian didn't even hold out for one calendar month. Again, impressive.

Conviction number 4, 4th December, 1978. Brentford Magistrates Court. Obviously didn't learn, but a mere four different offences.

1. Theft. Imprisonment 6 months.

2. Breach of suspended sentence. Imprisonment 6 months concurrent resulting from original conviction on the 17/11/1978.

3. Obtaining property by deception.

4. Attempt at obtaining property by deception (obviously got caught). *Imprisonment 6 months concurrent.*

Adrian would be sent to Wormwood Scrubs. There he landed up in a strip cell. It is a ward called G2. Ceilings are 20-feet high, along with the windows being a similar height. He was put in a Zoop suit—a rubber suit for people who are consider a suicide risk. It is like a rubber smock with rubber shorts. He was then put in a strip cell, which is nothing but a mattress.

In the hospital wing, he was in a small ward with Graham Young, the St Alban's poisoner, who later went on to hang himself. There was also a multiple rapist and Ian Brady, the famous 'child killer', whom Adrian described as a real *'weirdo'*. Ian Brady was the ward orderly; He was only allowed to work in the hospital wing, which is a small sealed unit, having two strips cell, Adrian being in one strip cell as he was in solitary confinement. The six other cells were for dangerous people. A ward orderly was a trusted prisoner. Ian Brady was trusted only to serve teas and dinners from that kitchen. Ian Brady served the other prison meals up at meal times. Brady would serve up Adrian Christmas dinner that year.

'*Adrian was only doing 6 months, they were doing life x 3.*'

He landed up in the strip cell as he had been rude, aggressive and lied to the doctor. This attitude did not surprise me. He could be that at the best of times.

His average time of serving was 18 months.

Conviction number 5 was when he reoffended. 19th April, 1979 Kingston Crown Court. Just one offence! Burglary with intent to steal. Non-Dwelling. Imprisonment 9 months wholly suspended two years. Supervision Order 2 years. This was probation for which he had to turn up once a week to see a twit. *His words not mine.*

Give him credit. He turned up for a couple of the probation visits and then didn't turn up for any after that. He'd just come out and was back on the drugs and reoffended. Again, he didn't learn. I would make comments to him about not learning from mistakes. He would respond with various facial expression and usually blame me or someone else.

It would be 11 months until his next court appearance.

Conviction number 6: 21st March, 1980, Kingston Crown Court. Three different offences.

1. *Breach of suspended sentence on power of criminal courts act 1973. No order to continue resulting from original conviction of 19/04/79.*

2. *Theft—Shoplifting*

3. *Criminal damage. Probation order 2 Years for both.*

Conviction number 7: Date of conviction 29th June, 1981. Ealing Magistrates Court.

If nothing else, he moved around. We were now at court number four. He had kept out of court for 15 months.

Offence 1. Criminal Damage. Imprisonment 3 months. Wholly Suspended 2 years.

2. *Theft—Shoplifting. Imprisonment 1 month. Wholly Suspended 2 years.*

3. *Failing to Surrender to Bail. Conditional Discharge 2 years.*

4 and 5 the same Theft—Shoplifting. Imprisonment 3 months. Concurrent Wholly Suspended 2 years.*

6. Theft—Shoplifting. Imprisonment 3 months. Wholly Suspended 2 years.

Three months later Ealing Magistrates Court.

Offence 1. Criminal Damage. Imprisonment 3 months. Wholly Suspended 2 years.

2. Theft—Shoplifting. Imprisonment 1 months. Wholly Suspended 2 years.

3. Failing to Surrender to Bail. Conditional Discharge 2 years.

4. Theft—Shoplifting. Imprisonment 3 months concurrent. Wholly Suspended 2 years.

5. Theft—Shoplifting. Imprisonment 3 months concurrent. Wholly suspended 2 years.

6. Theft—Shoplifting. Imprisonment 3 months. Wholly Suspended 2 years.

If nothing else, he most certainly was whacking up the theft-shoplift offences. No wasting courts' time with five of those in one hit.

Conviction number 8: 20th August, 1981. Oh, another court! Bow Street Magistrates Court.

Offence *1. Failing to Surrender to Bail. Fine £50 or 1 Day's Imprisonment in Default.*

2. Theft—Shoplifting. Fine £50. 1 Day's Imprisonment in Default.

Adrian choose Wandsworth Prison. £100 was a large amount of money in 1981.

Conviction number 9: 19th February, 1982. Guildford Crown Court. He had the book thrown at him here. Impressive.

Offence number 1. Burglary and Theft-Non-Dwelling. Imprisonment 9 months

2. Theft—Shoplifting. Imprisonment 6 months concurrent.

3. Breach of Suspended Sentence. Imprisonment 3 months Concurrent Resulting from Original Conviction of 29/06/81.

4. Theft—Shoplifting. Imprisonment 6 months concurrent.

5. Theft—Shoplifting. Imprisonment 6 months Concurrent.

6. Theft—Shoplifting. Imprisonment 6 months Concurrent.

Adrian went to Wandsworth Prison.

Conviction number 10: 16th June, 1983 Richmond Magistrates Court.

Offence 1. Attempt Theft—Shoplifting. Imprisonment 3 months. Wholly Suspended 2 years.

Conviction number 11: 30th June, 1983 (didn't wait long for this one, just 14 days until in court again) Ealing Magistrates Court,

Offence: Theft—Shoplifting. Conditional Discharge 2 years.

Conviction number 12: 9th December, 1983 (Not even a whole 6 months here) Blackfriars Crown Court.

Offences 1–3. Theft. Imprisonment 9 months for offence No 1. 2 and 3 were Imprisonment 6 months Concurrent.

4. Breach of Conditional Discharge. Imprisonment 1 month Concurrent Resulting from Original Conviction of 30/06/83

5. Breach of Suspended Sentence. Imprisonment 3 months Consecutive Resulting from Original Conviction of 16/06/83.

Adrian went to Wandsworth Prison.

Conviction number 13 was a bit more colourful. 11th April, 1986. Blackfriars Crown Court.

Offences 1 and 2. Supplying of Controlled Drug-Class A. Probation Order 2 years.

Offences 3 and 4 the norm Theft—Shoplifting. Probation Order 2 years.

5. Supplying Controlled Drug-Class A. Probation Order 2 years.

With the probation order in place, his words were, "I'd turn up once a week to see a twit, then couldn't be bothered."

Adrian rarely turned up for probation. He was never granted bail as he never turned up at court. He would go to Brixton Prison on remand while awaiting sentence. His worst offences were (apart from being stupid) in *conviction number 13* burglaries and possession of drugs.

Adrian went to Pentonville Prison; he was sentenced six months but served 18 weeks at HMP Northeye near Battle. He left just before the rioting when it got burnt down. Then went to Ford Open Prison. There he was allowed out in the evenings, he played pool, jogged around the perimeter. (He was not a natural athlete; he did try). He could have a joint there (cannabis). Oh, he got a job. Billet cleaner, mopping the floors in the huts. Adrian did very little in prison and getting a job was not one of his priorities.

HMP Coldingley: This was single-cell electronic prison; you'd press a button; this unlocked the door and allowed you to go to the loo. You would press the intercom when you returned to let the guard know you had returned. There were loads of drugs there, mainly cannabis.

Adrian loved prison. (Just as well). All his mates were there. He could detox, go to the gym, have a laugh, club together, make sandwiches. However, he was not the easiest of prisoners and not the inmate to get on the bad side of. I learnt that he and others would beat someone up for ½ oz. of golden Virginia. His ethos in and out of jail was to cause and inflict as much damage and pain as possible on his victims if they did not repay what they owed him.

He had lost most of his teeth; this was outside jail. On one occasion, he was hit across the face with a solid metal bar; he landed up in A&E one too many times.

Prison was known as *'bird'* by those who had been inside. *'Bird lime'* was slang for time.

Adrian would call me 'swoop'. This was a name given to people who had no cigarettes and when someone had finished theirs cigarette and dropped it on the floor, they would swoop down and pick the dog-end up and smoke what was left. I was called swoop because later in our friendship, I would tidy his flat on a regular basis. Then when he got home, things had been put away and he could not find them, or I had taken them to be washed. He would leave notes for me: *DO NOT SWOOP.* On his belongings. Now that must have been comical to see him trying to find his stuff as patience and tolerance were non-existent with him. Glad I wasn't there to witness these moments in person. A fly on the wall, yes I would have done that.

When I asked about the rapist and child offenders, he informed me that they would be done over in some form. The prison guards knew who they were, the prisoners maybe not. The guards were on a low wage so they could be bribed with money or cigarettes and they would leave cells open. The offender would be slashed or beaten up. You never wanted to be inside for that. There was always a way to get them. Not only that, their food would be pissed in along with rats dumped in the soup urns (Adrian's words) and they would be spat in the face.

Adrian now never got bail as he never turned up to court so was sent to Brixton, a remand prison, while he awaited sentence.

He was in solitary confinement five to six times. When I asked if that had happened, he said, "What do you think, a loud, foul mouth git like me always ends up in solitary."

He would always shout back his answer. At the best of times, I called him 'Billingsgate'.

In solitary confinement, you were allowed a Bible to read. Your bed was taken away in the morning. Solitary was not just in prison; it was also in various psychiatric units he was admitted to.

When he was released on one occasion, he had decided that when he got out, he would be going into a rehab to sort himself out. He was convinced about this. When he got on the coach with a load of Londoners going back to London on their release, the beer and the lager came out. You can only imagine the scene. Rehab didn't happen.

In total, Adrian would spend 9 years in and out of jail. His last sentence was in 1983, the year I got married to Michael. I was living a very different life.

My life had been very sheltered life in many ways. At 22, I didn't know anyone who had been in jail *except my dad* (He wasn't a bad guy) or anyone in trouble with the police. I did however know a few people who were on drugs.

Chapter Seven
My Life Was

While Adrian grew up and lived predominately in a city on council estate, my parents owned their own home. I would, however, end up living in a council house at the age of 17.

We had these things in common. Both Adrian and I would feel very insecure due to our family life, along with both of us having addictive traits. Our families were dysfunctional. We both wanted our own way over most things. This would cause conflict between Adrian and me. We would both be unhappy in our childhood, teens and to a degree adult life. Feelings were shown in my family. There was no violence. A certain amount of discipline was put in place by my father, my mother being more lax. My father was a notorious womaniser, same as Adrian's. Both our fathers gambled and lied. *That would be the trust issues we both suffered from.*

Where his parents were splitting up all the time and Adrian lived in many different places, mine was slightly more stable. There were constant arguments and my mother would say she was leaving. This led to even more insecurities for me and later even more would come along. Like not feeling good enough, lacking in confidence, being paranoid, thinking people didn't like me or were talking about me. Plus, the biggest would be money. We had none. Well, very little. Along with all of these, there was a massive inferiority complex. I felt out of place and that didn't really fit in. I would always struggle with close relationships. I was very shy, a bit of a shrinking violet. I was a quiet loner in many ways and had few friends. I was bullied in every school I went to. I sometimes now think did I have a tattoo on my head saying, 'pick on me!' I didn't get on that well with females and tended later to have more male friends. Adrian had very few friends. He mainly got on with females, had very few male friends. That is still the case today. I would find it hard to show my feelings. I was very emotional along with being very clingy. I only really liked one-on-one relationships. That meant I didn't have to share that person as it seemed that if there were more people, I was left out. I was terrified of not being liked. I had no confidence and was unable to stick up for myself.

I was born in 1961; Adrian would be 8 then. At 11, that's when his behaviour issues really started.

In 1964, my brother Robert was born; we were living in a cottage in Stokenchurch. It was a very run-down cottage that had no bath. There were baths locally. I remember being bathed in the sink. From my cot I could see the post office tower being built in Stokenchurch and the flashing red light turning on when it was completed.

We moved from there to Chinnor in Oxfordshire. My brother Jonathon was born in 1965, I also had an elder sister Dana. My other sister Vernie was more interesting. I never knew exactly what the relationship between my mother and Vernie was. At one point, I thought Vernie was my mother's daughter. Now I'm not sure how Vernie was related to my mother. Vernie was brought up by my mother's mother and her sister, Auntie Muriel.

Both these places were quiet and very rural. Before Robert, my brother, was born, my father had landed up in Winchester prison for selling stolen goods from his work. That is about all I know, and I didn't know that until I was 14 and found out by accident while looking through my mother's stuff. I found the letter from Winchester Prison.

At 13, Adrian was thrown out by his mother. I was 5 and went to St Andrew Church of England Primary School in Chinnor. I was not popular and had very few friends. I was bullied and picked on all though my school years. They called me Sargent Major as that was my surname and I hated being called that. I rarely fitted in. I was always the last to be chosen for anything! I was not intelligent and found it hard to learn, mainly because I was not interested in learning and thought it was boring. I never really got together with the three R's. I didn't want to learn. Plus, there was the additional task of copying from the blackboard in the classroom that was so boring, I would be forever asking my best friend Denise to do it for me. She did but I had to persist in asking her. Adrian was similar; he didn't want to learn plus he was persistent like me. He, however, was naturally intelligent. Had a brain, just didn't use it. I tried to get out of school whenever I could. Adrian just didn't go.

At the junior school I went to, St Andrew Church of England, they built a swimming pool. In the summer, we had swimming lessons and it was freezing. I didn't learn to swim in the lesson; I learnt by myself in the school holidays. They arranged a session for us to use the pool. Denise said she would meet me at the pool, which I was glad about as all the boys had told me that they would drown me if I turned up.

Denise didn't turn up. I had nothing to do but try to swim; that's what I did all through the session. Denise didn't learn to swim. She never turned up for any of the swimming sessions, so I was by myself in the pool, no one to talk with, so I just got on with it. I passed my 10 yard. The 20 yards, I was a short distance away and couldn't make it to the end. I was asked if I would like another go and said yes. I was so exhausted from the first try that I was worse the second time. It did show that I was quite a determined person and didn't want to give up. However, I was disappointed as in the first one, I was so near to getting it. Plus I had everyone in the class staring at me, with the boys afterwards telling me they knew I wouldn't make it.

End-of-term games were even worse as I would be put in a relay team along with the 100 metre or yard sprint potatoes sack and egg and spoon race. I dreaded the relay as the rest of the team would have a go at me when I didn't do that well, which was every race. Later, when I went to Icknield, I realised that I was very good at distance, not sprinting. Distance I could do. That made me feel better. However, my sporting life started and ended there. Anything with a ball was a total disaster. I did, however, like to dance and would be good at that. At that point my parents' relationship had got a great deal worse and at this point my mother was sleeping in my room. Dana was in the navy; Mum would disappear to Vernie's in Manchester without warning. I would plead and beg with her to come home. I told her the dates of my school plays, when I was singing in the choir for the school for I desperately wanted her to be there for me. I remember looking into the audience hoping to see her. I didn't. My heart would sink even lower. I never knew when she would return and I never knew when she would go.

My life until 1974 was growing up in a rural area, living between three farms. Two working, livestock and arable. The other was horses, goat and geese. Geese I didn't like. All my spare time was spent between these three farms. My clothes were casual and Wellingtons were worn most days. We had a dog, Nicky, a Border Collie that I walked regularly. I also had cats. Sam after Samantha from Bewitched. She had kittens, all white like her. I called them Tim, Tom and Tess. I also had guinea pigs, a tortoise, mice, rabbits and a budgie.

I would walk down to the sawmill on Saturday mornings and get sawdust for the mice. The farmers gave us hay for the rabbits. Quite often it was me who cleaned out my mouse cage. Dana did her own, and I also did the guinea pigs and rabbits.

To start off every school holiday, especially the summer one, I would spend a couple of weeks with my nana in Maidenhead. I loved it since I had no one to compete with for affection and attention. I had Nana all to myself.

Nana live in a terrace house and the neighbours were lovely. Mrs Young next door was older than Nana but she had a Jackdaw which I loved and always went around to see.

Not only that, I had friends there. My best one was Dawn, who lived next door to Nana. She also had a younger sister called Susan. Susan at times could get in the way as Dawn and I just wanted to play together. There were also other children my age there and it helped with my confidence as this was one of the only places I wasn't picked on or bullied. I fitted in and played games with them, bull dog being a great favourite.

Dawn and I would spend most of our time sitting on the small recreational ground which was built in a circle and had grass. We made daisy chains and buttercup chains; all the simple little things that girls did at that time.

I was always told off for climbing on a very small wall which was put there to separate the path from the grass as you walked in to Nana's close. I was told several times I would fall off and it was these small walls which caused the most damage. It happened eventually and I fell off and scraped both my legs badly. Not an A&E job, just plasters and Dettol.

Nana and I would go to church regularly. I wanted to walk everywhere but Nana wanted to catch the bus due to arthritis. Nana had Rheumatoid Arthritis. That meant nothing to me. To Nana it meant at times it was painful to walk. I didn't understand and all I knew was I didn't want to go on the bus as it made me feel sick.

Another favourite of mine was Nana taking me to Windsor to see the river and go to the castle, which we did a great deal.

We would walk to Auntie Madge, who was Nana sister. She had suffered from polio in her childhood and that had affected her legs, which she kept in a brace. Little was known about polio in those days. Auntie Madge never got married. I asked her why. She said there had been a young man, but he went to war and never came back. At that age I couldn't comprehend it. I did ask why but she said she didn't know.

Auntie Madge had a big house with the rooms upstairs converted into rooms that she could rent out. Uncle Tom, who was not my uncle, lived there and always helped Auntie Madge with everything. He drove her and Nana most places, and when I came to stay, we would go out and have cream teas, which I loved.

There was a large children's park just around the corner from Auntie Madge, and I would go there and play on the Witches Hat this went around in a circle and made me feel sick, along with the roundabout. There were also slides swings, and the seesaw.

I was more or less okay on the swings and slides but the boys on the Witches Hat and roundabout would make them go really fast. To add to it, at times these lads would pick on me knowing that I hated to go fast and preferred it when there were only a few. They also knew I came alone. No health and safety in those days; if you fell off, you got hurt.

I had everyone's affection and attention and nothing and nobody to compete with. *I loved it.*

Nana at times would say that next year I will have Robert over. This I was not happy with. This was going to be instead of me. *That never happened.* What did happen was I went for two weeks and my dad would drop me off and then I would call them on the telephone and say I didn't want to come home and could I stay longer? Which I did. I didn't return until a few days, maybe a week, before I had to go back to the 'dreaded school'.

Auntie Madge would at times drive in her disabled car to our home in Chinnor and would take us down the lane in it. It was great and we loved it. We had to sit on the floor as there was only one seat. Again, no seatbelts or health and safety there.

All of this would end when my mother went to work. I would have to stay at home in the holidays and help Dana. I hated it. My mother started working once Joggy, my youngest brother, started school. This is when things all started to go downhill quite badly in more ways than one. The home would not be a happy one. It would be full of arguments and conflict; Dana and our Dad not getting on. Mum and Dad always speaking of splitting up. Mum would take Dana and Dad would have Robert and Joggy. Where was I in all this, I had no idea. My mum couldn't and wouldn't take me. This gave me even more insecurities. Dad didn't seem bothered about me either. I would hear my parents arguing at night about what I have no idea. Probably my dad's womanizing and gambling.

Dana would look after us in the evening and school holidays. Dana became obsessed with housework and keeping the house clean. Our mother was not big into cleaning up and the house was a mess. It was and had been typical washing on Monday before she went to work. Roast on Sunday and a meal from the leftovers of Sunday roast on Monday. Housework rarely happened.

Then Dana started to do it. What was awful was I had two brothers from hell and a sister that insisted I help her every day. When I got home from school, the housework would start. I had various jobs which would be inspected and if not done to her standard, I had to do all of it again. During school holidays, I now had to stay at home and not go to Nana's as I also had to look after my two brothers. No lunch was allowed until the housework was done and that could take till 3 in the afternoon. I was not allowed to go out and play with my friends and more often than not, we couldn't have the TV on to watch TinTin, Bell and Sebastian, White Horses, Banana Splits, to name a few. One day, we got all the work done by 1 p.m., a first. However, the chimney caught fire so the fire brigade were called to put it out. They did that but there was dust all over the place, so we had to dust and clean *again.* Yet again, lunch not till 3 p.m.

Dana also had a problem with all the cats and Nicky the dog. Nicky was tied up outside and howled all the time, and the neighbours did make remarks about it. We had two cats left; both Tom and Tess had been killed. Tom must have been hit by a car and made it into our back garden. He was the biggest of the cats. Tim did try to take his place with my mother and she had noticed that. Unfortunately, Tess was under the wheel arch on one of the tyres of the car one day. My dad reversed and ran her over. Sam and Tim were left outside, clawing and starching at the door to come in. Dana did not want the mess of two cats and a dog. I hate what she was doing to them, and I thought she was awful for doing it. It was heart breaking for me to see but I had no control over it. All I wanted to do was let them in but couldn't. What Dana said when Mum and Dad weren't home, went. I thought she was cruel and a bully for this, along with the excessive housework. The animals came in when Mum and Dad came home.

Robert and Joggy were not allowed in the house if they were dirty; they had to completely strip outside the back door and were hosed down by Dana until they were clean. Robert and Joggy named her 'Boss or Bossy'. That was an understatement.

Dana was a very dominating, controlling person, and I was stopped from going to visit my Nana on several occasions so that I could help Dana with the housework. This was upsetting too.

Dana was constantly telling me and my brothers off over everything. However, although she was quite the disciplinarian, when my two brothers and I started to fight, all hell broke out. We would try to kill one another. I ended up falling through the French windows. Robert and I were fighting, and I was now doing the 'flight'. With Robert chasing me, I put my arms and palms up, thinking the door was open. It wasn't, and I fell through it. Remarkable as it was, I got one small piece of glass in my left shoulder. It is still scarred today.

Dana disliked Nicky and said he had bad breath, which I hadn't noticed. My dad and Dana clashed really badly. She totally humiliated him on a school trip she was going on for a week. We had little money, so she went around the neighbour's and asked if they would give her the money and Dad would pay them back later. They did but my dad was furious about it and felt ashamed that she had done that.

However, Dana was miss goodie two shoes in so many ways, Brownies, Girl Guide, paper round in the morning. Only thing I did was try the brownies for a few weeks and then stopped.

During Dana's O' Level exams, she was at home one day revising. She drank half a bottle of sherry. My mother, being so laid back, never told her off. My mother was so laid back that she didn't think about what tablets she was leaving out for young hands to get hold of. My brother Joggy got hold of my quells for car sickness. To this day, I always related hair spray to being carsick and I hate the stuff. I never wore it but my mother always did when we went out in the car. As I was sick so often, I took the quells; mum left them on the side and Joggy my brother took the lot. The ambulance came and Joggy was taken to John Radcliffe Hospital, where he slept it off and had jelly and ice cream and was as happy as can be. The neighbours did ask me why an ambulance was there. I said Joggy had taken some of Mum's tablets; I was ashamed to say they were my carsick tablets. Why, I don't know.

The good thing about that was I had tea at one of my schoolmate's house, Trudi. They owned a store in the village that sold games and other things. There were chocolate eclairs on the table. I'd never had one of those and my mum came to pick me up before we got to the eclairs. I asked if I could take one since I didn't want to miss that opportunity. Trudi's mum was nice and let me take one.

Another occasion that I hurt myself was when I fell over and cut my head open on the drain. In those days, the drain had a concrete barrier on the outside like a square, but the fourth part was attached to the wall of the house. There was blood everywhere. I screamed the place down and when we got to the hospital, I needed stitches in it as it was over two inches long on skull near my front of my forehead, I screamed so much that Mum left the room and let the doctor get on with it. That's how laid back my mother was.

Even when Robert threw a log at me one day and cut my head open at the back of my skull, my mother was completely laid back about that. Robert landed in hospital, where he scalded his hand from a boiling pan on the stove. He came back from hospital with his hand bandaged up, which looked like a doll to me.

Windows were forever getting broken in our house due to fighting, arguments, losing tempers. My dad was, it seemed, always replacing a window in the kitchen door.

My parents, not hot on housework, were keen gardeners, and the neighbours would praise them for our garden, saying that they should enter the gardening competition. They never did. They planted a Weeping Willow in the front garden at the bottom and it's still there today. I had my own garden patch, which had lovely flowers in it. Then our new neighbours moved in, whom we would call Auntie Alison. She had two boys. My mother saw me picking their front garden's flowers when they moved in. My mother was not so laid back over this. I had to pick a bunch of flowers from my garden and take them around by myself with my mum at the end of the drive to apologise. I was crying on the doorstep. It was that or my mum said she would take me to the police station, which was just over the road and could deal with me.

The other time the police station was mentioned was when Karen, Donna and I were out and decided to nick some apples from one of the big houses down Oakley Road. We came back bragging about it. My mum saw the three of us coming back and said, again, that I have to take the apples back or go to the police station. Again, another drive where she remained at the bottom and I had to knock on the door, give the apples back and apologise. I was in tears again.

So there were certain boundaries that she had and would stick to. Lying and stealing were not on her list to go unnoticed. As for trying to kill each other, she let us, to a degree, get on with it.

We all decided one night that we would have nicknames for each other. Joggy was either Jog or Joggy. At one point, he had been called John-Jo by me. Robert would become Robbie. I was called Cathy, not Catherine as I had been. Dana would be called Dalips; later in life I would call her laree lips. She never knew when to keep her mouth shut and didn't care what came out of it. She could be quite venomous. Dana definitely had a very ugly side to her, and I realised in my 20s that there was no point in arguing with her. She was always right, never wrong. The only two compliments I can remember her giving me were that I had a quick wit and a lovely face.

Dana did say when she got married the first time when I was 16, that my bridesmaid's dress was made correctly. Morag's, who was the other bridesmaid from Scotland (Dana's husband-to-be's sister), dress had been made by another seamstress and the lace around the neck and the bodice had been put on differently. Dana was very critical and attention to detail was her big thing.

They gave us both a silver cross and chain each as our bridesmaid's presents. I still have it today along with the heart-shaped St Christopher she gave me for a birthday. Dana married a guy she met in the navy; she got married on the 15th of October, 1977. I would get married to Michael, 15th October, 1983. We both separated and got divorced at the same time, similar situation. However, Dana came home to a note on the table and was heartbroken.

Apart from that, she was critical of me all the time. Later in life, I would put weight on due to drinking, and she would call me fat saying I had to lose the weight and look after myself. She was overweight herself, but I never mentioned it. She was really cruel about it and continued to put me down like when I was younger.

What Dana failed to realise is that although she didn't have a good relationship with our father, my mother adored her. She would do more for Dana in her life than anyone else. Dana's children would be Ma's favourite grandchildren. Ma really did love Dana more than us three. I wonder if she ever saw that. I saw and knew. It gave me yet more insecurities. However, my mother did love all of us.

To add to my low self-esteem and inferiority complex, they all called me big bum so that gave me a complex about by bum, and my mother didn't help. When I said something about wearing a mini skirt later on in life, she said my legs would be too big for that type of clothing. I did wear them, and I did look good in them. But the inferiority complex was there. I had worn miniskirts to school since before I was 14 even though they were going out of fashion; for the first two terms of the school year, I was wearing my uniform from the previous year. Just as well it was a stretchy material. I did get new shoes; that was it. No new school uniform when I went into my third year at Icknield. The fashion was going into longer skirts below the knee; that didn't happen for me. This made me very self-conscious of how I looked. Again, I felt inferior. I had no real clothes at home, a couple of tops and some trouser bottoms and Wellington boots, that was it. My shoes were my school shoes.

I never heard my parents swear and didn't know a swear word until I was 11 and went to comprehensive school, which I started in 1972. Icknield Secondary Modern School in Watlington Oxfordshire. Again, quite rural. All my friends from primary and junior school were going to Lords Williams in Thame but my mum didn't want either me or Dana going there.

My parents split up in 1973. My mother had gone to a friend's leaving party. When she returned, my dad would not let her in. I woke up and went downstairs to see what the noise was about. My mother was trying to get in and Dad wouldn't let her in. She asked me to help. I tried but he stopped me and called the police and said, "There is a woman here 'who is not my wife' trying to get into my house. Can you come and remove her?" I was sent upstairs. The police came and Mum went. I went downstairs and saw my dad was sat in a chair looking defeated. I asked where Mum was, he said that the police had taken her away. I screamed at him said, "Are you f***ing happy now? Are you going to let her come back?" His reply was yes, so I went to bed.

The next morning was awful I got up and made my two brothers their breakfast: porridge. When I got them up and they came down for breakfast, Joggy said, "Where is Mummy?"

I replied, "I don't know." I knew but what could I tell them? I was 12 years of age.

This led to a great deal more insecurities, inferiorities and in so many ways, shame. I was ashamed my parents had never married and more ashamed that my mother had gone off with my father's best friend and didn't even try to hide the fact that they were not married.

I remember that day so well. One of my school teachers was taking me to school in those days. He picked me up. At school, all I could think of was getting home. The anxiety and stress of that day was awful. Time dragged like it never had before. When I eventually did get home, I phoned my mum at her work. I asked, "You are coming back, aren't you?" Mum said she would see me and the boys later. I knew just knew I had that sinking 'this is it' feeling.

Mum came home but it didn't last long and the begging and crying did nothing. She had come to collect a few things and was not staying. *I felt lost, deserted, helpless and most of all unhappy.*

When my mother left, things were dreadful for me. I had two brothers from hell. Three and four years younger. My father would go away at weekends to his lady friend and leave me with my two brothers and quite often no food. It was just dreadful. Robert and Jonathon ran riot. Our language became foul, we all used the F word. Robert and Jonathon had very few boundaries put in place and were, I felt, quite rude and impolite. Not completely their faults. I was left to do the housework, get them up for school. My father did do some of the washing and some cooking.

To me it felt that I had become a slave to the house and my two brothers were never happy with what I did. It started with getting them up for school in the morning. The porridge was not like Mum's. Admittedly, it varied day to day, sometimes being like thick stodge which they refused to eat. I tried to get the measurement right but some days it worked and some days it didn't.

More insecurities came due to no school dinner money along with my father not picking me up from school. I had to walk the three miles home once the bus dropped me off at the Lambert Arms in Kingston Blount. I felt abandoned.

My father knew nothing about my school life. The plays I was in, the choirs I sang in. He turned up one evening when I was doing a rehearsal to pick me up. I was staying with a friend that night, so it was a wasted journey for him. Did he, my dad, know anything about my life?

A school trip for the day out with the school was a nightmare for me. I didn't know if I would have a packed lunch or not. Somehow my mum manage to smuggle me a packed lunch for one school trip on the rare occasion I was able to speak with her and let her know what was going on. If I spoke with her, it was always a tearful conversation, I just couldn't hold it together. I felt I had no one.

My father got a housekeeper with a little boy from up north; she went back at Christmas and didn't return. I was distraught. I had little contact with my mother due to my father not allowing it and getting sole custody.

Another housekeeper came, Irene. I liked her and we got on well. Her opening statement was, "Your two brothers cannot be as bad as the two Martin boys down the road." I knew who they were and I thought, *you really have no idea*. Her parting words were,

"The Martin boys are angels, angels compared to your brothers." Irene helped me a great deal; she could see the state I was in. It was bad. I was by all accounts on the verge of a breakdown. Irene got things sorted somehow; I don't know how or what she did. Social services took me away to live with my mother.

I asked her if Ralph was okay with me coming to live with them and she reassured me that he was. I was happier. That didn't last. In the summer of 1974, I went to live with my mother and Ralph in Haddenham, Buckinghamshire, another small village. My sister Dana was there and that was good for me. She was on leave from the navy. (One thing that our father did not want for her). We got on well at this point and she was very supportive. I had gone through a phase before going to live with my mum. I started to pull my hair out from the top of my head. I had a bald patch on the top of my head on the left-hand side. It was a nervous condition due to everything that had happened to me for the last year and how I just didn't and couldn't cope with it. Mum took me to the doctor's, and he suggested Johnson's Baby Shampoo. I didn't need anything; I just didn't tell them why I had pulled my hair out as I was ashamed of what I had done. Dana was quite concerned over it. Going to live with my mum stopped the habit, but I was very conscious of the bald patch on my head.

When we all drove Dana to London with Michael, Ralph's son, I cried when she got on the train. I felt deserted and abandoned again. Michael brought me a bar of chocolate which you could get from the vending machine on the platforms.

When I left Chinnor, Sam and Tim were left with Nicky. I did not want to leave my pets. They were my constant. The one thing I had, and especially since animals show love unconditionally. Nicky always waited for me on the drive when I came home from Primary and Junior School. The feeling of stroking Sam and Tim, giving them evaporated milk which they loved. Pleading to keep my animals. Why couldn't we take them? I was losing everything, I didn't want to lose them.

Ralph took Nicky to the vet's with me to have him put down. When the vet asked what he would like to do with Nicky, my dog, Ralph said, "Just throw him away." The vet had suggested to Ralph that I leave the room, but I didn't. I knew that Nicky knew what was going to happen, and he tried to struggle; I had to help hold him and say, "It's okay." It wasn't okay; nothing was okay. The neighbour had Sam and Tim put down. Everything in my life was leaving. I now was fearful of most things and felt alone.

I went back to Icknield School after the holidays. A teacher had to pick me up in Longwick. Ralph would drop me off at the petrol station. To come home, I had to get two buses. One was forever being cancelled. That caused more insecurities; my trust for people and things had gone completely. I didn't get home until after 6 p.m. I was a latch-door kid. I would remain at Icknield until the end of the school year in 1975, when I was 14 years of age.

The late summer-autumn in 1974 I can still remember feeling low.

Three things happened. Firstly, my mother came home from Dad's after seeing Robert and Joggy all black and blue. My dad had beat her up good and proper. Her face was just a mass of bruises.

Then the second thing, my mother wasn't in the best of states due to my dad not letting her see Robert or Joggy. I did feel for her and thought Dad was unfair. I hadn't expected her to feel as bad as she did. She was on various tablets and after a telephone conversation with my dad which landed her in tears, she took all her tablets and told me not to call the ambulance. I did but I got a crossed line; I was speaking to 999 and also people locally. I said where I lived but I had to repeat everything twice. The people from down the road turned up before the ambulance and then the ambulance came. I was in the house by myself as Ralph was at work. It was a Saturday. I left a note to say that Mum had been taken to the hospital as she had overdosed. She was in Stoke Mandeville and stayed there quite a few days. The people from down the road, a lady called Joyce who was also the post woman, took me back to their house until Ralph and Michael turned up. *Thank God for Michael.*

Ralph did the washing on Sunday and put all the whites in with the colours, so all my white socks were grey and looked awful.

My dad did go and see my mum in hospital, so did Ralph and I. I asked my mum what Dad had said. Obviously, not a great deal but Mum had to have her stomach pumped.

This was doing nothing for making me feel secure. Just another thing that added to it. Plus, I now had 'grey socks', which at 13 is almost the end of the world on top of everything else.

The third thing, I had to go to court and say to them that I felt that Ralph could be a good father to me just like my dad. My mum had told me I had to say that or I would end up going back to my dad's. My dad never forgave me, and we would then have a very distant relationship for years. Robert and Joggy would get everything by my dad, mopeds, cars, video recorders to name just a few. I got nothing.

My mother was at the start of a new relationship and only really had time for Ralph. She had very little time for me. She and Ralph were close and intimate. I felt left out yet again and going to live with my mother was not quite what I expected. I thought she would have more time for me and put me first, but again, I just seemed at the bottom of the pile. Michael came over regularly. He helped me in many ways. If he stayed the night, he would take me to Longwick in the morning and drop me off. This I preferred as, unlike Ralph, he would get up on time and I wouldn't have to be constantly asking him to get up. I hated being late for things and wanted to be on time. Ralph did not share the same attitude.

Michael became totally obsessed with me. This caused problems. He had at the beginning came over because of Dana as he quite fancied her. When he saw me at thirteen, he just fell head over heels in love with me. The record that he bought about us was *'Barry White You're My First, You're My Last, My Everything'*. Michael was like a security blanket for me. I didn't want a relationship as I felt it was too incestuous with his father and my mother. Michael and I would have a very on, more off relationship. Unfortunately, he would be the one who got hurt time and time again. Bit of a first for me, someone else getting hurt. Michael got hurt very early on in our relationship.

Michael spent a great deal of time at our home. One night he didn't come over and I was really grateful, and I had taken the day off sick from school although there was nothing wrong with me. I was home alone. My mum and Ralph would always drink Woodpecker Cider in the evening, and they kept it under the stairs. I was allowed to have a glass of cider with them in the evening. Having the day off school, I drank a whole bottle, got completely plastered, and my mother came home to me drunk and passed out on the couch. Michael didn't come over that night, thank God! I wasn't sick, but I felt really ill. I was seeing treble and could not go to school the next day due to my first hangover. I begged my mum not to tell him. She never did. I found myself a boyfriend from the village, Julian. Michael was mortified. That would be the first relationship I would get really hurt in. I was looking for security at 14 years of age. I thought we would get married at 16 and all my problems would be over. That never happened. It lasted two months.

There were also the added complications like my hormones. I had started to go off the rails. At Icknield School, I had started shoplifting with a few of the other girls. Melanie had introduced me to it and how to do it. She would steal money from me, which was upsetting. This was before I started on the shops. I spent a bit of time with Melanie; at one time, she was my main friend but it didn't last long. Cathy was from Australia; her family had come over with another family and shared a house. We got on well and became very good at shoplifting.

Then Julian's sister Michaela wanted to come on board. Julian and I had broken up. I was hanging out with her, hoping to get back with Julian. That never happened. Michaela and I went to Oxford. Cathy had found a great way to steal clothes from C&A. You took two skirts into the changing rooms on one hanger, one underneath the other so it looked like one item. Then you put the skirt in your bag and walk out with the other on the hanger. I was okay and got away with it. Michaela was useless. She couldn't work out how to do it. My biggest mistake was to help her. By doing that, we both got caught for shoplifting. We were followed out of the shop by a shop detective, who stopped us. We went upstairs to a room, where we were given the third degree. Two female coppers turned up to escort us out of the building to police cars, informing us on the way out not to run as they would be faster. Neither of us ran.

My mother and Ralph turned up along with Michaela's mum. Michaela's mum insisted it was my fault. In one way, it was, since I took her. Michaela wanted to do it; she had pleaded with me to take her. I did. We landed up on a Saturday morning in Oxford's police station. I defended Michaela. The same curtsy was not bestowed on me by Michaela or her mother. No charges were placed. I never did shoplifted again.

Now with my mother at least I didn't have the two brothers from hell to deal with; well, for a while at least. I did not want my brothers to come and live with us. That was the last thing I wanted. They did arrive and I hated it. My father had custody of my two brothers and my mother had visiting rights.

One weekend, they came over just before the start of the new school year. I'd had a year without my brothers, and I liked it.

I was resentful; I didn't want to share my mother with someone else. Ralph was bad enough. My mother never took them back to my father's; that weekend, she went over to Chinnor with all of us and collected the boy's belongings when my father was not at home. My father was livid but my brothers stayed with us.

It was sad for Joggy since we all started in a new school. Joggy John Hampden Junior School was about to be made captain of the football team at St Andrew's Church of England Junior Chinnor School. He had to forgo that for a year. Robert went to Lord

Williams Lower School in Thame. I would be starting at Lord Williams Higher. Only one bus journey and then home between 4:30 p.m. and 5 p.m. The downside was both my brothers were on the same bus. We started where we left off—trying to kill each other. There were fights daily.

As I was starting a new school in Thame, Lord Williams Comprehensive School, I had to see the headmaster, Mr Moore, about it. Mr Moore gave me a dressing down, saying he always asked the police about new students whether they had been in trouble in the past. I was informed that I would be watched.

At fourteen years of age, I was not doing too well in any area of my life. When I started at Lord Williams, I got in with the wrong crowd straight away. I was back with my best friend Denise from primary and junior school. My mother never thought much of Denise and looking back, she did have a point.

More problems came about by getting back with Denise. Also, due to another girl I would become friendly with, Hurlen. Boy, looking back she was bad news and had me up to all types of trouble—staying out late, not turning up for school, running away for one day, were all Hurlen's ideas. Another one of her ideas was hiding in her attic for the day, with police, teachers and parents looking for me. When I came down from her attic as she realised it was getting very serious, I was instructed not to say where I had been. That landed me in more trouble at school; was I going to be suspended? The shame of that was awful. It's just as well I had a good schoolmistress, Mrs Sadler, who I felt could see that there was more potential there and I could turn a corner. She did, however, put the fear of God in me, which in hindsight was a good thing for me.

Hurlen had me up to all things, going to disco, which were 18 years or older X-rated films. I didn't look 14, more like 12. Hanging out with older guys in their late teens, early twenties. I wasn't interested in them or them in me. Hurlen got all the attention and all the guys. She was welcome to them. I just hung around at discos, dancing and doing my own thing while Hurlen went off with some guy or other. Hurlen had got loads of boyfriends but always maintained she was a virgin. I was young, innocent and knew no different, so I took it at face value. However, there were stories about Hurlen from guys. I didn't want to know. We would occasionally meet some of the guys in Haddenham. She liked some of them but I liked none of them. They were okay but not boyfriend material for me. Once they asked us to go in the pub and buy a bottle of whiskey. They couldn't get served and Hurlen looked older than

14. We both went in with all the change they had given us. Real change, 1p's 2p's 10p's, get the picture? We went in to buy it, handed over the money, only to be informed there wasn't enough there. Hurlen had a right go at them when she got out of the pub, saying, "You have just made me look like an idiot in there. You didn't give us the right money." Based on how we were paying that alone, I was surprised they even considered serving us.

Michael would turn up at a weekend with his mates and their girlfriends. I remember one of the girls called Vanessa saying she thought I was 12. Michael would drive us all to London to go bowling or ice stating. Roller staking we did in the Haddenham Village hall. I liked all that.

I started seeing one guy; he was nice, called Anthony, but he was in a young offenders' prison. He would be allowed out for a weekend occasionally, depending on his behaviour and other criteria he had to meet. He was nice. When Thame fair was on and Hurlen had me going on all the rides that the guys were not letting us off and I was really ill, Anthony stayed with me until I felt better. By all accounts, he really liked me. I ended the relationship as it seemed pointless. Anthony being in a young offenders' and me in school, we couldn't really have a relationship as we saw each other so infrequently.

Hurlen and Emily, who was lovely and had actually been at Icknield School with me, came to Thame. We tried to have a séance with our own Ouija board. That never worked. We tried it a few times in a derelict house in Haddenham at night in the dark.

When Halloween came, the three of us decided to dress up and go trick or treating. Hurlen and Emily looked nice. I got the short straw and was dressed as a fat green gnome made from a large green tracksuit top and bottom stuffed with other clothes, a ridiculous looking hat and my face covered in black make up to look dirty, along with Doc Marten Boots. The three of us had a good time as we made a great deal of money and we were delighted with that. We did this in Haddenham, not Thame, where Emily and Hurlen lived. Haddenham was a really lovely village. The downside was everyone knew me, so I felt a complete twat saying at the end, "Hope you always have a gnome to go to."

I was, however, still out of control. I hitchhiked everywhere. I was popular with the boys at school; they all wanted to go out with me. I didn't like most of them except a couple. I did, however, fancy one who was going out with another girl; his name was Adrian Collins. I was very shy but foul-mouthed, used the F word a great deal. Within the first term, I had managed to get three detentions and one Saturday morning. That was so humiliating. Mr Moore took me to a wall that had graffiti on it and I had to clean it. I was there for two hours.

What made me change was that Adrian Collins was a boarder at the school. I so hoped he wouldn't see me washing the wall down. He didn't. After that, I changed, changed my friends. Literally, my registration class who I sat with, I changed, I just upped all my stuff and went and sat on another table sat with a different group of people and never looked back. So my first term had been a disaster. November was when I decided enough was enough; I didn't like what I was doing, and that's when I started to hang out with Katie. Katie wasn't in my registration class. We were in the same pottery class and sat together with Jane, with whom I had been at primary and junior school.

Katie would become my best friend, a true best friend, and I would say that the remaining time at school, Katie and I had a wonderful time. She really was a good person, plus out of every other so-called friend I brought home, Katie was the only one my mother actually liked. I felt none of my insecurities with her. Having Katie as my best mate also helped me change. She would never know it, but she did have a big impact on my outlook on life. I worked hard at school and got the progress prize my first year.

After the first term, I did make the effort. I had changed. I did hand in homework. I wouldn't say I was academic but there was a great improvement! Well, it would have been difficult to have been worse. Adrian and I did go out. I would get hurt again and it all ended in tears. Adrian was a nice lad but Julian was not so nice.

Despite all that, with my now best mate Katie, we had a whale of a time. It really was great, discos, boys, music. We would go to the same disco at Lord Williams Lower School in the gym hall. I believe it was on every two weeks.

The first disco at Lord Williams Lower School I went to, had been with Denise and some of her mates. Also Hurlen. They were all drinking alcohol, so I tried it again. I got a bit tipsy and spent the evening with one of the guys who wanted to go out with me. That didn't happen as I wasn't interested in him. The discos were great as boys would ask us to dance and we spent all night on the dance floor at the back dancing. We loved it. This was my big Friday night out. At Christmas, we would all turn up and the guys would be there. They all wanted to kiss us both before we went into the disco. This would happen every Christmas, Easter and summer end of term.

Katie and I went to Oxford, shopping on the bus, either the 280 or 282 red double decker bus; I will never forget those numbers. I was to a degree having a nice life outside of home. I was not happy at home, and Ralph and I never saw eye to eye.

I would have sleepovers at Katie's and stay for tea so often. I loved it and their family. By all accounts, her brother David had a crush on me. David was a couple of years younger than me but a nice lad. Katie was also a twin, not identical as it was a brother, not a sister. Katie also had an older sister who was very good at needlework. I can remember both Katie and I were not big on the bust size. We both were small. Katie's sister was the opposite, and they could never work out where that came from.

Katie and I went on two holidays, one with my mum and two brothers. Yes, the two brothers from hell. We went to Ilfracombe in Devon and stayed on a caravan site. It was 1976, the year of the heat wave. We went in the beginning of September, and it was cold and rained. After such a great summer, we got the cold weather and rain. We both had our first holiday romance with two guys form Oldham, Manchester, Wayne and Phil. We met them on the beach when we were trying to put our clothes back on after a quick dip in the sea. That happened once. They came to the beach and started talking with us. We agreed to meet them the next day. We hadn't sorted out who wanted whom on the beach, so that night, Katie and I talked about it. I liked Wayne and she liked Phil. How it came about was, walking along the beach, Wayne held my hand and Phil held Katie's. There was no talk. That's how it happened. We had a good time with these two lads. We would go back to their tent in the evening and after we had been to the TV room, we gave each other love bites. They both turned up the next day at our caravan with scarfs on to cover them. We went into town and did quite a few things with Wayne and Phil. Katie and I had booked to see 'Anne of a 1000 days' at the cinema. Wayne and Phil didn't come with us but we met up after we got out of the cinema. When the holiday ended, we were all upset as we had had such a great time. We would all keep in touch for years via letters. That only stopped on my behalf due to having an overly jealous boyfriend, Martin. I wish to this day I hadn't stopped writing to him. I have all the letters still that he wrote and the photo of us in a photo booth.

Our next summer holiday together was in Hayling Island, staying with Katie's grandma and granddad. They were fantastic. Katie's dad drove us from Thame to Hayling Island in a VW, I think, a camper van. Katie had warned me about his driving. It was interesting. Terrifying, at times. This holiday, there was no holiday romance. We did meet some guys at a disco and agreed to meet them the next day. They had locked themselves out of their caravan but Katie was able to get through its small window and open it for them. We didn't pursue them. We had to walk back to Katie's grandparents' and we had no idea how to get there. That caused both Katie and I to be stressed. We hitched a ride as I was doing it all the time. Katie had never done it. No one picked us up so we rang her granddad and he did. The other thing that happened on the holiday was before we went, Katie, who had always had long hair, had it cut much, much shorter. She hated it and was really upset over it and was in a state each morning. It didn't look that bad but it didn't matter; Katie was upset over it. She grew it back and all the time we were mates, she only ever had it trimmed at the ends. She has the same style today.

Katie was a very good student. I could have been better but I did try to skip school on several occasions and ask Katie to come with me. Katie wouldn't; she was scared of being caught. I just lived on the edge that way. I didn't skip school enough in those days for it to be noticed as I had turned over a new leaf partially.

Katie and I would get tipsy on one occasion together. We would have a few glasses of cider before we went to a local fête. It was quite funny, looking back. We both had our fortunes told by someone who was reading palms. Then we looked around at the stalls feeling slightly tipsy and laughing a great deal. Neither of us ever got really drunk, except on one occasion.

Katie and I had been invited to a party Adrian was going to and I was going to meet him there. It was at friend's house. Ralph drove both Katie and I to the party, which was in the middle of nowhere. We got there relatively early and were given red wine, which we drank. Adrian arrived but had to leave early as he was a boarder at school so he had curfews. I carried on drinking. Mum and Ralph were picking us both up at 11 p.m. I have no idea what time it happened and how much I had to drink. I was 15 and being really ill in the sink at someone house. Katie and a few of the older, more sensible lads actually looked after me and helped me. They were really kind and nice. We got in the car when Ralph got there. I was hoping to get away with it but unfortunately, according to Katie, it took us hours to get home as they had to keep stopping for me to be sick. Katie stayed at my house that night. The next morning one of the lad called to check I was okay. I said yes and thanked him for looking after me. Adrian heard about it. He found it very funny and wished he had seen it. There wasn't any malice there as he wasn't that type but I was so glad he hadn't been.

I also had a few drinks the night before my pottery O' level. I remember my mum saying that had not been a good idea and no wonder I didn't feel too great the next morning. "You don't have a few drinks the night before you are taking an exam," were her words to me.

Mum did mention Dana; when she did her O' levels, Mum came home to Dana being drunk when she should have been revising. Dana drank half a bottle of sherry. Dana would leave for the Wrens shortly after that, just after her 17th birthday in October. She left with instructions on how to make the tea for my two brothers and me, along with cleaning instructions! I took little notice of that but did do some cleaning. Nothing like before when she was at home on a mission! I was 12.

Katie and I both left school the same year. We both stayed on for an extra year to get some more O' levels. Katie would go to London to do a course in floristry; it was what she was interested in and, in all fairness, had quite a flair for.

1978 was a great summer. Before I went to college, I hung out with a load of guys who were great company and Angela, who was one of my main friends. She was incredibly attractive as her mum was from Cyprus. She was great. We had loads of different boyfriends wanting to take us out. Going to the pictures, we saw Alien one time. The guys were great to us. We went on the back of their mopeds or motorbikes. They didn't have full licenses, just provisional ones. At that age, you don't care and think of the consequences.

Unfortunately, in a couple of years some lads we went to school with were killed on their motorbikes. I lost one of my boyfriends that way.

At my second wedding, Angela would be my matron of honour. At her second wedding, I was going to be her matron of honour but due to the cost, she asked if I minded if I wasn't. I told her that no, I didn't mind. Angela had been so supportive to me when Michael and I broke up. She had been great and really did a great deal for me.

Her hen party had been really interesting; this was in the 1995. I had got remarried in 1994, for which Angela's second husband-to-be had done Gee's car up for going away. Dana also helped as I had put confetti and other bits and pieces in her luggage when she got married the second time to Dick. I would find confetti all over my house in various place for years.

Angela's hen party was a scream. We had Chinese in the local Chinese. It was great. I had gone into Ann Summers and brought a load of stuff for her to open at the table like grow your own penis, penis pasta, erection gel, bed stick basher and various sex toys, which proved to be a real laugh. The 'grow your own penis' didn't work, wasn't meant to. We put it in the water on the table and waited. We were all quite drunk at this point. After the Chinese, with all the sex toys, erection gel and fake jelly penis in hand, we headed to the Crown pub, which had a disco on. We caused havoc there. Twelve drunk women at a disco which was predominantly men who drank there. They knew us really well and we them, which was just as well. One poor guy, Ian's partner was very possessive and to this day, I have no idea what happened when he got home. We covered his shirt in lipstick kisses, which we all had a go at. We tried the erection gel on him and one of his mates. This was on the outside of their jeans. The guys we picked on took it really well but boy, would they have some explaining to do about lipstick and the front of their jeans covered in the red erection gel!

At Angela's second wedding, the reception was held at her mum's house in Haddenham, and they had brought a bass band in which was great. It was in the afternoon and notes had been put through all the neighbours' doors to inform them. That, however, didn't stop someone from calling the police about the noise. They arrived just as Angela and Richard were about to leave in the car that had been done up by us. There was confetti everywhere. Durex on the gear leaver window wipers and indicators, Ariel on the roof. We sprayed shaving foam all over the car and attached tins on the back of the car, with balloons completing filling the inside and outside the car. They could hardly get in the car. We threw rice grains in the car along with other things. Richard had said the next day, "Trust Cathy to go all out and too far." Angela had laughed. Angela also told me that they had had sex where they were staying by some lakes and people could see them. She would not walk past them and said to Richard they had to go another way back to the hotel. She didn't like her wedding shoes, so took them back and got a full refund. Angela and I had great fun together.

I left school with a handful of qualifications, not knowing what I wanted to do. I then went to Aylesbury Further Education college and studied catering and hotel management. Again, I became a mouthy and cheeky git. Dropping back again into a life I really didn't want and mixing with people I knew were no good; Martin would become my boyfriend at college.

Martin and I got together during the Easter break; we had all gone to the pub The Hen and Chicken, and I got absolutely plastered. *A sign of things to come.* Martin took me back to the college, where I threw up for what seemed like hours in the men's toilets. I can remember one of the guys saying to me that I made the loos smell dreadfully of sick. Martin took me to catch my bus home, and we arranged for me to go over to see him in the holidays. I can remember the day I was going. I can also remember getting on the bus feeling awful.

I met Martin the day we had decided upon; it was two bus journeys and he met me at High Wycombe bus station. There were students who had to get the Aylesbury to High Wycombe bus, a great deal of students. Mine was Aylesbury to Thame, not a long journey and not many students to get on the bus. There were also students who got the train to Wendover. None of the catering students were on my bus. It was either train or High Wycombe bus. When the High Wycombe bus turned up, as there were so many students wanting to get on, it was a massive free for all with everyone trying to get on the bus first or at least get on the bus. They would push each other out of the way. There was no orderly queue. Quite the opposite; it was like seeing a mass panic of people in danger of some sort. Martin always managed to get on first, regardless of where he was in the queue, which wasn't actually a queue as when the bus arrived, they just dived for the bus.

The first time I got really drunk at college was my 18th birthday. My friend Maria and I were going out with Mum, Ralph, Robert and Joggy to the Bugle Horn for a meal in the evening.

We went to the Hen and Chicken at lunchtime with most of the student from our course. When we had finished, neither of us could walk properly and I was crawling along the ground at times with Maria. I was lucky I didn't have to get the bus home as the guy whom I had brought a record player from was going to take me home with the record player. I can hardly remember picking it up but I know he took it to my room and set it up for me. That was before the incident of getting together with Martin.

With Martin, I would start to drink a great deal as he drank too. He drank pints of bitter or Southern Comfort. Later, he would drink a pint of bitter with Pernod and Black in it. Martin had once drunk Gold Label but got so ill on it, he never touched it again. I tended to go for Pills Larger but got so ill on it on one occasion, I switched over to brandy, with Baby Champ being my favourite. Then wine, Tia Maria or schooners of sherry. A normal sherry glass was just too small. Before Martin and I had our meal out, it was always a couple of schooners of sherry; sometimes he had one. Then we would leave the restaurant and go into the pubs close by, and I would move on to the wine and Martin either bitter or Southern Comfort. One thing Martin used to say was, if I die, when I get buried, just throw in a bottle of Southern Comfort and I'll get it somehow. Martin would also mention to me later in our relationship that my drinking had increased. I hadn't realised it but I took very little notice of it. This was in one of the local pubs just outside Thame, heading towards Chinnor. We both liked it there. There would be a couple of pubs we liked in my area and one was really good on the food side. Even though I had an even meal, I would always have avocado and prawn salad.

Martin never really seemed to be happy with himself and said he wished that his middle name was John and he could then be called Jack. Plus he wanted to talk like a Londoner and wanted to know all the rhyming slang. That never worked and he would know just a couple of rhyming slang words. Like 'tea leaf. Thief.'

Although I got in with the wrong crowd, I somehow left with all my qualifications. Martin and I were together quite early on in college. He was quite good looking, dressed well and had a rebel side to him, which was appealing. He had been privately educated as he had got behind at school due to illness. He suffered from Asthma, so had a great deal of time of school. His parents took him out of the state schooling system and put him into a private school.

Martin's parents owned two Men's Wear shops. They lived in a large house in Naphil. These few things drew me to Marin. It was a difficult relationship with me always feeling insecure; he would end the relationship due to his jealousy on a whim. I always ended up crying. That relationship did eventually end in tears and I wasn't enjoying the relationship. He had at one point got into CB radio's; that was boring for me.

We went on holiday down to Cornwall; that was a disaster. I went to his house and thought we would be leaving straight away. Martin had to gone to his mate Nick's house to check the car. This was in the afternoon. Instead of just packing up and going, we didn't leave until after 5 p.m. His car broke down on the motorway; the pedal for the accelerator broke. We spent more time getting his car repaired than having a nice time.

I had used sex to keep him interested but it was just plan awful. I ended it. It was after we left college; we remained together until Martin and I were 21. It literally ended a week after his birthday.

I just knew he was seeing someone else. I had this sixth sense, a gut feeling. I remember at his birthday party my mother saying to me that if he had someone else, she would be here. I said, "Mum, I don't think so. I just know there's someone else; she's just not here." I found out at my brother Jonathon's 18th birthday party. One of Martin's best mates was a DJ. I literally hounded him, saying, "Gareth, I know he is seeing someone else." He confirmed it and confirmed who it was. I was mortified and devastated; I really think I went into a state of shock at that point. The pain was awful. I had ended it because he was just making it terribly difficult to be around him. Instead of having the guts to tell me he'd met an ex-girlfriend, he let me give him the soft option and yet each time I saw him before the end, I wanted to say, "Is there someone else?" Yet another painful end-in-tears relationship. *At least I was consistent.*

This would be an area that Adrian and I would have in common. Any meaningful relationship ended in pain. We were both fickle in so many ways that we would have loads of casual relationships which lasted moments. Neither of us were really interested in these casual relationships.

I would work hard for my employer. My impression of Adrian was he had done little work. To me it seemed that his life was just drugs and prison. *It was!* This would reflect in his OAP.

My first full-time job after I left college was as a receptionist for a dental practice. I got this job in the early 80s, the recession. I got this job by pleading and begging Katie who worked at the practice to tell Mr Keene that he needed a receptionist. That is how I got the job. I persevered until I got it. Perseverance would be what made me successful in many areas of my working life.

Although I didn't really like working for David Keene, Katie and I were back together and again having a good time at work and out of work.

In 1979, my family moved from Haddenham, which I had liked. We had lived in a nice rented three-bedroom house. Ralph had rented it out. However, my mother was granted a council house in Thame. It was a new development and I hated it. I felt we were above that. I was ashamed to have to live in a council house. It did nothing for my self-esteem or self-worth; they deteriorated further. Later in life I would take people for who they were, not what they had, but I had a long way to go before that happened.

In 1983, I married Michael and we brought a house in Thame. I was a right cow from start to finish. The marriage ended in 1986, in tears for both Michael and me this time. The divorce took longer than the marriage lasted and cost more than the wedding! Again, I hurt him by seeing someone else. Michael was also seeing someone else. It was a complete mess and a shamble of a marriage. Michael had two sides to him. He could be great fun, nice, there for me. The other side was vindictive and full of malice and caused me a great deal of pain that way. He was also incredibly possessive and jealous, which didn't sit well with me, I felt trapped.

I was not very good at being faithful. Again, Adrian and I had that in common.

I got very hurt in this and it would have a very bad effect on me with regards to relationships. I was shutting after that myself down emotionally would not and could not let people in that way. The relationships I had then were not great.

Michael left me for Sue. I was devastated. Unbeknown to me, Michael did want to come back I learnt this years later. This is probably why I always felt he never wanted to leave. He went to live with his sister for a few weeks. Then Sue and Michael got a place but it didn't work very well. He went to live with his mum for a couple of weeks, then went back to live with Sue. I wanted him back and I wanted to stay married. It didn't happen.

Michael had in so many ways been my rock. He had always been there and now he wasn't.

Michael had insisted when we got together and married that I passed my driving test. I had taken one at 20 in a small mini metro with a guy that looked like Lurch from the Adams family. This was a disaster. I couldn't do my three-point turn as I panicked, and he must have taken me to the smallest road possible. Then I kangaroo hopped across a junction and Lurch hit his head three times on the windscreen. A real thumb, thumb, thumb, and I laughed. I passed my driving test in 1985 after three attempts and give up each time. It took me seven years in total to pass.

I had a few relationships after that and one I got very hurt by and that closed me down completely. I would not be able to open myself up emotionally or intimately until Adrian.

Dentistry

My employment at this point had been dentistry. I had gone from receptionist with David Keene to dental surgery assistant for Graham Barker. However, I wanted to be a dancer, so I left dentistry and went to work for Chris Farrow. His company was called

Chiltern Ceramics and they were dental technicians who made crowns, bridges and dentures. It was part-time, so I could pursue my dancing. Chris Farrow would be one of the best employers I would ever have.

I worked on the computers, doing all the admin invoices and orders. The job was fantastic and the people were great. It was such a laugh! There were so many incidences that happened, especially when Chris took over another company in High Wycombe, JB Dental. That was almost a derelict building. Once, one of the guys was walking through a doorway that needed to be repaired when a brick fell and just missed his head. Another guy went into the attic (it was in an old house). The electricity wasn't working so he went up to look at the wiring and decided to try to fix it, getting an electric shock. One of the other guys said he would take him to hospital, only for the car to have a flat battery. The guy who had the electric shock had to push the car while the other drove it to jump-start the car. Just two small bits of information to let you know how it was. No health and safety, SOP and EAP in place in those days.

I left Chiltern Ceramics but my dancing was also short-lived. I did a few things on stage but a hip flexor/groin injury finished the very short-lived attempt at dancing.

I then changed my employment to catering. It was a disaster and lasted only a year.

I was 28. I moved from Thame in Oxfordshire to Aylesbury in Buckinghamshire, where I brought a house. It was in quite a rundown area but it was all I could afford. In hindsight, had I known the property market was about to crash, I think I would have gone home to my mum's and waited. So many properties went into negative equity. Mine didn't as I had a large deposit to put down. I would, however, lose out financially.

I hated Aylesbury. It was nothing like Thame. Again, my self-worth and self-esteem went down. I did not like the area and felt I was above that.

I went to work for a company that manufactured car accessories and other car-related products. This was where I met Gee, and we got together. He was easy. I felt secure with him and I wasn't going to get hurt. I was closed off with Gee. He was insecure and scared of me leaving. That was one of the reasons I stayed, along with money. I felt financially secure with Gee. Not the best reason to stay with someone. He, however, came with his problems.

These problems were his family. He had two teenage children, and Scott, who was nine. That is where the problems started. I was not sure if I would be able to handle his family. He brushed it off, said I'd be fine. *I wasn't.*

I became resentful. I was in my late 20s, early 30s and wanted to go out and have fun. That didn't happen since we had Scott most weekends. I was fed up and felt tied down, restricted. That wasn't the only area I felt restricted in. He was not happy with me going out on my bike or walking; that had to stop. My friends went. I wanted people over but he didn't. I wanted meals at their house; he didn't. I put on weight and in some ways, this is where the drinking really started.

Gee was very controlling and, in many ways, a bully. Again, this would be another relationship where I would be a complete cow at times. However, I never out-performed Gee and his whole attitude towards me. His constant complaining. He was always so negative, saying this couldn't happen and that couldn't happen.

Gee moved in with me quite quickly. He had a house in Milton Keynes but he sold that; a stroke of luck just before the crash of the properties market and people landing up with negative equity. Gee moved in quickly for a few reasons. We were paying out a fortune in mortgages between the two of us. My lodger in Thame left as he didn't like Aylesbury. I couldn't blame him; neither did I. My father was meant to help me financially but that didn't happen and I felt insecure financially.

Gee selling his house meant we could do my house up to a degree. It would become the best-looking house on the road.

I eventually left the car accessory company and went into financial services.

Financial Services
This happened by chance. Steve Hardin, who was a member of Stoke Mandeville Lifesaving Club, introduced me. I had joined Stoke Mandeville shortly after Michael left. It became a big part of my life for 15 years.

For 15 years I would constantly be updating my Life Saving Certificates. Every Sunday we had a training session on life saving skills or training for the exams for the bronze, silver and gold medals. The people were great and the club wasn't cliquey. Although I had limited swim experience at that time, one of the trainers let me train with Aylesbury Swimming Club to bring my swimming up to a good standard.

It cost you £5 a year to be a member of the club. You also had to agree to do one lifeguard session a month and you were put on a rota. For that you got all your training and could use the swimming pool during public sessions free of charge.

Steve came around to look at my mortgage. I did nothing with him. I liked Steve and his wife Vi, who was also a member. That would not last. Steve was basically a Natural Born Liar (NBL). Not trustworthy at all; he did, however, have charm. An ex-copper, one of the most corrupt people I would meet.

Steve was put on jury duty. Glad it wasn't me being tried at that case. Mark, a work colleague, said to me, "Steve is going to have all of them going down, innocent or not." That was Steve. He would grass you up, let you down and be happy if you fell flat on your face. I joined the financial services industry at the end of 1989, selling life assurance, pension, mortgages and investments. It changed me as a person. I was not particularly good at sales when I first joined. Financial Services gave you no leads or clients. You had to find them yourself and it was commission-based. They would pay you a retainer to start and would expect a certain level of business. After you had used up your retainer, you would be commission-based if you had not achieved the level of business 'sales' required. I would say at this point most people went down that route and landed up broke. Some could take home £200 a month, others more, some less. It was dreadful. People dreaded payday. That's a first. I was one of the lucky ones. I didn't start off well. Gee and I had his salary so that helped. I worked mainly with men. They were the main providers in their homes and their incomes were important and essential.

When my retainer ran out, my business picked up. It took me six months from the start to get my head around the job and sales and what to do. I became the top producer of the Dunstable Branch. Shocked many who thought I would be out quickly.

I became more confident in many ways and could stick up for myself more. It did change me as a person and at that point not for the better. I was under so much stress that I would be horrible to some of the guys in the office and very negative.

I had to work in an office with nearly 30 men and very few women. It taught me a great deal about men. I heard all about their sex lives, women, marriages and living arrangements. It was very educational. It was also a great laugh. I got on with some of the men. Steve, whom I regarded as a crook, was liked. He became a manager based on the business he brought in. Ethically, *I doubt it.* Steve did get what he deserved. He went to work for another insurance company when all the financial services changes came in, in the 90s. Steve had a company pension and it reversed on him (The company decided to cancel it the 14 days cooling off period). The company had paid him and as it had reversed, they wanted the money back. It was over £30,000, so Steve disappeared. I never saw him again or found what happened to him.

There were a couple of the guys I struggled with. As I had changed, this didn't really help. As I said, I was more confident and was earning a great deal of money, even earning more than Gee. I found it difficult to cope with the rejection in the job. That is what made my attitude bad. I tended to hit out at people and wasn't that nice.

One guy Sharam, whom I really didn't get on that well with, was, I think, Asian. He had a chip on his shoulder and had the mickey taken out of him a fair bit due to being Asian. The lads said he had sex lessons. Sharam didn't like this and it wound him up completely. With 30 or so guys, it is not the best idea to show them that you couldn't take being wound up that way. He was crucified regularly. There were many things done, and pranks played, such as strippers turning up for birthdays.

One Guy who got stood up for himself and told off one of the guys, saw a banner up over his desk when he walked into the office, saying *'blown out boy'*. It just went on.

Financial Services taught me a great deal, not only about people but also about people and their money. There were two groups I found—95% were broke or just getting by; 5% were well off and financially secure. I found it hard to believe the mess people got themselves into financially.

I now was not this shrinking violet who wouldn't say boo to a goose. I had, as they call it, the killer instinct to work and get the business. This I did, but at a cost. I hated it and I drank. When I got in from being out until God knows when, I drank. I worked late into the evening to see people in their homes. I was winning all the prizes.

I wanted to leave and get another job. Gee didn't want that. His words were, "You're good at it and look at the money you are earning." I was earning more than Gee. I felt like I had become a commodity for him and I hated it.

I left when all the financial services changes came in 1994–95. Not just me but half the people that I worked with walked out and got new jobs. The paperwork which was involved for each sale was awful but a requirement now.

SB Pharma

It was early in1995 when I went to work for a pharmaceutical company, SB Pharma. I joined the sales side, handling dentistry by selling consumable product to dentists and hygienists. One of the reasons for the move was I didn't want to take any more exams. *That didn't happen.* I would work in the pharmaceutical industry until 2007 but I never stopped taking exams. All of which you had to pass. If you didn't, you lost your job. With one exam, the ABPI, if you failed three times, you had to leave the industry.

ABPI was the governing body who overlooked the industry to ensure that the company and you followed a 'Code of Conduct'. That rarely happened. Pharmaceuticals made financial services look like angels.

Again, I was the top person not only in sales but in getting access and seeing clients. I have no idea what the other reps were doing. I was informed by other reps that I should only stick to a certain amount of contacts a day and sales. If I didn't, it made it hard on the others. Basically, they would have to work. I didn't try to be the best rep. I just went out, did X amount of calls a day, did it methodically, and I just got the results.

This is where I met Julie P. In three words, Julie P was a complete shit in every way possible. She was very like Steve from my financial services job. She would grass up anyone she could and try to make herself look good.

Julie and Tam didn't work that hard. Tam, in all fairness to her, was capable of being a very good rep. Both had issues with the manager Lisa. Lisa didn't like them and saw them for what they were. Julie was very unfair to the other reps. If we had a large stand meeting which involved you showing your products to dentists and hygienists and the odd consultant, we normally had to stay away. Julie never did the early morning slot or if she did, she didn't turn up until 10 a.m. or after she had stayed up drinking; that's why she was always late.

At the Brighton meeting, Julie had arranged for all of us to have a shopping session. It's not like she was in charge. She was on the stand over three days once. What was funny about this was all the other reps were working and not happy with how Julie and Tam were taking the piss. They went shopping all the time. However, one day they came back quite quickly. I was informed by one of the other reps that Julie had been shat on by a seagull. I went to see her in the loo along with everyone else. She was covered, her hair, her face, her clothes. I laughed and my statement was, "If you shit on people, you will get shit on yourself." Then I walked out. It was mentioned to me that it wasn't very nice, what happened to her. I didn't care. There were many more things that happened due to her being a complete and utter shit and making people look bad by slightly altering what someone had done or said to make them look bad and as if they were not doing the job. I'll leave it at that.

Again, I didn't like it. I wasn't happy. I used to think if *I actually liked this, how much better would I be!*

This would be the case with all my sales jobs I got. I've got another three to go.

I was with SB Pharma from 1995–1998, that is when I moved to Hampshire. My manager at the time did say he would ask if I could get a job in the GP division but I turned it down based on my experience with them so far. They said one thing and then did the opposite.

It was something I never saw coming. The car accessory company Gee worked for was in trouble. I knew this but didn't realise how bad it was. Tim the owner was selling the company. They were based in Andover. One of the criteria for the sale would be Gee's employment that the company employed him with continuation of service. Which they did.

Moving to Whiteley

We moved to Whiteley on 27th April, 1998. The start was not great and it didn't come without trials and problems. Firstly, Gee found it very difficult to adjust. He had been employed for 25 years by the other car accessory company. Plus, he was doing a completely different job and the people at the new position were not great. He had a breakdown. However, things did improve for him eventually. The company was taken over again a few years down the line and he was given the position he had occupied for 25 years prior to that—he was made Operational Director. One of the criteria of the sale here was that the new owner wanted Gee to stay. Gee did.

I had got a job with a Japanese pharmaceutical company, so I had to go on a six-week intense training course while I was still living in Aylesbury. The position was for the Hampshire area, where I was moving. It was a GP sales rep position, which is what I wanted.

I went on intense training course (intense in more ways than one). It was full of 20 plus ex-graduates who drank for six weeks. It was an excuse for me to drink. At this point, I really didn't need an excuse and it was now '*problematic*'! More people that I knew were beginning to mention it.

The training itself was appalling; I came out not knowing anything about the cardiovascular drug I was going to be selling. I never applied for a cardiovascular position after that. The other therapeutic areas they trained us in were easier. I got to grips with them and felt reasonably confident with the information I had learnt.

On weekends, I went back home to Aylesbury. By the end of the training, I was screaming to get out. I wasn't really that sure about my manager. We got the moving date a week before we moved. I was in conference with this new Japanese company Monday through Wednesday.

Gee was moving the company on Friday. This meant I would have to go down from Cobham, where the training course would resume, on Thursday to collect the keys, so I was there to move in on Friday. Matt, my manager, wasn't happy about this and said it wasn't possible and we needed to speak to the MD about it. I should have known at that point that trouble was ahead. I was given the time off. They let me leave after the training on Thursday, so I missed out on the 'gala dinner', which was no great loss to me. I heard that everyone had got very drunk. Hardly anyone could work properly the next day as they were being sick during the training. One person even had a diabetic fit.

We moved into our house at the end of April, the Friday before I went out on territory. I was starting on Tuesday as Monday (thank God) was a bank holiday.

One of the criteria for the house we bought was that it should not need any work to be done on it. We got that. From an investment point of view, I wanted a four-bedroom house. From a personal perspective, four bedrooms meant there was room for us to consider having children, which I wanted. We also were just around the corner from my sister. Dana and her family were the only people that I knew in Hampshire.

The job was a contract for six months with a contract company. The drug they were promoting had by far exceeded what they expected so they needed a larger field force. We were all going to be taken in-house and working directly for the pharmaceutical company after six months; they just wanted to make sure we were good fits first.

Matt called me one evening from a pay phone to tell me that the contract was not to be extended and that come September, my contract would be terminated. Matt basically lied to me; his words were, "They have not extended the contract or taken other reps in from other areas; only a few are going in." Matt and I didn't get on, that was why he told this lie. He was awful to work for and had no respect for your own time. He took over calls when we were in there and once had both of us thrown out of a practice. I think what clenched the deal was I called him a 'prat'! *That, I'm sure, did it.* Although, no doubt I was difficult to manage. The main reason for that was I just wanted to be left alone to get on with the job and not have my time wasted, which normally happened with field visits.

September–December, 1998, I felt like I had been transported to the moon. I knew no one in Hampshire and I was lonely. I went for interview after interview with pharmaceutical companies like Astra, who I really wanted to work for as they gave their reps a large budget for 'educational meetings'.

Other interviews were with APC, Janssen Cilag, Nova Nordisk, Sanofi, Avensis, MSD, twice with Pfizer, the first time I thought it was for Viagra. The recruitment company got that wrong along with the territory the next time. I wasn't in the right location to be employed by them; I had to live on territory. What made it worse with recruitment agencies was that you attended an interview them first. Then one with the pharmaceutical company, and the third interview was normally if they were considering you and you went to an assessment centre or did a presentation for them. So all in all, there were three interviews you needed to get through.

I spent three months trying to get a job. Gee said maybe I wasn't suitable for it and should try something else but I was determined. In that three months, I learnt so much about different drugs and companies, it really did put me in a good position knowledge wise. I gained knowledge of assessment centres with companies, personality tests, presentations based on the pharmaceutical company's choice, understanding clinical trials and explaining them, product knowledge and RSA data. I went through the whole lot. I just didn't have a job. Being a GP rep, your sales are based on RSA data, since the monthly report tells the company how many prescriptions that area had produced for the medication you were selling. I was getting fed up with it. December came with no job. Dana had asked Gee and me to go to France with her and her family, Nick her baby born in April, Sebs, who tuned three in April and her husband Dick. We booked it.

At this point, I was now sick of interviews, sending CVs off when I looked at the jobs in either the Times or Telegraph on a

Thursday, and signing on with recruitment agencies. There were loads of jobs in the pharmaceutical industry for reps.

I got the paper one Thursday, saw a part-time position in my area in Hampshire selling HRT, which was the therapeutic area I wanted to sell in. I phoned, sent my CV to them and had an interview with a guy called Barry. As he knew Paul very well, who had been the divisional manager for the dental team at SKB, his first words were, "I shall call Paul and ask him."

Barry called me that evening and said he had spoken to Paul, who had said that I was a very good rep, just difficult to manage. This was true. Barry gave me the job saying he was not the one who was going to manage me, so I got a job with Kudos. This was all done and dusted by mid-December in days. The recruitment agency that Kudos had registered with had me on their books but they didn't put me forward for the interview even though they knew I wanted part-time work in the HRT market place. The recruitment company lost out since they didn't do their job properly.

The alcohol for me wasn't great. Adrian's would be worse.

Chapter Eight
Adrian, 1983–1996

In total, Adrian would spend nine years in and out of jail.

At 23, he had been admitted to his first psychiatric hospital, Tooting Bec. Going into jail so many times managed to keep his admittances down. When I met him, he looked like someone who belonged on a wanted poster to me.

Between 1983 and 1997, Adrian managed to stay out of jail but not trouble. On the outside, his life was drugs, crime, women and a mess. He rarely worked. There were jobs that he did do over the years while he was using drugs. They were always jobs that had no responsibility and he could either use or get drunk while on the job. One job was street-sweeping for Hackney Council.

However, he thought of an easier way to get money—theft. Louis Vuitton was a popular bag and normally there would be a Louis Vuitton purse in it. These were good items to go for. It stood for Luncheon Voucher LV for those on the street and tended to be an easy target. Owners of such bags were generally more interested in shopping and thus, were easy targets and you could snatch a bag or purse from them very quickly. Easy, there was your luncheon voucher. These items, along with money, were either given to dealers for drugs or the money used to buy drinks, cigarettes and sometimes food. However, food was not a priority. There were homeless places you could go to get food and cups of tea. When unemployed at this point in his life, Adrian did not sign on for benefits. His words: "It was too much hassle, all that waiting around, paper work and turning up once a week was not my thing!" Well, to give him credit, at least he didn't live off the state at that point!

I, on the other hand, had got married, divorced 1983–1986 and then remarried again to Gee in 1994. I have no idea why I got married again, just felt I should.

I had been in sales in financial services and earned a fortune with them. I had then moved from financial services to pharmaceuticals and had been earning a reasonable salary with them. I was a top performer/producer for the companies I worked for.

I moved from the Home Counties down to Hampshire. I was on my third sales job, which was a disaster due to my attitude and my inability to cope with my new manager. I had then started with Kudos, which would be the best sales job I would have. But my drinking was getting worse. This was very different to what Adrian was getting up to.

Adrian epitomised everything I disliked in a person.

In 1983 and onwards was when he really started whacking up the admittances to secure psychiatric units, along with A&E. Adrian was now on a real cocktail of drugs: Heroin, Crack Cocaine, Cannabis, Valium, Methadone, Morphine, Purple Hearts, Black Bombers, Crystal Meth, Sulphate, Dexedrine, Tuinal, Palfium, Diconal, Nembutal and Seconal. Plus a few more.

He robbed doctors. On one occasion, he stole 1,000 DF118. How he is still here, I have no idea. Adrian was basically very unhappy. He was known as 'Junkie Bob'. He did not change his name back to Adrian until 2004. That is one thing he said in an AA meeting that he did not like the name Junkie Bob.

He almost overdosed on Nembutal, in a police station in Houndslow. He had been arrested for burglary and forging prescriptions. They had the Nembutal taken away from him, but he stole them back from the sergeant and asked to go to the loo. The sergeant was going to go with him, but he pleaded for some dignity. They let him go, and he swallowed 59 of them, was rushed to South West Middlesex hospital and even pronounced dead. A nurse saw the eyelid flicker and brought him back. The charges were reduced as the sergeant should not have let him steal the tablets back.

In 29 days, he had 31 admissions to the hospital and he kept on overdosing on sleeping pills. Adrian was crushing them, injecting them into his groin, his arms and his neck. He was picked up by the cops and the ambulances. He went to various hospitals over London. They were going to section him at this point; instead, they put him in a strip cell. They detoxed and stabilised him on medications then kicked him out.

There would be years of wards and cells and rehabs in the wards. The men were given rubber clothes in the secure cellblocks, rubber clothes to save on laundry and also stop suicide risks. He was lucky not to lose his leg on several occasions as he had DVT and was injecting into his femoral vein in his leg.

One of his statements he made with regards to rehab was that if he left and picked up, he was fucked. It would also spiral into other areas of his life if he stopped the drugs for a while. He had a need (still does today to a degree) for instant gratification. He wasn't comfortable with being himself, which was why he used things. If it wasn't drugs, it would be sex, women, cars and money. One thing would take over for a while. His addiction would always be active; if not drugs, one of the above. That is the same for any addict, regardless of their addiction. For me my first addiction was exercise and the second was work. It then morphed into alcohol and shopping and could manifest between the four.

Provided he had his drugs, he was relatively happy. He was, however, lonely. He hung out with other drug addicts, dealers, plus prostitutes. He never paid for sex. He had no interest in his appearance and looked a mess. His body was becoming badly scarred. His veins had collapsed, making it more difficult to inject but he would find a way of injecting. When all veins in his arms had collapsed, it was the legs, groin, then the neck. To me they looked like a combination of snakebites and indents or large dimples you would see on someone's face when they smiled, where he had injected in these areas so much. These marks were on his legs and in his groin area. His feet were a mess. He would suffer from leg ulcers, which could also be on his feet. Both his feet and hands were swollen and remained that way. He had caused neurological damage, so his hands always shook, not drastically but I noticed it.

He self-harmed and tried suicide many times. He didn't care if he died. The women in his life would always come with a multitude of problems. All of them were on drugs and they would use together. He had no shame about where he had sex and undertaking sexual acts on buses along with shooting up with another junkie was normal behaviour for him. One of the women, Nita, was another real mental case, according to Adrian. The two of them bullied and threatened doctors to give them prescriptions for drugs. In those days, it was quite an easy thing to do if there were two of you. Adrian and Nita did this regularly. Sex was probably the second strongest addiction. He rarely cared about the women he slept with, provided he had his orgasm. That was all he was interested in. The women were then dumped. That pattern continued until he was using so much there was no interest in sex and he was not capable of having sex due to all the drugs he was taking.

The people whom he hung out with were dying from OD or accidents. One of the worst cases was Kim, who was in rehab and jumped out of a window, impaling herself on a spiked fence. That was from third floor. Another jumped from the 17th floor. At this point, he was seeing some quite horrific deaths, along with what he called the normal Ods. The list was horrendous. Death, Adrian stated, was an all too common place. You could go out in the morning and by 10 a.m. one of your so-called mates would be dead.

Adrian was constantly trying to go to AA and NA. He, however, did not quite have the attitude that was required. In many ways, he wanted to clean his life up but the addiction was very strong. In AA meetings and others, he could be abusive and violent. On one occasion, he kicked the table over where the chairperson and person doing the share were sitting. He would turn up at these meetings with drugs and use them or bring alcohol and drink, not what you ideally want in these kinds of meetings where people were really serious about their recovery. Adrian was convinced he could handle recovery alone. That would be an area we both had in common. I'd think the same.

Ambulance crew and A&E were on first-name terms with him. He was either there for OD or injuries that had been inflicted on him. He always carried a knife or some form of weapon and his intent was always to inflict as much pain and damage on the other person as possible. The other person normally had the same thoughts. In *conviction number 13* the weapon would be a World War I bayonet with a leather sheath. It would be this conviction due to which in later life, in 2009, he could not get a job with Winchester prison. Ironic that he couldn't get in!

On one occasion, he caught one of the guys he hung out with stealing his stash. He beat his face with a clay spade. There were broken teeth and nose, and his face was a bloody mess. He met that guy in prison later, disfigured. He said to Adrian that he would have done the same. Adrian beat up one dealer in front of his family for cheating him out of £20. He was not in with a nice crowd; you could get killed for an £50 of Heroin. Adrian would steal the stash from other passed out drug addicts. He stole money and other things from his neighbours and people close to him. This was his normal life.

He lived for a while with woman called Denise in Dagenham. In his words, "She was a basket case on drugs, a loner. She lived upstairs and I lived downstairs with my pedigree Staffordshire bull terrier called Cassie-Angel. I called her Cas."

When Adrian left, he left Cas there.

Adrian described himself at that point before he left as the same as Denise, a basket case. He tried to be normal but wasn't. He isolated himself and read books, whatever he could find. It didn't matter what he read, when Adrian was capable of seeing the words. Adrian, surprisingly, is very well-read due to the time he had on his hands inside and outside prison. Inside prison, he did very little. His mother brought books in for him to read; there were many and varied in topics. She also managed to get money to him. There were so many ways you could pass the screws. Of course, he took drugs in prison; that was easy along with alcohol.

He taught himself to ride a motorbike. That must have been interesting! He had four different accidents and was admitted to hospital for only one of them, where he had a hole in his leg and an infection. He had no motorcycle licence or insurance since that involved paperwork.

Adrian slowly went mad and started doing weirdo stuff (His words not mine). He watched 'The Shining' on LSD alone and other films like Straw Dogs Soldier Blue, Stigmata; all with deep, dark themes. His isolation was greater than before. He hated people and tried hard not to come into contact with them.

He had no boundaries and would inject anywhere he could. He would inject in stairwells, underground, buses, shop doorways, just about anywhere. He didn't care if people saw him. His priority was to get his shot in his system as soon as possible. He surrounded himself with weapons. At one point, he was convinced London was the haunt of vampires. He was suffering from psychosis. As I'd say, he completely lost it.

In 1996, Adrian ended up again in a locked psychiatric hospital called Bethlem Royal Hospital. He stayed there for nine weeks. In the psychiatric hospital, he displayed all the symptoms of post-traumatic stress, paranoia, anger-management disorder and obsessive-compulsive disorder. He went to rehab in Clapham for six months. There he had flashbacks and bad nightmares. These continued for some time after he left.

In 1996, he thought his life had hit rock bottom. That would not be the case. This is the year he met Mandy.

In 1996, I was working for a pharmaceutical company and two years later I moved to Hampshire.

Chapter Nine
Kudos

I, on the other hand, in 1998…was having interview after interview, assessment days, and in those days, acetate presentations on an overhead projector, interviews with the managers, human resources, other reps already in the company, trainers from the field and internally head office based…The list was endless. In most cases, it was a pointless exercise which really did nothing to ensure you got the job. The reason being most had already, to a degree, chosen the rep that they wanted. The interviews, assessment days and personality tests were all to make the pharmaceutical company look good and just to confirm that they were right and had dotted all the i's and crossed all the t's. If you failed at this point, you really had fucked up good and proper in some way. Pharmaceutical companies seemed to compete that way too. Who had the best personality test to give a rep to do etc.

I got a job with Kudos and I did not have to jump through hoops for them, unlike the other pharmaceutical companies I had been interviewed with. The one good thing that did come out of these interviews was I would have a great deal of knowledge about these companies and their products. In many ways, it wasn't a waste of time. It had been incredibly annoying, in some cases upsetting, and then there was always the rejection factor. *What was wrong with me?* Actually, nothing.

What I did find out very quickly was the difference between the two jobs. I was paid commission based on what I sold in financial services and I earned the most in the branch due to business I brought in. It was not subjective. In pharmaceuticals, in many ways, it could come down to just plain favourites. I was so often the best rep business wise, but I didn't get the highest pay rises. I brought some of it on myself with my attitude, which wasn't great. I was, however, a good rep. Just plain difficult to manage.

Gee and I came back from France early for two reasons. One, it was freezing cold in Dana, my sister's, cottage, which she and her husband Dick owned. I had been unsure about going as I was not well. I had a very bad chest infection and could not stop coughing along with trigeminal neuralgia. Plus, I'd missed the first week of the training course. Kudos knew this and were happy for me to go the second week.

Dana wasn't very happy about it but I felt that I really did need to be on the course. I thought I would miss out on the product knowledge and probably have to do them by myself. Then also the team building and bonding. I would feel like an outsider. Juliette was also aware that I would miss the first week as she had called before Christmas since she wanted to make contact with all the reps who were in her team. For me it was the best discussion, based on my first job in Hampshire with the Japanese pharmaceutical company, which I had felt I didn't fit in. Plus, I had a prat of a manager.

I had always felt that I didn't fit in and in so many ways. I didn't and people would say that I was different. One guy in rehab said he had never met anyone like me. I never challenged him on what he meant. How and why I don't fit in, I don't know; I just know I don't. Today, I'm really not worried if I do or don't fit in. People are people and I am me.

I went to Corby Northamptonshire for the training course on Monday, 4th January, 1999. Gee drove me to Corby; it would be a two-week training course in the Hilton Hotel. This was very different to what Adrian was up to. Adrian was half-way through his marriage with Mandy. That was not going well.

At the start of the training course, I was still not well. I had seen my GP, who felt I probably would not be able to go. However, I did. I was coughing and spluttering most of the first week.

The training course was nice and enjoyable, unlike others I had been on. This one only lasted two weeks. With one pharmaceutical company, the training course was 12 weeks. That should give you an idea how long they could be. I remember out in the field when I had finished the training course, one of reps said to me, "It's the best brainwashing course you can go on!"

Two weeks went quickly. We all had a great time. There was no pressure or the expectation of a high pass mark; they wanted a realistic one: 75-80% pass. Bear in mind, you would learn more about your products and the competition on territory. That happened with all drugs very quickly. On territory would be your main and most important learning place.

Our team had the advantage over other teams. We all got on well. All liked one another and to a degree worked together as a team as much as we could when we were competing to be top rep. This is something I never aspired to; it just seemed to happen. I remember Dot who would be one of my co-workers saying she was going to keep a low profile in this job as she didn't want the attention or the expectation or the pressure that would be put on you as a rep. This never happened. Plus her personality type was to be competitive and top.

There were three products, with the first line being Hormone Replacement Therapy (HRT). HRT was the area I really wanted to work in as I had noticed and taken on board when working for Japanese Pharmaceutical Company, that practice's like and wanted information on this therapeutic area. Second was a hypnotic sleeping table. Finally, a palliative care product for prostate cancer.

Juliette was keen, very keen on us being the best team with the best marks. We always got the exam papers the night before. We would go to one of our rooms that night and go through the papers and memorise the answers. Most of the team got 100%. We looked great to the others. However, if another team member sat near us, we would help them out discreetly with the answers. In our defence for literally cheating, I'd like to say we would have got good marks nonetheless, not 100% but above average. We would become the best of the best, you could say.

Every exam, 85% of our team got 100%. The others were in high percentages, except for one, Becky. She never joined us for any of the revision, should I say, sessions. Juliette had to take her to one side and help her. This was an upper management decision. Another pharmaceutical/contract company would have kicked Becky out. Kudos were different from the rest in so many ways. They would have the division which you have never seen before. By that I mean happy, relaxed and good performers, who went the extra mile, plus we all got on with each other. I remember when we got to Majorca, Barry, who interviewed me, said that he had never seen such team rapport before. That was our last night, at the gala dinner.

Our team seemed to know it all. We would be called South West Incorporative. Also, we were the best team in the field, best team for attendance and not having time off or going sick, *simply the best*. We just clicked; everyone liked each other. Even Becky, who didn't join in, and Emma, who could be really short with you. Everyone accepted her like that and said that was just Emma. Emma was also a super brainiac.

We shared stories about our lives with each other. We each had a story of sorts. Some stories came out on the training course, the others would come later.

Emma had quite a shocking one. She was slim and attractive, in her early 20s. We sat one night, listening to her stories, one about her boyfriend whom she had been living with and was engaged to. One night, they went to a party, where Emma would meet her future husband. Instantly, they were attracted to one another. Graham, even his name had the wow factor. The other did not. Emma landed up kissing Graham in front of her then boyfriend, who would soon be her ex, spending the rest of the evening with Graham and then going home with him. She returned the next day to her home, to her would-be ex, only to tell him that he had to move out since Graham was moving in. Emma's ex had put all the money into the property and had bought all the furniture. "He went." We were shell-shocked. Then it got better. She told him that he had to sign the house over to her and Graham plus furniture. He walked away with nothing. None of us could believe it.

Becky's story was funny; she had a flat full of gnomes. These had come to her in many and varied ways. Firstly, not one had ever been bought. She and her flat mate would take them from people's gardens, morning, noon or night. Normally at night after a few drinks. They put letters through letterboxes, telling the owners they were gone. They would knock on doors and run off with them. The flat had gnomes in every room. Becky went on what we called gnome-hunting. She and her flat mate would walk or drive around the Brighton area where she lived, which was also her work territory. When they had spotted one, they would come up with a scheme of how to nick them. They also introduced challenges and targets for getting these gnomes. How many gnomes could one get in one night? What was the most difficult gnome to nick? Who could come up with the best plan to acquire the gnome? Along with the gnomes, Becky's flat, should we say, had many decorative items which had been sourced in a similar fashion.

Based on that story, there was no way I was having Becky stay over at my place for the very first regional/team meeting we would have. It was suggested by Juliette that Becky and I should double up for the first regional meeting and just take one car, as Becky had to drive past Junction 9 on the M27. It was logical as I lived off Junction 9. It would also help with saving petrol along with being a team-bonding exercise. Becky wasn't fitting in and Juliette wanted my help. The stay-over didn't happen but the lift the next morning did.

Sian also had a very funny story. Being from Ireland, I always feel the Irish tell the great ones. Sian and her husband were on a ferry with some friends. They had gone to the bar to have just a few drinks. Things did not go to plan. Sian woke up in the morning naked next to her husband on the bar floor with children jumping over them. Sian had no idea what happened there. Sian also had breast implants; none of us knew anyone else who had them so we were most intrigued. We weren't happy until we had all had a feel to see what they were like. This would be normal behaviour in other areas with our team. We just stretched the boundaries.

Dot didn't really divulge any funny stories over the course but later, when we got to know each other better, stories would come out. One was about the time when Dot became pregnant with her first child, she worked for a newspaper selling advertising space. Every lunchtime, she would park the car and have a sleep for a couple of hours, then go back to work. Although she was a qualified teacher, she had opted, in the end, to be a supply teacher and would later sell various bits and pieces to schools, mainly books.

Dot would also let us know that in the first term and the first few days of a new class you go in hard to lay down the ground rules, so they don't cause uproar. Later, you would relax the boundaries. The class knew at that point what was acceptable behaviour.

My stories…one was about Financial Services and what had happened there. That was quite a hit in the office. When you work with 30 guys, you learn a great deal about them, along with the practical jokes that go with it.

One of the stories that I relayed to them was of a roly-poly striper gram. It was one of the guys' birthdays, Graham. He was very popular with all of us. A stripper gram arrived. Graham was allocated this lead, as they were called. We worked in an open-plan office, and only the management had offices. Graham had requested an office, only to be told there were none available and he would have to do it at his desk. All the reps were sitting at their desk discreetly trying to look like they were working but keeping an eye on Graham to see what was happening.

Graham, taking the whole thing seriously, being very business-like, was doing the 'fact finding' (finding out information that was required.). He was given a few minutes to get into the swing of things. The roly-poly started getting very friendly with Graham along with adjusting her clothing. Graham started looking around the room to see if anyone was watching and looked incredibly nervous and uncomfortable. There we were all pretending not to be looking. Then she started to take her clothes off. Graham started to look horrified. We then, at that point, could not contain the laughter. Thirty guys in one room and me. You can imagine the rest. Graham did take it very well and became laid back and let her get on with it. There were so many stories like that.

Another other story really sticks in my mind and I still find it funny to this day. When I worked for SB Pharma, I had a large territory. Middlesex was one of the areas I worked as a sales rep, selling to dentists. I was in Greenford and the traffic was, as usual, stop start. You really have to plan where you are going and who you are going to see and what for. Some would be basic call rates, a dentist or hygienist being a call. Then there were the sales. I had targets for both. One of the practices I turned up on that day was for a call rate; I just wanted to see one of the dentists. This was to hand over some samples that I had. These had been requested. They were an awful practice, one which I didn't like calling on. I'd never got in. Parking was horrendous. You didn't know if your car would be there when you got back. There was a high chance of you being mugged as you carried doctor's cases. Apart from that, all was fine. The first time I turned up in Southall, I was covered in gold jewellery. That never happened again. I looked at the area and decided sensibly it was by far too much of a high-risk area in more ways than one. Mugging, stealing, at best, and so on. When I got in the practice, I went through the normal 'would it be possible to see a dentist or hygienist'. You then get the normal reply from the receptionist. "They're busy."

"Would you mind taking the card and asking for me, please?" Then a few different tacks if that didn't work. At a certain point, you know you're not getting in. I wasn't, even though I had samples, which I grudgingly handed over. I was desperate for the loo. I asked for directions. The receptionist informed me she would have to ask. Ask she did but really took her time to come back; she left me waiting for over ten minutes. Desperation was setting in. When she came back, she said where the toilet was. She went out of her way not to make it clear where I was going. I was unsure but felt I couldn't ask again. I went through to where I thought she indicated. There were a couple of doors. I opened the first door. It was a broom cupboard and the dentist was in the broom cupboard facing the wall. There was next to no room in that cupboard. He was squashed against the wall and the sides. I shook my head as the dentist had his back to me and I was just closing the door. How pathetic is that to get out of seeing a rep? Then I saw the broom cupboard door had a key to lock it. I have no idea why it had a key. As he was so keen to go to those lengths not to see me, I felt that I should help him out even further. He could stay in the broom cupboard to avoid the next rep that came in. Very quietly and carefully, I slowly turned the key. My lucky day, it didn't make a noise when I locked the door. My justification was how pathetic was that to avoid a rep. I then went to the loo and afterwards walked out as if nothing had happened and put the key back. I was polite to the receptionist, smiled and said thank you. She didn't even acknowledge me and went out of her way to ignore me. Quite rude really, not having any intention of helping me in anyway. She had given me my card back so there could be no repercussions of locking the dentist up as she would not remember my name or company. This I was sure about based on the fact that she didn't look at the card. To this day, I wonder how he got out. Plus, I never returned to the practice. This showed my wicked streak. The team was horrified but could not stop laughing. And yes, I would do it again.

We talked about our sex lives. It was mainly females, just one guy called Dave; he tended to be a loner on that part and didn't join in with that bit. It was about our partner at home, how they were coping with us being away. Some well, some not so well. Food parcels had been left for spouses and children by some. Not by me. We talked about how everyone got on with their partner/husband. We found out each other's background, how stupid and irresponsible our partners could be. In many ways, it was a full-blown counselling session on relationships with the opposite sex. I wasn't convinced in Becky's case it was the opposite sex. More like same sex.

Emma's story, we felt, was the most mouth-opening one.

On Thursday, our cars arrived while we were doing role-play. This is going through the sales pitch with another person. The final role-plays were always done with senior management, which was not great. There was pressure and you got feedback on how you performed. I hated role-play but did well on this occasion.

In role-play, you use the detail aid with all the selling points on it. You would then go through this performance of doing exactly what they wanted for you to sell the product to the doctors. I would like to say at this point it was a load of shit; you never got anywhere using the detail aid with doctors. Doctors did not want to hear about this clinical trial that had been done and other stuff. On the whole, you went into the practice with the detail aid, didn't use it but would leave them a piece on the product and a freebie if you had one and liked them.

The delivery of the cars on a lorry transporter did take the attention away as we all wanted to look out of the window and see them. There were two choices; half the room could have the Toyota Avensis, the other half the Nissan Premiere. We got the Nissan Premiere, which I would love.

We were meant to have our car the first week but Graham, the MD of the company, was let down. The car hadn't even been put on the cargo ship. There was no way they would be ready in one week. The car was Peugeot 406. These were nice cars, and the management wanted to give the reps a slightly better car than would be expected. Gee also had one. By not having our cars that first week made it more difficult for everyone to get home. Public transport, partners coming collect etc. I was very lucky. Juliette lived in Romsey, not that far from me. As the manager with the best team, Juliette had been allocated a Mercedes to go home in and she gave me a lift home. It was a good bonding session. The downside was there was a fault with the driver's window. It kept on going up and down. It was funny to start with. By the time we got home, we were frozen, and it wasn't funny.

Juliette took me back to Corby on Monday, which was great. It would have been public transport for me otherwise. The window had been fixed, somehow, by her partner. It now could not go down.

On Thursday night, we had a real laugh. It was the night of the gala dinner. Four would be awarded a prize for being the best in certain groups. Emma was awarded a prize for best academic rep. Dot's prize was for best role-play. Juliette for best team. Then, I think, they had to give one prize to another team as we had cleaned the floor with all but one. If there was a prize for loudest team, we would have got that one too.

The gala dinner was interesting. Most of our table got absolutely hammered; not one of us was sober except Mandy. Most of us had a blackout period of what happened that night. For me, I was beginning to realise that I might have a bigger drinking problem than I thought.

I had spent Monday–Thursday not drinking on the course. It was just both the Thursdays that we sort of went for it. The first week was more controlled than the gala dinner.

In the Home Counties, I was drinking excessively and thought maybe I could sort myself out. That would not be the case. When I had no work for three months after I moved to Whiteley, at lunchtime, I drank a bottle of wine while watching TV and then had a few glasses in the evening, so Gee only saw the couple of glasses!

We had started off before the meal with champagne and brandy (Wicked Lady) in the reception area. By the time we got to the table, most of us had demolished three to four of these, so we were quite drunk before the start of the meal. The prizes were then awarded. Just as well by the end of the meal none of us were coherent, except Mandy. The meal then came along. The wine was already on the table, flowing freely, and we managed to get a hold of more wine from other tables who were, for a better word, pacing themselves. That would never happen with our team. Halfway through the meal, the fire alarm went off so we had to exit. We eventually got back to our tables; I have no idea what had happened, it was some sort of false alarm. It added to the chaos that was happening with our team; we were very drunk at this point. We then continued with the meal, got more wine and became more drunk.

Then the entertainment started. Now this was meant to be a comedy act, which was appalling. It had been arranged by the trainer (his brother, I think) who facilitated the training. We were making an uproar doing various things. Then I got up and started dancing around our table. Sian would call it snake dancing based on what I did with my hands; I made snake-like movements. The trainer was not happy or impressed and kept on asking me to sit down. The table didn't want me to as I was more entertaining and funny than the so-called 'comedy act'. I was up and down like a yoyo. Then some of the others joined in. The comedian was a lost cause; we had stolen his thunder. *If there was any.* The room was looking and laughing at us, egging all of us on. He stood no chance; the room loved us.

Another fire alarm went off and we left the building again. We were given silver foil while we waited outside. I really can't recall this as I had blacked out at this point. At our table, each one of us would have a blackout about what happened that night in a different area. Somehow, we put all the events together the next day by recalling certain things that each of us remembered. It was just the second fire drill that I couldn't recall.

On Friday, we were going through territory planning with Juliette. Her region was the southwest. The territory planning was to work out where we would spend our first week and become familiar with all of our territories, as well as their boundaries.

It was the managers and their individual teams together. Not one of us was well; we had hangovers and we were being sick. There wasn't a single time when we were all in the room together as one would be throwing up in the loo.

After territory planning, we were given our cars. There was only been one of us who wasn't over the legal limit—Mandy.

Our team consisted of Emma, who would work Berkshire and Oxfordshire; Dot, Somerset and surrounding areas; Sian, Gloucestershire and Herefordshire; Dave, Wales; Becky, Sussex; Jude, Dorset; Bola, Surrey; Mandy, Devon and Cornwall; and I had Hampshire and Isle of Wight. This I was delighted with until I went there, along the very edge of Sussex. No territory was the same; all had different ways of working and how you got to see.

Each region had nine reps. There were three regions and our division was called Kudos GP sales force. However, our team would be called Southwest Incorporated.

At lunchtime, we were allocated our cars and packed them up with our luggage, plus all we needed to start on territory Monday morning. That consisted of detail aids, plus a few giveaways, like post-it notes and pens which the receptionist would love. They were always in need of them and could beg, steal and borrow for you to hand them over. That still would not be enough to get you in. You had to be, by far, much more creative.

The cars needed to be filled up with petrol. There was one garage close by. So four pumps and 27 reps. There is always one person who has no consideration for anyone else. Would have you rolling your eyes and thinking how much longer were you going to be; can't you do that somewhere else and let someone else fill their car up. That would be Margarette.

Margarette was a bit of a snob and had come from a relatively good background. I should imagine she had been privately educated by her voice. She got to the petrol station and at the pump, sat in the car and fiddled around for ages before she got out. She then proceeded to stand and look at the pump. What she was looking at, goodness knows. Eventually, she took the petrol cap off and filled the car up. She then needed to find her purse to pay. That took another age. Finally, she went to pay. *That was quick.* She got in the car and who knows what else she was doing. Five minutes later, she left. In total, she had been at that pump for over 15 minutes. There was no consideration for the other 27 reps.

Margarette was the type of character who could make people feel not so great about themselves. She was very judgmental and opinionated. She tended to put people down quite easily, upsetting other people with no thought about how that person would feel, and would look down on them. She spoke the Queen's English.

She looked down on me. When I turned up at one hotel for a meeting for a brand-new HRT product, I was late for dinner. My friend Sarah said, "Just come down as you are."

I went down in jeans and trainers and looked presentable. Everyone was dressed casually but smart. "Oh, dear," I said, "I should have changed."

For which Margarette looked me up and down and said, "Most certainly. Not the correct attire for a meal in a restaurant." I didn't look that bad. It wasn't like it was a top-of-the-range hotel either. That was Margarette all over. It did nothing for my self-image at that point and was quite upsetting.

Despite her attitude at times, I must give her credit. From a sales point of view, she did incredibly well on the palliative care product for prostate cancer. This is about all I had to do with her. She was liked by most people and did fit in like the rest of us, so she can be forgiven for that. I really don't think she was aware of how she was making people feel. Had she known, I am sure she would have been upset. There was no malice or any real nastiness in her. Margarette just had a very high opinion of herself.

I loved the job. Well, it was my second-best job working for the second-best person I'd worked for, Graham. It was a contract company so we sold for various pharmaceutical companies. Other reps who worked in-house for pharmaceutical companies and some doctors and nurses did not always think very highly of us since we were contract reps, but it suited me and I was happy. On the training course, I had one moment when coming down for dinner. I was in my room, just leaving, when I became tearful and thought *what am I doing here?* That got sorted in my head very quickly.

I became very friendly with one member on our team called Dot. I remember her words so well from the training course, "I'm going to keep a low profile in this job." She also explained the reasons why. She didn't want to get noticed or be pressurised, just wanted to do the job. That didn't happen.

One of the reasons Dot and I became good friends was she had confided in me about a few personal things and I listened. The other reason was she called me the Monday we went out on territory to ask how I got on. I wonder to this day if she had not made that phone call, would I have phoned her so often, as I became quite obsessed with speaking with her daily after that one phone call.

My first day on territory, I saw no GPs and one rep who told me that the GP of the practice I was about to go into had gone. He did, however, tell me when they would see me. Havant was the area I worked that day.

Dot was one of the most popular people in the company and the favourite. This stood her in good stead with pay rises. Dot was a good rep. Dot named certain calls 'Micky Mouse' calls. That's where you see a doctor behind the reception desk, give him some information on the drug and just name it and walk out. That's a contact that could go down on your call report. It probably didn't sell the product but helped your call rate, and more reps than not were doing that if they wanted to make their life easy and keep their manager off their back. You did get field visits frequently if you had a low call rate and sales. So, it was a good idea to make yourself look good. Managers had a tendency to make life for hell a rep whom they either didn't like or was performing poorly. More often than not the rep left before being pushed out of the company or fired.

The team not only made an impression at the training course, we were about to make an impression on territory. First, Mandy was pregnant and everyone was pleased for her. That would explain the no drinking on the training course. That was fine. However, Juliette soon became a little upset, to say the least, when two more became pregnant one after the other. Some comments were made.

These reps were Emma and Jude. Juliette was angry with Jude. She said to me, "How ridiculous is that, not taking any contraception and not expecting to get pregnant." Jude was Irish Catholic and did not believe in contraception.

That was issue number one. Number two being:

Graham mentioned to Juliette, "I see your team is having a smashing time." The first incident with cars was Sian's. Living in Hereford, her car got flooded due to the floods that happened at that time. Sian didn't even get out on territory that day as her car needed sorting. Then Becky crashed her car, along with Jude, Dave and Bola. Five cars had been in some trauma. Juliette was not happy as none of the other teams had done any of this. Again, we excelled. Juliette pointed out that she would prefer no more accidents as it did not look good.

Field Visits

I did not like them. No one did. In all fairness to Juliette, she wasn't a bad manager to have out with you. She knew the game and didn't expect you to be any different. One of the first things she said to the whole team on the training course was—when we were doing our training on calls access and sales—"If I call you on your home number after 12:30 p.m., please answer the phone as if you don't have a lunch-time meeting you will be home quite easily by 12 p.m.." That was true.

My territory was one of the hardest territories to work, had the hardest access to see GPs and lowest of call rates nationwide. The average call rate was 2.2 GPs a day, along with being the hardest area to get meetings, by all accounts.

I learnt incredibly quickly to network and listen to other reps. I listened to the ones I felt were doing it. I remember one rep saying to me the most important thing is to get your territory sorted out within six months. Make sure you find out when the practices book their appointments for the year. Appointments for the year were booked in September, October, November and December. Then get all your appointments and meetings booked. If you work hard for six months, the rest would be easy. How true that was! However, as it was January, I had missed those dates.

Networking could take two forms. I chose option two. Option one was going to coffee shops at 10 a.m. and meeting other reps. I called them the coffee shop kids. They never tried specking after 9 a.m. and knew that the next specking time would be 10:30 a.m. earliest, or 11 and 11.30am. They rarely went into practice, just to build rapport with other members of staff or after 9 a.m. they would go home until later. Option two was turning up early, normally 7 a.m. at practices, waiting for them to open, hand your business card in and hope and pray they would see you either then or when you come back later at a set time. The first rep that got to the practice put their card in first. That's how it worked. There was an etiquette. This was a great time to network, meet other reps, talk about who they worked for, what they sold. There wasn't the rivalry you would expect in a sales job, the reason being that reps needed other reps. By that I mean sharing meetings, swapping appointments, letting each other know who was booking appointments and when. This was very good networking and I got a great deal out of it. Well, let's face it, being at a practice 7 a.m. in the morning that doesn't open till 8:30 a.m., what else is there to do except that or work on paper work and planning?

After handing your card in, if you had a call back, it was normally either at 10:30 a.m., 11:00 a.m., 11:30 a.m. or 12:00 noon. This was also the specking time to turn up at practices. Again, you would sit and wait. Just because they said that time didn't mean you would get seen at that time. You could be in a practice up to 1:30pm waiting to see one doctor. One rep once actually stayed from 10.30 a.m. till 2 p.m. to see a doctor. I think I would have given up. This rep used to be a private detective and told us about his last case. The wife of this elderly man felt he was having an affair. *He was.* What he had to do as a private detective was to follow the old guy, and he found that yes, he was having an affair. He said I didn't know whether to tell her about it or congratulate him on his stamina for having sex in a car so many times in one go. It was four or five times. That was a bit of a gobstopper.

Waiting to see doctors was another opportunity to see reps. Quite often, there could be up to six reps sitting there, waiting.

One day there were three GP practices in a building and we were all sitting there to see one or two of them. One practice didn't see reps full stop, then another was hit and miss—if you were lucky, they would let you see a GP. I did, however, get on well with that practice, and I did a very good CPR meeting for them with one of the ambulance guys from Havant.

It was good because you networked with the reps and had a general chitchat. I remember well a brand-new rep Karl turning up at a practice where five of us were already in the waiting room. Karl was wearing a black suit and it was torrential rain outside. The black suit just emphasised how wet he was. He was soaked to the skin. We were all stunned into silence. Then one rep said, "I've never seen such a wet person."

Karl, however, became an instant hit with all the reps. Karl was nice and a real, good laugh. I shared quite a few meetings with him. He worked for a company called Astra that later became known as Astra Zeneca. They had large budgets back in those days. Large budgets could make you popular with other reps as you would share the cost with them or you had the meeting booked and the person with the budget paid.

The two meetings I remember doing with Karl both were in the evening. One was down in Southsea at a restaurant called Truffles. There were many GPs there. We had a good time. Karl drove and it was in a period when the drinking had taken off but I could hold out till later and control it to a point.

After the meeting, Janet Sussex, one of the GPs, invited us back to her home. We went back and had a few drinks with her. Then Karl had to go and pick his girlfriend up from a nightclub. I said I'd wait in the car while he went in to get her. After an eternity, he returned with a very drunk girlfriend who could hardly stand. However, Karl was laughing. The girls with her were so drunk they insisted on painting his nails, which they did. Karl came out with bright red nails, which he would then have to go on territory with the next day as they had no nail varnish remover. As he was so well-liked with both reps and GPs, Karl could get away with it. The girlfriend, sad story. They married a few years later; she got pregnant before they were married. There was the potential of a drink problem at the time. He later divorced her as she became an alcoholic.

I could not comment about this since others would also say I was a heavy drinker. Jackie said my tolerance for alcohol was going up. That it was. At this point, I mainly drank in the evenings, occasionally lunchtime.

I sometime wonder had I eased off at this point, would I not have become an alcoholic? That I will never know. Plus, things were going to get worse for me.

The other meeting I shared with Karl was at Villa Romana, an Italian restaurant in Fareham. The munch bunch went there. Karl and I were doing the meeting. We had both driven there separately. I didn't drink but Karl did. I offered to take him home and the GPs suggested the same but he decided to drive. He lived in Hedge End and I was in Whiteley, so he lived two junctions down from me. He didn't get caught but he was way over the limit and said to me the next day that I should have taken him home and picked him up in the morning to collect his car. Most reps would drink drive at some point or the other.

There were other meetings that I saw Karl at, stand meetings. When we were together, we always laughed. Well, giggled. I don't know why but we just did. Karl would work for large Pharma companies. He did leave Astra and regretted it. Then he was with Nova Nordisk a short time, then went on to SB Pharma.

Sharing meetings was a big thing and one of the necessities of being a successful rep. Not only that, it was better for you if another rep was there; you felt more at ease since had someone on your side and to talk with. You had plenty of time to talk. If you set up before 9 a.m., when the doctors came in, you might see one or two at this point. The times you saw the doctors was at tea break and lunchtime. After that you packed up and went home. In between seeing the doctors you had time on your hands so you talked, got freebies from other reps and made appointments. Even swapped meetings and appointments if necessary.

My first two meetings were by myself. The very, very first was at an Indian restaurant in Basingstoke. It was in the evening and it took me 45 minutes to get there. I sat in the restaurant and waited. And waited. And waited. The guys who ran the restaurant said they normally phoned the order through. They didn't come. A meeting would consist of two or more GPs or nurses. When I told Juliette the next morning, she couldn't stop laughing. She asked how long I had waited. I said, "45 minutes." She even asked if I had a meal. I said, "No."

She said, "I would have done; I wouldn't have gone all that way, sat in a restaurant, felt like an idiot and not even eat."

I did.

My next meeting was in Liphook. It was a lunch meeting and a practice of five GPs would be coming. It was in a nice pub. I got there early and waited for them. They arrived on time. As we went to sit at the table, their introduction to me was, "We don't mind you being here and eating with us but can you only speak at the end, as we'd like to talk amongst ourselves?" This meeting lark was not great. If this was what they were like, forget it; I didn't want to do it.

However, meetings were the way forward. They were key to your success as a rep on call rate and on sales. If you didn't go to meetings, then you might as well hand the towel in, especially in my area as it was just not going to work. You would be pounding pavements, trying desperately hard to get in, and it would be soul destroying.

Juliette had given us a talk about meetings and what types there were. She didn't mention those two types! The meetings that you were likely to get were lunch meetings which could be either in the practice, where you would take the lunch in for the practice. That could be sandwiches with other bits and pieces with it. Caterers could be called in. (You got the numbers of all the caterers and called them, giving them the date) Restaurant meetings were either at lunchtime or in the evening.

Then there were stand meetings. These were large meetings that always had an educational element to them. There would be several reps there with stands displaying their wares. The beauty of stand meetings was you had access to items called freebies distributed by the reps. Freebies were popular with the receptionists. These were items with the drug's name on them that varied from simple little things like fountain pens to blood pressure cuffs, soft toys, soup mugs, USB sticks, picnic blankets, really nice key rings made of stainless steel, boxes of tissues, pens, post-it notes, staplers and diaries. They could be wall calendars, paperweights, beach towels, penknives, wall charts of the skeleton or muscular anatomy and even penholders. One which I really liked was a model of a few of vertebrae of the spine. This was to promote an osteoporosis product and was excellent for hanging your jewellery on so loads of doctors took it just for that. The list was endless. All the Pharma companies had similar items. These items were meant to be worth no more than £5 each.

One rep had a full kit of instruments for testing your reflexes on his stand. He even had scales to weigh yourself. Not cheap micky mouse ones but the real McCoy.

You tended to sort your friends and family out first with these items as well as yourself. Tissue were great as again you had your supply, family's supply and friends'. Soup mugs were great. I got two of them from Jackie, who was handing them out. Samples were good as well, especially Canesten, which would be one of the products we sold.

I got over the first two meetings quickly.

If you wanted an easy life, you got meetings, appointments, access items, call-backs and your card signed by the GP to say they would see you.

The average call rate face-to-face no meetings was 2.2 in my territory. My call rate was 5 face-to-face and then meetings on top. I got this call rate, meetings, appointments, specking sorted out very quickly. (Specking was turning up at a practice hoping to get in with no appointment).

This is when quite a few things started to happen in my life. 1999 was my first year with Kudos. The start was not brilliant; it was hard to get in. I was, however, cracking it. By the end of 1999, I had one of the highest call rates in the whole company. That would continue but along came other things, meetings both with the company and with practices. There were drinks, lots of drinks. Everything paid for in abundance.

By the end of 1999, there was a buzz in the air, with everyone excited about the new HRT product we would be taking on, Indivina. However, Juliette wanted her team to go out with a bang and have the highest call rate over all. Dot was very keen and said to me, "Come on let's do this." At that moment in time, it was a bit like 'do we really have to do this'. I complied and really went for it.

That Christmas was great. Gee and I had a lovely time. My mother and Ralph came to stay for the millennium. I was delighted, Gee less so. We went all out for Christmas Day with the works but on New Year's Eve we went a lot further. French onion soup, roast lamb and my favourite white wine to start. There was red wine for the main course and then 12 midnight champagne and our own fireworks party. We even had a cat called Buster who didn't flinch at the fireworks.

In Aylesbury, I tried to get him off the fence to take him indoors; he was having none of it and swiped me a few times. I gave up, left him there and he sat and just watched.

We drank the champagne and went to bed in quite a civilised manner. There were not going to be many more like that.

Adrian, at this point, spent the millennium in Paris with his wife Mandy. He was clean, dry and sober at this point and had been for a couple of years. *That would not last; both of us would be brought to our knees in different ways.*

I was now eating in the best restaurants and staying in top hotels. Everything was paid for.

These are the two things I learnt. One was, quite a few of the GPs I took out liked to drink and did. There were a group of GPs we called the munch bunch as they always went out and had their favourite places for lunchtime and evenings. These were good meetings as you had easy access via specking, and we all landed up getting drunk in the evening. I used to share these meetings with two other reps, Jackie and Geoff. Geoff drove; Jackie and I got drunk. Well, to start with, I didn't, but towards the end, I did. Jackie could drink and had good tolerance. My tolerance wasn't great to start but I worked on building it up.

I soon became one of the most popular reps; GPs loved me. I was great fun, the life and soul of the party and did all the meetings that should never have been allowed by the industry governing body, the ABPI.

These meetings consisted of defence driving courses (go carting), maintaining good health (Champneys Spa), water safety, (going out on boats) to name a few. I and many others blew the rules completely.

I also did CPR training; in practice, I got the ambulance guy from Havant to do it, along with fire training. One of the best ones that would be very relevant to me was when I actually got the police to come into one practice to talk about drugs in the local area Gosport. That was an eye opener as to how people took drugs in various ways. The police showed us piece of silver foil that would be used to wrap up heroin or cocaine and pass from a dealer to an addict. Plastic bottles would be used to smoke cannabis. This policeman said that a few years back the police had a real clamp down on cannabis in the Gosport area. They got rid of all the cannabis. However, it opened the door for heroin to come down from London.

Not only did I break the rules, I blew my budget big time. I spent more than my whole team put together. I was having a great time, and the job had become so easy for me. That was probably another downfall along with the drinking. I could go home and start drinking at lunchtime if I had no other meetings or appointments that day.

Tiger, Tiger was another meeting. That's a nightclub in Gunn Wharf Quay Portsmouth. The GPs loved that one. We had a private room to eat, drink and sit; then there was the dance area. The turnout for that one was incredible.

Even an Australian doctor came to it. He was saying at the Solent and had really taken a fancy to me over a cricket tour. I met him in the pool. The moment he set eyes on me, he didn't leave me alone. In the end, I agreed to take him to a lunch meeting with me in a practice in Titchfield. That was all I wanted to do. Well, I didn't even want to do that, but I needed to get him off my back. It was embarrassing when I was in the gym one morning. I was on the rower and he came in with only Speedo swimming trunks on. *Great.* In the mirror, I could see all the guys. My mates looked at me then at him, then anywhere but the two of us.

That lunch meeting is what got him off my back and into the pool, where he should have been in the first place.

I was sharing this meeting with Tia. She invited him to Tiger, Tiger. I could not believe that she had done that. The one good thing about Tiger, Tiger was that I brought Sue. I was driving so couldn't drink; Tia was coming later so she could look after him. I was leaving at 11 p.m., which is what I did, not without taking several bottles of wine which had already been paid for.

My life had changed completely. I was also becoming outrageous in many ways. My behaviour with the drink left a lot to be desired. Yes, I had turned into the life and soul of the party but there was a price. The price was I could rarely remember what had happened. Now, I was drinking at most evening meetings. I managed to give it a miss at lunchtime. Various things could or would happen at them. I was loved due to my appalling behaviour; it was outrageous. The fact was I broke all the rules—I kept GPs out till late and they would get home drunk.

This happened after I left Kudos and I was working for Pharma. The pattern and uncontrollable drinking had started. I managed to throw up in Geoff's car one Friday night. We had been to a meeting.

I hadn't drunk for seven months; not quite sure how I managed that, but I did. I went to Sardinia with Pharma and that would be the only conference where I would be sober while the GPs were there.

When they left, I decided Jackie and I could have a session, and we did. Not only did the wine come out but the Flaming Sambucas. Not flaming in the glass but flaming in our mouths. You tip the Sambuca in your mouth, don't swallow, hold your head back, open your mouth, then someone lights it. Pretty stupid but when you are drunk, it's funny. Probably funny to onlookers in more ways than one. The pair of us were getting really drunk; not only that, but I actually hadn't drunk for a while. Geoff took both of us home as usual. He dropped Jackie off first. I knew I was going to be sick, so I opened the window. He hadn't stopped by the time I threw up. I was hoping in my drunken state it would go outside the car. It didn't. Geoff was not too happy as he was driving to Manchester the next morning to see Man Utd play with his wife Angie. Angie was furious over it. They had to clean the car that night and it was past 12 midnight, plus they were leaving 5 a.m. Angie said to Geoff. "Why didn't Cathy clean it up?"

His reply was, "She was in no fit state and couldn't." This was normal, my 'no fit state'.

It wasn't just me getting into a state, it was GPs as well. We dropped off one GP just down the road from where he lived. He fell in the bushes and managed to stagger out. His wife found him in the morning asleep in the downstairs loo.

There were meetings after meetings. Well, to me it was just piss up after piss up. In nice surroundings.

Again, further down the line working for Pharma, I went over to the Isle of Wight for a meeting in a very posh restaurant. I did not like working the Isle of Wight. I hated the ferry and I felt stuck. Plus, it was like going back a hundred years in time. This is the one I got really drunk at and couldn't remember paying at the end. I went over with Geoff, Simon, one of Geoff's territory partners and Linda, another rep from another company. Linda and I got plastered. I went in and out of blackout. I can't remember Simon having to nearly carry me down the stairs of the ferry to the car, along with Geoff doing the same with Linda. Then Linda and I were kissing each other in the back of Geoff's car. I don't remember that. I also don't remember both Linda and I trying to see who could get their leg in the air the highest. Another thing I don't remember is while we were waiting in the car to come off the ferry, there was a cop car with two coppers in it looking at the car. It was next to us. By all accounts, they didn't miss a thing. I did ask Geoff if they had come over to breathalyse him. His reply was, "No they didn't need to. They saw Simon and I bring the pair of you down the stairs." This was just normal behaviour. In my defence, it was not just for but other reps too, but that is a poor excuse.

To deal with lunch meetings, if you picked up sandwiches from Tesco or one of the large supermarkets, you could get stuff for yourself. In all fairness to me, I didn't really abuse it. I would get a few portions of fruit and maybe some juice. I didn't kit my whole fridge out like a great many reps did.

I remember well one of my lunch meetings in Twyford near Winchester. I was early, so I went into ASDA and got the lunch. Then I decided to have a cappuccino. I got into the queue, got my cappuccino and was by the soft drinks that you get from a soda stream like dispenser when some big fat woman with children and another big fat woman by me went to get the cherry-flavoured one. I got sprayed with cherry-flavoured soda and my beige suit was covered. I looked like a cherry aid Dalmatian. I had to go to the meeting looking like that since I didn't have time to go home. The woman just looked at me, didn't apologise, didn't even offer me a napkin to clean myself up. ASDA was in Fareham and I've always regarded some areas in Fareham as constituting a Class C demographic type person and I wasn't wrong there. They were out in ASDA that day.

Some meetings were just plain embarrassing to remember the next day. Others were incredibly funny.

The restaurants owners treated us very well. As we supplied them with so much business, we had first-class treatment. Not only would they order things in for us, we always left with a few bottles of wine, on the house.

My average week had turned into a three-day week. This was probably my downfall as it gave me more opportunities to drink.

I had appointments and I did some specking. I didn't need to be there at 7 a.m. anymore. I could go in anytime and I'd get seen by so many GPs. They signed my business card at meetings with a message on it saying will see any time. This you handed to the receptionist when you went in. They couldn't have the same approach with it in black and white that the GP would see you; they had to take the card through. These were fitted in between appointments and meetings. My call rate both for face-to-face and meetings was the highest in the company but my mileage was turning into the lowest. There were two reasons. One was that for meetings, Geoff drove and occasionally, Jackie. I wasn't going out every day in the car. I didn't need to. The mileage and petrol made it seem as if I was never going out. I did. However, I had heard that other reps for Kudos had very low mileage. Juliette had told me Graham had said, "I've no idea what they are doing." Well, nothing as they weren't getting the meetings or the call rate required.

At one meeting, Jackie had driven. It was a stand meeting at the Rose Bowl in West End Southampton, a cricket club. After the meeting, Jackie and I went down to the bar and consumed nearly three bottles of wine between the two of us.

I did drive occasionally to meetings which I did alone. That meant I had to worry about driving. I would have to stay sober for the evening meetings. In case of the day meetings, I was home by 2.30–3 p.m. I would more often than not start drinking as soon as I got home.

I was working predominately in Portsmouth, Fareham Gosport, along with some of the outskirts of Southampton. Southampton I hated with a passion. There were many reasons for this; access was awful, but I did get in. It was just awful to drive around, with traffic lights every two minutes. They always seemed to be red. On one occasion, Juliette made me jump the lights. I was following her to the BMW garage since she had a BMW and needed to take it to the garage. I had no idea where it was and she knew it. I was then out with her for the day. All I saw when the lights changed was her waving her handing telling me to come, not to stop. I jumped the lights. To this day, I don't know how I didn't get hit. Thank God, there wasn't a camera there.

That was an interesting day. I had sent her my day plan of what we were doing. She did um and ah about it. Juliette had worked that area as a rep. I said to her, "Just trust me on this one." I got the real raised eyebrow look.

We had started off at Townhill surgery. Got in there, contact number one. We then quickly dropped off the BMW. I had said to her there could be no mucking about; we were on a schedule. These were all speck appointments, and I wanted to see them all. I was on a real mission. Not only call rate wise, but I wanted the sales. Off we then went to North Baddesley. The GP whom I wanted to see was there that day. The receptionist said he was working with a trainee GP in the village hall at the next village. We got in the car, drove there. Juliette was saying, "You can't do that; you can't do that."

"Why not?" was my reply.

The village hall was an old building and small. Very typical, what you would expect. The inside looked like they all do—cold, with wooden floors. We went through the main door on to the wooden floor. There was a door down the hall on the left opening into a room. Ah, that's where the doctors must be. I had heels on and I'm not light-footed. There was this loud clip-clop (me) which echoed through the hall. Juliette was laughing, asking me to be quiet, but I was on a mission. I marched to the door and there were the two doctors I wanted to see. One was important and made the decisions with regards to dispensing, what was brought in and used. He was the one I wanted to see. The other trainee was to make my call rate look good. Hopefully, I would get him on the side for a later date.

I politely said who I was and asked if they could see me for a few minutes, which they dutifully did. I spoke about the drugs and then I went into the dispensing. I mentioned that our drug worked out cheaper to their prescribing budget along with the practice making a better deal on the dispensing side. Of course, the main doctor said, "Like all reps, lying." He got the calculator out. It was cringeable as I had been true to my work and accurate, so he had to apologise. I felt quite sorry for him at this point especially as he had given me such a hard time in front of the trainee. It was a bit like the *rep fights back* but without the rep having to do a thing.

When we left, Juliette was in stitches over it. She could not stop laughing about my clip-clop marching across the floor. We then went on to Botley for a quick speck call, which I got and then a sandwich, in practice, then a lunchtime meeting. That for the day was four face-to-face contacts and five contacts in a meeting in West End. The meeting went well; the doctors were polite and listened to what I had to say. They asked sensible questions and didn't make me feel like a complete twit. It also gave Juliette the chance to have a chat with them as well. This I really didn't mind as she was good fun, not intimidating and she didn't overrule you. On this field visit, she actually bought Gee a card, saying how exhausting her day had been with me and asking how he coped with me.

Most of my field visits with Juliette were okay. Plus, you got taken out for lunch somewhere quite nice. It was like going out with your mates, a good laugh.

Juliette had been a rep for SB Pharma. She knew the company. We talked about them; I had been on the dental side. I didn't like them. Juliette had worked the Southampton, Winchester area as a rep. That was the worst area on my territory to get in. Sales potential was high so that needed to be considered, and it would be something I would have to decide on. This would be one of the most important sales and business decisions I would have to make.

Juliette came around to my home one day. We had a business meeting in my back garden. It was a lovely day. The point of the meeting was to discuss my primary care groups. Our new HRT product launch was for an HRT product called Indivina. It was to ensure that we were all on track. The PCT needed to be on our side as they, to a degree, controlled the prescribing budget; you more often than not needed your product on their formulary. If you didn't, it was not a good thing and this could make or break a drug. The same was true in hospitals.

Juliette arrived at lunchtime. I made her some lunch and casually asked if she would like a glass of wine with it. "Yes," she replied. We sat outside as it was such a lovely day and went through all the PCG stuff. Juliette was very impressed with what I had done. I had obtained all the information which was required to get the drug on the formulary. I had all the key people's names and what their roles were. All I needed to do was see them and get them on my side to put the drug forward for the drug to be added to the formulary. I mentioned what the drug was able to do and how it compared to the competitor and the distinct advantages, without actually naming it. All reps did that with a new drug coming on the market; they didn't mention the name. With the exception of Viagra, where everyone knew about it and wanted to hear about it before it was even launched.

Juliette could not believe the amount of work I had done. She was very impressed and mentioned that no one else in the team had anything nearly as good or in so much detail as me. I was pleased.

We sat in the garden and managed to demolish two bottles of wine. Then we decided to go and get another two from the Spar. This was just around the corner. Juliette got them and we proceeded to get drunk. Gee came home and was not impressed. We all had dinner. How I made it, I will never know. Juliette stayed the night and then drove to Wales the next morning to have a joint field visit with Dave.

I felt dreadful, so I went out on my bike before going on territory to hopefully get some of the alcohol out of my system. I went on a bike ride every day to keep myself fit. When I went on territory, I felt dreadful but I had to go as Juliette had stayed back. I went down to Portsmouth and worked the Copner area, and saw some GPs and Karl. Karl and I sat in the waiting room, and I told him what had happened. Karl thought I had a cool manager, which in many ways I did. At that moment in time, I was more worried about throwing up in the surgery. I didn't, which was more luck than anything else.

Everything was going great for me. Except I was drinking out of control at this point but was still a functioning alcoholic. Meetings had come together. I wasn't doing anything that most reps didn't do. I did get drunk but then again, so did a great deal of other reps. If I wasn't doing the lunch time or evening meets with Jackie and Geoff, I would be doing them with another rep. Normally, on these occasions, I drove and even picked the rep up, and they got drunk.

All I needed to do was keep this up so when Indivina was launched, I hit the floor running.

I remember the launch of Indivina well. One of the things I really wasn't happy about was that they changed the territory. The pharmaceutical company Arion employed their own field force, which worked a proportion of what I had worked. This led to more reps with smaller territories, which good from that point of view. I had to decide which area: Portsmouth, where I had access to most surgeries now, or Southampton, which had a great many more people on HRT.

I chose Portsmouth since I hated Southampton. What I really wasn't happy about was that I had worked really hard to get appointments and meetings. I had to hand them over to two other reps, and I got nothing back in return. The territory would change twice. Twice I should have handed over appointments but I didn't. Instead, I swapped with reps I knew on territory from other pharmaceutical companies. I would also see a great many Pharma reps, whom I would be working with shortly!

Now, my life had become drinking while working, drinking, socialising and drinking at home relaxing. At this stage, I couldn't stop drinking once I started. I kidded myself and others that I was a heavy and problematic drinker but I hadn't quite gone over the edge yet, or so I thought.

I should have looked at myself and done something sensible. Instead, I chose to make things worse. I carried on because I just didn't see it coming and was firmly in denial. Maybe I just didn't believe that things would get a great deal worse and affect every area of my life.

Does anyone see it coming? No, but everyone else sees it.

The launch of Indivina came around. The changes had been made and they were going to have more reps.

The launch was in yet another nice hotel in the Midlands. I managed to behave, not get drunk, do the work, pass the exam and go home not feeling wrecked.

When we met at the hotel, that was the moment that Margarette would look down on me. I had turned up late for the meal and came down in very casual clothes. Margarette was not impressed and implied that.

The pharmaceutical company loved her. They were all over her like a rash. Everyone had to turn up wearing some form of purple clothing or item. I saw nothing special about what Margarette wore. It was just a plain and simple purple top. Somehow, she won the prize.

They seemed to idolise their field force as though Kudos reps were second-rate contract company reps. True that we were contract reps, but we were not second rate. Kudos had much more than the pharmaceutical company; they had good leaders, managers and a field force which were second to none. There was just something special about Kudos, an atmosphere which you rarely, if ever, find. The launch happened. However, I had another area of my life which I wanted as a priority.

To start I could do all three, *Work, Drink and Exercise, Swim.*

Chapter Ten
The Club Whiteley and a Girl Called Sue

I had joined the Solent Health and Spa in June, 1999 before the drinking had got really got out of hand. Jo was the manager when I joined, and she came from up north. Jo was lovely, social and always let us in early. Not only that, to this date Jo would be the best manager the club ever had.

I started swimming again and I was a good swimmer. I lost weight as I was getting into the routine of going daily.

Things weren't that simple at the club. There was a clique, which to start with I most certainly wasn't in. I would then become part of the clique. I would become lane safer, this was known as the pool position where everyone liked to swim, which was by the wall on the other side of the steps. Later, I would also be the papergirl since I took the papers in for the night porters. I also found out that if you put your key in the door lock, you could slip the catch and get in. Later, I would be known as pool monitor. I would look out for people that I liked, and when I had finished my swim or warming down, I would let them have pool position as I always got there first in the mornings.

However, I was most certainly not liked when I first joined. Certain members had been there a while: Joyce, Liz, Ray and Iris. All were retired and all had been members since the club opened. All had their own positions in the pool. There were no lanes; it was a normal hotel type swimming pool, a nice one. Everyone wanted pool position as it was by the wall and to a degree, you didn't have to worry about other swimmers because you had the protection of the wall. The pool was 13 metres long and the width was about 11 metres.

As the new girl, I was told in no uncertain terms that pool position was not mine. Joyce had pool position, then Liz, then Ray. Liz and Ray where having an affair; he was married, and Liz was or had split up with her partner. Many things would happen in the steam room between them, and people would tend to not go in there. Talks of blowjobs were the norm.

Iris was in the next place but not popular as she was forever talking about her time in South Africa with her husband who had died before I arrived. Iris never really got over her husband's death and spoke about him often, especially in the month of his death. Liz's son had died in the same month due to a car accident. Melvin was also using the pool; this was because he had just had a hip replacement and could only swim for exercise, so he was not in the gym, which had been the norm for him.

I was then allowed to have what space was left. However, I would soon be given Joyce's space (pool position). This was due to the fact that I became very popular with them and was liked. Later, I would become one of the most popular and well-liked members not only with the staff but the other members. I could never work out how that happened. Maybe it was due to the fact that I very rarely moaned or complained about things. I also spoke to people and got to know them. I would let the others know about new members and they would be accepted into the circle if they were nice and sociable. If we didn't like them, they had no help whatsoever of getting anywhere decent in the pool with us. Because of my chatterbox nature, everyone got to know me. Comments to other members were, "Oh, you've met Cathy," or, "That must have been Cathy."

They would all turn up first thing in the morning before it opened and waited in the corridor for it to open. They chatted amongst themselves. To start with, Joyce looked at me as if I was some bug that should be crushed. However, she was polite and acknowledged me. This went on for a few weeks.

At that moment in time, I wasn't turning up every morning as I had to be at some practice to put cards in early or wait outside practices in the car until they opened. This would become the most terrific way of networking and getting to know other reps. You would also be given information about surgeries, meetings, where they were and who organised them. This would increase your contact rate incredibly. Reps would share meetings and even swap meetings and appointments. Funny, even if they were competitors, you would still get help with most but were also told which reps to avoid and why.

At most GP surgeries, if you had to turn up early, you would have to turn up at about 7–7:30 a.m. before the other reps got there.

This way, you could put your card in before the others and most of the GPs would say yes or no. Mainly, yes.

If I had to be out early in the morning, I would be then plan the club later. This would turn into another addiction; exercise had to a degree always been something I either did not do or went completely over the top; another addiction to add to the collection. I went to the club every day.

I would fit the club in around my workload, but I had now got to the stage in the job that I didn't have to drop my card off and wait for the practice to open at 8.30am. I now could get in at other times.

Depending on the workload, if I did have an early morning appointment or breakfast meeting, I turned up with the rest first thing in the morning.

When I turned up in the mornings, it was Liz who started to speak with me. She asked many questions about me. What I did, where I came from? As I hadn't been born and bred in Hampshire, that was the first strike against me. The second was that I live in Whiteley. It was a new estate that had been built on farmland and the locals called it Shitely.

I liked Whiteley; it was all that I wanted—rural, not over-built at that moment in time. There were no post boxes or shops. The doctor's surgery was in a portacabin and did just three sessions a week. The rest were done in Locks Heath, where their main surgery was located. It would take Whiteley years to get a permanent doctor's surgery built. There would be many talks and it was not permitted to build it where the portacabin was situated. The council had wanted to build houses on that site and make more money. At this point they had then put up portacabins for a pharmacy and a Spar. Pharmacy at one end, Spar at the other. My friend who was the pharmacist there said to me, "We know all the alcoholics here." That would be a while down the line when I thought no one knew. Everyone knew I had a drink problem.

Whiteley Surgery was going to be built at Gull Coppice, a small development in Whiteley. Due to ground conditions, they would have had to have far deeper foundations to support the proposed two-storey building; unfortunately, the council would not pay the additional cost.

Then it was going to a new business park which had been built opposite the Solent. They would only allow one storey so *that didn't happen*.

What happen many years later was the Spar went to Gul Coppice along with other businesses. The Spar would later become the Co-op, where I would eventually go every morning to get my drink at 8am when they served alcohol.

It was then built on the original site where the portacabins were and completed in November 2007. They had been working out of the portacabins full-time now for a few years. I loved them; they were cosy and not so clinical. Just a nice atmosphere. That is not a good enough reason to leave it as a portacabin.

The surgery was nice and the staff were friendly and good at what they did.

Back in 1998, *you either loved or hated Whiteley*.

It was not without problems and we would have power cuts, which reminded me of the 3-day week. These power cuts lasted all night. The Solent hotel was one of the area's most hit. Along with this, you could smell the sewers. The traffic was light, except first thing in the morning and rush hour in the evening; this proved more difficult but nothing compared to what I had left.

There literally was only one way in and out. Leafy Lane had been closed off with great big concrete blocks. I got my picture and comments about Leafy Lane in the local paper, the Daily Echo, winter 1998.

Leafy Lane was closed it due to residents complaining. They were under Winchester County Council, which was the most proactive council. We were under Fareham Borough Council. Then there was Hampshire County Council. Let's not forget Whiteley Town Council.

This would prove to be a problem as each council would say it was the other's responsibility for any changes to the road system within Whiteley.

The other way that had been blocked off wasn't a road in any form just a track which would lead you out onto the Botley Road. This had bollards. They would have to open both those exits very early after we moved in for a few hours. We were doing some DIY in the house and heard on the local radio station that the roundabout from the motorway had a gas leak and was closed so no one could get off from the motorway going east or west. Anyone coming from the other side of the roundabout, Segensworth, were stuffed as well. The only entrance and exit to Whiteley was closed due to the gas leak. There was gridlock wherever you were in the Whiteley area, trying to either get in or out. They eventually opened the Botley Road exit, along with Leafy Lane. Leafy Lane would prove to be a bit more difficult to use as the residents from the houses protested and came out and laid on the road. I believe the police sorted that problem out after quite a while.

There was a wedding at the Solent Hotel and that party had not been able to get through. The Solent provided drinks for the people who had managed to arrive. The bride and groom were several hours late.

Many people in Whiteley and outside of Whitley complained about the everyday traffic jams which happened during rush hour, or if there was a problem elsewhere which would affect Whiteley itself. Traffic lights were put in, which did ease it a bit but not a great deal. There would always be problems if something went wrong on the motorway, Segensworth roundabout or Junction 9 roundabout. You could be completely stuffed getting in and out. People would end up missing appointments or other commitments out of Whiteley.

When they built the new village shops and they opened in May 2013, in Whiteley, replacing the outlet centre, it became a complete disaster. Things got worse, much worse, immediately. People from all the surrounding areas would come here. On the Tesco side, if you didn't leave before 3:30 p.m. weekday evenings, you would not get on to the motorway roundabout for one hour. If I had driven my car up there, it would be the same amount of time to get home. I always walked up later in the afternoon. At lunchtime, there would also be queues from Junction 9 roundabout for getting into the village. If I was coming of Junction 9 to go to my house, I would get into the right-hand lane when I got on to Whiteley Way, even though I wanted to turn left. Near the roundabout, where the club was, there was another roundabout with a filter; it was much quicker to go straight around the roundabout. Many people who lived on the Tesco side would leave Whiteley, even though they loved the place; it was just too difficult to get out if there was a problem. As one person said to me, they had missed doctor, hospital appointments and late for work. It was dangerous as the emergency services could not get through and if it snowed a few inches or more, you weren't going anywhere on our roads.

Whiteley road infrastructure was non-existent. The only thing that had changed since we moved to Whiteley was they opened Yew Tree Drive on Botley Road. Nothing else was put in place. They were going to build another 3500 houses in North Whiteley. The council said the road system will be put in place, but they have now been saying it for 24 years.

People who moved to Whiteley normally came from outside the area completely, like Gee and me. They would then either love or hate it. If they hated it, they moved on relatively quickly. Several years later, that would change completely. Whiteley would become one of the most popular places to live with both the locals and with people outside the area. Houses would be put on the market and sold the same day. Unfortunately, Whiteley would grow enormously, with houses and business units put up in every area possible. Woods and open land would be built on, and we would lose so much wildlife, which I loved.

I walked and cycled around the area of the business park daily as they had three relatively large ponds with two swans in them. They were known by the security people as Gus and Gertie. Every year, when they had signets, I would go up and take photos. Gus went missing; he usually flew off for short periods of time and returned quite quickly. This time, he just didn't come back. When I asked the security guys where he was, they informed me that he had been attacked by a fox and the vet couldn't save him. The signets that were there were then old enough to look after themselves, and it would only have been a brief period before they would have been driven out of that area by Gus. Male swans are very territorial and will kill the signets if they don't go. The area was only big enough for one pair. The Canada geese stood no chance. Occasionally, a shag cormorant would come to fish. That was interesting as the shag could stay under the water for a great deal of time.

Gertie flew off and two of the signets later became a pair and that then became their territory. The male swan was incredibly aggressive when they had signets and I wondered why. It was because in their first year, when they laid eggs, some people from the bar in the business park had come out drunk and smashed all the eggs. The next year, some children started throwing stones at the signets but people working in the business park saw this and came out and stopped them. That was the final straw for the male swan. When I went up with Gee, my husband, to take photos, I saw the swan moving towards us in a very aggressive manner even though we were at a distance. I said this to Gee and mentioned we should leave. He didn't think so. He had not studied swans like I did. The swan got out of the water and came running at us with his wings open. Boy, did we run! It felt like we were running for our lives.

There would be complaint after complaint about this swan. A large metal construal fence that builders used would be put around that year. Then a sign went up in two of the large ponds saying

'Caution: Aggressive swan. Keep your distance.' This kept most people at a distance, but some idiots would not take notice of the sign at first and learn the hard way by being chased of the area. Needless to say, pictures of their signets never got taken by me that year or any year after.

The main reason for joining the club was the swimming.

I had been a voluntary lifeguard for Stoke Mandeville for fifteen years while living in Oxfordshire and Buckinghamshire. My swimming had come along great guns for two reasons.

I wasn't a good swimmer so one of the chaps who did the training there was also one of the coaches for Aylesbury Swimming Club and suggested I came along to some of the training sessions. This I did. I could only do the breaststroke to start with; my front crawl and backstroke weren't there. In fact, non-existent. I was put in with, I think, the ten year olds who were far better than me. However, between the two clubs, it brought all my strokes up to the standard. Front crawl become my best stroke, then back stroke.

The other reason was I did all the life-saving courses again and again when they ran out. Along with the proper lifeguard course, which was very different to the life-saving course. I had to do one to two sessions a month, which lasted two hours. After that, you really had had enough.

Moving to Whiteley leaving Stoke Mandeville was one of the hardest things to do, and I was incredibly sad about it. When everything was signed, sealed and delivered with the company, I told everyone. That was, however, one week before we moved. No for-sale sign had been put up. We had sold the house, bought a new one. Everyone thought we had won the lottery as we were moving from a very large two-bedroom home with a garage plus an outside utility room to a four-bedroom house in Whiteley. The prices of the house in Hampshire at that time were quite low compared to the Home Counties, which were mega expensive, Gerard Cross being the one of the most expensive places to live in the UK.

Everyone at the Stoke Mandeville was sad to see me go. I was finishing my training course with a Japanese pharmaceutical company at that time. Everything was done in the last minute— exchange of contracts, moving, Gee starting with a new job, with the company dealing in car accessories.

Gee organised the leaving do. I remember one of the employees saying to me that at the end of the do, when they were all leaving, Gee's face was dreadful; they could see the sense of loss in it and the look of 'is this really it, the end?' Gee had been with that company for 25 years

I was in that job for six months, then joined Kudos in January 1999.

The club I joined in June, 1999, I had tried to get in before; in 1998 they had a waiting list. The main reason I joined the club was the pool. The gym I had no interest in till later. However, Gee (who joined too) had to have a gym induction course. Gee would do the gym. I did the pool; we rarely went together, only at the beginning. That did not last long with Gee; he did not enjoy it. He hated the sauna steam room and Jacuzzi, saying they were too hot. He complained about most things, which took the joy of it from me. He would eventually cancel his membership as one year it was equivalent to 500 pounds per swim. His membership would be cancelled three times in total, and we had to pay a joining fee again. This I really was not happy with but Jo had left at this point and gone to Yorkshire to open the new spa that was part of the chain of the Solent; it was called North Lakes.

Jo had been the manager when I joined; she was from up north and a brilliant manager. The club had brought her in to sort all the problems out. There were quite a few, like the manager never being there and on the gold cause by all accounts, members not being happy, and the place not being maintained and kept clean. Jo sorted the lot out and was one of the hardest working people I know.

That swim which cost 500 pounds was done on Christmas Day. We went down at 8 a.m. in the morning, swam and had a bacon bap glass of champagne after. The bacon bap was got for us specially; this was before Jo left and she sorted it all out. The club didn't normally do this but made an exception as I was such a popular member of the club and the manager on duty was Jo.

She would be the best manager the club ever had and really put herself out to make sure everything was up and running. Jo put 110% into the job. She was also really liked by all the members. The staff respected her as she was fair and really fought for her staff to get better money; she also gave them better hours. However, they were not very pleased when the opening time had been changed from 7 in the morning to 6:30. This had been requested by several members, myself included, as this would give me more chance of a swim first thing in the morning rather than having to go later in the day. Jo left a few years after I had been member and went to open a club in Yorkshire.

145

Joining the club would cause another problem with me. I became obsessed with going first thing in the morning unless it was not possible like I could only get the appointment early in the morning. Most were local, either in the Southampton or Portsmouth area. However, sometimes I would have to travel a distance, so it meant an early start. Sometimes I had the chance to do both but it was a splash and dash in the pool and then hop foot it to the appointment after my swim.

In case of distant appointments, I would have to go early if the appointments were early. I would become such a popular rep that that would all change, especially in the Portsmouth area; doctors would write on my card 'will see anytime, let her in'.

To start with, my exercise routine was cycling before the club opened; that would be 5km. I had two routes; one when it was lighter in the morning. The other when it got dark in the evening. I then went to the club at 7 a.m. at first and when it opened at 6:30 a.m. I was there for opening time and I didn't do my cycling around the business park. The other was walking for an hour after work. I finished early as I worked part-time so I could fit it in early. That would stay my routine.

We used to camp outside the club at 6:15 a.m. onwards. Joyce and I were always the first to get there; this enabled us to get to know each other well. I found out about her two marriages; her first not being great; he was a womaniser. She left him and then married a guy called Gordon, whom her first husband put down dreadfully. She was totally in love with Gordon, the love of her life, but he had died several years before I joined the club.

Joyce told me all about her operations. She had had breast cancer. Two mastectomies and she was on Tamoxifen; this had kept the cancer at bay. Her breast cancer was several years before I joined the club; all of her ailments were. She also had an operation for an over-active thyroid gland; that by all accounts was her worst operation. Hysterectomy, that was her best one. Knee replacements, hip replacement. I'm not sure how old Joyce was but I imagine in her 70s.

Joyce was young at heart and loved her two granddaughters, whom she would talk about on a regular basis. Her daughter was another case, very difficult and had married a Jew. Before her daughter married him, she had to covert completely to Judaism, which she did, along with learning the language. Liz was not keen on the daughter. Liz felt and spoke quite vocally to me when Joyce was not there, saying the daughter was trying to take away things from Joyce like her car, her home. Reading between the lines, that contributed toward the difficult relationship with her daughter; Joyce found her over-bearing. The granddaughters were a different matter; Charlotte was a lot like her mother but tolerable. Becky was by far her favourite. Joyce spoke passionately about Becky and how well she was doing at college, then her job. This was over a two-year period. I looked after Joyce when Liz wasn't there.

Liz did not like the 6:30 a.m. opening and would regularly mention it to us, saying what a ridiculous time it was to open and that it was too early. However, she came down at 6:30 a.m. for meeting Ray there. They seemed to always arrive at the same time. Liz would, however, give up the early Saturday morning swim, which started at 7 a.m. This had been changed from 8 a.m. at the same time as the 6:30 a.m. opening. Many of the staff said it would not last, but it did. It was much better as there wasn't so many interlopers, these were hotel guests which members did not like as they tended to ruin your whole session while you were there—getting in the way, swimming across the pool, as opposed to doing lengths, and children getting in the way.

I would rename the interlopers 'Hotel Guessed'. I called them the Ku Klux Klan. This happened one day when I was in the pool. I saw a group of six guests walking in a line down the poolside. They were all in white fluffy bathrobes; it just looked so like them, without the white hood with slits for eyes only. Linda, whom we later called Linda big legs, (I'll let you work that one out.)—when I called the guest there on the poolside the Ku Klux Klan—said that she called them the white army, which I believe was another name for them. They would also be called other names by me. Overall, I know they were there to have a nice time; they were just a pain, would get in the way, be inconsiderate, make an appalling mess. At the weekends, if you went into the changing rooms, they had left their used towels and robes in the changing area everywhere. They would leave their towels and robes on all the sun loungers so no one else could use them. Generally, the members who paid a regular amount each month had their noses put out of joint and these spa day people got the priority, were looked after better and came first. From a business point of view, probably not the best thing to do. Later, the club would lose many members partly due to this but also because they were the most expensive club in the area and didn't provide the best classes or equipment.

Holly Hill was built. It was a sport centre with a swimming pool, fantastic gym equipment, loads of different classes which weren't cancelled at a moment's notice due to either lack of numbers or no trainer. Due to a mixture of things, the club lost 30% of their members.

Nicknames would become a norm with us and other members. I was friendly with most of members, and it was me who would come up with the majority of these names. But I give credit to other members like Melvyn. He came up with some good names as well. I will give you examples of some of the nicknames which materialised over the years.

Moaning Myrtle was given to a member whose first name was Maureen. Then the Cruesome Twosome, Linda Big Legs and Miss Personality Plus. That was a sarcastic name for someone who had no regard or manners for anyone else. FA Ian, Flipper, Neptune, Miss Poison Ivy, Poison Dwarf, Baloo, The Lemon, The Mince Walker, Mr Cuban Heals, Snakeskin Pants, Desperate Debs, Di Tetchy Di and Complaints Box Dee. (We all joked about that, saying Dee went home with the complaint box and brought it back in an artic lorry.) Grey Brigade were the older members of the club. The South Coast Witch, Beast from the East, Early Shirley, Dog Walking Shirley and Nora Batty. I was called Cathy 'Two Mats' by the guys; when I did my stretch, if no one was on the mats, I was inclined to take up two mats as opposed to turning around and doing it sideways on the mat. I also had the nickname 'The Look'. That was because I gave people at times a very hard glare. Umm. *Need to work on that one.* I think you have probably got the general gist of the nicknames; there were so many more, I could write a book on that alone. Nicknames were given to identify members who had the same name so you could identify the person when talking about them. Then came the not-so-nice ones for people who really were rude or a pain in the arse (PIA). PIA would become normal terminology, along with NBC (Natural Born Complainer). SOP (Standard Operational Procedure) could be used to handle certain people. EAP (Emergency Action Plan) to avoid people or get out the way quickly. So much with what would be the clique was said in code. Quite a few new members would come into the clique. Over the years, it got larger and the demographics of it would change considerably. In many ways, people got into the clique via me. Something if you had asked me, I would have said *'It wouldn't happen'.* It did!

My weekday routine at the club at the start when I first joined would be 198 swim lengths in different strokes. This number came about as the club would do intergroup hotel challenges. The club had a group of hotels. These intergroup hotel challenges consisted of various gym challenges and then there was the pool relay challenge. The club had never won the swimming challenge. They had, however, normally won the other challenges.

I was asked to enter the gym challenge; they wanted me to do the swimming. *Great,* I thought, *piece of cake.* Then I was told it would not be my main stroke but backstroke as they had no one else who could do it properly. In my swimming routine in the mornings, I made sure with all three strokes I did that I incorporated 'arms and legs only'. The main reason being to improve on my back, stroke which I did. I also improved on the other two strokes. Come the day of the challenge, I was nervous and did my normal twitching around with my hands and moving. Then it was the relay. So far, the Solent had won everything. Now they needed the swimming. Front crawl was to go first, followed by backstroke, then breaststroke, finishing with front crawl. When I got in the pool to do back stroke, I noticed that one of the competitors was all of 14. A girl. My heart sank; they normal are really quick, and in this case, I just knew she swam with a squad. We did win the swimming. I kept up with the 14-year-old squad swimmer but could hardly breathe when I finished. The team were elated, along with everyone else for all the other competitions. The club won overall. I did ask Gee how I did on the swimming and he said, "You did okay. It wasn't a white wash; you kept up."

I would start using the gym about six months later. That all came about doing a charity row down the outlet centre for the club. I went for a gym assessment with Caroline; she was one of the young fitness instructors. Caroline was nice; you just had to get used to her as she was a bit cold and unfriendly at the beginning. I just wanted a 30-minute maximum program with rowing only. Caroline said it would be 40 minutes since I would have to do the minimum. I would start on the bike, do some exercises with the weights, go on the rower and warm down. Three times a week. That started like that. By a week, I had added to my program a 15-minute walk, which would become a run at a later date. I was a good runner. I started with the swim in the morning, then coming back in the afternoon to do the gym. After a while, I was doing the swim every day and the gym Monday to Friday. The rest of the gym program was 15 minutes cross trainer, ten minutes rower and ten minutes cycle. Plus a few weights. The gym at this point always came after swimming. This was because I wanted pool position—the place by the wall. I would then go to work. This routine worked well for me. It kept everyone happy.

I was now obsessed with the gym as well as the swimming, still lane saver and paper girl for the night porters who provided me with all the gossip of what happened in the hotel. Sadly, later, that would change, but for a good 10, maybe 12 years, I got the gossip and loved the night porters and their stories. Plus, they always told me which football club was staying, which wasn't of any real interest to me but it was nice to be in the know. Man United had bouncers all over the place. Plus David Beckham, who was a Man United player, would sign the room signature form.

The bouncer would ask what you were doing there. Swimming was my reply.

Chelsea stayed and they had to close the hotel to stop any more people coming in. Man United stayed there three times; each time, they lost to either Southampton or Portsmouth. Alex Ferguson wouldn't stay there again due to losing three times already.

One of the night porters was my favourite, Graham. When I came down the club in the morning, I came in and met him in reception. Graham said to me, "You'll never guess what happened last night!" I had no idea. Graham then told me that they had a situation about 11 p.m. last night: Victoria Beckham turned up to see David.

I said, "What did you do?" He said, well I sat her down and said I know that you are his wife, but we are not allowed to disturb the players. She was quite insistent, saying it was important. Graham said, "I really can't, Victoria. I would lose my job."

"Oh," I said.

He played me like a fool and I believed it. I was really sucked into the story he expanded on; I said, "What was she like? Did she look nice? What was she wearing?"

He then started laughing and told me it was winding me up. I fell for it. That is what I was dealing with all the time. They all played jokes like that on me. It was such good fun.

Arsenal…it was dreadful for Arsène Wenger when he arrived; there were photographers all over the place taking pictures of him and stopping him from getting through. I was told this by Vicky who worked as a trainer and on reception for the spa area of the club. I met Arsène Wenger by chance and had no idea who he was. I was in the steam room and he came in. I always speak to people if they stand or sit still for 10 seconds. I asked if he was staying in the hotel or a member; he said staying. He had an accent, so I asked where he was from; he said Strasburg. I had been to Strasburg and been to the cathedral there and said how lovely it was. We talked a bit about his family. He was a nice guy. I got out and left him in peace and then the guys told me who he was.

The night porters did have stories about various managers from other football clubs and what they got up to, which were quite interesting. Plus they could also get free tickets if they asked. They were treated quite well by the football club staff. The morning before the game, you would always see the players walking around Whiteley somewhere. I assumed it was a warm up before the match or talk time.

On weekends, I used to have a long swim, which normally consisted of 252 lengths. The two lengths came about as I did one length under water and the next front crawl. Then I started my swimming program. This would become a very big obsession or addiction, probably both. I would get really bent out of shape if I couldn't do exactly what I wanted to do, when I wanted to do it.

As I had sorted the job out with Kudos, the business sales and call rate, it more or less ran itself. By that, I mean I had made all the contacts I needed for meeting access to see GPs. The job was simple. All I needed to do was maintain or increase sales and call rate. I had it down to a fine art. That was probably a very dangerous place to be for me. I would have more time to go to the club, but I didn't. Instead, I drank when I got home.

With my job under control and not getting in the way of the club, which had become my number one priority in life, I lost weight. I got down to a size 8. I looked good; I had my hair dyed from brown to blonde and I wore it in a long bob.

So originally it was the basic crew: Liz, Joyce Ray, Iris and then me.

Sue

Sue came along; she was small, slim and fairly attractive. Her entrance was she got in the pool, did a few lengths, then went in the Jacuzzi. She became one of us. That didn't go without problems. Sue was a 'Natural Born User' (NBU). She would take and gave very little. It would be a very one-sided friendship.

She had been married three times. Husband number one was basically dumped for husband number two, who would be the love of her life, and she was devastated when he dumped her for someone else. Husband number three walked out on her, leaving her on the doorstep, crying her eyes out for him not to leave. Sue wanted everything her own way and was very shrewd. She manipulated each of her husbands, so she landed up financially better off than them. In all fairness, she had husband number two and three sort out their finances when they first got together so they had no debt. Money was and is Sue's first love. She never wanted to drive, never had any money when she went out. Everyone else paid. Gee and I went out with Sue and her friend Jeff who wanted more but Sue didn't. In all fairness, Sue never led him along. Sue was happy for Jeff to take her out, spend time with her, go out socially with her friends and have sex. Sue did not want a commitment. She was a very popular member down the club; people liked her. I liked her but then things happened. Like money went missing. When we went shopping, some of my new clothes went missing. Things just went missing when she was around. I never challenged her over it. It wasn't worth it in the end. I saw what she was like with other people and I need no proof. I saw it. She had no respect whatsoever for other people's possessions and would take what she wanted. Yet, everyone liked her.

It was just after this that Shirley, who would become known as Dog Walking Shirley, came along. She worked in Winchester on the administration side for that company. She had swum regularly at a pool close to where she worked but it closed and the company was moving locally.

Shirley was accepted into the clique. She swam on the opposite side of the pool she was a nice person. Her backstroke was not always in a straight line but whose is? However, her stroke was much better than Melvyn's who, when I first joined, had had a hip replacement. He was, at that point, not using the gym, just the pool. His front crawl left a lot to be desired and his backstroke was referred to years later by Ray as the crucifix stroke. I never noticed it. It was mentioned by Liz, who was always very vocal about all things. Melvyn was a nice, good person and we would become very good friends along with Shirley.

At this point, Sue and I had become drinking buddies. The first time I went out with Sue was with Gee and Sue's partner, Jeff. We went to Port Solent and had a meal in one of the restaurants there. It would be one of the very few civilised meals that the four of us would have. Quite quickly after that, Sue and I just wanted to go out and get drunk. We went to Gunwharf Quay often to drink up there either with Gee and Jeff. We did go alone once. That was a complete disaster. Phil had come on the scene for Sue, Jeff had been kicked into touch. (Jeff was dumped.) Sue also had Peter in the background; he was married but she was seeing him quite regularly. They had been having an affair for about ten years. There was one boyfriend who came after Jeff; his name was Phil. Sue had literally kicked Jeff into touch but there would be one occasion with Sue and Jeff which showed how she really was.

Phil he had a very small one-bed flat, but he owned it outright. He worked in a fishmonger. However, he drank a great deal and had a drink problem big time. Unfortunately, it would not be long before I was like Phil where the drink was concerned.

Sue met Phil at Port Solent; it was a nice area full of restaurants. She met him with one of her friends called Jackie, who was also a member of the club. Phil even took me and Sue up to Gunwharf Quay once and then dropped us off. Sue and I went drinking in Tiger, Tiger. We had two bottles of Pinot Grigio and then got Phil to pick us up. We had arrived at Tiger, Tiger at 5 p.m. and left at 6:30 p.m., trying not to look drunk. Amanda, one of our mates down the club, was having a leaving do at the local pub attached to the club. She and her family were moving to Bristol. She was very nice. When we arrived, we got Phil to pay for all the drinks. I was just too drunk to sort payments out, plus I had no money left. I have no idea how much I drank. I made a complete fool of myself, sitting on some guy's lap who gave me his number to call him the next day. To this day, I have no idea why. Sue was the same with some other guy, his mate, I think. This was all in front of Phil. Then I was on the dance floor dancing around with the DJ saying, "I think one too many here." I fell over, hit the top of my eye socket by my eyebrow on the edge of something. A lump came up like an egg. Sue and Phil took me home before 8 p.m.

The next morning, I woke up on my bedroom floor with my clothes on. I'd also wet myself. Gee had just left me to it. This would become quite normal for him.

I walked around to Sue's as I had no idea what had happened. Just the normal drunk behaviour. She assured me my eye didn't look too bad. My sister was dropping my nephews off for a while before their birthday party. When they returned to collect them, my eye was turning black. I went to their party at Fun City, Fareham. There were other parties there, unfortunately some of the parents were members of the club. My eye was getting darker and darker; it was like tsunami wave, no colour appearing. Then it just turned by the second and got blacker and blacker. The whole eye was black. It would, by all accounts, according to so many people, have a black eye that a rugby player would be proud of. I wasn't. I had to go to work like that.

Gee and I went out and everyone looked at Gee, then back at me, then Gee again. Especially the men. I had a meeting up at HMS

Nelson. It was just after 9/11. I had to have my photo taken and a pass given to me. Every time I went back to Nelson, my pass had a picture of me with a black eye. One of the doctors whom I saw there that day, mentioned in passing that maybe I should take some more water with it. I did not understand the reference then. I do now. They could probably smell alcohol on me.

Sex was important to Sue, but it just didn't happen. Phil was unable to get an erection. Sue had great delight in telling us and laughing about it in one breath but then became frustrated in the next. The one time when it was dreadful was when we all—that's Gee, Ray, Sue, Phil and some of Liz's friends—went down to Liz's beach hut so we could see the fireworks at the end of Cowes week. She was really quite vocal about it to everyone; complaining about the difficulties with sex is putting it nicely. Sue really did not care who she told that evening. It actually was quite cruel how she was, and it was always talked about when she started drinking. Well, when we all started drinking. She would get very drunk and I got drunker. What happened down there and was going on I didn't want to know about and be involved in, it was so cruel to Phil.

Before Sue met Phil, the state of play was to get drunk somewhere with other people and have a laugh. We had that all right. We were like two naughty children when we got together.

Phil did not last long.

Now my drinking was really going to get a hold of me, and I really had got to the no-turning-back route. I had slipped over to the other side. *I was no longer a cucumber; I was a gherkin!*

At that point, I was and would be for a while a functioning alcoholic. When this happened, my life down the club changed. It changed in a way I didn't like and didn't want. Basically, when I got to this point, if I drank, I just could not make the club in the morning. That was beginning to happen at Kudos. It really happened big time when I joined APC.

Before the drinking really got a hold, the club and Kudos were my life. Dana, my sister, her husband and two nephews Sebs and Nick were also important parts. The club had really got a hold of me. Well, the exercise was and would be in so many ways another addiction. Where one stopped, the other took over. To start in my early 40s, I was unable to do both by the time I got to my mid-40s; it really was one or the other. Either I drank and couldn't do the exercise, or I exercised, and my drinking didn't happen. It was that first one. Always the first one that ruined everything.

I was at times functioning alcoholic, but the cross-over to non-functioning alcoholic was happening.

I didn't see it coming. I didn't want to know I was upset about the club and not going and putting on weight. As soon as I picked a drink up, nothing else happened.

Every year they had a New Year ball that was great, and I attended most of them to start. The first one I went to with Sue was very interesting. Our table got the drunkest, except Gee. It was the loudest and we got on the floor dancing first and had a real laugh. One of the highlights of the evening was me asking a couple—whom I would become very friendly with much later—while they were dancing, "Does your husband wear pants under his kilt?"

The reply was, "That was a very personal remark." True, it was. It just fuelled my recklessness even more. In my drunk state, while they were dancing, I put my hand up his kilt and confirmed that he was wearing underwear. That, unfortunately, would become one of my drunken party pieces. Especially at APC, I always put my hand up their kilts to see. Well, some did and some didn't wear underwear. That time was also the one where I really did look lovely and everyone commented on how nice I looked. I, however, do not think that either Sue or I looked great at the end. We were just terrible to be around if we were drinking together.

The summer ball wasn't great either. We both got drunk. However, we were not the highlight of the evening that night but a new nickname would come about. One of the spa staff Nigel's party piece was to strip off on top of a table, which he did. Sue and I, along with others, were looking, not really impressed and were both were just tipsy, verging on drunk. One of the guys who was watching obviously was not impressed, so he picked up an ice bucket and threw the contents over Nigel's private parts. After that incident, Sue and I called Nigel Dinky Winkey. You can work that one out. It shrivelled up completely.

There were loads of drinking nights with the club. Liz, Ray, Sue, myself and Peter, who then came on the scene more, started to go out. Gee came occasionally. This was always a drunken night which could start off at the Sailing Club or the Rising Sun pub down in Warsash but then ended up normally in Liz's house. We would then get smashed. Well, Sue and I would be completely drunk and normally not remember what happened, how we got home and, even worse, what we did. We were dreadful when we were drunk; no one was safe. Liz was great; she did reprimand us at times and tried to get us to behave but it never really worked out. Liz also couldn't quite understand why Sue had to marry everyone. Once was enough as far as Liz was concerned. If they had their house and you had yours when you had had enough of them that day night or whatever, you either told them to go home or you went home.

Ray arranged to take Liz, Sue, Dee and myself to the Isle of Wight one day. We met down at the club. I did my normal swim, then went home, and Dee came to pick me up and take me to Ray's yacht, which was on a swinging mooring down at Warsash. We had to row out to the yacht. Liz had never been keen on sailing in any form but as we all were there, she came and enjoyed it. We all went out for the day and then had a meal over on the island. It really was just another massive piss up, me being the worst, followed closely by Sue. It was a beautiful day and I could have got so much more out of it if only I didn't have the drink. Everyone had a lovely time even though I was drunk and so was Sue.

Dee was very good to both Sue and I and would take us out for lunch quite often or around his house. He was a very good cook and would cook traditional Indian meals. Again, it was always free flowing with drink. Well, I say drink; it was mainly wine. Dee even took us both shopping to Gunwharf Quay that weekend. Gee was away on business at that time. When he went away, then it really happened; I would really go with it. This shopping trip would be my confirmation that Sue did steal from me. We both bought some new gym stuff, exactly the same. In many ways, she copied me. This time, my socks went. She was in the back of Dee's car on the way home. She asked him to go to her house first so she could drop her stuff off. Sue informed me that she was sorting the bags out. I wasn't comfortable with it. I felt I couldn't say anything in front of Dee.

Sue sorted the bags out and my socks, which I had bought, weren't there. We had gone back to my house after that. We all went in for a drink. Dee left us and then Sue and I went for it drink wise. I did go upstairs, and I had left my bag downstairs. At this point, I knew the socks were missing, not a big item, but my handbag had money in it. In my drunken stupor, I called down and said, "Where is my handbag?" Sue already had it in her hands. She was clearly nervous about handing it back to me. I had almost caught her in the act; she just hadn't completed it. My money, this time, was safe.

Prior to that, Sue had taken £10 from Gee's wallet. He had left it on the top in the kitchen. We went out for a walk and then when we got to the pub for lunch, miracle of miracles, Sue asked to pay. I was struck dumb. This never happened; she never had money on her, she never wanted to drive. Sue was just a very tight person with her money. She had £10 on her and paid for it. Gee later asked me if I had taken £10 from his wallet. That's when I put two and two together. Sue had stayed over with Jeff once and left before Gee and I got up and a load of my mouthwash had gone missing. It was in her bathroom when I went around a few weeks later. Not big stuff. But my stuff.

At the club on these occasions, when things went missing, I would be distant towards her and others. I would let it go quite quickly but on one occasion, Sue said, "Liz and the others keep wondering what's wrong with you. I tell them Cathy will be back shortly." I did come back and throw myself back into the actives with her. It wasn't just drinking but that became and was the biggest part.

The music at the time that I liked and listened to was Enrique Iglesias' 'Could I Have This Kiss Forever'. That was one of the records that was played at Sue's 40th birthday party and on our local radio station. That would become Ocean FM.

Sue held her party at the wine bar on the business park in Whiteley. Kylie was also in there in a big way, along with Toni Braxton and Madonna. ABBA had made a revival in my life. That was the basic music. That was around that time for me. The 40th birthday party. This was the very first, over-the-top drunken evenings. The first of many. It would be this party which would spur on all the other events with Sue and myself. Phil had not arrived on the scene at this point and Peter was definitely under cover.

When the wine bar closed, some of Sue's family were staying at the club. Her mum and Jeff were sleeping at Sue's. Sue lived just around the corner from me. We all went back to the club. Needless to say, Gee, who remained sober all the time, had to endure more drinking at the Solent. The price for a glass of wine was expensive to say the least, well over the top. We managed to get a few drinks there by putting it on her sister's room and then giving her sister the money. All of us, except Gee, were hammered. Jeff couldn't even stay awake and the night porters kept telling him not to go to sleep. Jeff was just slouched in a comfy armchair. Eventually, we left. I'd like to say that that was the end of the drinking. However, it was not. Sue, her mum, Jeff, Gee and I all came back to Gee and mine.

Gee was not happy, but he had to contend with three very drunk women and one very, very drunk man. I knew there was drink in the house; at this point I was on the sparkling wine when I drank at home. It would change from red or white wine to sparkling. I never worked that one out. We proceeded to open and drink the, as I called it 'sparkly warkley' or 'sparko demarko'. Where those names came from, who knows. Just more name changes. Like the nicknames. I went to the fridge in the garage, brought in a couple of them and opened them. Sue, her mum and I were drinking. Jeff was now out of it completely. Gee was just plain pissed off with the lot of us. He got even more pissed off when the ABBA CD went on and even though he tried to change the music, it just didn't happen; he was outnumbered. I changed it back to ABBA several times and in the end, Sue and her mum just stood guard over the CD player. Gee just gave up and went to bed completely pissed off with everyone.

The three of us proceeded to drink three bottles of sparkling wine. Jeff then looked in a better state, that he could make it to Sue's house by walking. From the club to our house, Gee and one of us helped to carry Jeff back. In all fairness, it was mainly Gee dealing with Jeff as we were just completely drunk, no help whatsoever and were laughing at the whole situation. *No wonder Gee was completely pissed off.*

Gee was okay about Sue to start with. He did, however, say we were bad together. Our drinking was similar but out of the two, Sue was better and would stop drinking. I didn't.

Sue, Jeff, Chris and I went away to London for the weekend and stayed in the Thistle Hotel just off Park Lane. Sue had a discount weekend. So up the four of us went. This weekend came with a huge amount of problems. Peter had come on the scene big time. Sue was keeping Jeff quiet. Jeff was more or less off the scene then and only had come as Sue had kicked Phil to the curb several months earlier and Peter could not make it.

It was yet another drunken weekend. Firstly, Sue manage to piss both Gee and me off as soon as we arrived. We were leaving later than Sue and Jeff due to Gee's work. When we set off on the Friday, it was rush hour traffic. When we got to London, we got lost. We had arranged to meet about six-ish. I kept in touch with Sue, letting her know our progress. We then agreed to meet in an Indian restaurant just around the corner so we could have a meal together. That was the first thing. When we got there just after 8 p.m., Jeff and Sue had already eaten. Sue didn't want to hang around. Normal behaviour; once she had what she wanted, she wasn't interested. I wasn't happy. We then agreed to meet them in one of the bars in the hotel after Gee and I had something to eat.

Gee and I went to that bar. It was nice, had a piano, wasn't packed, had a reasonable amount of people in there. Sue and I then threw ourselves into our reckless behaviour. Drinking. Some guy at the bar said I looked like Phoebe from Friends. I had never watched it and didn't know who she was. Sue said she was lovely, and it was a compliment. Gee was his normal self. "Oh, now here we go again." He wanted to leave quite quickly, and he could see what was going to happen. It did. Sue and I got drunk and made a nuisance of ourselves with whoever, wherever we were. It was total reckless behaviour, not thinking or caring about the consequences. That night we went into the loo, swapped tops, thinking that was funny. Gee became very insistent that we go back to our room. We did but not before I took Sue's top off in the bar and asked for mine back, which she gave back to me. Both of us took our tops off in this bar and neither of us remember doing it.

The next day was when all the fun and games happened. No one would be happy with Sue; she would piss the lot of us off. Peter was not aware that Sue was with Jeff. He soon became aware and was very angry as he and his wife had now parted. Sue assured him that Jeff had a separate room. *That wasn't the truth.*

We went out the next morning to have a look around some museums. Sue was on and off the phone to Peter all the time and Jeff was getting annoyed. We all were. Everything would have to stop while Sue was on the phone trying to pacify Peter and reassure him of the bedroom arrangements and why Jeff was there. Sue was becoming more and more upset as she felt Peter was with another woman. It would transpire years later that he was. Eventually, Sue and I left Jeff and Gee in the museums and went to Oxford Street for shopping and met them in a Costa later. Sue was on the phone with Peter most of the time.

On Saturday night, Sue was on the phone to Peter a lot. In the room, Sue was on the phone with Peter. When we checked out, Sue was still on the phone with Peter. When we went to get the cars to leave, Sue was on the phone with Peter. Jeff at this point had really had enough, saying that she had ruined a good weekend. Which she did as it was constant phone calls from the moment she had mentioned that Jeff was there but in a different room. Peter could not be fooled that she was there with just Gee and me.

It was yet another drunken weekend which would be the norm for Sue and me when we were together. Not only that, Sue worked a great deal from home, if that's what you could call it. She spent more time down the club on her days at home than she did at her laptop. Her words were, "I've logged in first thing this morning and done some email. I've got my mobile. I will check on things when I get home." Basically, it was a full-on jolly for Sue doing what she wanted to do. *I could hardly judge on that part.*

To give her credit, she was good at her job. Later, she would be made redundant. There was another job where she would not get on well with her manager who was female and again would be put in a situation where it would be best that she left.

I also worked from home, but I had to get on territory to see GPs. I would feel dreadful some days. I must have been over the limit for drink driving more often than not. My doctor mentioned it to me several times saying considering the amount I drank, it would not be out of my system by 9 a.m. in the morning. My GP also informed me that I should contact the DVLA about it. I chose to ignore it. Just as well as I would have lost my licence.

Later I later lose my licence for a short period of time but that was more by default than by actually drinking. The consultant who I was seeing at the time filled the DVLA form incorrectly. One of the drugs I was on for anxiety was also used for alcohol withdrawal. It was a complete mess; I lost my licence for 6 weeks until I put a complaint after which it was reinstated. However, to this day, I think it was karma.

That was the basic behaviour for Sue and me. We would more or less part just after I joined APC in 2002, based on her selfish behaviour, lying and stealing, plus I had to drive and pay for everything. To give her credit for this, she did try on several occasions, when the drinking really got a hold, to get me out and do something with other club members, going out for meals or coffee. Or water aerobics classes down the club. It just didn't happen. I just wanted to drink then. The final thing for the end of our friendship other than to acknowledge one another and make pleasantries when we saw each other was when I asked if I could stay with her for a few days as Gee and I were just getting on so badly. It was all arranged and then at the final hour, she came around, told me to lock him out, and that she wouldn't have me at her house. There was a long spiel with all the reasons to change the locks and not let him in. I didn't do that for obvious reasons but did ask one of our mutual friends from the club, Shirley, if I could go to her as Sue had let me down. Shirley did tell Sue that I had called to ask if I could go there as Sue had let me down, which was true. I did not feel any guilt whatsoever about Shirley saying that. I was glad Sue knew how I felt about her letting me down yet again. She had done it so many times to so many other people. She was only there for herself.

One of the last drinking evenings with Sue was with Gee; Peter was there as well. It was dreadful for Gee. We had gone out for a meal. I was not quite the worse for wear when we got back to our house. We sat outside as it was a hot summer's night and finished the wine. Three out of four were now well on the way to getting drunk. There was no wine so I thought we can do the 'Flaming Sambuca'. This was a trick I had learnt when I joined APC. Gee was really not happy with this and took the Sambuca away, but I got it back and we went indoors to continue our game, leaving Gee outside. One bottle gone; how many times we would light the stuff in our mouths, I have no idea. I just know the next morning I was asleep in the spare room when I woke with no idea how I got there. The bedroom stank of Sambuca. I came downstairs feeling dreadfully hung over. The kitchen stank even worse than the bedroom. Gee greeted me with, "You better clean up this mess. It's all on the tops and the floor, and I am not doing it." The floor was sticky and the tops too, probably from spilling it in the drunken state that we were in. I did attempt to clean up. Gee, in the end, told me to get out and he would do it.

I did get out and went down the club for a swim. It was Sunday lunchtime. I felt dreadful. I did 100 lengths; how I did that, I have no idea. I remember speaking to one of my neighbours in the pools, saying I felt dreadful. I must have stank of drink. That was my life with Sue and that was really one of the last occasions we had out together. The only other thing I did for Sue was again working for APC. It was when I first joined them. Peter and Sue were going through tough times again and splitting up. I was down in Bournemouth, and I spent most of my morning on the phone with both, passing on messages from the other, trying to calm the situation and get them back together. It worked. They did get back together; they even bought a place together and did it up. Sue never trusted him and always felt there was someone else. Peter was actually seeing someone else and they split up. They both had their sides of the story to tell. I will leave it there.

My obsession with exercise was very obvious to everyone who knew me, those who didn't know me well as well. I had started in the gym, doing three times a week which was probably excessive with my swimming. There should have been a better balance. I could not achieve a better balance and would not listen to people who commented on the amount I swam and then commented even more when they found out I was doing the gym in the afternoons. I did stop the gym in the afternoons and then shifted it to the mornings after the swimming. This was because if work got in the way, I would have already done it. I remember one hotel guest who saw me on a Saturday morning in the pool asking me how long I swam for. At the weekend, I did a long swim and during the week just 198 lengths. That guest would see me in the gym that day in the afternoon. He said to me that I would make myself ill and could land up with Chronic Fatigue Syndrome. This, to a degree, would be true and would probably add to my illness later as I was so tired and never rested my body. It was another complete addiction; I could not cope with not doing my routine.

My priorities were wrong. When we went on conference with Kudos to Mallorca, before we went out again—this was just after 9/11—I increased from three times a week to five. This was to compensate because I would miss some days. We were only going to Mallorca for four days. I lost more weight in the three weeks that I increased my time in the gym. Audrey and Ali, two gym members, mentioned it to me. The five days would not stop once I got back; they continued. I was tired all the time. I found it difficult to get up and I had to make myself. I took on the attitude that well, athletes did this and I should do it. I didn't take into consideration that that was their job. The gym wasn't mine.

I was entered into and asked to participate in all the club challenges after I had started in the gym. I was good at rowing so I was asked to do the rowing and the backstroke in the relay swimming. I always won the rowing. The club would win the swimming overall. There was only once that I was beaten in the backstroke in the relay. That was because it was against a 14-year-old girl who swam with a swimming squad, a potential Olympic. I'll let that one go. It was not a white wash and I did keep up.

We then had a staff versus members challenge. Of the two challenges I was asked to do, one was the rowing. Again, I won that one. After that, I had an hour to recover and then I had to do the triathlon. That really was a challenge. This would all be timed. Two people at a time started together. It started with the cycling. That was the easy bit. Karen, whom I was competing against, I knew was a very good long distant runner, really fast. I got off the bike first; it was three kilometres. The run on the running machine was two kilometres. I normally ran at 12 kilometres. Karen, when she got on, whacked it up to 16. I was in panic mode; she was going to catch me up. I increased mine. I could hardly breathe and Gee, who was with me to support me, kept on saying to concentrate on what I was doing, not to worry about her. I got off the runner seconds before her and went into the changing rooms to get out of the gym kit. I only had tracksuit bottoms on, trainers and socks. Plus, my swimming costume. This was taken off and just thrown on the side. I got in the pool. Luckily, there was no pool position and it was 'only' 20 lengths. It was like hitting a brick wall when I started to swim. I knew Karen was in the pool. At this point, I didn't care. All I could think about was not where I was, in front or behind, but just to do the 20 lengths, which felt like an impossible task at that moment. I counted my lengths. I was good at that due to counting all the lengths I normally did. Vicky, one of the staff who was overlooking all this and counting, informed me I had finished. I knew it anyway. Boy, was that a relief! It really was and I thanked God that was all over. Karen still had several lengths to go. I was quite surprised; swimming was not Karen's thing. She was good, however. The overall outcome was I came first out of the women and second overall. The guy who came first was in his 20s and did all the iron-men challenges. I felt very pleased with myself. Not only pleased but I was the only one who got two medals, so I was on par with Kelly Holmes, who in the 2004 Olympics at the time won two gold medals. There was a nice presentation for all of us. I was still, at that point, in the game of keeping fit. Drinking but still could 'just' do both.

I went in for the race for life with other club members one year in Southampton and again came first out of our club. *I was still going quite regularly.* People were saying to me that they aspired to being like me. I thought, *if only you knew about the drinking.* Would they be aspiring then?

Things were changing down the club. Night porters would come and go, Mike being one of the funniest. He was always picked on by Liz and Ray in the mornings. He would bring the papers down to take through to the club, and Ray and Liz would bounce on him to get the Daily Mail. Mike was an ex-landlord of a pub. His words were that he could spot a drunk at a thousand paces. Did he spot me! Maybe, maybe not at this point; it was very early into my life at the club. He always had remarkable stories about things that had happened in the pub.

My two favourite night porters would be Graham and Keith, then Ahmed. These had the most interesting stories of what had happened the previous night. However, the one who would see me for what I was would be Ian. He was an ex-copper. I remember so well the occasion he told me. I was sitting at the club in the car park in my car. I was drinking and had only gone down there that morning to reassure Gee. If he thought I was exercising, great. That was all I had to do. I remember the day so well. I was just waiting until he had left the house, sitting in the car with a bottle of drink, well wine. Just waiting. Ian came over to the car. I remember thinking, *oh God don't let this happen*. He came over and I put the window down, so he could chat with me. I smiled sweetly. "Morning, Cathy, how are you?"

What do you say to that? Can't exactly say, "Well, actually I'm waiting to go home to get pissed good and proper but my husband is still at home and until he has cleared out of the house, I'm stuck here."

So I replied, "Just sitting in the car, thinking." Ian asked if I was going in the club. I said I wasn't sure.

Ian said to me, "You're drinking, aren't you?" How on earth does he know?

I replied to Ian, "Why do you say that?"

Pitiful as it is, he said so kindly, "Cathy, I know. I've known a long time. I think you should go home." He never said another word about that conversation. He did, however, always ask how I was with genuine concern.

Graham and Keith worked together for quite a few years at the Solent. Graham came after I had been at the club for about three years. He was the perfect gentleman. Melvyn knew Graham well since they had grown up together, played football together and lived in the same area. It was at this point that the previous night porters were giving me the weekend supplements from the Mail and the Times. I had at that point turned into the papergirl. I took the papers in. At the weekends, they would save the paper supplements from the Saturday and Sunday papers which were the Times and the Mail. After several years, the Times would be replaced with the Independent. The local newspaper, the Daily Echo, was there for a while but that went also due to cost cutting.

It was also when us members found out you could open the club door with your membership card. It was quite easy, you just put it in between the door and the doorframe by the lock and it opened. This caused many problems as you can imagine, and they did change the door completely.

Firstly, members were getting in. Now this only happened when members of staff were late. We went through a period with one of the staff called James; he entered all the Mr Universe contests and had won Mr Universe South Coast. Rumour had it, he was using steroids. It was not something I was interested in, and to me, he didn't look like it. However, I didn't know what someone who was using steroids looked like. He was forever late, morning after morning. One day when he turned up on time to set up, I was early, and he dropped all his stuff on the floor, and when I went to help him pick them up, he said, "No, no, I can do it." That made me think about what he was hiding.

I would turn up with the rest and the club was in darkness. Waiting in the corridor, you knew no one was in. So, it was normally me who was allocated to knock on the night porter's door and inform them. To start, they had no idea what to do but after a while, they had the rota and it was always James. The duty manager would have to be called to oversee everything. Certain people were rude to the night porters, and Graham was upset by two members who were very vocal to him about it. It was not Graham's fault but being a manager, he got all the flak. Members who knew how to get in got in. Then one night, some hotel guests got in. They were completely drunk, and Graham had one hell of a task getting a load of lads, who were completely plastered, out of the pool Jacuzzi and the wet area.

Due to this, the door was replaced so this could not happen again. Then there were other problems. The staff came in but couldn't find the night porters or keys so we had to wait. Before, we did the card trick on a regular basis.

Graham and then Keith, who joined as a night porter, had to deal on Friday and Saturday mainly with drunken guests and wedding parties; later, it would be hen parties when they built the spa. That came about in 2002 after they refurbished the gym and some of the poolside into a member 'terraced area' and changing rooms. Plus, they added and built a spa where you could go for treatments. While these renovations were being done, we were put in portacabins, which were freezing cold. Plus, within 24 hours, someone had stolen the showerhead. The ladies' changing rooms were renowned for things going missing. The hotel changing room, both male and female, would be turned over a few times, once by some professional who came in and took everything from the lockers. On other occasion, I was convinced it was either a member or a staff member who had a master key. They knew people's routines and it would be them who had wallets, money and watches nicked. One of the worst things to happen was one of the girls left her Rolex watch on the cross trainer in the water bottle hold. It had the footprint of the baby she had lost on the back. Someone took it. She even put a notice up for a reward, but it was never found.

The new spa was lovely from the hotel's point of view and business wise. The members would and did, however, suffer. How they suffered was in many ways. Firstly, our so-called 'Members' Terrace', the area which they had taken away from the pool side and built an indoor terraced area on. That part of the poolside was used by the members to have food and soft drinks. Dana and I would regularly have lunch with my two nephews Nick and Sebs there. That stopped; if we wanted lunch or a snack, we had to get dressed since we could no longer eat on the poolside with our swimming costumes on.

We came to terms with that quite quickly and accepted it. However, what all the members would find increasingly more difficult to tolerate were the 'spa days'. This would normally mean the terraced area was reserved for these days and now we couldn't even have a coffee overlooking the pool from the terrace. In the reception area, it was not a very comfy place to have coffee, plus there were only three tables. On two tables you could get two people around them, and one you could get four people around, but it was a low table so it was not great for reading the paper. The members were just kicked out. It felt like the club had a zero-tolerance policy for members.

They were their bread and butter money, and they just didn't seem to care. Things would not be working, and it would take months to be repaired in the gym. The wet side being the worse, one item would be out of action like the monsoon shower, steam room, sauna or Jacuzzi. The swimming pool would go from so hot you couldn't swim to so cold you didn't want to get in.

The club would lose over a third of their members when another gym and pool opened in the area that I believe, the council ran. They would have better equipment and classes. It would also me much cheaper to join, about half the price. The club also lost their members since they were going to other places locally. People were getting fed up with the problems and lack of hygiene and problems that were never resolved or heard. It wasn't good, but I loved it when I went down there. I had all my mates there, but things would change.

There are just too many stories to tell about the terraced area and what had happened; I could write a book on that alone.

This was my life at the club. Meanwhile, Adrian was on his knees with his addictions. He had lost everything and he was dying. How could he get up from the depth of despair he had got to at this point where he had nothing and really no one.

Chapter Eleven
From Launch to Field to More

The Christmas party that year, 2000, was in Coventry. Juliette and I went together; she drove. When we all came down for drinks, we noticed that a football club was there. It was Fulham. Obviously, some of us were interested. I wasn't. It was a great evening, but boy, did I play up good and proper.

The normal brandy and champagne to start, again our area was the loudest and most outrageous. Unfortunately, it was mainly me. I was not completely drunk but had a far few down the line. I can't remember who said it, but someone said go and get some Durex from reception. This was to play a prank on the divisional manager Neil. Jane and I went up and got them, then gave them to Neil. We never asked for one; we asked for several. After a while, getting drunker, the lot of us were finding it amusing and funny. Neil was not. So, we changed the game. We decided to have all of us on the dance floor. Well, I decided that we needed to get the men's ties. Why, I have no idea, but it seemed funny at the time. All our team were in on this except Dot, but I always called her 'Miss Goodie Two Shoes'. I had them all hanging around my neck, dancing around. Then Jane pointed out to me that there was still a guy with a tie. Poor guy ran from us, thinking he was safe in the men's loos. Oh no, I was in there, but was soon escorted out by the guy on reception, who probably saw it all the time and thought, *not this again*. Well, he had to get me out three different times. In the end, I left the poor guy alone. I had abandoned all the ties on the table, had a few more dances and drinks and went to bed before 12.

I remember waking up as I needed to have a wee. I got out of bed; I had forgotten my nightdress so I had just put a T-shirt on. I opened the bathroom door, went in. The door closed and locked me out. Oh, fuck I was in the corridor with a T-shirt which didn't even cover my bottom half. Not only that, to make matters worse, I could hear all our lot downstairs, partying. I couldn't walk down to reception; all the guys would see me. What was I going to do? I walked along the corridor one way, then back the other. *There is a God*, I found a phone. I picked it up, spoke to the guy on reception and explained my situation. He was up within minutes. It was the guy whom I had been getting Durex from all night, the same guy who had escorted me out of the male toilets. He put the card in, opened the door and just walked away, leaving me to it. The '*oh no, how can this happen?*' went through my mind. I was so tired, I just got into bed and went to sleep. I am not sure the night porter saw it that way. I should imagine he thought I had been thrown out of some poor guy's bedroom.

When I informed Juliette in the morning on the way home, she could not stop laughing, asking me why hadn't I just come down to reception? I explained to her again that I was wearing a T-shirt. Not extra-large but a normal, micro, mini T-shirt. This is where drink was taking me. People were also noticing and making comments. In my defence in this case, I could have locked myself out sober as I was always disorientated in hotels. The launch of Indivina had been delayed. This was due to APC, the competitor, blocking it for a while. How exactly they did it, I don't know. The launch was meant to happen in the middle of the year; instead, it began the start of the New Year, 2001. We were already selling one of Arion's products— a real shit product but oh well, it was HRT and it was different from the others, that was about it.

Kudos would have Indivina for one year. Day one, I hit the ground running. I had done all my preparation. I knew who to see, when to see and how to make it fun. My diary was completely full. The only thing I was a bit aggrieved about was that I had so many appointment and meetings that I had had to hand over to the Arion Southampton rep and one of the Kudos reps, due to the realignment of territories. We were told that obviously, we would get appointments and meetings back. I didn't get a single meeting or appointment from the realignment of territories. I just set someone's diary up, so they would do well.

Juliette was concerned about the amount of appointments and meetings I had on the outskirts of Southampton which I had to hand over. The Arion team had their own manager, so Juliette would not get any credit for that area, which had the biggest growth potential.

My launch plans were all in place when this happened. With the budget that I had been allocated, obviously, it was better than before, not massive but workable and I could share meetings with other reps.

I had all my appointments in the diary. There were one year's worth along with meetings. I came up with my own great marketing plan. In plastic sealable bags, I would place the leave piece of Indivina along with a pen, post-it note and three Cadbury roses. I chose three as there were three different strengths to Indivina that could be used. If one failed, try another, that simple.

In January, I gave up drink for one month and put my leave pieces together for Indivina.

Every single GP I saw on an appointment got one of these. Admittedly, it did take time to put them together. Meetings, the same on the stand, there would be the normal give away items and my own marketing parcels. By putting the chocolates in, GP opened the bag to eat the chocolates but also read the leave piece. Normally, you leave a leave piece and they would chuck it in the bin when you had left or it stayed on the desk with all the other paper work and was forgotten.

So, my meetings varied between somewhere at lunchtime and in surgeries, sandwiches or a caterer. The occasional breakfast meetings, that could be either a caterer again doing a cooked breakfast but normally it was just a continental breakfast. So far, so good. Nothing wrong there.

Then you had the big stand meetings normally with the local Primary Care Trust. To cover the cost of education and room hire, reps were brought into play. This was all legitimate and above board. GP nurses came. Your area of sales opportunities was in the breaks when they came out from the educational talk for a coffee break and then lunch break. Most of the GPs and nurses would come to your stand. We had give-aways, excess items, so they were quite keen to have these. You either gave them to them then or got your card signed to take it into them. The company also did postal campaigns with a give-away; they just had to return the card and the company sent them to you to go in with the give-away. At these stand meetings, reps stayed for the afternoon teas ones. We'd all gone home. At the morning coffee and lunch, the doctors did come to the stands out of politeness even though they might not want anything, which was good of them.

My real interesting meetings were the other ones. The defence driving course (go carting); GPs loved that one, then health benefits and Forest Mere Champneys. That consisted of a stand, a speech and then various spa treatments. These were at really posh hotels and restaurants. I can't quite recall what us reps put down about the ones we did on boats. However, on one of the boat meetings, a tour around the part of the Solent, the Golden Princess was making its maiden voyage. Everything stopped for that, and we had one of the best views you could have of the Golden Princess. These meetings were loved. Also, interestingly enough, they liked the army training days. This was for GPs to look at serving in the armed forces. They came along for a training day to see if they would be interested in joining up and what the benefits were. They were very good. However, I for one hated it. I don't do tanks, shot guns and get into trucks that the troops travel in. I didn't know how to get off the tank. I was terrified; I had a young shoulder offering me a shoulder lift but I gave that a miss. He was really good at helping me. Plus, with the truck that would take us from one bit to another part of the course, everyone got in the back. I got in the front. No way was I jumping out of that. The guys in the army were brilliant with me. Obviously, they could see I was scared stiff of some of the stuff we had to do, and they had kitted us out in overalls, which were appropriate for the courses we were doing. When I refused to take part, one of the troops would look after me. We had a laugh that a career in the army was never going to happen for me.

I didn't have a single worry about the call rate. All I needed to worry and think about was sales. After a few months, we were taking on another company's product. Now that I did worry about— a treatment for osteoporosis.

The training course was down in Bournemouth, so it was great for me at last; I was quite close and didn't have to travel miles. It was a charming hotel, one of the best in Bournemouth, and five minutes from the beach. You dropped your car off at the front and they would take your keys and park your car somewhere, then collect it for you when you were leaving. I had a new Ford Mondeo black. When I got mine back, it was covered in seagull shit on the roof and bonnet; it was dreadful.

It was quite a civilised training course; not many of us got drunk. I didn't. The training course was for three days. What was interesting is that Juliette had lost loads of weight along with one of the other girls and me, spending every morning down at the club swimming. I had dropped from a size 14 to 8. I no longer needed to be at the surgeries, camping out at 7 a.m.

We all left the training course after lunch but as there were so many reps waiting for their cars, I went shopping in Russell & Bromley's in Bournemouth. I spent a fortune as the compulsive spending had come into play big time. As soon as I got back to Whiteley, I was at the club doing my swim as the hotel had a lousy pool. This new product was not my cup of tea. However, I didn't need to worry. Walking along the beach between appointments, obsessing about exercise, fitness and staying slim, the club, swimming and my walks were priorities. Juliette called. She asked me how I was, and I said I was struggling big time with this osteoporosis product. I was genuinely upset. She talked me through it and said, "Catherine, don't worry about it. It doesn't matter, it's not important. What is important is that you are the number one performer and have the highest sales by far for Indivina." I was floored. Speechless, over the moon. All my hard work had paid off. I'd done it. Every month, my sales would increase far greater than any others. My call rate was the highest by far due to all of my so-called 'educational meetings'. There were just so many more meetings coming on board which got raised eyebrows, but reps were doing them; some organising them, others helping with the paying for them. I would like to add at this point that I did put together some very good ethical meetings, which were educational for not just GPs but their staff.

The whole of 2001 would be much different to previous years with Kudos in many ways. I had done all the work; there was very little for me to do and by that, I mean I had put the hard work in. My diary was full of appointments and meetings. Even if I needed more meetings, I could get them with other reps. That was standard. Although, I tended to do most of my meetings with Jackie and Geoff. Both did my head in in different ways. Jackie with her constant panicking or in a meeting having a meal, with head down, almost under the table, talking to one of her children on the mobile phone. Now that really did piss me off.

Geoff, who would be our driver, had no idea about time keeping; he was never on time and I am not talking five or ten minutes. I'm talking half an hour or more. Boy, did he get *hell* from Jackie and me when he eventually turned up. I hated being late. I was always on time or early, early being the preference.

Now things were getting out of hand with the drinking. I could do the job within a few hours a day due to all the planning. That left time on my hands. A great deal of spare time. Even though I did my paper work, I continued to make appointments. The time was there, and I used it. I used it to drink.

I can remember one day practice in Romsey; again you had to book a year ahead to see the GPs. I got there just after 8 a.m. and I was home by 10 a.m. Job done, call rate was there, I had seen four GPs, got the commitment to try and call backs.

On my territory, the average call rate was 2.2 GPs a day. That's the data the pharmaceutical had worked out, with all territories being different.

I had time on my hands. I did the shopping. I'd been doing my own grocery shopping on territory for years now. But it was clothes. I spent loads. I did network with other reps, the occasional coffee and stuff like that, but they were few and far between. I could have gone back to the club and relaxed. There were loads of options open to me. No, instead, I went home and drank.

I was drinking a great deal more at meetings. At home, I was drinking more. Gee and I were really not getting on well. The relationship wasn't great at the best of times, but the drink just fuelled it. He'd come home, and I was drunk. This was not an everyday event yet, of course, I was drinking on weekends. At this point, I thought the drink hadn't quite got me and brought me to my knees and made me a complete 'slave' to it. That was literally just around the corner. *I was constantly in denial.*

All of a sudden, I was doing so well and better than the rest of the team and the whole division. I even managed to get Indivina on the hospital formulary, being the only rep who would actually do that in 2001. Arion managers at the head office wanted to come out with me on field visits. This, I was not happy with. One reason was I didn't want anything at that time getting in the way of the club. I wanted to do my 6:30 a.m. stint and not have to be out on territory until 9 a.m. Plus, I felt uncomfortable. I wouldn't be able to leave territory when I wanted. I think the biggest thing was having someone with you actually makes you less productive, and they really do get in the way. And the GPs don't like it.

Juliette wasn't too bad; she basically let me get on with it as I would do it. Juliette also had her own agenda. She didn't want to do field visits. Dot and I found out she was making up that she was doing joint fieldwork as Graham had said to Dot, "How did your field visit go with Juliette?" Dot didn't land Juliette in it but we did chuckle to ourselves.

So here I was making the grade, going to the club, eating and drinking in all the best restaurants and staying in the best hotels. Then drinking at home alone becoming more frequent. Sue was still on the scene. There were a few things which were about to happen.

I had to do joint fieldwork with one of the guys from Arion. I really was not happy about it. Not only that, I had planned a fair bit and I didn't need someone slowing me down or putting me off. Juliette was insistent; she cut me no slack. She was not taking my,

172

well he can't come this day that day or any day attitude and why. It was a given; Steve was coming out with me for that day. I had sat with Steve on occasion when we were doing training. He never drank alcohol. I asked why and his reply was, "I don't drink on these occasions." I did persist but that is all he would say. I did ask if he drank. I now wonder was Steve an alcoholic?

I picked Steve up from the Solent Hotel at 9 a.m. since I didn't need to start earlier. I had brought a sandwich lunch already for a practice down in Portsmouth. That's where we were headed first. I handed Steve the agenda for the day. It was a hot summer day. I was wearing a T-shirt type fitted top, a pink skirt just above the knee with a slit up the front of the left leg and high-heeled sandals. I was slim; my hair was in a medium-length blonde highlighted bob. By all accounts, I had great legs. Steve was wearing a business suit.

We discussed the agenda on the way down to Portsmouth. The day was planned like so:

1) Lake Road: Pop sandwich lunch in and book the appointments.
2) 9:45 a.m. appointments with GPs at Gamble Road
3) Call in at Cosham to book appointments
4) 12:30 lunch meeting at Bognor Regis (rep only, no manager)
5) 2:30 appointments with GPs at Wittering's practice

None of this had been set up to make me look good. There were no Mickey Mouse calls, which was the norm with reps when they have their manager out with them. They set the day up with GPs with whom they get on well with to look good. The GP might or might not be using their product, but it made them look good and working. We won't go down that route as it's a minefield of fake appointments etc.

At Lake Road, I said to Steve, "Just stay in the car for this one as I just need to drop the lunch off and make the appointments, so I will only be a few minutes." I didn't even realise I had done it but just on automatic reflex, I locked the car. It was a hot summer's day; even that time of the day, it was hot. Really hot.

I just came out in a smart T-shirt-type top and a pink short skirt with a slit up the side. Plus, I had parked in the blazing sun, no shade. The poor guy was sweating buckets when I got back to the car. Steve was not slim. He was what you would call on the rather large size. I did apologise. Steve looked a mess; his shirt now was soaking wet.

He got out of the car to take his jacket off as he hadn't been able to do it while he was sat in the locked car waiting for me. When he got back in, there were beads of sweat on his face and nothing like a tissue to clean himself up with. Steve had to come into the appointment at Gamble Road looking a mess. The appointments at Gamble Road went well. We got back to the car and drove to Cosham. Steve asked me many questions; I answered them and we chatted. At Cosham, I said, "I'm just making appointments. Do you want to come in or stay in the car?"

He chose the car but not before saying, "Don't lock the door," With panic etched on his face.

We then drive over to Bognor Regis. This is the meeting where I had decided he was not coming in. The GPs were nice but could be challenging. Plus, it was a sandwich lunch meeting. Also, my mate Tia was sharing the meeting with me.

We arrived at Bognor, I had informed him that they didn't have managers in with them, so he would have to wait in the waiting room. We arrived about 12 noon; the receptionist took me through to the meeting room. I set the food up, sandwiches, fruit, muffins, donuts, crisp fresh fruit and some fruit juice, paper plates with napkins folded between each plate so it was nicely presented.

The GPs came in (Tia, another rep renowned for being late was still not here). I was doing my bit but had to wait as there were a couple of GPs running late. One o'clock came around. Tia then arrived with her 'manager'. I wasn't too happy about that but got over it. Her manager did actually ask me about Steve, and I did say well, four of us would have been much too heavy, which is true. Three wasn't great either. It could have been totally intimidating to some GPs. Plus, we would be out-numbering them. I do know that Tia had asked to join this meeting as a favour, she wanted to do an audit in that practice, so I agreed to let her share. What an audit was I had little knowledge; I just knew we didn't do them.

I left them at 2 p.m. Steve had been in the waiting room alone for two whole hours. He did mention Tia and her manager going in. I brushed it off by saying they were doing an audit. We got to the Wittering's. This was a brilliant call. It made up for me being a complete cow and leaving him in the waiting room in Bognor. I was due just to see one GP. The practice manager knew me well, and I introduced Steve to her to give her credit where credit is due. "Oh well," she said, "if you're out with Catherine today, you need to see her with a few more GPs than just one. It will give you an idea how they all differ with regards to prescribing."

It was a dream. The GPs were great. They involved Steve, asking him a few questions. He asked them some back and I did my sales bit. We saw four GPs at that practice.

As I said, I really did now have this job under wraps, so I wasn't always at home by 10 a.m. I did make it look easy and that you can see six GPs in a meeting, two GPs face-to-face by appointment and then another GP with appointment, with three more from that practice coming in on spec. Not many reps have days like that. Well, not on this territory.

I took Steve back to Solent, dropped him off and went home. Juliette called asked how it went; I told her the complete truth. She wasn't happy about me leaving him in the waiting room for two hours. I didn't know how angry she was. I knew she was out with Ketan the following day so had every intention of calling Ketan after his field visit with her to see what she had said.

When I did speak to Ketan, he was very evasive and continued down that route. He kept on saying she'd mentioned it but not much was said. *No way was I believing that.*

I kept on until he cracked. "Okay," he said. "She was really pissed off and angry that you had done that, and it was an unreasonable amount of time to leave someone in the waiting room: two whole hours!" The discussion continued with the basic outline that I had done it on purpose, and no one was happy. Well, tough luck. Arion should have taken a bit more notice of their bread and butter reps. Kudos was right at the start.

Autumn was coming. Sue and I were still doing some of the very occasional weekend stints of drinking. Gee was always complaining and moaning at me. Our relationship was dreadful. I heard it time and time again from everyone. "If you cut back on the drinking, things would improve between you and Gee."

Tia's word were, "Get really amorous and when you're drunk have sex with him, and Gee would be better about the drinking."

Sex now was non-existent, and there was no way I was capable of sex when I started drinking; I just passed out. So that was not going to make the relationship any different and even when I didn't drink for a few days or a week, it made no difference except I could hear what he was saying. Being drunk blocked all that out.

Three things happened, one after the other. The first thing was Sue and I went out early one Friday night; she was sort of with Phil. Well, she used him to pay for things and pick her up or take her places. Peter was still looming, or should I say about to blossom into her life. This Friday, Sue got Phil to take both of us to Tiger, Tiger in Gunn Wharf Quay. It was September, just after 9/11. Phil was to just drop us off and then pick us up later. It was happy hour, so bottles of wine were half price. We ordered three bottles of Pinot Grigio wine. Phil was then under instructions from Sue to pick us up at 6:30 p.m. to take us to a party. One of our friends from the club, Amanda, was moving to Bristol and having her do at the Parsons Collar, which is attached to the Solent hotel.

When we got to the Parsons Collar, we were worse for wear, to say the least. Sue decided that Phil could buy all the drinks, which he did, on his credit card. I really don't know how long we stayed there; all I know is I was dancing on the floor by myself with Sue. I must have lost my balance, fell over, hit my eye socket where the eyebrow is. We both went into the loo and it had swollen up like an egg. That didn't deter me. I went out and made more of a fool of myself and even landed up on some bloke's knee along with Sue. I was so drunk at this point, I said, "Sue, ask Phil to take me home." Don't forget, he had been paying for all the drinks. We hadn't bought one, which really was out of order. I can't remember getting in the car, out of the car, in the house.

I woke up in the morning fully clothed on the landing. Gee had plenty to stay about that. Not only that, he told me straight I had to sort myself out as we were or, as he put it, I was looking after my two nephews and taking them to a party at Fun City in Fareham in the afternoon. I didn't feel too bad but not great. I just needed to work out which way it was going to go. I checked my eye. It looked fine, a bit swollen, but fine. Perfect. Except I had the guy's name and phone number on a scrap of paper in my pocket. Um, let's not even think about that one.

My sister and Dick, her husband, dropped Sebs and Nick, two of my nephews. Gee did not let up on me one bit. It was obvious he was going to have to drive and go to this party at Fun City, which he had no intention of doing. I was going to do it alone as I did everything with the both of them. But because of the state I was in, he actually had to help.

Fun City was no fun for me whatsoever; we got there at 1 p.m. We were there for a few hours, as you usually are. It was embarrassing, all these parents with their children and some were club members who knew me. When I went to the loo, the colour of my eye socket, and I literally mean the whole eye socket area or call it panda eye if you like, was changing. It was light in colour to start, but every time I went back to the loo to look, it was getting darker and darker. I am talking full-blown blue-black left eye.

Dana and Dick came to pick the two boys up. Their shock when they saw me was comical. They were stunned into silence. Quick wittedly, I said, "Your children!" They looked very concerned then. I put them straight. They came and went and I was left with Gee, who read me the riot act. I still had a drink that night. The old upstairs-downstairs thing. I did, however, agree to go out with him for a meal down at The Watermark in Port Solent on Sunday so that his weekend wasn't completely ruined. Gee would be quite helpful on Sunday; my eye looked so bad that I wanted to get a patch or something to cover it up. We looked in various pharmacies on Sunday but it was waste of time, with us finally buying an eye patch that didn't even cover it.

We both liked the Watermark; it was the first place where Sue, Jeff then Gee and I ate. It has a friendly atmosphere about it. We arrived and Gee knew I wouldn't limit my drinking. We got a table, sat down and ordered our food. Gee was completely oblivious to all this. The guys were checking me out. They were looking at me, then Gee, then me. It's not rocket science to work that one out. I could tell they all thought it was Gee who had done it. That continued everywhere I went. People commented on it all the time. In appointments, meetings down the club, friends, other reps, the list was endless.

On Monday, I was meeting Juliette at my house; we had some work to do and we had decided to do it at mine. Juliette arrived and was again another one 'stunned' into silence. She asked what had happened. I relayed the story. Her words to me were, "You can't go out like that."

My reply was, "I've got to, I have many appointments and meetings that I've got to attend." Which I did. There were many comments. One was, "Many a rugby player would be proud of a black eye like that." I got sick of talking about it. One of my meetings was at HMS Nelson, a navy base down in Portsmouth. To make matters worse, first I had to have my photo taken (great, with a black eye) which meant that each time I went back, that picture would come up. Then because of 9/11, the security was very tight and all vehicles were checked thoroughly. Boot, inside the car, underneath, and oh dear, bonnet of the car. I had the new Ford Mondeo. It was a nice car and I really liked it. The bonnet on the Mondeo opened differently to other cars. I had two military guys either side of me with great big guns pointed at me while I tried to open this bonnet; it took me 45 minutes to do it. Just as well I got there well ahead of time. 'Female, blonde hair, black eye, can't open car bonnet.' Then just to add to it, I did the meeting with the GPs and the one who was walking me out said to me, "You should take more water with it." I didn't get the reference then. Maybe I smelt of drink most of the time; I don't know.

A memo came from the head office that the whole field force had to go to a meeting in Coventry. For what, no one knew. Dot, who tended to know most things, wasn't sure either. All we knew was that Arion had decided to take full head count of its field force, which meant Kudos would no longer have the Indivina contract from the end of the year. There was no massive panic since we sold and detailed other products. The company had said that the second product we sold and detailed would fully support Kudos with the loss of Indivina. No problem, we still had a job.

I turned up for the meeting in Coventry. It wasn't a crack-of-dawn meeting; it was at a reasonable hour, so I could leave early but not ridiculously early. When I arrived, Graham came over to me. He asked me about my eye but before I could answer, he said, "I bet you're sick of being asked." I had to agree. Juliette said it looked better. Dot was shocked but knew the whole story. Ketan didn't say much either. Then there were the normal double takers, looking twice as if they couldn't believe what they were seeing.

There were other people there as well, not just the Kudos field force. A woman got up on the stage to talk. Her name was Jackie. I can't really remember too much about her except she worked for APC and was a divisional manager. There was talk about our third selling product, which we sold for a treatment for prostate cancer on the palliative care side. I knew that. Then there was talk about flu vaccines. Jackie's basic message was that they were recruiting a new field force using Kudos as the contract company. It was a full-time sales reps position and not what I wanted. I was now not part-time but had gone to three-quarter time. Then came the fear of God speech. They would be giving those they chose to employ a good pay and what it was straight across the board. Although employed by a contract company, they would be treated the same as any in-house representative. However, they would be expecting us to work hard and do the job properly because here it came, "I will know and don't think I won't because we always know." What do they call that, fear management? Well, that's what I called it. Others who had worked for APC for a while called it 'Big Brother is watching!'

What none of us realised at this point was that when Jackie said she expected us to work hard, that meant it would take over our lives completely.

We were then given a break to talk about it and those who were interested in the position were to let them know and they would be interviewed. The job started February, 2002. Dot and I chatted; she quite liked the idea of the job, but it was 'APC'. None of us were a fan of APC. Ketan wasn't going for it. He said it straight away. Dot would and did go for it. Me, I thought I just don't want the full-time work; I liked part-time. That was one bone of contention, the other was yes it was 'APC'.

Dot went for the interview and got the job. This wasn't done straightaway; the interviews would be towards the latter part of the year. She requested to go out with one of the vaccines reps to see what it entailed. Plus, sus the job out, what it really was about and ask questions about the 'manager'. That was important as you really did not want a bad manager in the pharmaceutical industry. She reported back to me and said I really should go for it. After her joint field visit, the manager was going to be a piece of cake to manage by all accounts. He was supposed to be nice. His name was Richard and he was young. He had also done the job so knew what it entailed. So, there shouldn't be any unrealistic expectations. Dot started to sell me the job, saying I would still be able to do my swimming and gym plus my walk later in the day. Not only that, the rep that Dot went out with, Bruce, said Richard generally left everyone alone to get on with it.

I ummed and aahed about it and then decided I would go for it. So, I phoned Graham and said I would like to go for the job. His response was, "Well, most people had applied for it over a week ago, you're quite late on this, but I will see what I can do. I don't think they have a rep for your territory yet." While Graham was contacting APC, I contacted Ketan and then sold the job to him. If I was going and Dot was going, I wanted at least one other person whom I liked working with and that person was Ketan. Ketan said okay. Great, I had mates. All that needed to happen now was us both getting interviews and both getting the job. Simple.

APC wanted both Ketan and I to go for interviews, but they weren't doing any more interviews until the new year. That suited me and Ketan just fine. In the meantime, a few more things had to happen.

Arion wanted to get into dispensing practices. Dispensing work is something I had never done but I went with the flow, found the practices and yet again, I was the one who got the first dispensing deal and then the most dispensing accounts. What was everyone else doing? It was simple. GPs wanted to see you as it meant money. So again, I got another gold star.

Then Arion pulled the plug on the budget; there was no more money, that's it, no meetings, nothing, everything had to be cancelled except for one. Mine. I had booked a speaker meeting at the Solent Hotel with a consultant to talk to GPs and practice nurses about HRT. Now, this was a joint meeting. I had agreed for the Arion Southampton rep to come in on it, Jill. I told her exactly what she needed to do. She would have to literally contact by letter every single GP on her territory in that area. It had to be a mass invite with SAE for them to reply yes or no. I gave her the template of the letter. She kept on saying yes, she would do it. I couldn't emphasise enough the importance of 'mass invite'. I also said when the letters had to go out. The reason this was a joint venture was because part of Jill's territory had GPs which shared the same hospital consultants as me. I worked the hospital; Jill didn't. I sent all my letters out, my replies started to come back, there was a good percentage of no's, but I did have yes's. Most of mine had replied and I was still waiting for Jill's to come. They did! Not en masse like mine. It really was one or two here and there. Jill hadn't done it. I'd done these meetings before sending out invites. I knew she hadn't done it. I wasn't going to challenge her about it. The GPs that eventually came from her territory in the end, came because I invited them because I knew it was a therapeutic area they were interested in.

The meeting, for me, was a remarkable success. There were a total of 30 GPs, 28 mine, 2 Jill's, for which I went into the practice and gave them the letters myself. *You only have to set up the job right once.* Do the work and it will come to you; it will be a breeze. I can't emphasise this enough—you really have got to do the groundwork; if you don't, you're stuffed. Yes, I was working fewer hours but on the days when I needed to put effort into getting results, I did. Like spending an entire day doing letters. Boring, but it needed to be done. Plus, it kept me off the drink, which was well on its way with me.

Arion had asked Kudos if I would go and work for them. The simple answer was no. I don't know why I came to that conclusion. I just knew Arion were not for me. But was APC?

Kudos had had a blinding year business wise, and they wanted to reward their field force. This had been mentioned and booked earlier in the year; we were informed of the dates which had to go in the diaries. It was not up for discussion, it was compulsory. They were taking us away on conference to Mallorca in October, 2001. It was for four days. Over a weekend, and needless to say it was a few days away in the sun. I was really looking forward to it. So were Dot and Sarah, who was now on our team due to the realignments of the territories. She had moved from Corby where she lived when she first joined Kudos to Cornwall.

Here lay the problem. 9/11 had happened and certain members of the team didn't want to fly. They were reassured by Juliette and Graham in a memo but they weren't convinced. In the end, Juliette told them it was compulsory and they had to be there. I wasn't exactly ecstatic about flying but I did fancy a few days away with company, staying in a nice hotel and a bit of sun in Mallorca.

The previous year they had taken us to Jersey, which had been great, it was really nice to get away for a few days. I can remember going shopping with Dot when we were out there, I found this beautiful ball gown. She really would be the belle of the ball. I insisted she tried it on. There was the discussion of the money and she didn't want to spend that sort of money. I insisted she tried it on. Eventually, she did and she looked stunning in it. Dot was very attractive, about 5' 6", with highlighted blonde hair and she was slender. She had to buy the dress. I told her it was made for her. Eventually, she did. Now she was adamant that I spend a similar amount. I bought some Jersey pearl earrings. Dot was not stopping there. So, I bought some other bits and pieces but didn't come close money wise to the dress. We were only in Jersey for a couple of days. We did have to work, do some training, but it wasn't too bad. At the gala dinner, as predicted, Dot really did look the 'belle' of the ball; she was stunning. The tables were set up, so everyone was mixed up. I was lucky I did get Ketan on my table, so I had someone whom I got on with. They were a nice few days; nothing outstanding happened. I did behave. With the drink, I was still not quite there yet. Before the meal, we had a group photo taken of us. It is a lovely picture and Dot outshone everyone.

Juliette and I travelled up together to get the flight to Mallorca. She drove. There were quite a few comments about my case—how large it was, how heavy it was and what the hell was I taking? I had been over-obsessive about clothes and worried I wouldn't have enough or the right ones!

There were many comments made by the rest of the team. I said to them that I couldn't decide as I had so many clothes that I couldn't decide which ones I wanted to take. I didn't take a lot, but 40 T-shirt-type tops might have been a bit obsessive. Juliette was laughing on the drive to Heathrow Airport.

Juliette was fuming, in a complete rage with Jane, Ketan and one other member of our team who pulled out on the day. They had phoned that morning and gave reasons why they couldn't go. Juliette was beside herself due to the expense to the company and the fact that it was compulsory, which was quite normal for the pharmaceutical industry. Conferences were compulsory unless you have a genuine reason not to be going. They didn't!

We arrived at the hotel. It was lovely and over-looked the harbour. Well, there were a load of big fancy boats moored there. We had a lovely meal with our small team that night. I remained sober and only had a few drinks. Then the next day, we had to do some training but had time later in the day for ourselves, then we went out for a meal in the evening.

I did get plastered at that meal and staggered back to the hotel. Dot said she had watched me staggering all over the place, walking along the road to the hotel. Then staggered in the hotel lobby and up the stairs. I was told the next morning that it was quite impressive to watch. I woke up on the bedroom floor. Juliette had hysterics over it. The following day was a day out on a boat, a catamaran. What had been good was I had been able to swim each day and go for a run in the mornings.

The catamaran sounded lovely, and we would get to see a bit more of the island out there. Dot, Juliette and I were near the front, and the guys who were crewing it thought it incredibly funny to steer it in such a way that the people at the front sunbathing got soaked. We did. However, I had come prepared; I brought some dry clothes.

I knew we were going to moor up near a beach and those who wanted to go to the beach could. I had already made my mind up that I was getting off; I felt sick. There was one crew member who was rowing two people at a time to the shore. He was a small lad, very slim and about 5'5". No wonder he was so slim with all the rowing he had to do.

I got myself dry, sorted, ready and waiting. I got into the rowing boat with another girl from a different team. Sarah was already on the shore. She wanted to get off too. I felt sorry for this poor chap who was doing all this rowing. He explained to us that when we got near the shore, we would have to get out of the boat in the water at a certain time. He would tell us. Simple! He got out of the boat to steady it. Then he said wait until he said go, then get out. This we did. This went terribly wrong. Of course, I could see everyone on the shore looking at us before anything happened. Both of us were catapulted out of the boat by a big wave that came at that moment. We did not see the funny side. He was quite apologetic and genuinely felt bad. He even said a few words in his native language. I have no idea what that was. Probably, oh fuck! He asked if we were okay. Yes, we were okay, just soaked head to toe. He got back in the boat and rowed back. He only did a couple more rows and it did take 10–15 minutes there and back. He had, had enough and was shattered. He must have rowed there and back at least ten times.

On the shore, the others, obviously, were laughing at us. We were informed that ours had not been the worse mishap. They told us we weren't the best or funniest one but I wasn't interested. I was soaked, hair, clothes, shoes, the lot, plus there was sand. I don't do sand either. Not when I'm soaking wet. Sarah suggested, "Why not think about it as exfoliating?" She got the look. Basically, it meant 'fuck off'. Now we were on the shore. I had no intention of going back on that boat. We did, however, sit on the beach and watched a few more that he rowed out to us. We all knew what was likely to happen. It did and I must confess we were all laughing and waiting for it to happen to the next few people who came by the rowing boat.

Three of us, Sarah, Ken—who was the company's accountant—and I decided we would get a bus or a taxi back. I had no idea where we were in relation to the hotel. Ken took the lead. We went in search of one. By some miracle, we found a bus stop and someone who spoke English was there and informed us the next bus could take us to a stop near the hotel. My attitude still hadn't improved and would continue to nosedive as people started to turn up at the bus stop, looking me up and down. Sarah and Ken looked fine. When the bus arrived, Ken sorted all the payments out along with where to drop us off. People were staring at me when I got on. I went to sit down in a space next to someone who really did not want to share the seat with me. They begrudgingly moved along so I could sit down. We got dropped off in the town. Ken said something about going for lunch; Sarah was all in favour of this. I said yes but I needed to get some dry clothes. I quickly changed in my room, and the three of us had a nice lunch.

My better attitude had returned, and I was laughing about it all. After lunch, Sarah wanted to do some shopping in the town, and I was up for it. I was not a greater shopper with other people, rarely going out shopping with others, but I was happy to go with Sarah. She wanted some clothes and boots, which we found, and they all looked nice. I just bought some pearls, nice stud black pearl earrings and a black unpolished pearl necklace traditional to the island. I had always liked the look of rough unpolished pearls. Also, some perfume, Mademoiselle by Coco Chanel. This perfume always reminded me of Mallorca and that conference every time I wore it.

This would be the start of me buying jewellery which was relevant to the area and the country I was in. I always got earrings with stones from that country. Later I would buy other pieces of jewellery too.

The real spending would be when I went to Capri with APC; I spent thousand on earrings necklaces, bracelets, rings, all in coral and gold and not at all cheap.

The night of the gala dinner, we were taken out to a restaurant in the middle of nowhere. It had been someone's home, a chalet-type building that had been converted and was beautiful, old and traditional to Mallorca. It really was a lovely evening. There were a few things I wasn't expecting. I didn't realise that there was going to be a presentation for 'me'. It was done at the end of the meal, and I hadn't drunk much; I wasn't really in a drinking mood. One of the reasons was that we had travelled there by coach so I wanted to make sure I could get back on it without help. It seemed to me everyone knew about the speech but me. Neil, the divisional sales manager, gave a speech about me and how well I'd done, calling me Whitey, I think a dog from one of the soap operas. I was then presented with a lovely gold pin with a ruby in the shape of K; the ruby was on the cross bit of the K. I really was taken aback and quite touched as I really had not expected that.

Later in the evening, we were all on the dance floor enjoying ourselves. Graham came over and had a word with me as he wanted to say a few things that he felt Neil had left out. It was lovely. Then Barry, who interviewed me for the job, came over to speak with me. Barry said, "Look, you just don't see this sort of thing, I've never seen it before."

It was the atmosphere, the people all enjoying themselves, a kind of serenity. I knew exactly what he meant. You just don't get that feeling with a field force. It was worth its weight in gold. This would be a one off. No one had known this to happen in the pharmaceutical industry or any sales industry before.

But things were changing and all I can say is, I was so glad I was there for the special moment that I had never seen in my life anywhere else and to date still haven't.

The only thing that ever came close was with Chiltern Ceramic and Chris Farrow; he was a brilliant boss and there had been great people to work with. I had been lucky in life, had two great jobs working with people who were great.

We were leaving the next day and going back home. The flight was late, so we had time to do things. Sarah and I went shopping again.

My one regret is regarding a beautiful Moschino red cocktail dress I had been at Heathrow Airport. To this day, I regret not buying it. I had enough clothes and I didn't need it but I just liked it. They do say it's what you don't buy that you regret the most and I did regret that.

Our flight was delayed by a couple of hours. Graham, I know, wasn't happy but there wasn't much we could do. Juliette informed all of us that the three who hadn't come had been informed that they needed to be in Winchester head office Tuesday morning at 8 a.m. They were given hell and being there at 8 a.m. meant that the three of them would be leaving before 6 a.m. to get to the meeting on time. Juliette lived in Romsey, so it was close to home. Ketan, for example, lived in Esher Surrey. Jane lived near Brighton. Juliette informed them via memo that they would be working as they had missed the conference and we had training out there and they wouldn't be finished till 5 p.m. She kept them there until after 5 p.m. and really made them work.

The Christmas party was a bit sombre. It was like an end of an era. It all going to be different. In 2002, Kudos would still have a field force and anyone who had a job with APC would still be employed by Kudos. They would just be the APC contract team, which would be looked down upon by my GP divisional team with APC. I can remember Liz, a girl I saw in the field. She was forever on her way home after a 7.30 a.m. sit and wait speck.

The people who remained with Kudos would be selling a treatment for osteoporosis and an antifungal cream and pessary.

Ketan and I were given our interview dates. We had to do a presentation, a business plan of how we worked our territories. Dot had already informed us of that. Plus, there would be a personality test. It would be three people who would interview us.

Gee and I were going to Lanzarote for Christmas; this would be the last Christmas on which we would go away for a while. Lanzarote was a complete disaster. I spent more time drunk than sober. I was drinking the sparkling wine at breakfast by the large tumbler full. I must have had two bottles of the stuff at breakfast alone. Then I was just too pissed to do anything and Gee was left to doing things by himself saying, "What a life you live with it." It must have been dreadful for him as I was just constantly pissed.

Chapter Twelve
APC

Christmas 2001 had not been a great success for Gee and me. I had always found Gee hard work on holidays. Before we went, there would always be some form of negativity. Like, "Oh if I don't get this done, we won't be going." Always that type of statement. Every single holiday. It had got the stage where enough was enough and I would stop inviting people around for a meal or for anything again, due to his negativity and the pressure he put me under. Gee was constantly complaining about it. He really stressed me out and then the enjoyment was always gone. Although when it happened, at some point it could be quite nice. The build-up beforehand from him was hell on earth.

The other thing Gee would do was after the meal, with my family or whoever I had invited, he would either go upstairs on his computer or put the telly on. Especially with my family. However, it was completely different when his family came. He was more than helpful and did so much to help. Not with mine; it was difficult to get him to carve the meat if we had a roast.

In 2001 we stayed in a hotel Batiz in Costa Teguise. It was a pleasant hotel, had a gym, which is what I wanted, and a lovely spa area where you could go and relax in bubbled water, hot tubs, a steam room and an ice-cold dipping pool afterwards if you were brave enough. I did the lot; I thought it great fun although the holiday wasn't great. Gee didn't want to do any of it, he just wanted to sit in the sun. I wanted fun and that was fun. Plus, I wanted to drink; he didn't. I did go all out on the drinking.

I wanted to go walking but Gee didn't. I wanted to see things; Gee didn't. Gee just wanted to sunbathe. Ugh. This was what holidays were like. I came back with a suntan and a mega hangover. As I was drunk more often than not. Plus, some earrings and a Raymond Weil watch, as well as fatter due to the amount of food and drink I had consumed.

I mentioned it to Sue when I called her on holiday, and she couldn't wait to see me. She was very competitive like that and always wanted to look the best, be the slimmest. I would, however, lose the weight very quickly when I got back as I threw myself into the gym and swimming. I was back to size eight by the end of January.

January 2002 would be a hard January to take. I was still on the Kudos GP sales team, working but not selling Indivina. APC called both Ketan and I in for interviews in the first week in January. Dot had pre-warned both of us what to expect and what to do.

The interview was at APC's head office Taplow in Slough, so it was not a difficult journey. The time was 11 a.m. which made it ideal; I could avoid rush hour traffic.

I arrived in good time, 10:30 a.m. so was pleased with that. They brought me straight through. Security was very tight. I remember they had this revolving door which you needed security to swipe a card to let you in. That didn't necessarily work. This revolving door had a way of throwing you out. Quite scary really. The revolving door threw me out twice before I could get into the place. Maybe that was a sign from something that was looking out for me. Higher Power, God, I don't know. I just knew I never felt right.

I was greeted by Jackie, who informed me I was to take the personality test. Well, it was called aptitude, personality and skills test. I had done loads of these and I hated them. Half the time, I didn't have a clue what the questions meant. I was informed that I had one hour to complete the test.

I finished just on the hour. Then I waited a while and was interviewed by Jackie, the divisional manager; Richard, our regional sales manager, and Carly from HR. I did an overhead projector acetate presentation. It was on my territory, how I had worked it, what results had worked and what hadn't and why. They were particularly keen to hear about my dispensing deals and how I did with those.

I was then quizzed about it by all three. Jackie, however, said to both Richard and Carly, "This is your territory." She repeated those words several times in the interview. Carly from HR, to give her, her due, was a really tough cookie. There was no messing with her. She really did not take prisoners. Richard, who would be my manager, was easier; Jackie, however, was tough. I was then asked the question! The question that I did not want to answer. It was one of those sinking moments. Oh no, please, not that question. The question was, "What have you done in the job that you were asked not to do but did?" Oh, I knew the answer, I just didn't want to answer. I tried hard to wriggle out of this.

In the end, with Carly from HR pushing me, I confessed. My words were, "I went over my budget…"

There was shock and horror on Carly's face, which was followed by, in a shocked and horrified voice, "You went over your budget?"

"Yes," is all I could say, hoping that would be the end of it.

It got worse. Carly said, "By how much?" Jackie and Richard were just both looking at me. It was cringe-able. One of those dire moments where you just wanted to fast forward out of this subject and on to the next ASAP.

I replied in a very low, even-toned voice, "A few thousand."

Carly, "A few thousand. How many thousands?" It was getting worse by the second. This is it. This is it; they really are not going to want me after this. I hadn't overspent on my budget. I had blown it completely.

My reply was, "28,000 pounds." Can you imagine the look on their three faces? It was comical in one respect. Horrifying for me in another. Now there was no way they would employ me based on that.

They did ask one question. "How did you get the money?"

I said. "The other reps weren't spending their budget, so I was told to carry on spending until I was told to stop." However, even when I was told to stop, I did still spend some more money and got away with it somehow. Probably because I was 'the best'.

Carly then changed tack. She asked me what my budget had been and why I had done it. So, I told her the truth. "My budget was 3,000 pounds. I spent the rest as other reps were not using their budget, so I just kept on spending until I was told to stop. I was bringing in more business than anyone else and seeing more people and doing more meetings. It was just the thing to do. The money was there, others weren't using it, so I did."

"What did your manager say?" Carly asked.

"Juliette informed me that others weren't using their budget; that was straight across the board not just our region but all regions." I had some very big meetings and talked about the meeting I had at the Solent. It was a speaker meeting on HRT with a consultant coming to talk, then a meal after. Before they went in for the talk, they looked at the stand and asked about Indivina. One thing that had gone wrong was my chairperson pulled out at the last meeting.

He was a local GP, so I had to find another and I did. I phoned one of the GPs I knew. He was male and had worked at Winchester Prison. Obviously, didn't know about HRT so when he got up to do the opening speech as the chairperson, he made it very funny. He was a great GP. He would be one of the GPs who said to me about my mother and her COPD that she probably had another five years left. That was normally the case at that stage of COPD.

Carly Richard and Jackie were very interested in that meeting. Jackie asked, "How many GPs did you get there?"

My reply was, "30."

Jackie then said, "As it was a joint meeting, which one of you got the most GPs there?"

I replied, "I did." Because it was true, I did. They wound up the interview, and I walked out having no idea as to how I had done. I just couldn't see me getting the job. I got in the car, spoke to Ketan. He felt the same as me. No idea, how he had done. We were both perplexed.

Graham phoned me. I hung up on Ketan to say Graham was on the phone. Graham asked me how the interview went. I said I didn't think I had done that well and couldn't see me getting the job. I had no idea. Graham asked a few more questions, which I answered. He then said, "They've offered you the job." I was at APC's head office, sitting in my company car, having spoken to one of my work colleagues, now speaking to the owner of Kudos, my boss's boss. And I had been offered the job. Graham asked how I felt. I said I was feeling fine. He asked if I wanted the job and I said yes. He told me the salary: £27,000 basic pay with an earnings potential of 15% basic salary. That was the bonus, but the exact details would be confirmed at a later date. There was health insurance, life assurance and contributory pension as well as a company car, £6.95 tax-free lunch allowance, evening meeting allowance £35 but taxable and finally, twenty-two days' holiday building up to 25 days after four years. Graham had confirmed about the holidays they could not be taken between September and the end of January as this was the flu vaccination season. Except for Christmas and the New Year week, no reps worked then.

It was normally standard in all pharmaceutical companies that you take Christmas as part of your annual leave. I was used to that, so I didn't mind. Plus, I normally went abroad for Christmas to the Canary Islands.

The contract would be put in the post, and I needed to sign it and send it back to them as soon as possible because the start date was 4th February, at Metropolitan Hotel, Edgeware Road, London. It was the APC annual conference and my brother Robert's birthday. Kudos were doing some pre-conference induction training from Wednesday, 30th January – Friday, 1st February, 2002. This would be on the set up of the NHS.

The position was Porstap/VSS Representative (full-time). That's the bit I did not like: 'full-time'. I enjoyed working part-time. That is what I had wanted when I first came to the South Coast, a part-time sales job.

My territory was 87B. Basically, it was most of Hampshire and the Isle of Wight was included in it. I had always wanted to work the Isle of Wight. *That changed rapidly. I'd really dislike the IOW.* Along with Dorset and some of West Sussex.

I was not good in January and I couldn't put my finger on it. It wasn't the drink as I was being good on that front, but my anxiety levels had hit an all-time high plus I had a small rash on my face on the right-hand side, just above the chin and below the lip at the side. It itched like mad. I am not the best person with spots at the best of times; I can make a small spot look like a mascara on my face. I was constantly itching and scratching it. It looked dreadful and had a circumference of about one and a half inches.

I was very apprehensive about going to APC. I couldn't put my finger on it and was getting more agitated by the day. There was also the problem that I liked Juliette and working with her. We had our differences but overall, she let me get on with the job and was a good laugh.

The week leading up to the induction course, a couple of things happened. Firstly, Buster, my cat, was seriously not well. I don't know if he had had a stroke or what, but he would meow outside the house on the decking to come in. We had a cat flap bur even in the pouring rain he stayed there just meowing. He was a very vocal cat and everyone had commented about it over the years. He was a rescue cat. I was not having a male and definitely not a ginger one. Buster was both. In Aylesbury, he was only allowed downstairs and didn't really care too much for Gee. In Whiteley, he wasn't allowed upstairs by Gee. However, every afternoon that I got home working for Kudos, I would have a kip or do my paper work upstairs in the office.

If I was in the office, Buster was in the office with me upstairs. If I was having a kip, Buster was on Gee's side of the bed, sleeping with me. It was the perfect setup. It was so perfect that I knew exactly when Gee was home before he got in the door or the car on the drive because Buster just got himself up and went downstairs. Our secret, which I enjoyed and laughed to myself regularly about it.

Buster, as I said, was not well. He wasn't eating properly. It looked like he struggled with his body to eat his meal. He stopped using the litter tray. He would urinate on the kitchen floor, which you couldn't see, so I normally ended up walking or treading in it. This didn't make me that happy, but I was really concerned about him.

I had this new job, an ill cat and I was getting no support from Gee. I kept saying, "Will you look after Buster while I am away?" Gee gave me no reassurance whatsoever, which made things worse. What was I going to do? I made an appointment with the vet one afternoon. It was Tuesday, 22nd January. I got to the vet's. He was a very nice man, and I explained everything to him. He said he would keep Buster in and give me a call late afternoon early evening.

This is where everything started to go really wrong. Talk about being alone on this one. Which was the norm with Gee; when I needed help the most, he could be at his worse with his attitude towards me.

My father phoned; he thought my mother had been taken in to hospital, Stoke Mandeville. He didn't know what was wrong with her, but he saw an ambulance outside her house taking her away. I asked him where he was. He said in Thame at the moment. Um, not too bad. I said, "Dad, go to Joggy's, and I'll find out about Mum and get back to you."

"No, I'm going over to Stoke Mandeville."

"Look, Dad, we don't know if she is there. Go to Joggy's and I will call you. Let me make a few calls, please." I had a non-committal reply.

I phoned Joggy. I said, "Jogs, you have got to stop Dad from going to Stoke Mandeville. Ralph will be there."

Joggy's reply was, "Well, it's up to him. I can't stop him from going; if he wants to go, I'll let him go." At this point, I was almost losing it with him. I was in Hampshire. Joggy was in Oxfordshire, 20 minutes from Stoke Mandeville and so was my dad. I didn't want my dad to go to Stoke Mandeville as Ralph would be there, my mother's partner, who had been my dad's best friend. My mother had lied over the years to Dad about Ralph, implying he was no longer on the scene. This had been done so that Robert would inherit Dad's money. Not Ann, Dad's partner. This lie to my dad had been going on for the last ten years plus some, saying that Ralph wasn't around, so Dad would come over and stay once a week on a Tuesday with Mum. He lived in Peace Haven but was a sales rep for King Flexibles. He had a massive territory, so it suited him to come to Thame once a week, stay and do that area of business over two days. This was the night he would normally stay. I called the hospital and they had no admissions for her in A&E. I called my dad back to tell him that she was not at Stoke Mandeville, to go to Jogs, and I will call her doctor and speak with him. "I'm going to the hospital," my dad informed me. Now I was really stressed. I was visualising a massive punch up in A&E, police being called, my dad arrested or Dad or Ralph in hospital due to injuries they inflicted on one another. My imagination was running riot. I called the doctors' surgery, explained who I was to the receptionist and she said she would get Dr Straddling to call me back. I knew him since I had been one of his patients, but he also went to the same church as me when I lived in Haddenham.

The next move was to phone Joggy to get him to get Dad to come to him. "Hi Jogs, it's me."

"Yeah, what do you want?"

What I wanted to say was for fuck's sake help me here, please, because if you don't, all hell is going to break loose in that hospital. Dad hated Ralph with a passion. Dad also called Ralph a *completely spineless person.* "Could you get Dad to stay with you tonight and I will find out where Mum is and he can go and see her tomorrow, PLEASE?"

Jog was being very non-committal and my stress levels had increased by a 100-fold. Eventually, Jog agreed to do that. I spoke with Dad; he agreed to go to Jog's. We still didn't know where Mum was. I called the hospital back; no, she wasn't there but they took my number. Dr Straddling called me, said he had made a house visit to my mum's and called the ambulance because she had pneumonia and could hardly breathe, but she wasn't happy about going and had put up a bit of resistance. He had stayed with her till she was in the ambulance and they had left. Ralph had called him and also insisted that Mum go to the hospital. That was over an hour ago. I said Stoke Mandeville said she wasn't there. He said to call them back and say she was a new admission who just come in via ambulance. I did that. No, she was not there. I called Jog and Dad made sure all was okay there. Dad was with Jog, staying the night at his house but he was not happy. Tough, I really didn't care about him not being happy. I was more worried about Ralph and him meeting and the potential consequences.

What to do now? Stoke Mandeville called me. It was like an angel on the other end of the phone. She said my mother had just come in via A&E and was in a critical condition. That was all she could say, as that was all she knew. I made my mind up. It was now 7 p.m. I called Dana, my sister, told her about Mum, said I was going to Stoke Mandeville tonight to see how she was and that the hospital said it was critical. Did she want to come? If she did, I was leaving now with her or without her. I was not in the mood for her playing me up. It was yes, you are coming or no, you're not and you will be ready when I get there; if you are not, I will be leaving without you. It was said just like that. I really was not in the mood for her saying, "I'm too busy; I can't just drop everything." Again, it seemed like one of those moments when something was looking out for me as I had not had a drink yet. I had no worries about driving. Drinking now was the last thing on my list.

I went around, picked her up and informed Gee I was going to Stoke Mandeville. In the process of all this, I vaguely remember the vet talking about calling me. That had turned into a non-priority. I was worried that Mum could potentially be dying. She smoked and had chronic obstructive pulmonary disease (COPD). Basically, no lung capacity for oxygen and to be able to breathe that well. She could hardly walk 100 metres without having to stop due to being so breathless. I was worried, very worried that this was it.

I picked Dana up; we were in Stoke Mandeville hospital by 9:30 p.m. I went straight to A&E and thanked the girl who had phoned me. I was eternally grateful to her; it meant so much to me that she had made that effort in such a busy job. She informed me where my mum was in the Critical Care Unit. She hadn't been given a bed or a ward yet. We went to see her. It was dreadful; she could hardly breathe, hardly speak. She was concerned that we were there and was saying we should go home. I spoke with a nurse. We talked about her breathing or lack of it. The nurse explained it was the COPD; she had pneumonia. They would be giving her antibiotics, and she was on oxygen to help with the breathing, but they were limited as to what they could do for her. I stayed with my mum until after 12. The nurse informed me she would be moved to the high dependency unit as soon as they had a bed, which should be shortly. It was heart breaking when my mum started to panic as she couldn't breathe. There was nothing more the nursing staff could do. They were doing it all. They dad her on oxygen. I did say, "Mum, don't panic, as it will make everything worse."

They were not sure when she would be in the high dependency ward but they had a nurse checking on her every 15 minutes. That was good. Mum had said Ralph had gone home but would be coming back in the morning. Okay, that was good. Dana and I left as Mum was quite concerned about us being there so late. I didn't want to go but there was nothing else I could do. She was ill. The nursing staff and hospital were doing the best for her. I could do nothing else. I drove home, dropped Dana off and got into bed about 3 a.m.

The next morning, I phoned the hospital; she was critical but stable. I spoke with Ralph and yes, he was going to see Mum. I spoke with Dad and yes, he was going to see Mum. The question was when. This caused more stress. I liaised with Ralph, informed him when Dad was going into the hospital, so they wouldn't bump into each other. No other member of the family seemed to be bothered about the potential consequences of Ralph and Dad meeting. Not just that but the pain it would cause my dad if he found out Ralph was still around. I know he had Ann, but my mother had been the love of his life.

My day work-wise was simple. I had a stand meeting I was sharing with my friend Tia. She had set up. I told her about my mum. The stand meeting was in Chichester Hospital. When I got there, she told me to go home and see my mum. I said look, there is nothing I can do. My dad is seeing her. Ralph is seeing her. I phoned the hospital and they informed me of what was happening and what they were doing for my mother.

That morning the vet called me. I felt dreadful. He said he had tried several times to get hold of me last night. My thoughts were, *He must think I'm a dreadful cat owner. Dump the cat at the vet when it's sick. Don't bother taking any phone calls. What a great owner we have here.*

I explained about my mum. To me, it felt unreal. It was obvious that nothing could be done for Buster; I was beside myself. I asked him could I see him as obviously Buster had to be put down. He told me when he was working, and I booked an appointment. Then I called Gee and told him he was going to have to come home and go to the vet with me because Buster had to be put down, and I could not do this by myself with everything else that was happening.

Gee came home; we went to the vet's. I thought I would be okay and wouldn't cry. I was a mess, in tears, nose running, eyes streaming, dreadful. I spent a few moments with Buster, just me, and Gee said how much joy he had brought to my life and that I had, over the past three years, enjoyed our secret moments of him sleeping on Gee's side of the bed while I had a kip and Gee not knowing till now. I couldn't give a shit how Gee felt about that. Asthma or no asthma, Buster slept on the bed. He didn't have an attack even though Buster was in the office with me. Gee was still alive and kicking. Although he did have three full-blown asthma attacks when we first moved to the south coast but that had nothing to do with Buster. It was the moulds from the tree and the pollen which set them off. Now they were scary. On all three occasions, Gee ended up in hospital as the ambulance staff could not get his blood pressure down and his response to the nebuliser was not that great.

Buster was put down. I was in a dreadful state. The vet asked what we wanted to do with him. I said Gee would bury Buster in the back garden, which he did. The fact that it was torrential rain and it took him over 45 minutes to bury Buster under the tree he used to sit under was neither here nor there. I was no help whatsoever. The only thing I did was pack all his food, toys, blankets, basket cage, and Gee had to get rid of them. He took them to work the next day and gave them to one of his work colleagues who had a cat and needed all that stuff. I just wanted everything out of the house, gone.

My mum was in hospital in the High Dependency Unit. My cat Buster put down and a *new job*. Great! Not only that; it was a new job I was not sure of and I had just had these two things thrown at me. Again, Gee was very little help in my hour of need. *Things were going to get worse.*

I went up on the weekend to see Mum with Gee She was hardly aware that I was there. Ralph said he would keep me up to date. Dad had been in to see her and let me know what she was like. So I was praying that Ralph and Dad's paths would not cross in Stoke Mandeville. It was just so stressful for me. The rash on my face was now getting much worse.

Dana and Dick went with the two boys, Nick and Sebs. Dana said that Sebs looked at Grandma very strangely and asked about all the tubes and whether she was going to stop smoking. He was coming up to seven years of age; Nick was almost four years old. I felt incredibly low. I felt let down by Gee in some ways. I knew and felt he had no interest in looking after Buster when I went on this training course with Kudos and then APC. I had no choice but to let him go. It just would have been nice if he had said, "Yes, I will make sure Buster is okay," but it never happened. I asked for another cat; that was a 'NO'. Just like it had been with us having children. In

Aylesbury, he had said before we moved. *No children now, no children ever.* I wanted to know why not; I wanted something. So now the situation with Gee was no cat, no children, no nothing. He had three children by his first wife. "Great!" I said, "what about a dog?" *It was no dog, no nothing.*

I was scared of dogs but I tried to assure him that if I had one, I would be better. All I got was, "Catherine, until you can prove yourself to me that you are not afraid of dogs, the answer is *NO*."

So, he had three children. I had none. Before we got married, Gee had said that we could have children and then like so many things, he went back on his word. *Again and again and again.*

He would go back on money. As for spending money on holidays, I would be left with nothing. If he wanted something, he got it. If I wanted something, all hell broke loose.

Gee never intended or wanted to have children even with his first wife. However, Wendy his first wife became pregnant three times. She was pregnant before they got married and again shortly after. Gee helped with the birth the second time as the baby had gone into distress as the umbilical cord was around her neck. There was a changeover of staff. The midwife just said put this on; we've just got to do. That was it. The baby was born and the baby was okay. Then Wendy waited a few years and had another. They would have two boys and one girl.

What a life! I had nothing. It was all what Gee wanted. I felt like a commodity. Someone who could earn a great deal of money, which Gee liked. The fact that the jobs in the past with the exception of Kudos caused me stress, especially in Financial Services was neither here nor there for Gee.

All I heard was, "You're good at it. Look at the money you are earning." That was a high price to pay. The highest price was about to come.

We had the induction training. It was in the Cotswolds, the hotel. I can't remember the name of the place, but it was in the middle of nowhere. I had never heard of the place. It was just past Evesham near Stratford upon Avon, in the middle of nowhere.

This would be the sign of things to come. I was one of those people who was always on time. I was not on time for this. I had planned my route, worked it all out and was confident about how I was getting there. It was, however, all A and B roads, but it looked like the quickest route on the map. The M40 took you away from the location then you came back on yourself. The A roads were the most direct. This didn't work out very well.

Firstly, I was over-tired. I had been doing too much exercise and was exhausted. My left eye kept twitching, which was always a sign I was over-tired. I could hardly keep my eyes open, so I stopped for a coffee. That would have been fine, and I would have arrived on time if I hadn't got lost, which I did. I had never heard of this place and being in the middle of nowhere didn't help; it just made things worse. I had to stop. I called Ronni, the Kudos company PA and told her where I was. I was literally stopped in the middle of nowhere. I could have been on the moon. There was nothing around. She guided me in, and I turned up 45 minutes late. There was no reprimand.

Here I met all the new Kudos team in this division. APC, however, had in-house (head count) reps for this division. It was a mixture of contract reps and head count reps. This training was for the Kudos contract team only.

The hotel was quaint and very Cotswolds. The training was on the 'NHS'; how boring could that be? Exactly, very. Not only that, we had to do the exact training again with APC when we went on their training course.

During this training, my anxiety levels had hit an all-time high. I was really agitated and could not stop starching my face. I didn't drink much on the course. I took on board all the information and had a good understanding of what the NHS was all about. Ketan and Dot were great to be with and the others who were new were great too. Some had worked part-time on the Prostap contract, with APC. They were very knowledgeable what was expected of them with regards to Prostap. Each rep who had worked on this contract did a presentation on switching from Zoladex, the competitor to Prostap. What was interesting was this part-time field force had been told that the position was for one year and then after that they would be taken on as 'head count' with APC. They had not been told it would also involve taking on the flu vaccines and the position would be full-time and they would have to apply for the job with no guarantee they would get it. I found that out from Lynn the three days I was on the course. Lynn had been one of the part-time Prostap reps with Kudos for the contract with APC.

Lynn would also be the person who noticed the clothes I wore were designer. The names meant little to me I just liked the clothes. Lynn would also be the person in the London Metropolitan to do a handstand in the ladies' loos while I was smashed out of my head at the gala dinner.

The hotel was nice. Not what I would have stayed in myself as there was no gym or pool and when I went running outside, it became obvious that I couldn't do that as it was pitch black with no streetlights. The food was good and Dot, Ketan, Graham, Barry and Ronni were all great to be with. On Friday, we finished at lunchtime. I got home and went straight to the pharmacy. A friend of mine was a pharmacist, Caroline. I went in to ask her about my rash. Her comment was, "Catherine I know you really well, and you are not right. You seem over anxious, and the rash looks like rosacea, which can come on due to stress, and you look severally stressed." Was I? Was it that obvious? She suggested I make an appointment with my doctor about it. Now that was going to be difficult as I was up in London Monday morning. I did manage to get into see the doctor after London. He said it was rosacea and was brought on, or could be brought on, by stress. He gave me some cream which helped and cleared it up. However, rosacea would always return to the same spot whenever I was stressed. That was going to be a great deal.

Gone were the fun, carefree days. They were about to be replaced by stress, paranoia, overwork, panic, victimisation, bullying, false accusations, plus a few more negative things thrown in on top!

London Metropolitan is a very interesting hotel. You could get lost in it very easily. It was like a maze, but you had two different mazes to deal with. It had two sides to it. One side had one set of elevators. The other side, which was down a very long corridor, had another set of elevators.

I got the train from Southampton to London Waterloo and then the tube to Edgeware Road and arrived in good time. I went to the check-in point for APC, where I met Dot and Ketan. That was great. Graham was there too.

There was a main conference room for everyone. Then there were individual rooms for different divisions. We started in the main conference room, then divided into our divisions. Dot, Ketan and I got lost. It was an overwhelming maze. Richard, who we thought to be our manager, found us. Jackie did not like people being late and didn't tolerate it. He had covered it for us. So he said; whether that was true or not, I don't know.

We sat down. We then heard what we didn't expect to hear and had not planned for this change of events. Jackie announced that there were going to be some changes. Firstly, Richard, our manager, had been promoted and was going into marketing. He was being replaced by Gail. Ketan and I looked at each other. "What, who's

Gail?" Gail stood up and introduced herself to us. Then Jackie informed us that she had been promoted and was going to be in charge of arranging all the conferences, so we would have a new divisional sales manager. They hadn't found one yet. This is not how it was meant to go. Dot seemed more relaxed about it than Ketan and me. Dot had done all the groundwork and assured us we would be fine with the set up that was. It now was a different set up. *How would this work?*

We were then sent to a different room; this was regional. We would meet our other teammates in our region. Mates is not the word I would use. The team consisted of Caroline, who seemed okay; Laura, I had no problem with her. Bruce and Ray. These four were the head count APC reps. Kudos' contract reps for that region were Dot, Ketan, Russell—who was a very young lad in his early 20s who would be great and a genuine, really nice guy—and me.

Bruce and Ray would turn out to be complete snakes in the grass and shits. Bruce was sly and two-faced along with being a complete shit and snake in the grass. Ray was difficult to describe. He had his own agenda; you had to watch Ray and by that I meant, he would have your knickers off quicker than you could say Jack Robinson.

There was definitely a them-and-us situation. Ray was sarcastic and any intelligent question you asked was mocked by him, L=like you were a stupid idiot. I did not like Ray or Bruce and every single warning bell came on. *Another time when something was looking out for me!*

I wasn't completely sure about Caroline; a sixth sense said beware. Laura, no problem, she was okay.

We did what we had to do that day. Then it was the gala dinner in the evening, where everyone who had done well was presented with prizes on stage. Before the gala dinner, I checked out the gym and had a quick work out. I got ready, I wore a pink fitted cocktail dress with straps and a flared skirt with black stiletto sandals. I had dyed blonde hair in a long bob. Ketan looked nice and Dot looked lovely, as she always did.

At the table, we started to play a drinking game. That was mistake number one. Carly from HR was on our table, and boy, could she drink! This drinking game was dreadful; if you did the wrong sign, you had to literally drink your whole drink, which was wine. We were getting drunker and drunker. The only people who seem to be keeping it together and getting everything right were Ketan and Graham. The rest of us were getting trashed, really trashed. Then all of a sudden, a record came on. Music had been playing for quite a while; we had finished our dinner, the prizes had been given out and the drinking game was over. We were smashed. Ketan, who drank rarely, was sober and Graham was also sober.

I was definitely one of the worst.

S Club 7 came on, *Reach for the stars.* I loved that record. That was it. Did they want me to dance on the table to S Club 7? Carly, Gail, Laura, Caroline, Bruce, Ray, Richard, Russell, Dot, not so much Ketan, and Graham were up for it. I got up on the table, and in a room full of probably 600 plus people, danced on the table to S Club 7. I finished the dance and Ketan helped me off the table. I carried on drinking after that and got even drunker. Ketan kept on saying, "Come on, Catherine. I'll take you to your bedroom, I think you've had enough." This was to no avail. I was on a roll and Ray was on a mission. Ray kept on asking me to come to bed with him in front of Richard. I made no comment, just went on the dance floor drunk and probably made an even bigger fool of myself. I can't remember going to bed.

What we all had missed was the argument between Caroline and Gail. Caroline was telling Gail she was not management material and a few other things were thrown in like, "I'm not happy working with you as my manger as we are on the same level." Gail had been in tears, and Laura had come to Gail's defence and told Caroline to shut up, give her a break, now was not the time, and not to take all the enjoyment away from Gail and her new position.

The next day, I woke up. Ketan rang my phone in the room but I was already up. He wanted to check whether I was okay. Well, I was sort of okay. I didn't think I was going to be ill. My head was okay as was my stomach. Yes, I should be all right. I did actually go to the swimming pool and did a quick swim at 6 a.m. in the morning. This was before Ketan called my room.

We all met up in the conference room again, then divided into regions again for some work. Graham came up to me and said, "I've had a word with Jackie about your dancing on the table last night, and she has assured me that there is no problem with that." Um, not great, first thing in the morning and not great first night with a new company, dancing on the table! Graham did look out for me, and he was a very good boss to all of us but he would take no nonsense.

Graham also needed to talk with me about a meeting which I had done. Geoff, who worked for Nova Nordisk, had taken the meeting on for me as I had no budget left and it was at HMS Sultan. We did the meeting together. However, Geoff was made redundant shortly after this and didn't put it down on his expenses. The military contacted Kudos as the bill had not been paid. Graham and I discussed it. I said I had done the meeting with Geoff but explained that Geoff was meant to have paid it. He probably forgot or couldn't be bothered because of the redundancy that was coming up.

As we were sitting around the table doing whatever we were meant to do, a French girl called Pascel, who was part of the administration team for APC flu team, gave me a picture. Someone had taken a picture of me dancing on the table and wanted to find the person it belonged to. It was shown to Pascel. She knew instantly who it was as she had been at the table and gave it to me. I still have that picture today. I did look a bit drunk in the photo. We had lunch, did a bit more work of God knows what and then got the train home.

Wednesday, Thursday and Friday we spent at home studying Prostap and flu vaccines ready for our training course of three weeks starting Monday, 11th February, for three weeks.

That weekend, I went up again to see my mum; she was still in Stoke Mandeville. I phoned Stoke Mandeville every day to see how she was and went to see her every weekend until she came out of the hospital. She was in the hospital for a total of six weeks. It was the first time I ever saw my mother with colour in her face; she had a lovely glow and soft red cheeks. All my life, all I had seen was her grey-looking face with no colour due to smoking and the morning cough that was there every morning. She was moved from the high dependency unit to the general ward after a week. Because of the pneumonia and the COPD, she wasn't well enough to come home any sooner and when she did, it would be to stay with Dana for a while. She would spend three weeks in Stoke Mandeville till she was somewhat fit to go home. I remember her saying to me that she could not remember a thing about her time in the hospital, she was that ill.

So, I had made my debut performance with APC on the 4th February and now we had the training course. It was at the Swan Hotel, Stratford upon Avon. The good thing about this hotel was that although they didn't have a gym, they had passes to the local swimming pool and gym, which was literally just over the road. I was still obsessed with going to the gym five times a week and swimming every day. The pool was longer than the Solent; it was 30 metres, which is a strange length. I did 30 minutes most mornings that I stayed in the hotel. The club's pool was 13 metres.

I got the passes, so I could swim most morning and go to the gym each evening. Each evening, I went to the gym after we finished the training between 4 p.m. and 5 p.m.

Due to arriving late for the Kudos induction course, there was no way I was going up Monday morning. I went Sunday night to make sure I was there. A few others also did the same, those who lived quite a distance away. The Scottish reps were flown down. People from up north drove down Sunday evening; the others like Ketan who did not like being away from home came down Monday morning, including Dot. Ketan really liked the room he had been put in so he requested it every week before he left. It was a lovely room, much better than mine or Dot's.

11th February was the first morning. We then got to meet all the reps, 27 in total, for three territories. This is where them-and-us came in, and it was almost in three categories. There were the APC head count reps who had sold flu and a pneumococcal vaccine. They now only sold flu as APC had stopped the pneumococcal vaccine, which by all accounts was the best on the market due to the presentation of how the syringe and needle were attached, making it easy for the nurses to administer.

Then you had Kudos' part-time Prostap team. They just sold Prostap on a part-time basis and had been assured that after a year, they would go in-house. However, they had not been told they would have to reapply for the job, and there had never been any mention of flu or full-time. In-house they did not go. They were part of the Kudos/APC contract team.

Then there was the almost new team. That was Dot, Ketan and me. We had sold Prostap. Last but not least, there were also some completely new people who had sold none of it and were brand-new to all of this.

We were assured that being contract people, we would not be treated differently in any shape or form. We would have the same budget. True, we did. We were told we had the same expense float, but that wasn't true. Why say it if it's not true? It would have been better to have known than find out the way we did. We had a float of £300, APC head count had £500.

On the training course during the training sessions, there was a strictly no mobile phones on policy. If you had your phone on and it went off, you had to stand on a chair and sing a song. Bruce led the way with the first song.

The training course was strained in many areas. Firstly, Ketan, Dot and I sat together with Bruce and Ray next to Dot. People are naturally territorial, so everyone sat in the same seat each day.

This should not have caused a problem and it didn't until we were put into teams to go away and do various training things we had been asked to put together. They consisted of three groups of five and two groups of six. We would then find a quiet spot in the hotel and put together a presentation to take back and deliver to the whole team. Easy. Except Ray and Bruce did absolutely nothing. They would just disappear and leave the three of us—Dot, Ketan and me—to get on with it. We were one of the groups of five.

It was not great teamwork. Not only that, either Dot, Ketan or I had to present it then to the other teams. This happened all the time over the three weeks. We just let Bruce and Ray get on with it. It wasn't going to matter what we said. They were going to do their own thing and that didn't consist of help for the three of us.

The only good thing that Ray and Bruce actually did was to steal a copy of the questions we were going to be asked in our exams and getting them photocopied. One was on Prostap. That was easy for Ketan, Dot and I; we had already done the training and sold it. Flu was a bit different. There was quite a bit to learn about immunology. It was quite a complex area. Plus, there was also the selling it into practices and the dispensing deals as well as how the practice made their money by buying the flu in.

Practices were under pressure to hit certain targets and criteria with the flu. For the 'at-risk' groups, they had targets; they had to vaccinate 80% of those groups. They then got a payment for hitting that. Flu vaccines were big money for practices. They would get a dispensing fee along with another fee and would be reimbursed for the cost of the flu vaccine at full price. The practice would buy the vaccine with a discounted rate. This maths part was a bit of a nightmare for me to start with, but I got there in the end. It took a bit of time though. Dot, being excellent at maths, had it sussed straight away.

We also had the NHS training again. I really felt for the Welsh and Scottish reps. They had to sit through training which was not applicable to them. *Twice.* How it worked in Wales and Scotland was completely different. Goodness knows how they felt.

Valentines that year was interesting. It came on Thursday. There were a couple of things here. Firstly, my friend Tia was getting married on that day and I was unable to go due to the training. I had, however, bought her wedding present. That was an interesting relationship. I spent one New Year's Day with her down at the police station based on his threats. She had spent New Year's Eve with me, Gee and her daughter Jez. We had all written a list of new year's resolutions. Jez was to keep her room tidy. Tia, I have no idea what she and Gee put down. Mine was to lose weight, be a better person and swim every day. I did lose weight. I went down to a size 8 by June.

In 2001, New Year's Day we spent down at the police station. This was for harassment and threats and a few other texts to her from him, along with him getting her sacked from a job. She had lost her licence for drink driving but still had the old licence. That is what she showed the company and that is what he doped her in for. He informed the company of this fact and she was dismissed. She did, however, get a job straight away after that. Then she married the guy in 2002, on February 14th. Two days later, he's gone. Tia was upset. She was, however, a very strong person and got herself together very quickly, within days. Literally days. There are many humorous stories about Tia.

On Thursday, the 14th, most of the girls had some Valentine present sent to them by their other halves, which would be brought into the training room. They came in fast and furious. It was lovely to see. Ketan's wife owned a flower shop so it was one of the busiest times of year for her. Normally, Ketan would help with the deliveries but couldn't this year as he was stuck on the training course. Then the really big one came. Ketan said, "Now this is a serious one." It was a bouquet of 14 red roses from Gee, the number corresponding to how many years we had been together. Of course, when all these things arrived, we would have to go to our rooms and put them in water, so it was quite a disrupted morning. Just as well Valentine's Day was a Thursday that year. Ketan did say to me that Gee obviously loved me, and I should work hard on my relationship with him. If only he knew how difficult things were with Gee…Like so many, he would probably say leave if he knew it all.

We got through week one. I called Stoke Mandeville every day to see how my mum was, then I went up to Stoke Mandeville either the Saturday or Sunday when I came back from the training course. This was along with unpacking, washing, drying, ironing, packing, shopping and cleaning the house. It was exhausting, and I felt severely stressed.

I was tired. I was drinking. Not quite like the head count APC reps. They were in the bar ordering drinks at 5 p.m. as soon as the training had finished. That would be doing that for the whole three weeks. Now they did look rough after a while. Really rough and I didn't look that great either.

I went to the gym at 5 p.m., did my hour, came back, had a shower and got ready for the evening meal. It was always at 8 p.m. I hated it. I liked to eat between 5 p.m. and 6 p.m. We all joined the rest of them in the bar between 7–7:30 p.m., then had our meal. I would be drinking before the meal, during the meal and after the meal. This was where it started to go completely wrong with the drinking, also the depression.

Some mornings, I was just too hungover to go for the swim. I really did not feel great. How the others did it, I don't know. They were in the bar, the same group of them drinking from 5 p.m. till could be past 1 a.m. I was in bed by 10 p.m. plastered on certain nights. All the drinks went on our room number; we then had to pay for it at the end of each week. APC realised this was a problem for the Kudos reps so one APC rep would get one Kudos rep account transferred to their room number and they would pay.

The second week, Dot wasn't there for three days, which was fine by me. Jackie wasn't happy but had been informed before Dot took the job that she had booked this holiday and Graham had agreed to it and defended her corner.

I really did not feel right. I can't recall exactly what was wrong. I was tense, stressed, agitated, anxious and paranoid; I felt very down, insecure and unsure of what I was doing. It was like a flick of a switch; I just seemed to break down.

Ketan noticed it and put it down to Dot not being there. I wasn't going to disagree with him as I just didn't know what had happened to me.

Week two's training in the hotel was similar to week one. We just knew a great deal more about the others on the training course. Ray and Bruce's behaviours got worse, not better, and Dot did actually say something to them, but nothing happened; they carried on the same way.

One morning I was coming downstairs to go swimming. I was early. The fire alarm went off and everyone congregated outside. I was the first to sign my name and said I was going swimming. One room had not come down. I would hear later that it was the Irish rep Wanda. The kitchen was on fire. They went to get her. They knocked on the door and said, "The fire alarm is going off; can you evacuate your room?"

Her reply was. "Is it a bomb or a fire?" They said a fire. Her reply was, "I'm going back to sleep." This was at 6:45 a.m. Unbelievable to me but true.

In week three, we finished the training course and gave all the necessary exams. I have no idea what our results were as none of us were given the marks. The only good thing that happened with the exam is we could do it Thursday night instead of Friday morning.

This came about due to the Scottish and the Irish people's flight. We had also got to the point where Ketan and I were so sick of some of the reps, we would go out for dinner somewhere else. It was much better and we both liked to eat earlier.

I got home exhausted and the worse for wear with three weeks of drinking and going to visit my mum every weekend when I was back from the training course. My cat was dead and there was no real help from Gee except arguing with me over everything.

He argued about how inconvenient it was to go up to Stoke Mandeville every weekend and that it wasn't how he wanted to spend his weekend. I did say I would go alone, but he didn't want that either. So, it was just hell for me. What made it even worse was the parking. There wasn't enough space. Plus, it cost a fortune. That caused even more arguments. We could and would never be able to be in each other's company for more than a few minutes without some form of argument or bickering; it was exhausting and very challenging being with Gee.

That, in the end, was why we had and lived an upstairs-downstairs life. I wasn't allowed to watch what I wanted on TV downstairs. He had everything recorded that he wanted to watch, and I had no say. I was an inconvenience where the TV was concerned so I left him to it.

The only few things I can remember my mother saying about Gee was he was negative, unkind, selfish, had no patience or tolerance and was inclined to be cruel. *The only way to deal with that type of person is to treat them the same way.* That's what she meant. She also felt I would be better off by myself as someone like Gee would never change. She saw clearly that I was very unhappy.

After the training course, we then had to spend three days at the Potteries in Fareham for computer training. All of us also had to stay in the Meon Valley Marriot Hotel.

It was quicker for me to get to the Potteries from my home and a shorter distant as well as less money to the company. Alas no, it was team building. More time away from home. More drinking. Ketan drove me each morning to the Potteries from the hotel.

This training was a complete nightmare for me. I really was completely computer illiterate. The course was bigger as it involved the hospital reps as well. We needed to meet them as we would be working with them in two ways.

Firstly, to help them sell flu to hospitals, and secondly, one of the products that they sold into hospital and tried to get it on the hospital formulary was Prostap. So, they would be key people for us to work with! My hospital rep was Maeve. I will not give you the low down on her, except she was useless, didn't keep in touch, didn't work with me and had no idea of potential best areas to work. We did the training and set out the territories I was going to work. Two weeks later, she said she had looked at the sales data for the competitor and we should be working another area. She had been working that territory for four years, and she had only worked out the largest potential sales area! I was sticking with my plan; I knew what I was doing and how do it. We were meant to meet monthly. That was either a complete shamble of her not being prepared or cancelling at the last minute. I liked option two; cancelling at last minute meant I wasn't wasting my time with someone who I thought was hopeless. I think the whole time she was my hospital rep, we met up once and that felt like once too many times.

Eventually, we went on territory. Things were different, GPs were no long the main target; it was practice managers or the person in the practice who ordered the flu vaccine. Going on a newish territory with a new product to sell in areas you are not familiar with in March is not great. The reason being that the flu season January–March is when most of the business had been signed up. All that was left to do was ensure you stayed on top of the discounts that the other companies were giving and try and keep your business. I had been reasonably lucky here; Paula, the head count APC rep, had worked the territory and had signed up a great deal for me. I still had work to do. She had done her job.

That cannot be said of every territory. Dot's was a nightmare. Bruce was meant to have signed up her business and had done nothing. It was the only time I saw Dot burst into tears. Dot burst into tears with me on the other end of the phone. I did not like Bruce, and this was just more confirmation of why not. He was a lazy, selfish git and a snake who would grass someone up for nothing. The only thing he was good at was stashing flu so if there was a shortage in the season, he could take care of his customers and maybe help a few of the other reps who needed it.

We had been told on the training course that 'no one was to stash flu vaccines'. This had been a very big thing for all the APC reps in the past. It meant they would have a holding source, usually a pharmacist, and when they needed extra, they would go in and do the credits and debits with the pharmacist and practice they had taken them to. We heard horror stories about flu season. We also heard that flu season 2001/2002 Solvay had blown the discount levels by going up to 50% discount. Along with not taking the other competitor's business away from them. It was common practice to leave their business with them and then we would maintain ours. How did that one work? It worked or was supposed to work in that they didn't touch your accounts, you didn't touch theirs. Is that sales? How were we going to grow the business because that was what was expected of us? Now it was getting accounts to order more. Plus I did get some of my practice to order a small amount of their flu vaccines from me.

We didn't go out on territory straight away; our first week would be the week commencing 4th March. My diary from January was blank anyway, so it would have been a month of specking only as a GP rep. That was simple for me and the remaining time I had with Kudos as GP rep, that's what I did.

Gee went on a Power Boat Course the weekend of 2nd March, which meant I had time to myself. We had gone to see my mother in the hospital on Friday. She was looking so much better; she had colour in her checks, a lovely soft pink glow, even more than the last time I saw her.

It had also been decided by Dana, Dick and Ralph, her partner, that Mum would stay with Dana a few weeks while Ralph went down to Devon where he had a bungalow which he was still renovating. That would be yet another project Ralph would never finish. He did the kitchen, living room and one bedroom. It had three bedrooms and a bathroom. The bathroom was passable, just… Ralph was mean with money and never got a job done quickly. He was not one for cleanness in any shape or form. The place was a filthy, dirty dump which needed knocking down and rebuilding, if you ask me.

I had made several appointments on the phone with regards to flu customers. That had been easy. My diary was a mixture of meetings with practice managers who were really important to see and GP appointments along with the odd nurse appointment who would see you about the flu and arrange clinics. The delivery date had to be confirmed. On the whole, I tended not to make appointments with nurses as you could get in to see them quite easily. Well, I could, and I liked to do nurse meetings. They loved them, and I would always have a speaker for them, a consultant specialising in the area I was selling in.

The week commencing the 4th was Monday and blank, so it was specking for the day with flu customers whom I hadn't got appointments with yet. Easy. On Tuesday, I had a GP appointment; easy, I could see the practice manager, nurse, talk flu and Prostap with them and the GP. The good result was I got a flu order. Plus I saw more people. Wednesday was a speck day so more practice managers. Simple. Thursday, I had a GP appointment on Hayling Island. The other GPs knew me well so I was guaranteed to get in. I just needed to see the practice managers. They were now more important in many ways. It was an easy day. I got to see three practice managers as three practices in one building, four GPs and got a flu order plus potential switch from Zoladex to Prostap. Then I had a hair appointment at 2 p.m. in Fareham, which was cut and colour, so it was a three-hour job. This, I did not feel comfortable about. I was working full-time. Although my call rate was good, and I had got sales, I felt guilty like I wasn't doing the job and I had an appointment at the sports injury clinic at 6 p.m. for sciatica. This I had suffered from on and off for years. They sorted it out with a couple of appointments, which were very painful. The treatment was very effective.

On Friday, I had a lunchtime meeting at Villa Romania. I would be sharing with another rep. You never knew how many GPs would turn up. It was a regular meeting, and there was always a table for us. It never had to be booked; the waiters knew the system. There was also one in the evening. These meetings were booked through two different GPs; as a rep you just had to go in, ask for a date, be given a date, then find another rep to share it with you to help cover the cost. At lunchtime, there was normally one other rep. In the evening, you needed more than one; it was a big meeting and you tended to bring your partner at times and the GPs all brought theirs. The evening ones normally had about four reps. There could be up to 20 plus people. Plus, it was against the ABPI Practice Authority. The Prescription Medicines Code of Practice Authority (PMCPA) was established by the Association of the British Pharmaceutical Industry (ABPI) in 1993 to operate the Code of Practice for the pharmaceutical industry independently of the association itself. Pharmaceutical companies were all members. It was important to them. The only company I knew that had got kicked out of the ABPI was Astra and they were one of the companies I had really wanted to work for before Kudos. Their reps had a £30,000 budget. I could use and do that easy.

Reps had so many get-out clauses with the ABPI like the GPs paid for their partners. That never happened. One even brought his daughter as well and gave me a £20 cheque for it. I tore it up and threw it away in front of him. Plus, the meal was over £30 per head. Again, against the ABPI. There were certain amounts you were only allowed to pay for lunch and a larger amount for evening. It never happened. All reps were the same. All did the same thing; it was the only way of getting the contacts. You didn't buy GPs to prescribe your drug. That never happened with any rep. What these lavish meetings did was get you access to them. Some never saw reps. These meetings enabled you to talk with them and get appointments, something I was very good at. You got your business card signed by them and then you either went to the practice and saw them there or appointments were made. I had hundreds of cards signed with different messages on some. 'Make an appointment'. 'Will see'. 'Will see any time'. Now that was a first for any rep and I got that on some of my business cards. With Kudos, other company reps just didn't know how I did it. With APC, I had almost instant access due to the flu. If I got in with that, I was made in so many ways with Prostap.

The GPs who were most difficult to see and for whom you needed to get these meetings were the cricket meetings outside in the summer and in a sports hall in the winter. I played at the indoor once and never played again; it was dangerous, and I hated any ball sport. It did the job and that got me in. All this was with a restaurant in Southsea and Havant; you had to go in and see the owner of the restaurant to book them. These were very important meetings to get as you then got access to practices you would never get in.

My first week had been a dream. My second week wasn't quite a dream. First thing was I was now doing the Isle of Wight. I had always wanted to do it but the Kudos rep who did Dorset with Kudos did it. The Isle of Wight would not be a joy for me. I hated the island from the start. You had to get a ferry from Portsmouth to Fishbourne; that would be the one that I would use. Another was Southampton to East Cowes, I would later use that one to go to Osbourne House with Adrian when I was doing all my 50 years of age stuff. Then Lymington too Yarmouth. It was known as the most expensive crossing in the world. At that time, one passenger and a carry cost just under £50. It took about 45 minutes and according to Jackie, it took a great deal to cancel this ferry. It really did have to be rough at sea. She had told me that waves were coming over her car on one occasion and they still sailed.

The island, however, was big flu business for me. It was over 15,000 flu vaccines. That was big business. Again, Paula had done an excellent job. The APC flu reps had massive territories; there were only 12 of them to do the whole of the UK and Ireland, so you can imagine. My first visit to the island was with Jackie. We had a lunch meeting at the White Mouse restaurant, an inn; it was a very popular place to stay. This was a regular meeting for doctors.

The other thing about the island was that reps did not go over there in the summer months due to the fact that the ferries got booked up and the traffic was dreadful. To me, this island was like going back a hundred years in time with what seemed like a maximum speed limit of 40 miles per hour. Because of the flu and the potential Prostap business, I was on the island every other month. It was great for getting out of joint fieldwork with Gail, my then manager. The ferry was booked; you had to be there and once on that island, you weren't off until you finished. I felt like I was being caged in going there. You booked your ferry back but nine times out of ten I always got an earlier one as I couldn't wait to get off and back on main land.

You showed your ticket; it was getting in that lane and then simple, you got on. I never had to wait for the allocated time on my ticket.

I will not forget two meetings on the island. One was with Jackie; we had a speaker to talk about HIV along with a patient. It was a very interesting meeting. When they finished speaking and we had eaten, I said to Jackie we needed to go. Jackie was good on talk time. I kept on saying we need to leave. Eventually, I said, Jackie, we are going to miss the ferry. She looked at her watch and said, "Oh shit." Driving to the ferry in an almost all 40-mile-an-hour zone didn't happen; it was like being on a rally course. Jackie went through red lights, overtook on bends. I just kept my mouth shut and prayed. We saw the ferry and I said don't stop just drive on in case it goes. We were okay; we had just a few minutes to spare and had a laugh on the ferry about it. Neither of us wanted to spend the night on the island; that had been the alternative.

The other meeting on the island was with Geoff. Again, an important meeting for me in a restaurant. When we had eaten, I went and asked for the bill and explained how it needed to be done, split in two. This should have been a simple process. It was not. Firstly, the waiter kept on getting the bill wrong. The added complication was he took his time doing it. In the end, Geoff and I knew we were now getting close to missing our ferry and the next would be an hour later. We went up to pay, both of us, and got them eventually to make the bill as we required. Now all we had to do was pay, say goodbye and rush to the ferry. Geoff wasn't worried, said we would be okay, we had time. He was right. That is, until we got outside. It was like a scene from *The Hounds of the Baskervilles.* Fog everywhere. We missed the ferry and waited one whole hour in the car for the next. I got indoors at 1 p.m.

My first week to Bournemouth, now that was interesting. I have not got the greatest sense of direction, and I am terrible at map reading. How I ever got anywhere I'll never know but I did. I had an appointment on Thursday, 14th March. I got completely lost. I called the practice manager saying I was lost. He asked where I was and I explained. He directed me to another point and asked me to then call him. I did that. Four times I had to call him, and he got me to the practice. I had a map and he had sense of direction. This was another big account. The first time I met him, I sorted the flu out, plus talked about Prostap. He agreed that he would talk to GPs about what I had said, and to call him back and he'd inform me of the outcome. This was normal practice. This is how you got your Prostap business. Flu was millions to APC. Prostap was hundreds of millions.

On 26th March I had joint fieldwork with Laura on her territory. It was Peterborough. I was not happy about having to drive all that way. She was an original APC flu rep. I travelled up the night before, booked myself into a hotel which had a gym. Laura picked me up at 8:30 a.m. in the morning. The day seemed to be spent with most of the time in the car, travelling miles. We saw four people in total and she only spoke about the flu and left a Prostap leave piece only. She never spoke about Prostap. That would be the case for most of the APC in-house reps. They had been so used to doing flu only that Prostap took a back seat for them.

Wednesday, 27th March to Thursday, 28th, there was more computer training at the Potteries Fareham. I still had to stay in the Meon Valley Marriot Hotel, Shedfield. How ridiculous was that? It was good to see Ketan and Dot and some of the others but that is where it ended. It was boring and there was going to be a new program for putting flu vaccines sales on the system; it just wasn't ready yet. This was done by an IT guy who by all accounts drank a bottle of vodka a day and could still do the job and turned up at a conference in jeans and a T-shirt. He was, however, excellent at his job. No doubt an alcoholic, but I didn't judge him like that. I was still under the impression you had to be falling over to be an alcoholic. He didn't fall over.

Mum had been staying at Dana's for a few weeks now. Dana, Dick, Nick and Sebs were going to their place in France as it was Easter. Mum was coming to me on Thursday, 28th March. Dana was suspicious; she thought mum was smoking. Mum was now on an oxygen tank every day for a certain number of hours plus a tonne of other medication, nebulisers, inhalers and tablets. Also, her vision was not that good.

Gee was not happy. At this point in our relationship, he wouldn't go around to my sister's with me. He wouldn't come baby sitting with me for a few hours as they didn't have Sky TV. He didn't like the boys coming to ours, or Dana and Dick. If I invited them for a meal, he moaned for weeks, then after the meal instead of joining in with the conversation, he would leave the table and either go upstairs on the computer or watch TV. This really pissed me off. I was also getting very resentful. I had looked after Scott, his youngest son. He would stay the weekend and Gee would clear off with his mate Roy and Winston if it was breezy and the wind was good and go to Mudeford. It was a two-hour journey there and two hours back as well as a whole day windsurfing.

I had had my late 20s and mid-30s written off. We didn't go out anywhere since we had to look after Scott. There was no baby sitter, no cinema, no fun. And now, 'no children' for me. That he made very clear when we moved here. Gee made it clear he didn't like my nephews at our home when they come over and made it obvious. When they did, they weren't allowed to play with his remote-control cars, which he had. He took them away. He was horrible. He made it obvious to all that he didn't want them or any of them around.

So you can only imagine the uproar there was when my mum was coming to stay for a few weeks with Ralph joining her later after Easter. He moaned about it, saying why did she have to stay here? The fact that she had almost died was neither here nor there and Ralph coming later…Why did he have to stay? He didn't want Ralph and my mum here. The pressure he put me under with the moaning was intense. I wasn't feeling great as it was; I was a bit of a mess now and this was just dreadful. It was so one-sided; he was not like this with his family and the resentment on my side had set in.

We had a regional meeting on Wednesday, 3rd April. I was lucky it was at the Fifteen Head Manor Stockbridge. My territory just down the road, about 30–40 minutes with no traffic. It was a bit different in rush hour. We had to be there, should I say, Wednesday evening for a meal and team building. Basically, a piss up. That morning Wednesday after Easter, Gee had been dreadful over Easter towards my mum. She was quite upset about his behaviour toward her and me. What made it worse was Ralph was going to be joining my mum at our house on the Thursday morning. He planned to be there by mid-morning. Gee was going to be looking after my mum on Wednesday evening.

Gee was so bent out of shape on Tuesday morning it was unreal. He was saying why couldn't Dana take Mum to France with her? Why should we be left with her? The fact that I had looked after his dad and let his dad stay here when his mum died was neither here nor there. He had acted dreadfully then. His dad stayed with us for a week. He took no time off work and I had to juggle my appointments around his dad. He didn't eat one evening meal with us. One of the classic moments, as I would call them, was after his mother's funeral, he sat in the living room with his dad and watched *Death Wish*. What a film to watch when your father has just lost his wife! The second best was Friday, Gee finished at lunchtime. I remember I had a big meeting; Dot was saying Thursday night and then we were out all day that Friday. I talked to Gee about his dad and asked if he could be home in the afternoon. No, he couldn't do that. He had to go into Portsmouth to sort out his personal number plate on his car.

This is what I constantly had to deal with—his selfish attitude. He spent what he liked on what he liked. He was spending to excess at times on clothes and his latest gadget. He was, however, in many ways a good man. That is what all my friends, especially Tia, were saying to me.

Gail, our manager, was on holiday for Easter and returned to work on Wednesday the 3rd. On Tuesday, Gee was throwing a fit in the morning before I went to the club saying he didn't want my mum here and he didn't want Ralph here. He said Ralph stank, which is true; he didn't wash, which is true; and ate us out of house and home, which was also true. I said, "Look, you only have to look after my mum Wednesday evening; make sure she has something to eat and takes her medication. I've left their lunch for Thursday and I'll be home Thursday evening."

Gee's reply was, "I'm not doing that; why couldn't she go to France with your sister? I don't want this. She's your mum, you do it." He brought that up yet again, then promptly walked out of the house, slamming the door on the way out! SOP, Standard Operational Procedure.

Great, Gee at his best. Well, it was not the end of the world; Gail would be back on Wednesday. I would explain the situation to her on Wednesday morning and say I will be there first thing Thursday morning. I'll just miss the team-building piss up meal.

Bruce the snake called me Tuesday. "I want you at Fifehead Manor at 2 p.m. Wednesday." *What the fuck for*, I thought. He had some must-do training with me. The fact that he had left it till the Tuesday coming up to 12 noon to inform me was neither here nor there and his so called 'must-do training' was nothing of importance whatsoever. In fact, there was no must-do training; he was just being a complete shit.

I explained to Bruce very nicely about my situation, leaving quite a bit out, just said that I was going to speak with Gail on Wednesday about my mum and see if it would be okay for me to arrive on Thursday morning. Bruce informed me that couldn't be done. I had to be there Wednesday. I had to be there for his training, and I had to be there that night. It was unacceptable. Calmly, I said would he mind if I spoke with Gail about this situation. I asked him not to tell Gail but to please leave it to me.

The snake phoned Gail first thing Wednesday morning as she was on the phone to me at 8 a.m. about it. I explained my situation. I also explained about Gee. Then I explained that I could make the evening meal as Gee, after being a complete shit on Tuesday, had come home Tuesday evening saying he'll look after Mum and Ralph. Now all I needed to do was pop home at lunchtime to give her some lunch. She couldn't get it herself. Apart from not being able to breathe that well, her sight was not good. My mother had told me when she had been around my sister. I had gone around to see her and asked her why she hadn't had the soup that Dana had left here. Her reply was I couldn't see the controls on the microwave to do it.

Gail was understanding but it was really the beginning of me not getting on very well with certain team members. The meeting was dreadful, with Bruce and Ray making snide remarks about me whenever they could and me being stupid enough to retaliate. Caroline was not being exactly warm to me. Laura was okay and thank God for Ketan, Dot and Russell. Russell being so new to this industry was a bit like a 'bunny in the headlights'. It was like a game of tennis between Bruce, Ray and me. I wish I had not taken the bait and just ignored all their comments, but I was really defensive and was feeling over-stressed with everything.

The first year with APC was hell for me. Not only did I not get on or like certain members of my team, the GP team who I was meant to work with had it in for me too. Except two.

The others I knew very well. I had seen how they worked on territory. I called them the coffee shop kids. They were always in coffee shops with other reps from 9:30 a.m. onwards till 11ish, or they went home and came back out at 11ish, or they didn't come back out if they had got to a practice at 7 a.m. seen a couple of doctors that morning till about 8:30 a.m. Then they picked their children up from school. That was their full-time job's day's work. I am not saying I was a saint, but I did work. I did get appointments. I did sit in waiting rooms with the appointment I'd made, got seen; they didn't. That was just how it was. I was getting the job done as a GP rep for Kudos, they weren't.

They felt threatened. Why? Because they felt I would grass them up. I had no intention of doing that. I couldn't give a damn what they did. They were meant to be able to help me. You have got to be joking; they couldn't help me. I could have helped them a great deal but that didn't happen. That didn't happen due to the fact that they picked on me; they sent false accusations about my work via email to manager. The top guys at head office saw them. This caused much more stress. The implication was 'I wasn't doing the job. They were.' They were stupid. Due to every single thing they accused me of, they were made to look stupid as I always had someone with me to prove my innocence—Gail. It was remarkable how it was but Gail was with me each time I had been accused of not doing something. This was making me ill. Very ill.

I went to the doctors; I felt like I was falling apart. I was drinking. That didn't help. He prescribed Prozac. I stopped the drinking, took the Prozac, felt much better but the victimisation, bullying and false accusations were still happening. I turned up at one of their stand meetings to help them. They didn't acknowledge me and Barry, who was one of two reps I got on with and was a trainer. Barry said, "Can you please say hello and acknowledge Catherine?" It was brought to an end a few years down the line. I was, however, going to have to suffer and suffer until then and I did.

I was unhappy and didn't like the job. Graham called me one Friday evening, concerned. I was now a bigger mess at this time and I said many things. At one point he said, "You sound to me like you don't want the job." I can't remember my reply. Graham talked me around saying Gail was new to this and to give her some time, and to keep doing what I was doing and try to ignore the general division. Bruce and Ray weren't worth getting upset over. Graham really was in my corner. I even met him and Gail for a talk about things. Was I in a state? Why? Was it just the alcohol? Yes, I was drinking again, but I wasn't drinking all the time. It was *just one bottle* in the evening when I drank.

I didn't stay on Prozac for that long as I started to feel better. I came off it as I told my doctor I was better now. I genuinely thought I was. I was able to do things again and wanted to go down the club and do my normal exercise routine.

I had gone through a phase where I would just lie in bed staring at the ceiling, not wanting to get up, and when I did, it was about 8.30 a.m. for a quick shower. I didn't bother to do my hair since I could put it up.

Everything was going hunky dory on the flu side. How wrong I would be!

A new and very aggressive flu company came in, Chiron. They didn't muck about; they were late to the market place, end of April beginning of May. All flu companies at this stage had their flu vaccines signed, sealed and, what they thought, delivered. We all thought that. Chiron came and put the 'cat among the pigeons'.

Everyone thought all we had left to do was dates that the practices wanted their flu vaccines delivered and check they were happy with their reserve amount of flu. This was instead of the stash. They could have 10% of their total order as reserve, which meant if they didn't need it, they didn't have to use it. We didn't do sale or return as most of the competitors did. However, APC did always sort these accounts out, so they weren't left with unwanted flu vaccines. It was good business practice. As the rep, you just had to reassure them. APC made a very big mistake; the rest of the competition, not so.

Chiron came to the market place with 40–45% discount, just 5% lower—depending on the size of the account—than Solvay the year before who had blown the discount market. Our competitors were Aventis, Evans, Solvay, Smith Kline & Beecham. They took a few knocks but not as bad as APC.

This was not good news for us. The regional managers were Gail, Carol and Ross plus the divisional manager, Jason. We now had a divisional manager. I liked Jason; however, Jason would not budge over 35%. Jason was new to this position; he had worked in the general division, which was very different. It would take him a while to get to grips with this position. Coming from GP land, he thought the business was seeing GPs, especially with Prostap. He was very wrong, and we would meet him for the first time at the Chelsea Conrad Hotel London. It was a very foolish, costly business move. Chiron were not interested in your bread and butter accounts, the 500 vaccines here, the 200 there. They went straight for the over 2,000 vaccines. They got them. By the time management had decided to shift the discount rate up, it was too late. I lost, so did the rest of us, thousands of vaccines and really good accounts. I didn't, however, lose the Isle of Wight. I kept all my business on the island, even though I hated the place.

My appraisal with Graham on the 18th of September was in Winchester, his head office. I was not in a good state of play. Winchester was my territory and my appraisal was at 9 a.m. in the morning. I should have got there easily but I got lost again, my map-reading skills and sense of direction being crap. Winchester had an awful one-way system which people have said in the past they had no idea how to get out of it.

I arrived at 9:30 a.m. Graham did not tolerate people being late and the only reason I think he went easy on me were several factors. He had seen the victimisation, bullying and the accusations. He saw first-hand how Bruce had been towards me but also to Dot and Ketan. He had also earlier in the year had a meeting with me and Gail as I was in a state. I told him the doctor had put me on Prozac. Graham would always stand in my corner. I wasn't going to the club. I found it difficult to get out of bed with or without the drink. I felt a mess. I was, however, a very, very good rep. I wouldn't say I was let off. He did say that I did work Winchester as a territory and had no excuse for being late and that he would let it go only this once.

As for flu, I was 86% off target. No one reached target that year. However, my growth over 2001 in that territory was 12%, which was very good. I also had the second highest selling price of flu, £4.35. That was excellent. For Prostap, in my whole territory, I had switched 52 patients; again, this was one of the highest. They just needed to sort that discount rate out. I had £1,600 of budget left at this stage. That would be blown by the end of the year along with some more.

I encouraged awareness and uptake of childhood vaccines and fully met the company standards for reporting and territory management. Paper work was always on time. I reported every night to head office, so they had my daily activities and appointment meetings I'd done that day. I also had an excellent relationship with my customers. Gail saw this on joint field visits. I had already started on the flu business for 2003. I had 11 practices in the process of switching from Zoladex to Prostap, discount dependent, and one PCT. That one PCT was worth millions to APC. Millions. What did need attention was computer skills. I was crap. Internet, what was that? Excel, what the hell was that? Word, I could do. Excel was just awful. I never got to grips with it. At APC, I always struggled even when on course, where I lost the will to live and walked out thinking, *What the fuck have I learnt?* Nothing, except I still couldn't do it.

Other skills that needed attention were people skills with other team members. By all accounts, they weren't that good with Bruce and Ray and not great with the GP team. No, I had issues with them and their manager Trish. They were just awful, a load of lazy, lying, bullying, victimising idiots who needed to concentrate on their own job, not show and have so much interest in mine and supposedly what I wasn't doing.

However, the real issue that Gail had was we would have regional and divisional meetings. We would be here for two, maybe three, days in some big flashy hotel like the Chelsea Conrad. When the meeting finished, I just got up and left. That wasn't acceptable. I was meant to hang around and speak with my other team members. Fuck that, I wanted to go home. That was what Gail would have an issue about. I just took it. However, my thoughts were, *I've been with them for a few days, can't I just go home?* I had enough enforced socialisation with some people I really did not want to be with.

The Chelsea Conrad hotel was a very interesting meeting. Firstly, Dot and I got there early as I wanted to go to Oxford Street early to get some shopping done. We didn't get there that early as Dot, who lived near Bristol, was faffing around at home doing her housework. By the time I met her at Chieveley Services, M4 halfway house for both of us as we were taking just one car, it was late, so Oxford Street was just a quick shop. The taxi driver wasn't worried about the amount the taxi was costing and the traffic. He said, if we could afford to stay there, we could afford his fare. No amount of us telling him that we weren't paying, the company was, didn't cut the mustard.

This is where we would be meeting Jason for the first time. The meal in the evening was fine. I didn't drink that much. However, the others were really going for it, including Russell, who I really liked; he was just such a likeable lad. Which for Russell was just as well. Russell would be late for two divisional meetings due to heavy drinking the night before. If he had not been liked, he probably would have been asked to leave.

The next morning, I got up to go to the gym at 6 a.m. I believe it was this hotel. I got in the lift and it started to go up and it was glass; I was terrified of heights. When it got to the bit, I could see it was glass outside, so I dropped down on the floor on my hands and knees. When I crawled out of the lift on my hands and knees, there was a guy there to get in the lift. Goodness knows what he must have thought; I just said I was scared of heights and carried on crawling.

I didn't fancy a swim. It was at the top floor. I got into the gym, but it wasn't really that well-equipped. So, I decided on the stepper. I had never been on one. I did that for half an hour. That was it, back to my room, showered, changed, breakfast meeting for 9 a.m. Jason would always be a reasonable divisional sales manager that way. He didn't do these silly o'clock meetings at 8 a.m. with nothing to talk about after about 11 a.m. just filling in with stuff. He did that bit. They all did that! What could take half a day always took two days, maybe three.

We were all in the meeting room. Jason was standing up, introducing himself. We were all listening. Russell opened the door. He was 45 minutes late. You could cut the atmosphere with a knife. Gail did not look happy. Jason had stopped talking, he was just looking at Russell who apologised. Jason just told him to sit down. Gail had words later. It was not the best of starts with the new divisional manager.

For Russell, the next divisional meeting was at Alton Towers. We got there. On day one, we had a short meeting, then we went to the bar. Alton Towers did not have a pool for me to swim in; it was for kiddies only, so I went for a run in the morning.

Day one we had all been in the bar early, 5 p.m. Paul, who was new to the team and had taken Ketan's territory, was there. I will always remember these three things. Firstly, Paul was ordering scotch after scotch after scotch. Boy, could he drink! Secondly, when I said, "Oh, dear, it's all over now for me," when I was on drink number three, a guy called Steve said, "Why change a habit of a life time?" Thirdly, I never made it back to my room to change for dinner; instead I stayed like so many at the bar and got hammered. The next morning, he was talking about his alcoholic mother-in-law who had vodka on her cornflakes for breakfast. He obviously knew I had a drink problem. Paul would later say to me and a few others when we were talking generally that he was probably an alcoholic.

When Paul moved to Canada with his wife Janet and our region had a get-together, at the dinner table just before we were all leaving, he said to me in front of everyone, "And you shouldn't drink." He knew I had a problem. I did know but didn't want to do anything about it. I was at the stage where I stood a very small chance that I could possibly get it under control. *That didn't happen.*

Day two was a few short hours of training and normal meeting stuff. We then all went to the theme park to go on the rides. Russell excelled himself at Alton Towers. He was not there at 9 a.m. day two and Gail was seriously not happy. I was quite concerned about the trouble he would get into. This was Jason's second meeting and Russell wasn't on time for the second. Admittedly he was in early 20s, so he probably went for it the night before like all of us. It was really cringe-able when Russell walked into the room. Jason stopped speaking and told him to sit down; he was nearly an hour late.

Russell told me and Tanuja the full story once we were in the park. Gail had met him on the stairs coming down; he hadn't showered and looked a mess. Gail told him to go and sort himself out and get into the meeting room ASAP.

Everyone wanted to go on the ride Aire. Russell, Tanuja and I didn't; instead, we went on the pirate ship. That was terrifying. We were screaming. When we got off, it was obvious that the chances of finding the others were remote. After that ride I said, "Come on, let's do the tea cups, they are easier." I was only joking; we did go down to the teacups but didn't go on them. We met the rest, went on the log flume, the rapids. I got soaked. Top to bottom soaked. Then the oblivion. Funny that because later I would drink myself into 'oblivion'. We had a fun time.

The first flu season with APC was simple. Farillon, the wholesaler and distributor for APC's flu vaccine, had got their act together; they had been appalling in the past. Farillon held a special meeting for us to go through how the flu season would work, what they would be doing and what we would need to do. It all seemed too good to be true. This first flu season that I was with APC, they were excellent. Plus, they dealt with Prostap sales along with Phoenix and Williams, the other wholesalers. The APC reps who had sold flu before said it was the most boring flu season any of them had known.

The 2002/2003 flu season was piece of cake. Prostap wasn't going that well. I had done the most switches in the company to date, but the main drawback was discount. Practices were not happy with a 10% discount rate. Zoladex gave a much better deal, which meant the practice earned more money on the dispensing side.

APC change the discount rate for Prostap based on the amount they ordered. For each practice which switched 15 patients, they would get a 20% discount.

Between 2002 and 2003, this happened: Russell had been taken on as head count in September 2002. It would be announced at conference in Portugal. Dot was livid. They did it in a way that was based completely his performance and other factors. Russell was well-liked by top management. We all liked Russell. I was pleased for him. However, Dot did have a point; he really had only been in this industry for five minutes. Ketan left twice; the first time, I was really upset. The second time I understood why; it was called 'APC'. Bruce moved to another position in training. I felt sorry for the trainees but thanked God. Ray got asked to leave. This was when we were on conference in Portugal in 2002.

In Portugal I had two problems. The next morning after we had flown in, we had a big meeting in the conference hall. Then we were divided into teams to perform certain tasks and get information; it was a treasure hunt. I would have enjoyed that. My team were more keen on drinking than doing the treasure hunt. So I drank with another girl called Karen, who was picked on by her regional team, which was also my regional GP team, who I was meant to work with. Even now at the conference, it wasn't working. I went back to the room, got plastered on the drinks in the mini bar. I didn't think anyone would notice. They noticed I missed the meal. They had to break into my room as they were worried about me, which not a great start. I couldn't remember any of it. I just knew I wanted to drink, and I did that and passed out in my room. The next morning, I phoned Dot's room to check whether she was still going on the jeep safari as our day out. She had said she would come, and she did, and we had a great laugh. It was just so funny and the most enjoyable part of the conference. We had four days over there.

In the morning, Gail also informed me that they had broken into my room and she had told Jason about me being drunk passed out in bed. This pattern would now become one of many occasions of me being so drunk that I'd have to be put to bed. I was still functioning and starting to get really good results, business wise. I'm sure that contributed to me not being sacked.

There would be another problem which would come my way, and I would get raised eyebrows. How these things happened to me in front of people who I really didn't want to witness them, I don't know.

Before we got on the coach to take us to the airport, I had seen some earrings in one of the shops below the hotel. I went down to buy them. The long and the short of it is the shop's Visa machine wasn't working; she had had a problem with it for a few days. I suggested using another shop's machine. However, that wasn't possible. One hour had gone by. In the end, I said look, can't we do it manually. Eventually, we did. Now one and a half hour had gone by, and I had to run to get back to the coach to be there on time.

At the airport, I was doing my normal mooching around, looking in shops, having a coffee, not taking much notice of what was going on. Siobhan from another region said I think I heard your name called out over the Tannoy at the airport. This was mentioned to me again by another team member but since I hadn't heard anything so didn't take any notice. We all got to the departure lounge just about to get on the plane, hundreds of APC employees or contract teams. Then two big security guards and a woman came in. She said, "Is there someone called Cathy White here?" Gail and Caroline both looked at each other with raised eyebrows and turned around. Everyone else looked at me. I was asked to go with them.

I said, "I can't, I'm just about to get on the plane." They assured me it would not take long. It didn't; they just needed my passport number for the shop I had spent one and a half hours in. Wouldn't have mattered what it was, it just added fuel to the fire for Caroline, Bruce and Gail to see me as a problem. I could tell by everyone's face they thought I was trouble and a problem.

Tanuja joined but she had a difficult job as she changed territories three times all within our region. Gail kept on pulling her up on not being productive. Tanuja pointed out, "I'm starting from scratch. You can't expect me to be performing like I've been on since I joined." Gail still didn't give her any slack, said she was an experienced rep and should be up and running. That is not how it works.

Laura got asked to leave along with Ray. Caroline became pregnant. Bruce was now in training. Tegan joined. We had a nice team. My GP rep team were still awful. I was still in a dreadful state but was trying to hold together, sort of.

It was September, the beginning of the flu season. 2002/2003 was a walk in the park on a sunny day. All the horror stories we had heard just didn't happen; it went really smoothly.

I got a new hospital rep since Maeve left, thank God, and went to head office working with Jason. Colette took her place and she was excellent.

Gail and I never really hit it off. I just didn't feel right with her; I couldn't put my finger on it. She did tend to leave me to it. She moved to Colchester which was miles away, and she did work hard, but she wasn't the best of managers. Our new divisional manager was good, Jason. He really did reward us when things really did get very tough for us.

The flu season in 2003/2004 was a bit busier. In 2003, Dot was taken on as head count by APC. She didn't tell me until conference in Barcelona. I knew she would be taken on. Why she didn't tell me as soon as she knew, I will never know. She said she had been told that day literally, which just wasn't true, and it was hurtful, but I was a mess anyway.

At conference in 2003, during the meeting in the Metropolitan London, the overall manager, Paul (APC had a load of higher management equally, they had too many lower-ranking people) told us many times that they had an extra place that year for President's Circle. This was one of the top awards you could get. It meant you were literally better than the rest. The other awards were five star being top, three star being second, and first star being last. These were good awards to have, so four people had the chance to win one of them. This spare place that Paul was mentioning all the time, I just knew it was going to be Dot. In all fairness to Dot, she did work hard and was a good rep. That you could not take away from her. Dot won the extra place mention for President's Circle. Bruce, somehow, had won the other place. He really didn't deserve it, but he got it and hadn't left yet. They had also changed how they handed out these awards; instead of over dinner, it was done during the daytime conference. Sebastian Coe was the person who handed over the awards. Dot was delighted as he had gone to Loughborough University and so had she.

This was a much better way of presenting the awards as the meal had taken forever in 2002 since between each course, people were going up on stage to collect their awards. People just got drunker, me included, and the 'dancing on the table' stunt happened.

The 2003/4 flu season involved more work but was still manageable.

I was quite well-behaved, better than 2003. We went to Barcelona for the conference. For our trip, I went to see the church that had never been finished. Plus, the football stadium—the only stadium I had ever been to. I think it a very famous one. I could be wrong on that. Tanuja went shopping so we had lunch together; she went her way to the shops and I went to the stadium.

Prostap wasn't going well; they had upped the discount. My hospital rep Colette, as I said, was excellent. We worked really well as a team. To win President's Circle 2004, the hospital reps would have to choose which territories were going to be their key accounts. The hospital reps had two Provac reps; Provac was the shortened name for our team.

At the divisional meeting, I had given my presentation of where I would be working. That was Portsmouth, Eastleigh and the New Forest. They would be my key accounts for President's Circle. All Colette had to do was decide was it my territory that would be her key accounts for the hospitals or was it Paul's, who had taken over Ketan's territory? Colette choose mine.

The 2004 conference, Metropolitan Hotel London, arrived on the Monday. We dropped all our luggage of which would be taken to our room later. I was with Collette, was faffing around in my bag and my electric toothbrush went off. I was in a state of panic and said to the very young porter, "It's my electric toothbrush, not a vibrator."

Collette was in fits of laughter, saying, "What is she like?"

The GP division had been hell to work with. Well, I didn't work with them, but they were just still dreadful to me. I was doing really well business wise. They still accused me of not seeing a key GP. Gail went into the call reporting with me. She had access to where they had been and how many times they had seen this 'key GP' who was so important to them. Not one of them had seen that GP ever. The only person who had seen this 'key GP' was me, twice. What were they playing at? What were they doing? Not much except picking on me; that's where all their time and energy seemed to be going instead of doing their job.

I was very upset at this conference. When I came down in the morning, I was in tears over this GP division. I had, however, got really pissed with them over things that they were accusing me of. I thought, *hold on, you're accusing me all the time of not doing things and basically saying I am a no-good rep. Where exactly is your team on the sales side?* Our division had three regional teams. Their division had 30 regional teams. Where were they on the sales data scale? I never did something like this and this was the only time I ever did it. I checked on them and they were second from bottom. Second from bottom! They had been accusing me of not working and they were second from bottom!

I told Gail this fact. When we met in the morning to go into conference, I had been in tears in my room and in the elevator

226

coming down. I meet Tanuja and she said, "Don't let them see you like this. They will think they have won." I said I would try. Gail was good. She kept on saying during the conference that they were second from bottom. We all sat together as a team. I was now very close to Tanuja and said that I could blame the red, watering eyes on contact lenses.

It was time for the awards. I had no idea of who had done what and what had done who. All I did was go out and do my job. I had done well on flu and very well on Prostap. I had switched loads of practices and had the New Forest PCT in the process of switching the majority of it practices.

Colette had informed me that she had seen Dr Mark Hammond, and she thought he would be doing the awards. I'd never heard of him. Mark Hammond did announce the awards. Top management was up there; David Miles was one of them. I knew his wife, she was a GP rep. Not only that, he lived just around the corner from me. He was a nice guy and his wife was lovely. Tracy was a good rep, and I liked her. On territory, she had said her husband worked in the industry but never mentioned what he did.

The star awards were being awarded; this was a large sum of money where APC paid the tax, so you got money that was stated. First star was £1,500; two people from each division were awarded that based on their business. Three stars was £3,000 with just one rep per division and five stars was £5,000, again one rep per division. I was called out for the first-star award. I was as pleased as punch until I got to the stage. Jason and a few others said to me, "Catherine, don't go up, come and sit here." Jason explained to me that they had got it wrong and I had won an award but not that one. Mark Hammond handled it very well, he made a joke with each award saying is it. Catherine White?

I had won the top one, the five-star award. We had a break. David Miles did come up to apologise to me about what had happened. He really was a nice guy. We went back in, for the President's Circle award. This award was given to the two best reps in their division. That was the GP Divisions. GP had several divisions, selling different products, Bio Tech Division, Hospital Division, Provac Division and APC's field force was over 400 reps. Out of every division, only one rep would get 'President's Circle Award'. I won it for the Vaccines and Prostap Specialist Division (Provac). Mark Hammond then said on each award that was handed out, was it Catherine White? A guy behind me said, "Who is Catherine White?" I turned around and said, "It's me." I won

President's Circle along with Colette, my hospital rep. She chose the right rep to back.

I had won all the top awards that you could win. Not only that, Tanuja had won President's Circle as well. Gail was pleased for me; she won regional manager's award, Dot got three-star award, Russell got first-star award, I got the five. So she won the five-star managers' award. Her first comment to me was, "Second from bottom."

The next morning, I felt much better, got up feeling hungover and still drunk but not bad enough to stop me swimming. Some of the guys came in to use the steam room and sauna.

I met up with Dot and Tanuja to go back to the conference room together. We got in the lift. A guy got in and asked which floor. My phone then went off. I answered it and had to give them the number. This poor guy was pressing every number I was calling out. I didn't notice but Dot did and she found it hysterical, the way that he was going from one number to others.

I didn't get too many problems from them after that, a few, but it calmed down. That is how it was with them.

We went for our champagne reception, I have a lovely picture of Dot, Russell, Gail and me along with Stella from another region who got an award at this reception.

They were second from bottom, not at the champagne reception!

The President's Circle was in Marrakesh. It was a top hotel, first-class flight, everything paid. Gee and I had a great time; it was with partners. It was champagne all the way and I did behave. That could not be said for Cannes.

We went to see the Yves St Lauren Gardens along with some other great sites, all by horse and open carriage. I would like to say at this point there is no way I want to come back as a Marrakesh horse. In the evening, they had put on a typical horse display, which was good, and a tent where you could go in and have henna tattoos put on our hands. Tanuja was keener than me. She was also used to this. We went shopping in the 'souk'. I love them but they were like a maze and you could get lost easily. I was, however, not that keen on the snakes that they had for you to have your photo taken with. That was in the square area before you got into the souks. That I did not do. I did have a massage and manicure plus went swimming each morning in their swimming pool, which was nice.

The evening of the gala dinner and presentations was lovely. We all dressed up in the traditional dress. That was good fun and it had been provided to us. Plus, each evening that we went back to our room, there was a present for us. It was great and the food was great too. I loved it and so did Gee.

2004–2005 would not be a great year flu wise. It was obviously a bit more of a panic with practices on the flu side but it was manageable. Chiron had and was a serious competitor, but these things happened. The massive panic was over bird flu. Personally, I didn't think it would be a problem but everyone wanted the flu vaccines. The flu itself wasn't a big problem. It was the massive demand, the general public, 'the worried well' as they are called, plus a few others. What people failed to realise was that the flu jab did not contain the bird flu strain. There weren't massive deaths from the bird flu unlike the Spanish flu, which killed millions. It just caused major panic; the up take was greater than ever. We would also have swine flu to deal with. The press and media really have a great deal to answer to here. Swine flu was actually worse than bird flu. That would be 2005–2006. Again, the general public didn't realise or understand that only certain strains were cultivated each year, normally three, and it was decided by the World Health Organisation, who study the northern and southern hemispheres.

In 2004, I had also won another trip for two to Bruges. Gee and I went first class by Euro Star. Again, we had champagne. I did behave. Bruges was lovely. We stayed in a Best Western Hotel, 'Navarra'. It had a swimming pool and a gym so that was the priority. I went swimming every morning. The swimming pool had been built in the cellar, which was lovely in one way but eerie in another. It sort of reminded me of an Egyptian tomb. Not that I had ever been in one. It just had a strange feel about it. I enjoyed my swim each morning, and we did a tour by horse and carriage. It was as different to Marrakesh as these horses were well-looked after. They did 15 minutes, then stopped for food and water for 10 minutes. They started again, and the horses were rested till they went out again. Each horse worked two days only.

We went into load of museums plus the church, which held the scared blood of Christ. I actually put in the request box for prayers to take this hell away from me that was the drinking and depression. We went to a brewery owned by a family and saw how the lager and beers were made. In days gone by, the workers who were working with the fermented lagers and beers, even though they didn't drink, as they were around and treading in the alcohol every day, they went home drunk. These used to be young lads. It was all very interesting, and we tried a couple of the lagers they made there. We had some lovely meals out with me actually remaining relatively sober. I had a lovely time as I behaved.

In 2004 we went to Sardinia for conference, which was good. I was sober and had stopped drinking now for several months so there were no horror stories to report. I had done incredibly well business wise.

At this point, Adrian, had done nearly six months in rehab after his near-death experience. However, he was in the process of being kicked out. I was sober too.

November was my mum's 80th birthday. I was sober for this. I hadn't drunk for a few months so it was a relief to everyone. She stayed with us and we all went out. Dana, Dick, Sebs, Nick, Joggy, Thomas, not Caroline his wife, Robert my brother without his two children. Lisa, his partner, wouldn't let him take them. Lisa only liked my dad as she thought Robert would inherit all of Dad's money. That was going to be the case. However, there would be twists and turns in years to come that changed many things.

At Christmas, I went out to Lanzarote sober with Gee. That would be our last holiday out there together. It was just too stressful with him. I just drank a few glasses of champagne on New Year's Eve where the main meal had been venison. (Bambi on a plate, as I called it).

By picking up that drink, by mid-January, I was drinking to excess when I went on conference. I was dreadful.

At conference in 2005 at the London metropolitan, I was sitting with Russell, who was now in marketing again. I enjoyed that conference even more as APC had put on a tai chi show with swords, which I loved. The awards were handed out by top management. Dot didn't like it that much, she was definitely not into tai chi. She much preferred Mark Hammond. I won all the top awards; when I went up for the five-star award, I got back, and Russell hadn't bothered sitting down; he knew I had won President's Circle which was in Cannes. I was sitting with Russell at this conference when the awards were given out.

At this conference we had some fun in London, going to various places and getting pictures with policemen. We went off a big MOD boat, no idea what it was, but in the evening they took us to see Ben Elton's *We will Rock You*. It was great. I went back after the show as everyone else was going on the piss and I didn't trust myself.

Gee would not able to go to Cannes with me as he was away on business and was very disappointed. I took Sue as I just thought I would have a bit more of a laugh with her. We weren't really hanging out together, which Gee was pleased about. I told Gee at the last minute that Sue was coming. I now had a dog called Holly, so we needed someone to look after her. Holly had come to us via an email that went to Carl's wife, one of Gee's work colleagues. Carl's wife worked for a county council. I read the email and Gee and I decided to go to Basingstoke to see Holly. We took her home straightaway. However, we were concerned about the next weekend as we were not going to be around; we would be away for a few days. We got that sorted. Carl, who loved dogs, took her for the weekend.

Mum and Ralph had come to stay. Gee did not want them staying or looking after Holly and had asked one of his work colleagues if she would as she had dogs in the past, and Gee felt Holly would be better off there. However, the drinking was now so bad. I wasn't sober enough to be able to take Holly to Christchurch, where his colleague lived with her husband. I had stopped before in Sardinia was also sober over to the Christmas period. As I said, I picked up after seven months on New Year's Eve. 2004 was going to be worse. It was worse than before. This was the start of the downward slope...

We were in Cannes, staying in the Charlton Hotel. I had won President's Circle and I had taken Sue with me. Sue and I drank pink champagne at the airport's first-class lounge at 6 a.m. in the morning. With the award, you travelled first class.

We were in Monaco the day after Prince Rainier of Monaco's funeral. Went to the aquarium and museum, which was great. Also saw the casino. In Monaco, it takes 6 months to put the Formula One track together and a few months to take down. We saw Princess Stephanie's house. We were informed that she really did not like Monaco and spent little time there.

We went to Nice and had a great time. Colette and her husband Tim wanted to spend time with Sue and I; we were really a laugh. I took Sue as I wanted some fun and I did. I never got a thank you note; she never paid for a single cappuccino when we were out. I got nothing, except it went on my P11D.

The year before had been a Waterford crystal fruit bowl that had been presented to us. This year would be a Waterford crystal lamp. The hard part at Cannes was staying sober at the gala dinner, so I could get up to get my award as the previous evening I had been very drunk and fallen over behind the bar. Esther, one of the reps who I knew well, told me to go to bed and put me in an elevator as I was so drunk, plus we had all been drinking on both days during the day. After I had been up to get my award, I really started drinking. When I got back to my room, I ordered champagne. I couldn't think of another champagne to order besides Dom Perignon. Two bottles, not one, but two.

When I got home, and the clocks went forward, I can remember Ralph telling me that the clocks had changed. I said, don't worry, Chris will sort it out. I then opened the Dom Perignon and drank the bottle for breakfast and went on the piss. How I looked after them and fed them, I had no idea. At that point, I was getting up at 2–3 a.m. to start drinking and would watch Kingdom of Heaven over and over again.

There had been a divisional competition that year. I can't remember what the criteria was, but our region won. This was just done as a divisional award, not in front of the whole company. We were all screaming about it when we went up to collect it and what made it even better was Russell was coming too.

Not just once but twice I went out to Cannes, in March and May, as our division and the hospital division had won a prize. What for, I can't remember. I just know I went out and spent a fortune on a Louis Vuitton handbag, purse, trainers and sandals, to name a few. I must have spent well over a £1000; the only problem with LV is they take so long to pack things up. It's presented really well when packed, but it takes longer to do the packing than the choosing.

We would also do Nice and Monaco.

We were on different flights; we all got very drunk when we arrived. There were three different flights: Midlands, Heathrow, and Bristol. The Scottish reps flew to the Midlands. I went from Heathrow. Bristol. The Midlands' flight was at the hotel first. When we arrived, there was champagne. They had made a great start and we joined in. I was thinking, *what on earth are the Bristol reps going to think when they come?* They arrived, three of them. Dot, Russ and Cheryl. They were hammered. They had drunk two bottles of champagne at the airport between them and a whole bottle of vodka on the flight. We went out that evening. I have no idea where we went and I have no idea how Dot and I got on the coach. Dot was hammered. I had to help her get ready; at this point, she was worse than me. We were all dreadfully drunk.

We all had such a laugh and the stories came out like they did the first time in Cannes, the really funny stories of what people had done, Fi's being the best one. Her husband's mother asked them to look after her poodle, which Fi hated. Not only that, but the poodle had to sleep on the bed with them. That made things even worse for

Fi. One night, Fi woke up and there was an awful smell in the room. The poodle had crapped on the bed. Fi, seeing the poodle on the bed, kicked it off the bed and it hit is head on the wall and was unconscious. The bottom end of the poodle was covered in crap. So Fi went and got some Dettol, cleaned the poodle's backside and end with it. This bleached the black poodle's backside and surrounding area. The poodle came around and was running around the house. Fi let it out on the grass; the poodle then started to scrape his backside along the ground. The only problem Fi had was this black poodle had a white arse, so Fi got some hair dye and dyed it. That poodle never liked Fi after that and never stayed at their place again.

We managed to lose a team member in Monaco. No one could remember who it was, and the coach had left without them. It turned out to be Russ. Russ had gone into the casino, so he didn't see us all getting together to leave. We had been told about the famous hotel where people liked to have their picture taken with some statue. I wasn't interested; by all accounts, it was very difficult to get past the doormen. Even if you are staying there, you are quizzed due to the photo taking.

We went back for Russ only for him to say he didn't know what to do so he called his mum. We all laughed and asked how was she going to help. Russ did try to make contact with Mary on the admin side for flu but couldn't get hold of her. It was just one big party and then…

I had won a prize to London, and we were going up to London to stay in the Marriot Hotel in Chelsea. We were booked on a boat trip on the Thames and the London Eye. We went in June.

When we left Whiteley quite early, it was throwing it down with rain. We both thought it was going to be a disaster on the Friday afternoon early evening trips. It wasn't when we got to London; it was just overcast, and we enjoyed both the London Eye and the boat trip, which pointed out all the landmarks. What was very interesting was no building was allowed to advertise on their building. However, Oxo had been very clever and did it via the brickwork, so it spelt out Oxo.

The next morning, Saturday, on the front of the Daily Mail stated that Holiday Inn Fareham was struck by lighting and basically was not usable, along with a few houses in Whiteley. Not ours, thank God. So the South Coast had had a real storm and quite a bit of damage done. The only part of the Holiday Inn that was usable was the gym. That was it.

We did some sightseeing in London, the tower of London and the Crown Jewels plus saw the houses of parliament and Big Ben, to name a few. Again, it was good as I didn't get plastered.

In 2005-2006, Evans, one of the flu providers, went down so out of six flu companies, one had gone down. Their flu vaccines failed. They had none. The reps didn't answer their phones they went straight to answer phone. The company didn't answer the phone either. We knew.

I called a few practices who I wanted the business from who were with Evan. This, I was not meant to do. I had a window of one day to get them sorted and then I would not be able to help. One practice asked why I was doing this as she didn't believe me. They tried to get hold of their rep to no avail; they spoke with the GPs. I faxed over the information I had, saying, 'They could not show this to anyone except their GPs'. They gave me their word; it was a memo from head office saying Evans had gone down. I saved that practice from a potentially disastrous flu season and not hitting any targets they needed to.

It was an awful flu year conference in Athens in September 2005 as we had phone call after phone call after phone call on our day off. Tanuja, Gail, Sima, who was new, and I went to 'The Temple Athen Nike' and also saw the Syntagma Square. Dot did the Pompeii trip which sounded really boring.

The conference aboard was aimed at the golfers. There would always be a golf course nearby. However, there were other activities which people could do. Like sightseeing. Now for the 2006–7 flu season. The World Health Organisation chose the flu strains, normally three. They chose a strain that they couldn't culture. Every company's flu season was delayed due to this. They had to give us another strain to culture. We went down due to this and our flu vaccines failed. We had to buy from other companies. It was a disaster. Our phones didn't stop ringing during the flu season; September–December; we were constantly on the phone. I did one meeting with practice managers in Oxford Street, Southampton. When I got back to the car, I spent two hours sitting in the car, returning phone calls and taking phone calls.

We would be on conference in September 2006, day one being in the conference hall, doing what they do. At this conference, our team had to go to a meeting with Jason. At this meeting, he would inform us of the state of play with flu. It was not great but it was sort of workable, just about. The flu vaccines team didn't get a break, we were making phone calls, getting back to customers who had left messages and sorting things out. The other reps always had their phones blocked so they couldn't make international calls. We didn't. The stress was unreal. I remember on our day off, Tanuja said she was turning her phone off; she wanted to enjoy the day. I didn't. It was hell. She kept saying, "It's your day off, Catherine. Don't take it." I should have taken her advice. That conference was in Sorento. On our day out, Tanuja and some of the rest of our team went to Capri for the day. It was lovely. I did, however, blow the credit card up with a lovely coral gold bracelet, earrings, a gold coral ring with a single coral setting, coral necklace cameos, small leather change purse, plus loads of other stuff. Tanuja liked to shop and although normally I don't do shopping with people but the team members who came with us were great and we had a real laugh. Dot did her own things.

I had also come clean with Gail about my drinking in 2005. Dot had said it was becoming more obvious, and I was phoning people drunk. Gail took it well. I asked her not to say anything, but she told Occupational Health. That probably saved me from losing my job but also, I was given time to go to Spot Light and Avalon Centre to help with my drinking. These are government programs for drinking that the GP will recommend.

I got help with controlled drinking but that didn't work. I saw a consultant had CBT. The one thing was at these places when I turned up, with the exception of CBT which was at the Bay Trees, I was surrounded by people who were still drinking or on drugs and using. I kept up with the CBT but dumped the rest. I hadn't won the highest award in 2006; I had won the first-star award for £1,500. At this point, I was becoming very ill. The drinking didn't help, and the depression just made it worse.

I didn't even turn up for conference as I was ill. Mark Hammond was there to give the awards out at the Grand Metropolitan. When my name came up and it was announced, I was ill. Dot told me Mark Hammond said I probably hadn't turned up as I hadn't won top prizes. Prizes now weren't and had never been the reason I did well. It all came naturally but now I was just ill with the depression and the drinking.

Gee had gone to Germany to pick up his new Mercedes CLK 280 AMG soft top. When he got back, I was on the couch drunk. Gail had to pick my laptop up at conference as they had some work to do on them. She offered to drop it off at my house but I told her to give it to one of the people who worked at the potteries and that I would pick it up from there. I didn't want her to see me in the state I was in.

I was a mess on Christmas, 2006. Gee's father stayed. I was just drinking an incredible amount at times. At one point, I went up to six bottles of red wine a day. I would start in the morning, pass out, carry on; it was 24/7 again. My drinking, however, was very on and off. They call it spree/binge drinking. I called it massive binge drinking at that point. I did not know what was happening to me. Clearly, when I did drink, it was always too much. Tia, my friend, said to keep Gee off my back with regards to drinking by enticing him with sex. Well, that was impossible. I would just pass out and was incapable of sex. How I never ended up in bed with someone at conference, divisional or regional meetings, I've no idea, except I was probably so over the top and my behaviour was so dreadful, funny by all accounts, incredibly funny, I must have scared most men to death.

The drink ethos at APC seemed to be if you wanted promotion, you were in the bar drinking with management. Drink seemed to be forced on you and there were only a few that didn't drink. The majority went all out. Duty of care was not there. The occupational doctor said there were quite a few who had drink problems in the field and head office. That didn't make me feel any better. I always tried to avoid the 5 p.m. in the bar as it was a total disaster for me; if I started at 5 p.m., I would be in bed passed out by 8 p.m. Tanuja had become my mate to put me to bed. Dot never did. She was always enjoying herself. She got drunk as well but didn't do the spectacular scene that I seem to do. It was just awful being told what I had done the night before.

The drinking ethos was beginning to change; everything was beginning to change as the government were doing an investigation into the pharmaceutical industry to see where all their money was going. A good percentage went on the field force and sales. The government put a stop to many things, one being less money for sales and more money for R&D. Then all the exams came in, and the ABPI started dictating what could and could not been done anymore.

In 2006, I had passed one major exam diploma on the NHS. This had to be passed and done and it was accredited by the ABPI. It was a very important exam and the whole industry had to do it. The job was changing big time. I passed the internal exam, a living the values award. This was for performance, clearly demonstrating

236

our values and contributing to our business's success and internal exam, which had to be passed.

I wasn't going to the club that often; if it wasn't the drink, it was depression or both. I won one award, the tour de France challenge for the club. I could have won the rowing one but didn't as I didn't turn up enough times. Martin, an accountant, won it. He had been told by everyone Cathy won't let you win; she always wins. Normally, I did. Not now, I was going down.

I was a complete mess in 2007; I remember very little. I remember we had a meeting which was role-play and would be video. Management would be behind one-way glass. Plus, my friend Sarah who had worked for Kudos and now was with SmithKline & Beecham selling an Asthma product Seretide. It was the best preventative on the market for Asthma. Sarah was not that happy with Smith Kline & Beecham, so joined us, we were called the Provac's team. As we sold Prostap and Flu Vaccines. Little did I know then what was in store for us all, and I would feel guilty about Sarah, and she had left a good job. She had performed well for them in the Devon–Cornwall area.

Sarah had gone through quite a lot since Kudos, in her personal life. When I saw her at this training, she looked fantastic. She had really changed and had a big makeover; she had lost weight, wore lovely clothes and looked great.

In the period January–March 2007, I remembered Sarah and the conference. I only remember sitting in the conference hall and hearing the awards. I got nothing. It wasn't at the London Metropolitan. I can't even tell you where it was, that's how bad I was. We had a new divisional sales manager; Jason had moved on. Jason had really looked after us during those horrendous years with the flu. We got extra bonuses of £70 quite a few times to have a meal out with our partners. Carol did nothing.

I had been a great advocate of her. I really thought she should have the job and would be excellent at it. Paul had refused to give it to her. She got the job several months later and I was really pleased. She could have been excellent. She wasn't. She was demanding, unrewarding, applied pressure like I had never known before and kept putting more and more on us. My head was spinning. I was working from 5 a.m. in the morning till 10 p.m. at night at times. I was still managing to function as an alcoholic, just about. I didn't know where to start, neither did Tanuja. You just thought you were getting on top of things and more was added. It was dreadful. She was awful. She had her favourites. They were the ones who won.

In 2007, I didn't win anything. I didn't deserve it. I was too ill by the end of 2006 and would not be very productive. I did work but not effectively. I was at the doctor's, where we talked about my drinking. He sent me to a place called Spot Light and Avalon, who dealt with and helped people with drinking problems. The only reason I didn't get sacked was that Dot, before she left vaccines and went to the hospital division, told me to tell Gail about my drinking and depression. What came first, I don't know. I told Gail; she told Occupational Health. She said she had to. I saw the nurse and the doctor on several occasions. Plus, I had telephone conversations with them. Each time I saw them, I wasn't drinking but the depression was just dreadful. I was allowed time off for group support with drinking and depression. That was in 2005 mid-year that I came clean to Gail about it.

From January–March, we had exam after exam after exam, I can remember that. How I passed, I don't know.

The Provac team were going to take on the hospital position with Prostap, and I think that was the final straw for me. I hated working hospital and we had enough work without adding to it. Collette had gone into training and my new hospital rep was nowhere near as good as Collette. She tried and was nice but would be doing Prostap for as long as our team would be.

I started on the hospital training. I did one day, then got sick with sciatica in both legs. I stayed at home and got drunk.

All I can remember is calling Occupational Health. I was drunk, in a hell of a state. I called them three maybe four times, as well as Gail. Plus, my own doctor who called me back three times as I had called him three times. He told me that at a later visit to him after the Priory.

APC got me into the Priory for my drinking. I remember going in. I couldn't stop being sick. I was put in the waiting room with Gee; there were other people there too. I had to keep leaving the room with a sick bowl to be sick. They gave me a room and the doctor came to see me. He said I could have an injection to stop me being sick. I didn't take that choice. Today, I wouldn't have taken the tablets. As I was being sick already, they wouldn't work; I would just throw them up. If you start being sick, the only thing that will stop it is the injection; tablets don't work. I remember asking the doctor if I should be here, did he think I was ill enough for this. He said yes. I had several days where I was on the Libram to help with the withdrawals, along with vitamin B and Thiamine. These helped protect the organs against alcohol damage. I had a blood test to see

238

if I had any liver damage. I didn't, so the vitamins were all I needed to take. If things were really bad with your liver, they gave you vitamin B injections.

The consultant came to see me and he put me back on Prozac. After several days on this combination, I was put into an alcohol-counselling group, basically rehab. It followed the 12-step AA program. We had to do AA. I had had several days where I just rested up. I was there a month.

I had gone from being a top producer for Financial Services, winner of top achiever's award for key contacts (by a wide margin again) at SP Pharma, winner of national high achiever award 2001 at Kudos, winner of President's Circle and Five-Star Award 2004 and 2005, First-Star Award 2006 at APC, to this. Being one of the elite athletes at the Solent (club), people would say to me I aspire to being like you. Club members asked me to teach them how to swim properly, they wanted help with gym programs and asked me how I did so many athletic things; I was what others wanted to be like. I had my own gym and swimming programs. I did at times get a personal trainer to help with the gym programs but swimming, I did my own.

My marriage was a disaster zone, it really was. I was upstairs when he came home. We didn't watch TV together or have meals together. I refused to go on holiday with him; I'd had enough of the negativity and moaning before and when we were there. It was always his way. He had no respect for my things and my family. He had told Ralph when they were staying that he didn't want them in 'OUR' home; he wouldn't eat with them. He brought me a hamster, not a cat. I did get a second-hand dog in 2005, Holly, a Collie, one of the most adorable dogs you could ask for. Even that didn't help; we went on a few walks, and it was always arguing. There was no joy. He spent money on what he liked and I had to sort it out. My spending would go out of control due to my illness, I would find out later.

Gee watched me break down and did nothing except complain about my drinking. He did have a point. The stress he put me under 24/7 was unreal. I felt like a commodity, someone who brought money in. He liked that. He would not help make my life easier. When I had to go away with APC, he didn't help with Holly. I was left to sort that out. At APC, the stress was unbelievable. Then at home it was just as bad; I had no let up. I was living an upstairs-downstairs life in hell. The club I went to every now and then now gave me no release in the end. Gee would complain about that, me getting up early to go to the club. If I didn't get up and go, he complained about that. He complained about everything; he never stopped and when he wasn't happy about something, which was most of the time, he couldn't tell me once. He would repeat it so many times, faster and faster, that my head would be spinning. There was no let-up in any area of my life. I just fell apart completely. I had not one area in my life now which I was happy with.

Now I was in rehab. I was broken in every area. For the first time in my life, I was glad to get away from home. I just wanted to escape. I had left all my appointments for Gail to sort out. This was a first. The first time I felt like I knew I couldn't do it. I had just completely broken down.

On 25th March, 2007 Adrian was three years clean and sober. His full recovery and change had not taken place, he still held on to too many ghosts. I would help him release the ghosts.

I was about to start mine. Or so I thought. Instead, I struck the blue touch paper.

Chapter Thirteen
1996–2007, Mandy to Southampton

Adrian was clean and sober again. Mentally, he was not in a good space. His paranoia, anger management—that can still be an issue today—obsessive-compulsive disorder, along with the flashbacks and nightmares…Those two I can relate to. They still haunt me today. Especially APC and the drinking dreams; you wake up, think you have drunk, and the relief when you realise it was just a dream is immense. They still haunted him. He was also unhappy and felt worthless. Some would call it depression; others could say it was the damage he had done to himself over the years with mood-altering stimulants.

In 1996, Adrian met Mandy. Mandy was from America and was an American Jew. She had been adopted at birth. Adrian met her a few months into rehab. He hadn't been discharged yet. He was anorexic but his face was puffy and pale from the detox. Mandy was the first person to be interested in him for years. He said to me, "I was in love the first time I saw her."

Mandy was working in a holiday shelter for the homeless, Crisis Open Christmas. Adrian was doing the same shift when he met her. Adrian's description of the place was: a filthy dirty warehouse with all the scum of the earth who have nothing coming in and don't want to change. *Bit rich coming from him!*

By all accounts, Adrian would be the love of Mandy's life. Within a few months, Adrian had gained weight, was eating properly and was looking well. Seven months of being together, Mandy proposed. They got married.

They married in a United Reform Church in Brixton. The church was a small two-storey house with a green neon cross. The reverend was an American. The people who attended were from NA and AA, along with Adrian's mother. Mandy's biological parents were there and gave her away. Mandy's friends Will and Helen, along with Mandy's first husband Amos, were there too. Mandy had married Amos so she could stay in the UK, and she kept on asking people to marry her. In the end, Amos did marry her as she always wanted sex with him. This had then allowed Mandy to stay in the UK to live and work. Adrian said that he knew as soon as he put the wedding ring on his beloved Mandy's finger that he would not be faithful to her.

Adrian was very proud of Mandy's biological father. He was a millionaire and lived in LA. Adrian loved the idea that he was married to a millionaire's daughter. Mandy had only just met her biological parents.

I remember asking Adrian about Mandy. More to the point, I was shocked that someone like him go to know her, with crime written all over his face, a walking multi-coloured tapestry of tattoos, no life or living skill, spoke like someone from Billingsgate, every other word being either the F or C word more often than any other words. His lack of education, a long list. How had this all happened? (I did not know that Mandy had been adopted at that point).

He had no idea what Mandy had seen in him. He also had great reservations about it working but went ahead anyway (like so many people do, all for different reasons. My first marriage was to escape home. My second as I thought it was wrong to live in sin.) Adrian loved her.

Mandy was, in Adrian's words, very intelligent and witty at times with a really serious side to her personality. She spoke six languages and had a BA in Russian. She played the piano and was very focused on her writing career. She had a job working for Tellex as a communication transcriber. She did belly dancing in their front room and also went to classes for that. She went running most days along the embankment in London by the river Thames

Adrian had managed to get himself a flat in Kennington as soon as he got out of rehab. They lived together more or less straightaway.

He went to Clapham College for three years and got qualification in RSA diploma 1 and 2 (Certificate in Counselling Skills, CPCAB Certificate in Therapeutic Counselling, CPAPB, 1998) along with in 2001 Certificate of Credit – Mediation level 1.

Adrian then got himself a job; the first one was in a treatment centre, working with recovering addicts. Then with the Richmond Fellowship, Mental Health and Substance Misuse. He knew that one since he had been in there as a patient. Adrian would also work in a homeless hostel in Victoria with a nun called Breda. He would later steal £40 from her on his relapse.

Adrian now was earning money legally. He was working very hard as was Mandy. She was working and writing a book. She managed to get a book published for which Adrian said he was very proud of her.

He had a Golf GTI and was driving it without a license. Money, a job he liked, flat, decent food, clothes, some personal possessions, a beautiful wife, he always claimed. His life should have been made. It was what he wanted.

Mandy and Adrian went over to America early in 1997 to stay with Mandy's biological father. Getting into the States was a miracle based on his criminal record. So he lied. Adrian got in to the States on a technicality. Mandy knew there would be problems as soon as they got there. She did her bit to get in and passed passport/border control. Adrian was in a different area. As soon as Mandy had done her bit, she flew around to where Adrian was. Mandy informed the USA customs that her brother worked for the IRS. American customs guy panicked and let Adrian in, with no questions asked. When Adrian tried to get back in a while later, he was declined before he took off from the UK.

Mandy had wanted to move back; that couldn't happen with Adrian. Their words were, "You're a felon, there is no way we would let you in the country, and if you had lived here, you would still be in jail for life."

Adrian loved America and the Americans loved him. His language, the way he spoke! He was the perfect package for success with the Americans. They loved Cockneys. He wasn't a Cockney but knew all the Cockney rhyming slang. Plus, it was only a technicality; they didn't need to know that. They just needed to know that he came from London.

Mandy's biological father owned and lived in Charlie Chaplin's House. Adrian was there, staying in the same home. He went to an AA meeting in Hollywood with her dad, who was also a recovering alcoholic. Mandy and Adrian then went to the Redwood Forest in California to meet Mandy's mum, who worked for NASA. They had three weeks of luxury, then went back to London and cashed his giro at the post office. This was the first lot of benefits he had claimed. It was very different to what he had been used to.

Adrian had been an instant success with Mandy's biological family. Her father liked Adrian, and they got on well. Mandy's parents were not married when she was born, and they weren't together anymore so her biological mother decided to have the baby and have her adopted into a Jewish household. Mandy was raised by another Jewish family. This was not without problems; her adopted brother and Mandy got on well. Mandy's adopted mum would commit suicide after trying it many times. What killed her adopted mum was there was no one there that time to call the ambulance. Nothing else. There was just no one around. Her adopted father did very little except watch porn movies. The place was a tip, no cleaning or tidying was done. They lived in a three-storey house. They each had one section of the house. Her adopted dad got married. His wife did not care too much for Seth, Mandy's brother, or Mandy. When Mandy's adopted dad died, he had left money to both Seth and Mandy but the new wife never handed it over. Seth and Mandy never asked.

A short while after the wedding, the problems started. Arguments and Adrian losing it big time. The undercurrent was already there before. Adrian was, at that point, losing his temper. Mandy was messy and she did not like housework. Adrian could not cope with mess. Hair in the plughole would cause a major row, along with books, clothes not put away, covering not done or the kitchen not cleaned up. I found that quite hard to believe!

Adrian liked to play what I call God-awful music loud, with the walls banging. Mandy liked peace and quiet to write. Adrian had no tolerance or consideration for the neighbours and one of them, Cassie, was a black woman who also liked to play music loud. She had a child. Skinhead boyfriend would turn up for sex. Adrian then lost the plot completely. *The dark side* as I would call it.

Adrian would go up to Cassie's flat, rant and rave about the noise and loud sex. He confronted one of her skinhead boyfriends. Telling him to "keep the fucking noise down. That black c**t has had your kid; sort that out too". Boyfriends would be thrown out regular by Cassie to be replaced a week later by another of the same kind. The saddest thing was Cassie was a nice person. She would help Adrian a great deal near the end. Most of the people in the block were African. All the black kids were drug runners. There were users and dealers everywhere.

Adrian and Mandy had got to the point where there were now constant arguments. Adrian would be telling her to fuck off and leave, throwing her books at her, telling her to take them, or any other item he could get hold of that belonged to her.

He wanted a dog. They got one that lasted two nights. I asked how come. His reply was, "It kept me awake at night, sniffing." I raised my eyebrows at that and to this day, refer to that dog as Snuffles.

Mandy tried to introduce Adrian to classical music, reading the classics, opera and the beauty of the spoken word. (He definitely needed that). "Fuck all that," he told me, "I could not concentrate, sit still and did not like being trawled around museums." Mandy liked to go to all the Jewish holocaust museums when they went on holiday. Adrian's attitude was, "Give me a beach and dinner!"

"Some things just don't change, eh?" Adrian's quote, not mine.

Angry and feeling lonely, Adrian was attending AA with the wrong attitude. He met a crazy 'crack' lady called Jackie in a meeting. It was only a matter of time before he started using drugs again. Jackie and Adrian were using in his flat. The marriage had gone down the drain. Adrian overdosed on drugs and Jackie ran a bath and dunked his head in the cold water. That was more likely to kill him than the overdose of the drugs he had taken. He managed to break his leg while stoned out of his head and ended up in hospital.

Mandy came to see him. She asked who had called the ambulance, he said, "Jackie." Mandy knew he had been unfaithful, so flew back to America. His words were, "There was no discussion with Mandy; she went." She demanded the wedding ring back and by all accounts threw it in the Thames. Whether she did that, he didn't know. Mandy got a divorce immediately, saying that they had not lived together for two years. Adrian was very hurt and could not believe he had fucked things up so badly. Adrian had almost had it all. The pain was terrible. He decided, on a couple of nights off, to do drugs, then he would sort himself out. Just two night, that's it, two nights. That didn't happen. All addicts say just one night, one day, one drink, just one. This followed by it won't happen again. Addicts have good intentions. The addiction is so powerful and such an awful illness that it just does not work that way. Once you start, stopping is so very difficult. It takes hold of you and takes over your life. The obsession is so great; you are powerless over it. This illness is awful and it should never be underestimated.

His words about Mandy and how he treated her was, "I was a complete cunt to her." That was 2001.

For him 2001–2004 were the same as before, drugs, women, violence, crime; this time, he was caught with a World War 1 bayonet with a leather sheath. His intention had been to sell it. However, he did need it as there were not very nice people after him. He got off, no charges, just a caution.

In 2004, Adrian landed up sleeping in a bin shed and using. He still had a flat. His words were, "When Mandy first left, I had money. The dealers came to me. When the money went, I had to go to the dealers. The bin shed was easy, provided I had my crack, drugs, a can of Tenants. I didn't care."

His flat had been taken over by Jamaican drug dealers. They had these scales which were so accurate that you would know if a very small amount had been taken. He stole cocaine from one called Luciano, one of the Jamaicans, who liked him a bit so didn't slap him up. He was lucky. For that, he could have been killed. His debts had escalated, and he was about to be evicted from his flat.

The only person who seemed to care about him and helped him at his point was Cassie from upstairs. She had seen the state he was in. She would take him in and provide him with meals from time to time. If nothing else, Adrian always described Cassie as someone with a big heart. They had, some time ago, managed to sort the noisy skinhead disturbance out!

He was admitted to King's College hospital with deep vein thrombosis. His legs were blocked with blood clots. There was a high probability that he would lose his leg yet again but didn't. He was bleeding from his anus and mouth and was chronically underweight. Mentally, he was a complete mess. His total possessions were in a black bin liner. He was put in a ward for two weeks but managed to use and drink. Adrian was then sent into a secure ambulance to a secure detox unit at Bethlem Hospital for five weeks.

For five weeks, a guy from NA called Mark, Scottish phoned to check if he was still there and how he was doing. "Every day for five weeks, this guy checked on me to see if I was still alive and still there." Adrian is still emotional about that show of concern today. After five weeks, his keyworker managed to get him into a rehab. This was Francis House, Southampton, the only place that would take him. He was put on a train. He was in Francis House for six months. Well, nearly!

When he arrived at Francis House, he was very ill. He had been off medication for three days from a five-week detox. He was given a job (all people were given jobs). Adrian had to hoover the second floor every morning. He was so weak, he could not carry the hoover up the stairs.

His attitude was not very good at this point. He was angry as hell that he was back in rehab, being told what to do by people who were less qualified than him and having to listen to 'twats' in group therapy. (Not the best attitude for recovery). However, it was quite similar to mine.

Adrian started going to predominately AA meetings with a few NA ones thrown in. He was not grateful one ounce! "I had lost everything, and I had to listen to people who had somewhere to live, money, cars, and I had fuck all."

He did his benefit claim with the help of the staff at Francis House and went to the Citizen's Advice Bureau to sort out the bailiffs and debts.

He was kicked out of Francis House early due to his attitude and acts. He would not engage with the staff or the program, their words. He was also sleeping with some of the women, which wasn't allowed.

Adrian was moved to a 'dry house' on Payne's Road in Southampton. He met a woman in AA, Sarah. She had a flashy car. Sarah dumped Adrian. He could not cope with being dumped again so he took an overdose. However, he woke up the next morning and the overdose didn't work.

He was struggling to walk to AA meetings due to his health. He did, however, walk to all his AA meetings; he turned up religiously every night. Most were at least half an hour walk away. These meetings were Shirley AA meeting, Salvation Army, Oxford Street, Ordnance Road, Bugle Street. St Marks NA, to name a few. Adrian was too proud to ask for a lift. He was, however, taken home. People liked Adrian and would soon rally around and help him.

He got a sponsor to help him with his steps in AA. His first job was moving furniture; that was '50 quid', his words, not mine. In September 2005, he got himself a job based in a homeless hostel as a support worker. He also passed his driving test. He did not like being a learner driver, he referred to the L on top of the car as "L for lemon". He mentioned this in various AA meetings. It was pointed out by a very nice lady in AA that the L stood for legal.

He could drive a car legally now. However, he had never filled a car up with petrol. At a petrol station, he had to call a mate to ask how to do it (Hard to believe).

In all fairness to him, he was trying to pull himself together and get a life. He was now living in Lawn Road, Supported Mental Health Accommodation. According to him, he was still completely fucked up. His boundaries with regards to women had not really changed, and he would sleep with whoever he could, sex being one of his addictions which now had really taken a hold. It was women from AA, work, wherever. His attitude now was just 'fuck them'. Provided he had his orgasms, he didn't care. At times, he didn't even care about that, he would just stop and walk out.

He was now nearly two years clean. In 2006, he met Angie. Like attracts like!

Angie had issues, serious issues. Adrian fell head over heels in love with her. He was totally smitten. She would, however, cause a great deal of pain to Adrian. Angie had the potential of causing a serious relapse for Adrian. She was untrustworthy, unfaithful, a liar, and would let Adrian down time and time again. She had many issues and came from an alcoholic family. She had no awareness of her own issues, one being an eating disorder, and would blame Adrian for everything. They got engaged. As soon as that happened, she left. Adrian was devastated. She came back, then left again. This cycle continued. When her brother told Adrian that she was seeing someone else, he flipped completely. He turned up at her house, threatened her brother and completely lost it. He left, only to return with all of Angie's stuff like sex toys, promptly dumped them in the front garden and left.

In between Angie leaving, there were a multitude of women, one named Anna, whom he worked with. She was a nurse. Their relationship was very short-lived. One reason for this was Angie came back and Anna found out. She was incredibly hurt. The other was she became pregnant very quickly but wanted nothing to do with it. He didn't want that life; it wasn't him. Anna was going to terminate the baby. It was decided. She told Adrian, who was quite happy with that. Anna, however, could not do it. She got to Bournemouth but left pregnancy intact. This caused Adrian and Anna to have a rift. They were not to speak but having to work in the same building.

Anna would later say to Adrian that she was a 'wanker magnet'! This was with regards to the few men who had come into her life.

The next woman was Deane; that was on and off due to Angie. Deane finished the relationship in the end, saying, "I can't see you being faithful to me." He would tell me later he had no intention of being faithful to her. Then Louise from AA, who already had a partner. Adrian slept with her at their place. Her partner was always suspicious. Louise wanted more but he didn't.

Then Loretta. She was very young, in her 20s and Adrian was in his 50s. I asked why he had slept with someone so young. His reply was, "Because I could." There was another young one, which just felt wrong to him, so he got up and left. The list was endless.

He would tell me about this later when we got to know each other better. The information was like pulling teeth, but I got it.

This type of behaviour would continue for quite a while, with Adrian being all over the place and women galore. Adrian still had an anger management issue, insecurities, paranoia, to name a few. There would be a few key people who would help him. A friend of his called John did a great deal for him but in the end, had to walk away as he said he could do no more. His sponsor was very supportive and both of them listened to his tale of woe along with a few others.

He had been told by the council when he first moved to Southampton that there was no chance of him getting a flat based on his debts and past. He now had friends in AA and where he was employed who were supportive and made suggestions of how to apply for a flat, which he did. His debts were high, and he needed to prove that he could take on responsibility and make payments for his bills along with the debts he had incurred. With the help of a lady where he worked at Patrick House and his GP, he applied. Adrian needed an assessment with the council. In supportive accommodation, they asked him if he would like council or housing association accommodation. He didn't mind either. At the interview, he pointed out that he worked for Patrick House as a bank worker. This was a hostel for 60 homeless people that helped them get accommodation. He did get a permanent job as project worker. He then had a client base to support and helped them move on. It wasn't a pleasant job. Police and ambulances were called daily. Fights would break out. Alcohol wasn't allowed on the premises but got in. Adrian was throwing people out daily due to the trouble they caused, only to get home and see that they had managed to move in, under him at Lawn Road. Adrian's life had started to improve. However, he was incredibly unhappy.

This was all pointed out to the council and got him the points that were required to get a housing association flat. He moved in November, 2007.

April, 2007

'The fuse' was lit when I was in Marchwood. I went to an AA meeting held there. Someone grabbed my arm, I turned to look at him and he said, "You look so much better than you did last week." I was stunned that he had touched me, flattered by what he said but was still in a daze from the medication I was on. I looked him up and down. He was covered in tattoo and scruff and looked like a thug and a moron. No one else said that I looked better before.

This was at Marchwood, a Thursday night AA meeting on 12th April, 2007. That was the night I meet Adrian.

My 2004, 2005 and 2o06 had been hell at times. I never realised how ill I was and it would take me years to realise that I was and had been seriously mentally ill. Adrian was getting better and making progress into a better world. Me, well I had to live my life. I would know hell like I had never know before

Chapter Fourteen
After 37 Days

In many ways, I thought I was doing well.

Going back to my diary, Wednesday, 15th August, this was what I did that day:

Addiction Treatment Programme Daily Diary:

My name, Cathy, 15th August, 2007.

I had a very good day. This was because:

I wrote a letter to Marchwood Priory informing them of my days that I can do my addiction recovery plan. I went to Tesco with my nephew and got some jobs done.

Today I learned:

"Therefore, I tell you whatever you ask for in prayer believe that you will receive it and you will." (Mark 11:24) This was from the Gospels, why I put that down, I have no idea. I was forever reading the Bible. I knew that quote by heart so why I thought I had learnt something, I don't really know. At that time, I was thinking if I asked to win the lottery, then God would do it. *That never happened.*

Today I enjoyed:

Having my nephew with me. He's 13 and taller than me (his dad is 6 ft. 7 in). I did my swim and went to gym and did a spinning class. Then I picked my nephew up after that and had a kip (sleep); he watched TV.

Today I did not enjoy:

Dana being too busy to pick my nephew up. Noticing the weight I have put on due to the 40 days relapse and then all the food that I ate at Marchwood. I need to resolve that, lose some weight and get back to just under 9 stone.

My weight and how I looked would become yet another obsession of mine.

Today I feel I have made progress in the following areas:

Doing more with my nephew, which is important to me. Reading more positive material. I have just finished reading *Came to Believe.* Now going to read *The Prophet.* I haven't read that in years. It's a really good book.

This was a couple of days before I saw Adrian.

I was doing nothing to help my recovery or depression. In fact, I was on the path to destruction in so many ways and I could not see it. I had become obsessed with another person. '*How and why, to this day, I have no idea.*

The only two things I could think of now looking back was

1) I didn't want recovery enough and did not understand the dangers of addiction and how ill I was. The path I would take would be long, dark and painful and get worse each time I relapsed.

2) If Gee had moved out and given me space, I might have looked at everything very differently. I might have moved on without him in my life as it was a very destructive relationship. We may have *resolved so many issues we had and maybe started a liveable, happier relationship.*

As none of this happened, I went down the *Dark Path.*

Thursday, 16th August, 2007

It was the night at the Marchwood AA meeting. I would ask him if he would let me know when he was sharing from the chair at a meeting. I had to wait for him to come out as he was talking with people. He asked for my phone number, but I said no and took his phone number. I still wonder today if I had given him my number and waited for Adrian to call, would he?

He told me years later that he had seen me in the rooms pretty much like him—negative and not wanting to be there. Also, when I was asked to do something in AA like read, it was pretty obvious I didn't want to do that. And what's more, I never wanted to share from the floor.

Adrian would also say that he recognised how ill I was based on his experience. I looked so like him, defeated in so many ways and really struggling with AA and everything else that was happening to me.

Adrian recalls seeing me at the coffee machine getting a cappuccino and talking with another AA member. He thought I was nice, funny and attractive, and he liked me.

That day my dairy read:

I felt good, happy in the gym. I have arranged for Leza to put the Pompey sticker in Paul's car. *He supports Southampton.*

(Paul and Leza were married and Paul took the piss out of me good and proper. I took it and did the same to him; it was continuous banter)

That day I found this on a post-it note in my bag: 'One meeting a week made you weak'. This was an AA slogan

Think of your worst drunk before you pick up. *It would take me more than few years to learn, believe, and understand that one.*

In the Big Book they talk about *'YETS'!* It was one of the AA slogans I thought did not apply to me. I was immune. I never dreamed the stories I heard would happen to me.

That night before the AA meeting I had a depression group. It was interesting. One guy was having an affair; and his wife knew nothing about it. Then she found the letters from the woman he was having an affair with. He went through what had happened and said he wanted his wife to find the letters.

Another person's son had just been jailed for dangerous driving; he was 19.

Then another person spoke about working with dying children and finding it very hard. I was with her on that one.

Listening to other people with their problems, I was beginning to think maybe mine weren't too bad.

It was depressing, just being in the group and it really was not helping. I should have stuck with the counselling. Maybe one-on-one sessions as I had issues, big issues. They would need to be addressed before I could really get well.

My recovery from alcohol would take time. I was an alcoholic who had been diagnosed with Bipolar Disorder type 2 by the consultant in the Priory.

The Bi-polar had always been there but not to the degree it was now. Even my doctor, when I lived in Haddenham, pointed out that I was an 'up and down' person and would have to live with it.

They had changed my drugs in the Priory; I was on three different types: two mood stabilisers and an anti-depressant in the class called MAOI, the generic name was Moclobemide. I would start on a low dose and it would increase to 350 mg. The consultant had talked about me taking a low dose of diazepine. I was having none of that. They could use the drug that they had given me for alcohol withdrawal; it was in the same class, a benzodiazepine, Librium 20mg. This was for anxiety, and boy, did I suffer from that! It was not as addictive and definitely would never be my addiction of choice. Diazepine was, on the streets, known as 'Vallies'. It was highly addictive and you would have to keep upping the dose to get the same effect as you became tolerant to it. Adrian would tell me this when I asked him about his many addictions. Adrian said to me his relapses always started with three pints of lager and then he went straight on the Valium. The rest was history.

In that AA meeting after the depression group at Marchwood, Adrian was there. This was his share from the floor. Adrian thought 'A good night out, before he got sober, was a bottle of Jack Daniels with a couple of prostitutes, a porn movie and some crack'.

I got Adrian's number. Now, any normal, sane-minded person would have left well alone. I was ill, not just with depression but with addiction to alcohol and I needed to recover. AA says when you first come into AA, don't make any drastic changes in your life. Just stick to the AA program. No relationships, no pets, no big decision-making. Focus on recovery, get a sponsor and stick with the winners. Buy a plant. My depression counsellor said the same. I had to keep things simple, with no changes unless they were helping to combat my stress and anxiety.

Really in hindsight that should have meant Gee and I separating and never ever going near Adrian with a barge pole.

I started to see Adrian. I did not recognise what and where my illness was taking me. *Turmoil.*

After meeting with Adrian, he texted me all night long about meeting again, and I agreed to meet him on Sunday.

I had told him all about APC when we met the first time and he said, "You can't go back to that job." True, at that moment in time, I was not well enough to do a job. He knew I called on GP surgeries so he suggested meeting at his GP surgery in Belmont Road. He did not trust me at that moment with his address.

I couldn't understand why. We were going to have a chat. We did have a chat at his flat. I had already thought to myself that I shouldn't go into his flat but I did. I felt nervous and unsure of this situation. We had a chat in his flat. I was wearing jeans and a strappy top. I was facing him and suddenly, he pulled the straps of my top down. I wasn't expecting that. He must have seen the shock on my face but then his attention was drawn outside and he said there was a dealer there doing a deal. How did he know that? When I left, Adrian was leaning against my car and I was looking at him. He grabbed the lapel of my coat, pulled me to him and kissed me passionately. He had his arm around me and another in my hair, holding my head in place. It was such a shock. I was not expecting that and I was overwhelmed.

This was not *Cary Grant*. How that saying had come about was his sponsor at the time had told him to behave like *Cary Grant* as he was a foul mouth yob.

Adrian was about as far removed from a Cary Grant character you could get. I stepped back, he then kissed my neck and said, "Text me, text me." I was overwhelmed by all that was happening my head now was in a spin and definitely in the wrong place.

That morning, I had gone swimming and done a 3K swim. I had also had a conversation with Gee about moving out. Gee was also not happy with me because I had not been around all day. He had to do his speech for his daughter's wedding. That was on Sunday, the 26th.

I was dreading the wedding. Everyone would be drinking, and I just didn't feel I was going to be able to cope with it all. Gee and I decided I would just come on the Sunday and not go to the Saturday night do. It was just as well as Gee's elder son got really drunk and his wife slapped him around the face.

I only went to the wedding. His son's wife, whom I had never liked, said to me when I arrived on the Sunday, "You're doing really well; stick with me as I won't be drinking," What a load of shit that was! Not only that but my Russell and Bromley shoes which cost over £100 were ruined by his other son's girlfriend, who managed to spill wine on them.

On the 20th, Adrian texted me first thing in the morning. I was running late and had just arrived at the Priory. *"R u ok, hun?" That word could go; I hated the word 'hun'.* It was just an annoying, irritating word to me.

"Yes," was my reply.

"I know you don't like to text but that really is a short reply."

Later in our relationship, my reply would be *"K"*, which meant OK. That would really piss Adrian off!

I replied, *"You left me last night on fire. Everyone is saying I am absolutely glowing, and I can't think why."* I'd never sent a text like that to anyone and would never even consider it before this.

What was I doing? I didn't particularly like the texts as they all implied sex and that wasn't what I wanted to read. I still had some romantic notion that he would and was madly in love with me. I don't think I wanted that either. I was lonely like Adrian and I just wanted some attention that was nice. To be appreciated and to feel good about myself. No conflict. To have a laugh. Just something so I felt I had some purpose for living. I hated the upstairs-downstairs life but nothing was being done to resolve that in any shape or form.

His next text was: *"Would you like me to douse your fire?"* I didn't reply to the text as I didn't know what to say and I didn't like these particular texts. They were a bit to vulgar for my liking

I phoned Adrian because I had just arrived at the Priory and one of the guys that I had been in with for a month was sitting on the steps; he looked dreadful. He had been drinking. Adrian told me to leave him, just let the counsellors sort this out. He was right, that's what I should have done and today that is what I would do, but I didn't. I was too new to all this. With a few years' sobriety behind me, I would possibly be able to help, but not then, not with only days of sobriety behind me. I was jeopardizing my recovery.

I went over to him, asked what had happened. It all came out. He got back on Friday, went to his normal shop, asked for a small bottle of whiskey, no a medium one, er, no the large one. It was all over. He had drunk all weekend. I was upset and took him home that night because he had got a taxi here as he was over the limit for drunk driving. He looked a pitiful mess, that whipped dog look.

Adrian never had credit on his phone and you always had to call him. He would send a text, *"No credit, can you call?"*

I can probably count on one hand the amount of times he called me on his mobile phone and that's in 11 years. Since he's had WhatsApp, it has been different; he has used that often.

On 21st, Tuesday, I met Adrian at an AA meeting. Afterwards, we went to the Kentucky Fried Chicken car park. Adrian came to sit in my car. He pulled me towards him from the other side of the car and kissed me really passionately. His hands were in my hair, roughing it up, and he also started kissing my neck. Then his hands were in my blouse, caressing my breasts and nipples. I was really turned on and really worried. What the hell was I doing? He then put his hand on the outside of my trouser and moved them up and down.

His comment was, "You're very hot there." Too right I was, I was really turned on and wanted him. But not here, not now.

The 22nd should really have been my wake-up call for me. I should have walked away from all this but no, I didn't do that.

Adrian texted me at 3:19 p.m.:

"Hey hun (that word again) I can't do Romsey 2nite (AA meeting) gotta a mate who needs 2 go 2 na meeting but still on 4 2morrow afternoon if ur fire still needs dousing."

Adrian also panicked since he thought he had sent a text to me which was meant for someone else. He panicked, one sure sign of guilt. I said I had not received the text but I did notice he had cooled off! Um. This was on Tuesday, the 21st. I was at Marchwood, having therapy.

I wrote in my diary, that sounds like he got a better offer. He did have a better offer; her name was Deane. I found that out later. I knew it. Even then that there were other women, *Helly, a neurotic, mad, serious, no-fun alcoholic whom he worked with. They went for dinner and to the cinema. He spent the night sleeping on her couch and walked away.*

Louise, another alcoholic, she was a midwife. They slept together many times and she was around for a while but that all ended when Adrian said the sex was all he wanted, she wanted more.

Anna, Angie back and forth plus a few others.

Yet I still pursued him. Adrian was not good looking, but he really was a woman magnet. He had something, I have no idea what it was, but women were just drawn to him. He also had no problem dumping them or as he said, 'jogging them on'. Like a twit, I was going to see him on the Thursday at his place to have sex. Why was I doing this? He was a thug, moron, uncouth, foul-mouthed commoner. Did not know please or thank you, and was rude. This list of his defects was outstanding. *Why, oh, why?*

I had been to Adrian's place, supported mental health accommodation, which was a studio flat. Once and for a short while. It was one room with a bed, a kitchen and sitting area. He had a separate bathroom and loo. It was dark, dingy and the walls were a dark, awful orange colour. The kitchen was a mess and was filthy. The tiled floor looked like a mop had never been near them. I wouldn't see the bathroom till Saturday, the 25th. Now that was interesting. The loo's bottom was black and the bath, well, that left a lot to be desired. Clutter everywhere. I would later call him a 'clutter bug'.

On Thursday the 23rd, I bottled it. I couldn't do it for two reasons. My period had started on Monday and was still going strong on Thursday. I had spoken to my brother Joggy and asked him what he thought. He told me straight that Adrian just wanted sex and once he had it, that would be it. I took no notice of that. It was a pointless phone call.

I was kidding myself that maybe he did like me. *He did like me but I wasn't the one he wanted.* What a fool I was being!

At 7:59 a.m., Adrian sent a text, *"Morning x its Thursday c u 2ish x."*

I texted back to say I couldn't make it.

At 8:08 a.m.: *"No prob hun (that word again) lookin 4ward 2 ravaging u but hope u r ok c u at meeting."* I had said I would be at Marchwood that night, made up some fairy tale about my cousin being in an accident.

At 11:47 a.m.: *"N we will get 2gether 4 some serious debauchery wen u r ready. Stay strong babe x"*

At 3:59 p.m.: *"Hope u r ok should be kickin u out of bed now 2 make a coffee x"*

Really!

I went to pick up Gavin in the evening from his mum's house. I had been in rehab with him. It was a disaster. I got there and he had been drinking; his mum was in a real state. I should have just walked out. *Yet another relapse person in such a short period of time.* I seemed to be drawn to them.

I agreed to take him to the Priory meeting at Marchwood because his mum begged me to. Once in the car, he asked me to stop at the pub, so he could get a drink; he would be a few minutes. True to his word, he was a few minutes and had two pints. Plus, he brought a bottle of beer for the car. I was not happy. How was I supposed to handle this situation? I called two of the girls I had been in rehab with; they were on their way to a different meeting but said they would meet me at the Priory. Gavin at this point was still in the car.

Adrian texted me at 7:44 p.m., *"Where r u? x"*

I texted him back to say I would be there in a few minutes. I walked in and the guy was drunk. The meeting was packed. I had to sit on the floor.

Adrian text me at 7:52 p.m.: *"U look fuckn georgous x."* I was wearing a pair of black Moschino trousers, a Moschino white top and a white Versace leather jacket, stilettos and black ankle boots. Adrian was wearing tracksuit bottoms, T-shirt and tracksuit top and trainers. I texted him to let him know that the guy was drunk. 8:07 p.m.: *"I want ux."* I said we would make a date. His text at 8:10 p.m. was: *"Wen wen wen! x."*

After the meeting, Adrian came over; the two girls were waiting for me in the waiting room and Gavin was drunk. Adrian said the best thing you can do is all go home and leave him. Gavin ordered a taxi. The two girls went home and Adrian disappeared.

I texted him asking where he was and why he had left. It was pretty obvious he was seeing someone else. I just chose to ignore it. I did find out later that it had indeed been Deanne.

9:43 p.m.: *"Saturday beautiful! Make it up 2 u tenfold xxxxxx."*

I responded with, *"I am upset you didn't stay and just went."*

10:10 p.m.: *"Don't be disappointed darling x big hug x nite x spend a nite wiv me! Tell ur hub u going to convention! x"*

I couldn't do that, could I? No, I couldn't do that for two reasons. One, I had Holly to look after and Gee was going up to the home counties for his daughter wedding on Saturday for a get together and party for everyone.

The service was happening on Sunday, when I would go for the service and then leave. I couldn't stay since I had to be home for Holly. Easy.

Friday, 24th August

7:13 a.m., *"Morning x u r in my head n I cant wait till 3 tmoro x pay day hurray busy day x want u bad."*

I didn't reply.

9:04 a.m.: *"R u ok hun? X."* (That word again.)

I still didn't reply until 11:57 a.m.: *"Yes cant wait I'm on fire"*

11:58 a.m.: *"Me too hun x (That word again.) cant wait x c u 2moro."*

"Good," was my reply.

I sent and read all these texts thinking, *what are you doing sex is not what you want need.* I needed some stability. Not someone whom came with turmoil and chaos.

Friday, 24th August, in my diary I wrote:

Gee just does not listen to what I've got to say about the split, and I am scared of being left in this middle-class, boring life where there is nothing for me. Not one thing, it's all dead and has been for a long time. Some of Gee's family came over to see us—Leigh, his eldest son; Louise, his partner; Finley, Gee's first grandson; and Maddie, Louise's daughter by another guy. Maddie was scared of Holly, the most unlikely dog to be scared of, but we sorted it. It was Finley's first birthday.

My feelings were mixed. I was terrified about tomorrow, how I will feel, will I enjoy it? Will it be a let-down? Should I? Shouldn't I? The answer to that was simple, *No, I shouldn't.*

To add to my stress, Neil from rehab called me to say I never should have picked Gavin up. I had put myself at risk; I should have left him there in the pub or not even taken him when I arrived at Gavin's mum's. Neil was right. (I liked Neil; we got on well. Unfortunately, Neil would die in a car accident a few years down the line. It was very upsetting. He was from Portsmouth. His family was big into horses. He had a serious gambling addiction but he

259

wasn't an alcoholic. His funeral was at St Mary's Church in Portsmouth, a very large church. It was the biggest funeral I had ever been to—people were standing outside; they couldn't all get in the church. There were hundreds of people there. Neil's coffin was brought in by a horse-driven carriage. He left behind two daughters and a partner whom he had been engaged to for over 20 years).

Adrian and I exchanged these texts:

I sent a text to Adrian, *"Do you want me to bring anything?"*

At 12:26 p.m. he replied: *"wot like? Stockings? Toys? Strawberries? Yes yes yes x."*

"Pls make sure I can't see the wine glassesx. (I had been in his room once and I had seen large wine glasses on the side, um, not good.) *Is hold ups all right if not go buy what you want and I'll give u the money. I don't like this texting but I like what you send especially?! Xx."* I sent that at 14:05 p.m.

"Hold ups fine just bring ux wine glases gone."

At 2:26 p.m.: *"Just brin u hunx* (that word again) *don't be nervous just come and cum x."*

At 2:26 p.m., I replied: *"I'm terrified."*

"Thought you might be x me too x." Did he seriously think I was going to believe that?

"Yeah right x."

2:29 p.m.: *"True hun x."* that fucking word again.

2:31 p.m.: *"XX."*

6:03 p.m.: *"Have a good evening think of u x lots x."*

He probably was thinking of me but only as another person with whom he's thinking of having sex and I was being an idiot thinking that the outcome won't be what I thought it would be.

I text back 7:30 p.m.: *"U2"*

The day, Saturday 25th August, I had written that morning. When I woke up early,

I was thinking about the obvious and what the outcome will be. This is going against all my moral values. I knew it was wrong, and I would feel dreadful after. But I wanted it.

Freedom, fun and life back, the other wasn't really in the equation (sex and Adrian), and I'm terrified. Well, I'm either going to be disappointed. I could get emotional. I could be devastated. I could be unexpectedly surprised. Well, it will be all over tomorrow and then it will be business as usual with the outcome that I expect. No word, no nothing, that's life. I just want it over with and to get on with my life.

So today my sobriety is what is important to me. (I had listened to nothing in AA and counselling; what I was doing was dangerous to me).

To detached myself, my goal was to enjoy the few moments I had left. I could always not go; I had a few hours left.

However, by 7:19 a.m., the texts started. *"Morning u awake x."* *"Yes,"* at 9:24 a.m.

"Well hello x n I'm waiting."

I reply, *"You going to Marchwood?"*

His response was: *"That's the one! Off to Marchwood then pool then ux".*

12:45 p.m.: *"2 hours and counting."*

I am now in a right state, having lunch, with a friend then going straight to Adrian. Oh dear.

2:02 p.m. *"Out of pool, heading home."*

2:23. *"Scummers playing 2day parkin shite will leave space next do mine x."*

My lunch with my friend had taken longer and I needed to go to a pharmacy to get some condoms and KY jelly just in case. My friend Mark said he would go in the pharmacy and get me my bits. He didn't know what bits I needed; he only said that as I was on double yellow lines. I was married so how could I ask him to go in and get condom latex free as I was allergic to latex and K-Y jelly? *"Oh, they're just for a mate who wants them."* I don't think so. I said, "It's okay, Mark, it's female stuff that I need." I was so glad I had got a big bag. I texted to let him know I was going to be late, hoping he was not angry. I am meant to be there at 3 p.m.

2:55 p.m.: *"Course I'm not angry x."* I was so used to Gee being angry.

3:56 p.m., I text, *"Get the kettle on."*

"OK."

The reason I asked if he was angry was because if that had been Gee and I was late for him for anything, he got angry. Anger was what I knew well in a relationship. Everyone was angry with me.

The whole thing did not feel right. When I arrived, I was nervous. I was in a studio flat in a dubious part of Southampton. As I got out the car, Adrian greeted me. Jeans, no top, tattoos all over his arms and two tattoos on his chest. One saying, 'In God, we trust', which was very American. The other was 'Not forsaken' on his back, his left shoulder. He had a dark blue tattoo of Bob Marley. It looked awful. *Definitely a backstreet boy. Plus, no body like Beckham*! Nina Simone was playing. I was wearing a corduroy black short shirt with tassels at the bottom. It was Moschino with a strappy multicoloured top and black stiletto boots and a mac over the top. I had, as always, nice silk sexy underwear plus holder ups. That bit was easy for me. I liked nice underwear and spent a fortune on it.

He made us both a cup of tea. He had Earl Grey, what I drank. Yes, I was shocked. He did make a comment, "I bet you didn't think I would have Earl Grey." I felt guilty about what I was doing. This was not me. It wasn't satin sheets and a nice romantic setting; it was a dark orange dingy studio flat which was filthy dirty with a very small fish tank. Um, interesting, what's with the fish. However, no wine glasses. I had a problem with wine glasses; they reminded me of drinking. I didn't want a reminder. I had become very suspicious of Adrian over the last week; something had changed. He wasn't quite as full on as he had been in the past. There was someone else and something going on. I could hardly talk; I was married for goodness sake. I just had this sixth sense that something or someone had happened about a week ago. I would not be wrong.

We sat on the couch with our tea which he made. He asked me to take my coat off, which I did. He pulled me towards him and started kissing me. I was enjoying this part and I am sure he was too. He then started to kiss my neck and caress my breast. I was beginning to feel turned on. Adrian lifted my head and started to kiss me. He was taking everything very slowly at this point. Not a quick fuck then. He was tender, and it made me relax.

We then went to his bed. It should have been good. I shall spare you some of the details. It was a disaster. Firstly, Adrian hated condoms. Most men do. There was no way I was sleeping with him based on his past without a condom. The sex didn't work or happen for either of us. I was slim, and he liked my arse; he thought it was sexy.

I turned up in sexy gear but he just didn't do it for me, and I didn't do it for him. He did not have a body like Beckham. He was skinny from the waist up and he had flabby thighs. Being an ex-drug user, he obviously shot up in all different part of his body. Once the veins in his arms were shot to bits and had collapsed, he used his groin and legs. They had big indents where he had used. I called them snakebites. His calves were a complete mess. A mass of red, thin-looking skin, his toes and fingers were large, slightly swollen, looked puffy.

We stopped trying to have the sex. It was not working for neither of us. I went and had a bath. When I came out of the bathroom, I asked about all the toothbrushes and who they belonged to. One of many lies he told was that he liked toothbrushes and liked to have many.

Yeah right, he hardly had any teeth. It was hard to believe plus oral hygiene did look like it came on top of his lit.

Out of the blue, he said okay let's go to Winchester AA tonight. We did. Adrian needed a meeting. He shared from the floor that he was going to an AA convention next week and didn't want to go but had to as he was doing one of the shares. He didn't want to go as his ex-girlfriend Angie, her parents and brothers would be there, and he never wanted to see them again. Clearly, he felt quite strongly about this. He had not mentioned Angie in a lot of detail at this point. The only thing he had said was when I went to his flat the first time. It was about their split, a bit about how he met her at an AA meeting with her dad, followed by the sex, which had been brilliant. Angie was doing Adrian's head in. He said he hated her and never wanted to see her again, but that was not the case. Adrian loved Angie and was besotted by her. Angie would cause Adrian a great deal of pain. That was all still to come.

The next part I couldn't understand, and this did lead me a bit into a very false sense of security. After the meeting, he asked me to follow him in his car, which was a green soft-top MG.

Adrian had asked me if I thought it was a hairdresser's car, as clearly someone had said that to him. I'd never given it much thought, just thought it was a bit of a wreck; the soft top was broken in places. I would call this car the Money Gobbler. This was because he would spend so much money on getting it repaired.

I followed him; he stopped and then got out of the car; so did I. He said, "*I really want to see you again. I'll text you tomorrow and we can meet.*" He kissed me several times. Oh, well, maybe it wasn't that bad for him. Maybe he did like me and wanted something between us. I thought I'd got him, how wrong was I! I drove home and took Holly out.

10:23 p.m. "*Ur civic is fast babe x nite x sleep well x No KY next time hun x*" (that word again I am going to say something about that. I do not like being called hun).

I text back, "*Nite x.*"

On 26th August, the wedding was a civil wedding. Adrian did not text me first thing in the morning at seven-ish like normal and I was distraught. I couldn't get out of bed and go to the club. I was upset. I did not want him to make me feel like this, yet I knew this would happen, and I had only myself to blame.

At 9:02 a.m.: *"Keep urself safe 2 day don't pick up n get back sober x Im off 2 Bournemouth 2-day wiv mates x beach n meetin x."*

My reply was, *"c u x."*

I thought we were meeting! Um.

The 11:08 a.m. text: *"Just stay sober."*

I replied, *"I'll be home ASAP."*

"Good x a drink won't make it better or happier will only make things worse x stay strong." That was at 11:13 a.m.

I sent a text, *"R we meeting?"*

This was classic, and I really should have seen it coming. At 11:20 a.m.: *"Driving to Bournmouth at mo x stopped 4 coffee x not sure wot time I'm back but we got plenty of time hun x (that fucking word again). Just get back sober call me if u need surport x."*

That really pissed me off, and I was now really hurt. Adrian had the grace to text me at 12:55 p.m.: *"R u ok so far? x"*

He was going to Bournemouth with Deanne, I would find this out later, but was not convinced by the mates bit. Did he really think I was that stupid? Okay, I had acted that stupid. My sixth sense told me everything was wrong; it was no good, would not work, that I should walk away, and there were other women.

I drove to the ceremony, saw them all, stayed for a while and drove home. I wasn't in a good frame of mind, with Adrian being distant, being with Gee's whole family was not the best place I wanted to be. I felt stress under normal circumstance with Gee's family. Now I had added to it.

Monday was a bank holiday. Adrian had said we could meet up on Monday about 11 a.m. as he was not working, which was great. He had said that on Saturday night. He'd also said we would meet up Sunday when I got back and look at all the texts I got.

Gee wasn't home, so it would be easy to get out. I had spoken to Adrian on the mobile phone on my way home from the ceremony. He asked if I was okay. I was jolly and liked speaking with him. He gave me no clue that it was just a fuck and he wasn't interested.

Monday, I called his mobile and left a text, *"R we meeting?"* I got no response. Now my sixth sense told me it was just a fuck. I sent him a text, *"Thanks 4 the nice time and making me feel good luv C xx"* What a lie that was. I felt good for a while. The thrill of something new, a fantasy excited in a state of ecstasy which was taking me away from my dull dreary life, but that was before the sex happened. Now, I felt awful.

I felt dreadful, used, stupid, foolish and rejected. All the emotions you don't want. Plus I didn't want to go to the club so that didn't help. Adrian had done this to me. No, I had done it to myself. Joggy, my brother, was right. I called him. His words were, "Don't analyse it, just get over it and move on. It is what it is." I was so upset. I deleted Adrian's numbers and turned the mobile off for obvious reasons. I did not want to continually look at it all day like a love-sick fool. That was it. If only.

I couldn't keep the mobile phone off forever as friends would need to contact me. I turned my phone on a few days later. There were three texts from Adrian.

On 27th at 12:56 p.m.: *"Sorry hun having a great garbo day may c u at totton? Stay strong x"* (That word again plus what the hell is a great garbo day)

On 28th, 12:28 p.m.: *"R u ok? X."*

On 28th, 7:33 p.m.: *"R u ignoring me? I can deal with that (of course he could it had just been a fuck) but I want to know if u r ok, x."*

I replied, *"Just got your messages, thought that was it, did leave voice message, mon 2 c if u wanted me 2 come around. No reply from u so thought that was it. Thanks 4 the nice time and making me feel good. Luv C xx."* Well, that should make him feel like shit. Nice time, yeah, right.

On 28th: *"Well I started 2 feel guilty hun bout u being a newcomer n u r lovely n I don't want 2 use u n I want us to b friends n I fancy u rotten but u need a bit of time not a sicko like me n u made me feel good 2x."*

What a load of bullshit! Adrian actually did feel guilty, and he had done one of the things in AA you should not do. He 13-stepped me. That, basically, is a member of the opposite sex coming on to a newcomer. Adrian had over three years of sobriety, I had days. He never should have pursued this. I never should have either. So that was it. It was hell. I was very upset and it was my own fault.

I went to my therapy group all day Wednesday at Marchwood; it was nice to get out and was enjoyable, but I wasn't okay. On Thursday, I wrote when I woke up:

Did not feel right when I woke this morning, still got colic and felt incredibly tired. Didn't want to get up. My first thoughts were, I don't want Adrian to do this to me. (I was letting him.) I didn't go to the gym or had a swim. I've just stopped over the last few days all the things I love. I might be a bit upset and still emotional and tearful. (That was an understatement) But this will pass, and I really did want to carry on with my life. Business as usual. I haven't got myself sober for all this to ruin it. I want my life back, freedom, peace, calm, tranquillity, serenity, all these things that are priorities in my life. There is nothing more important in my life than my sobriety. At that moment in time, I really did mean that. All of the above would not affect it. I had to put my sobriety first. Then I finished with,

I have no unresolved issues.

Who was I kidding!

On Friday the 31st, I felt a bit better. I was still waiting for a text, which was not going to happen. I was still dreaming. This external factor would not affect my sobriety. *Really, what planet was I on?*

I guess I was acting as if it's an unresolved issue, but it's not; it's resolved. I just needed to accept it, walk away and put it down to experience.

I got my act a bit more together later so went up the club. I wrote in my diary that Gee was looking for a place. He wasn't speaking much at the moment.

I was, however, still dreaming away, hoping for a different outcome; would Adrian come back to me? Who was the other person? Was it Angie or was there someone else? I wanted to know.

This would be the start of a very different relationship. Neither of us would realise how big an impact we would have on each other. Where one grew the other would wither. With heart breaking events.

I had for years always dreamed of writing a book and started many but never really got much further than a chapter or two. Plus, they were pretty naff, and my heart wasn't in it. I didn't have passion for the books I started. I remember years ago when I was married to Michael we came to see Dana and went to Southsea. I saw a fortune-teller. He was a guy. He told me loads of stuff about myself and what I was doing now and what was wrong. He really did hit the nail on the head. He then said I had a passion for writing and should follow that path. Write things down and keep a diary. I did all this. But still didn't write the book until now.

Later in life, I would realise that I really had a passion for photography. Not people but sunset, sunrise, flowers, the moon that would be something I would look at, along with my passion for writing about my life. I wrote a diary every day. I had everything written down. All I needed to do was make myself readable.

Chapter Fifteen
If at First You Don't Succeed

At this point I should have walked away and forgotten the whole lot and learnt from experience. I didn't.

Adrian worked at Patrick House for Two Saints in Southampton. He had told me that once he came out of Francis House, it was important to him to try and help someone else. More importantly, he did not want to subsist on benefits. He started doing voluntary work. He was offered a part-time job with the Salvation Army. It all went wrong as he took nude photos of Angie on the snooker table. His boss at the time looked down his phone and saw the photos and he was asked to leave. Not a great thing to do to keep a job. He was, however, ill, and I do mean ill. Adrian then got a job labouring in a factory and hated it. Someone told him to apply to Patrick House, which he did. Forty-two people went for the job and Adrian got the job. He had a caseload of ten clients, all homeless people. All alcoholic or drug users. It was his job to challenge behaviour, keep people safe, help them move on, sort out their benefits and help with their budgeting. Now that a=was a joke. Adrian was dreadful with money; he couldn't budget himself, this is all to come.

There were 55 people in Patrick House. All were dysfunctional, with lots of drugs and lots of mental health issues. It was a madhouse, all under one roof, along with a staff team with lots of issues including Adrian.

Adrian was a keyworker-support worker.

In Patrick House, they would call the police regularly due to violence and fights that would break out, ambulances were constantly called due to overdoses or injuries. Adrian and other staff members could unlock someone's room to find them dead. This was just normal stuff—a complete mad house.

I had thought it would be a good idea to write a book about Patrick House and Francis House. This was more because I thought, well, maybe I could get to see Adrian by using this as my in. I didn't know enough about these places then to write a book. My knowledge would have only just made an essay. I still don't know a great deal. But I have learnt a lot over the years by talking with Adrian.

No, Adrian was not going to disappear from my life. I just needed to work on a plan of how to get him in my life and I wanted to be in his life. That was all I could think of. So what did I do? I put myself right in front of him at Marchwood Saturday AA meeting. When he saw me, he laughed nervously at me. I went straight up to him and asked him how he was. He was nervous and uncomfortable. Good. He asked me how I was and made some lame excuse about not contacting me. I got straight to the point with him. "Yes, I would have liked you to have contacted me. Can we have another go at that sex thing?" He was surprised.

He laughed and said, "Okay."

Now all I needed to do was wait. Wait I did and then it all began.

The fuse had been lit and the blue touch paper was on fire.

All that was left was to wait for the fall out.